IMPLODE

TOXIC DESIRE
BOOK 2

VICTORIA DAWSON

PAPER HEART PUBLISHING LLC

Publisher: Paper Heart Publishing LLC

Cover Designer: K. B. Barrett Designs

Editing: Happily Editing Anns

ISBN (Paperback): 978-1-959364-09-2

ISBN (ebook): 978-1-959364-08-5

AUTHOR NOTE

Implode is the second book in the *Toxic Desire Duet* that follows the same two main characters throughout both books. It is advised to read the books in order.

It is also advised to start with the *Entice Series* (*Spark of Obsession, Rush of Jealousy,* and *Taste of Addiction*), as story elements are present in those three books that assist in character development and world building.

Trigger Warning: This book portrays what it means to be in a toxic relationship. The physical, emotional, and psychological abuse featured in this book may be triggering and not meant for anyone under the age of eighteen.

To my family members who continue to read my books…

Please stop making this awkward.

1

CLAIRE

The feel of ice cold water splashing over my face causes me to jump out of my sleep. I fly off the couch and cover my face with my hands in case another blast happens.

"What...the...hell!" I'm shivering so hard I can hardly get the words out.

I take a few steps back and wipe my face frantically with the edge of my shirt. My eyes open slowly, and I groan at the sight.

"Just staging your intervention, Claire Bear."

"Blake!"

"Shhh...or you'll wake up Henry and he'll probably invite you to his orgy."

I rub the sleep out of my eyes, as my body adapts to the sudden cold. "What time is it?"

"Ten till six."

I toss my hands up into the air in frustration. "You cannot drench me with cold water ten minutes before my alarm is set to go off and call it a fucking intervention!"

"It's all about making our own rules."

"Is it? And what is it that you are trying to intervene on? Huh?"

"This…" He points at me. "This…"

"Just say it!"

"Oh," he sighs. "I don't actually know, but you are not acting like yourself, and I know it is over that hot specimen of a man. The one with the broody personality and the abs that can open up pickle jars. So, snap out of it before you lose yourself entirely. I want the old Claire back. The one who didn't take shit from anyone and wiped asses."

My eyes narrow, and I prop my hands on my hips. "Wiped asses? Really?"

"That's not what I meant to say. Wiped floors *with* asses," Blake corrects, making me laugh.

I let out a sigh. "I'm still me. I am just trying to navigate two breakups within a short amount of time, find an apartment to live in, manage a start-up company, and actually earn some money. I am overwhelmed and lacking the skills to handle everything with grace. So bear with me. Please."

"I'm sorry, please forgive me."

"I ate Oreos last night," I confess.

"Okay."

"The entire pack," I clarify.

"Okay."

"A family pack."

"Well damn."

"Yeah, it wasn't my finest moment." Maybe I do need this intervention after all. I feel like I'm living someone else's life and not feeling like myself.

"What brought on the processed foods binge fest?"

"Nic interrupted my evening last night," I blurt out without thinking. I am careful not to mention the agency and keep things vague. The last thing I need is to be sued for a violation of the NDA. He is annoying enough to take me to court. I just know it.

I thought I knew Nic. I thought we connected beyond just the physical attraction we have for one another. I obviously thought wrong. I don't know him at all, and he sure as hell doesn't give a damn about me. It is a hard pill to swallow when you realize that everything you thought you knew about a person was some fabricated fantasy in your head.

Blake's face changes as he makes sense of my words. "His cock get cold, and he needs your personal warmer?"

I shake my head over Blake's flowery descriptions. He sure has a way with words. "Not sure. But you basically just described Ethan's proposition to me."

"Ew, gross."

"Exactly."

"Did he proposition you before or after you beat the shit out of him?"

"Before."

"Well, let's get back to Nic. What do you think his deal was?"

"He saw me out having fun with other men and decided he wanted to control yet another situation."

"Well, what does Angie think of this whole situation? Nic is going to be her brother-in-law, after all. I can't imagine she is thrilled over this development—especially this close to her wedding shindig."

I glance away from Blake and mutter, "She doesn't know about it."

He snaps his fingers to bring my focus back to him. "So, you've been hiding that you had a relationship with Nic Hoffman?"

I shrug. "You know how much stress Angie was under last year, and now with the upcoming wedding, the last thing she needs is to worry about everyone's feelings, including mine. Knowing her, she would probably try to rearrange parts of the wedding to keep us from interacting, just to keep the peace. I don't want to do that to her."

"Because you are a ray of sunshine, Claire Bear. That's why. No man will ever deserve what you have to offer."

I give Blake a hug and he slinks backward, making a face. "What's wrong?"

"You are wet."

I make a face. "I wonder how that happened," I say with a laugh.

"We are spending the day together," he says with certainty. "Nope. Do not even open that pretty mouth of yours. No arguments. I've been needing some pampering and you are going to come with."

I shake my head at Blake. He knows just what will cheer me up. "Where's the first stop?"

"Hair salon. Or maybe a breakfast shop? No, let's get food delivered to the salon. Or should we hit up the gym to release some endorphins? Oh, the possibilities. I am getting so excited!"

"I can tell." I giggle.

"But first, get dressed and put on fancy underwear."

I look at Blake with confusion. "Why on earth for?"

"Because life is too short for wearing the boring kind."

"I'm not sure," I say, looking in the mirror as the male stylist—who Blake can't stop checking out—stands behind me and mimics what my hair would look like with five inches cut off. "Seems drastic."

"Do you want to live in the past or make an epic splash into a new outlook on life?" Blake asks, hovering to the side of the stylist. He studies me in the mirror and smiles.

Blake's been on a pep talk kick since we left the loft. The whole car ride here was full of motivational messages and speeches. It's like he's preparing to be a keynote speaker at a conference about my life. I do appreciate it though.

"Fine. But let's make it seven inches so I can at least donate it to the foundation that makes the wigs for little girls going through chemo."

"You are going to look extra sexy and sassy with this weight off your shoulders," the stylist says, bouncing my hair up between his fingers.

"See? Even he knows that this is a great figurative and literal way of ridding your life of the extra baggage."

"Now, let's discuss color," the stylist says, smiling at me in the mirror.

"What's wrong with my color?" I ask, holding up a lock of my own hair to examine the shade. I have dark hair that I assume came from my biological father who is Filipino. He's also credited for giving me my slightly darker skin tone that makes me look golden all year round. But all of this information is speculation. I never met the man and, without anything short of a miracle, never will.

"Have some trust in the expert," Blake scoffs. He turns to look at the man wielding the hair tools and makes a gesture toward me. "Sorry, she's very much a work in progress and has deep-seated trust issues."

I snap my fingers. "Hey! I'm right here, you know!"

"Obvi, Claire Bear, that's why I didn't even try to whisper."

"I think just some auburn highlights would really bring out the beauty of your eyes. Make them"—the stylist smacks his lips at the same time his hands mimic a firecracker—"POP!"

"Ummm, I don't know," I say reluctantly.

"That's why we are here to help you make these lifestyle decisions," Blake says, as if I'm deciding on which college to attend or something equally as important.

My mouth tips down into a frown. "This just seems highly impractical and totally out of my budget."

"My treat," Blake says, rubbing my shoulders from the salon chair, while the stylist digs through booklets and fake hair swatches until he finds the color he is looking for.

My eyes meet Blake's with confusion. It's not like he is rich or anything to be able to afford paying for these deluxe treatments.

"I found myself a Sugar Daddy, and he is loaded in more places than one," he says, filling in the blanks. "If you know what I mean."

"When?" I ask. Last time I noticed, Blake was very much single.

"Yesterday morning. On a dating app."

My eyes narrow at him. "Blake…"

"It's legit this time. No catfishing. No bait and switch. No fakeness. Promise."

"So you met the man?" the stylist asks, narrowing his eyes at Blake, who is growing annoyed over our interrogation.

"Not yet," Blake says. "But hey, this isn't about me today." He smacks his hands together and returns his attention to our reflection in the mirror. "Give Claire the works. A new chapter in her life deserves to be rewarded with a new book cover."

It takes about four hours to get my hair cut, highlighted, blown dry, and styled. Neither man allows me to see the finished result until the big reveal time. Blake even snatches my phone out of my hand so I can't use the front camera to sneak a glance.

"Drumroll, please!" the stylist cheers, hitting his workstation with his hands to produce a drum sound.

Blake spins me around in the chair to place me directly in front of the mirror.

"Wow!" I say, looking at my finished result. My hands go to my hair that is now slightly below my shoulders. Soft layers add some volume and drama to my otherwise flat look. I am styled with loose curls. I can't believe that just a little color and a new cut could cause this much of a difference. I definitely feel lighter. Free. And my eyes do stand out more with the auburn streaks. "Thank you!"

"You look amazing, Claire Bear. Simply amazing."

My face can't stop smiling. Blake was right—as per usual. I needed a change. As we handle the bill, Ethan and his ex-wife walk into the shop hand in hand. I turn my head to try to hide behind my new waves but it is too late.

"Well, this is awkward," Deena snips, making a face.

"Only because you're making it that way with your inability to keep your face from turning ugly," I state coldly.

"How does it feel to be second best?"

"How does it feel to be attaching yourself to a lying narcissist?" My eyes meet Ethan's swollen ones. I got some good hits in on him, that's for sure. He looks like he is trying too hard to use makeup to cover up the marks.

"Stop following us, Claire," Ethan hisses.

"I was here first, you idiot."

Sidling up next to her man, Deena leans into his ear. "Call the lawyer, Ethan. Enough is enough." Her words aren't even muffled, despite her putting her hand near her mouth to pretend to shield them from my ears.

"You are only serving as the butt plug to his asshole. But I guess you do belong together." Not sure if she can stand any closer to him without falling over.

"Keep it up, Claire," Ethan finally says with warning in his tone, "and I'll sue you for harassment and for assault."

My mouth opens and then quickly closes. He cannot be serious. Is that what Deena meant by telling him to lawyer up? "What did I ever see in you?"

"A huge bank account. Obviously," Deena answers for him. She gives me a smug smirk and steps closer to her man for added emphasis that he is hers. She can have him. I don't need that type of negativity in my life.

I have nothing else to say to them. I am done with this toxicity. I turn to my stylist. "Thank you so much. I love my new hair. Let's go, Blake." I pull Blake out of the salon and drag him down the street until we are out of sight. "I hate him so bad. Lying cheating bastard."

"I am proud of you."

"Me?"

"Yup. You walked out with dignity, and no one needed to call the cops. That is progress."

"I wanted to mace his face," I grumble. "Shave his head bald and tweeze out all of Deena's eyelashes."

"Ouch!" Blake winces. "You need to keep your eyes to the sun. I didn't just stage an intervention and a makeover for you to undo all of the good we have done on your spirit today."

I take a few cleansing breaths and close my eyes. I tilt my head toward the sun and allow the warmth to surround me. *Look toward the sun, Claire.* I imagine my vision board in my head of the goals I would like to accomplish for myself. I cannot get things done by sulking or sitting around and waiting for opportunities to land in my lap.

"I'm getting a tattoo."

"Say what?" Blake asks, shaking my shoulders. "Are you being serious? Because I really need you to be serious right now." He snaps his fingers a few times in front of my face. "Or is this just one of those figurative representations? Like the washable kind?"

"A real one."

Blake holds his hands up for me to stop talking. "Let me relish this moment for a second."

"Okay, how—"

"Quit rushing it!" He turns around so his back is to me and lets out a "squeeeeeee."

I wait until he is facing me again, laughing over his

reaction. I think he is more excited about this than I am, and I'm pretty dang excited. "I have always wanted to do it. So, why not today?"

Blake thinks about it for a second and then eagerly shakes his head. "You promise not to pass out?"

"No guarantees. I am terrified."

"Over the pain?"

I shake my head. "No. I am scared the artist will mess up and it will turn out lame."

Blake laughs. "Then, there's only one place I suggest going…"

"Ink Coat?"

"Exactly."

"Well, let's do the damn thing before I change my mind."

"There's really only one last thing to do to commemorate this revenge body makeover and moving forward ritual," Blake says, as we eat ice cream cones on the street of Portland from a local shop specializing in all-natural ingredients. We just finished up at Ink Coat and are on the celebration kick.

I'm surprised I went through with my tiny tattoo. I have wanted one for so long but kept putting it off. I'm tired of placing my desires last on the list. I am a one-woman show now. I'm done compromising my happiness for others.

"And what's that?" I ask, licking my dripping ice cream before it lands on my clothes. I am a bit sore from the procedure, so I sit awkwardly on the bench but still can see Blake in my periphery.

"So, you are going to have to trust me…"

"Nothing good comes from addressing your idea with that line, Blake."

He makes a face at me. "At least I got your attention."

"Just get on with it," I say. I can't help but smile when we are together. He is the best kind of antidepressant.

"Okay, hear me out."

I take a deep breath. "I always do."

"You need to send Nic a little gift. To say thank you."

I can't hide my confusion. "*Thank you*?"

"Yes, you need to thank him for fucking you over, but also tell him that you are better without him. Trust me, it will make you feel empowered and refreshed. Plus, who doesn't like gifts? It is like reaching the ultimate level of kindness. But in the most beautiful passive-aggressive kind of way."

"Ha. And how should I go about telling him this? I'm sure you have a plan in mind."

"Always the best for you. You need to send him a box of dicks."

"Real ones or fake ones?"

"Don't get cocky."

I cannot keep myself together. There are tears starting to roll down my cheeks from the humor that only Blake can bring.

"Focus, Claire Bear. This is important," Blake says with a straight face.

"I'm trying." I take a few deep breaths to keep the giggles at bay.

"Get creative. But make sure they are pretty. If they are edible, even better."

"Of course, you would say that!"

"I mean, who doesn't like dicks you can eat? So, make sure they're tasty."

I can't stop laughing. My attempts at stopping have all failed. People walking by our bench give me dirty looks, as I drip ice cream down my hand and onto the sidewalk. I never thought this much discussion about the male genitals would be so much fun.

"Okay. Got it."

I just planned Angie's bachelorette party in Vegas, so I surely can find some edible dicks here in Portland to send to Nic as a parting gift. Maybe Blake is right in thinking that this will help give me some type of closure.

We walk back to the loft, and Blake gets ready for a trip to the gym. I start Googling for bakeries that specialize in odd requests...which leads me to an ad for revenge gifts... which then sends me on a winding journey to YouTube. Here I spend the next thirty minutes watching cute videos of animal bloopers. But that is how YouTube works. It sucks your free time down the drain as you jump headfirst into the rabbit hole. I feel cheated.

I put in my orders for custom-made accessories, featuring Nic's dick pic he sent me. Who would have thought that him sending me an obscene picture during our Vegas trip would come in so handy? Glad I thought to save it. I hope Nic enjoys showing off his member to the world.

I decide that a cake with the picture printed on an edible sheet would be special enough. If only I could see his face when he receives his package—*I'm so punny*—at his desk in his HH office. I give very specific instructions and even make sure to have the delivery person check in with security prior to arriving to help everything run smoothly. When I'm confident that I have everything ordered and arranged, I close out of my browser on my phone and run through my to-do list in my head. Tomorrow is going to be a big day, and if I want it to be a success, I should prioritize sleep.

2

CLAIRE

From the time I wake up to the time I fall asleep, I have Nic on my mind. It has been happening so frequently that I've stopped trying to prevent it. I just need to learn how to cope with this new chapter that doesn't involve him.

Thus, I'm surprised I am able to push through the weekend and start Monday morning with a semiclear head. I spent last night sending out my applications for a studio apartment, all within a price range I should be able to afford. I just need to get a few dates from some of the Entice database men—off the record. What Nic doesn't know is that I already programmed a few phone numbers into my cell from the mixer event.

He is just going to have to learn that I'm not a woman who can be controlled. I have gone through life on my own terms, and now that I'm not under any man's thumb, it's my time to shine. Maybe being single is what the universe is telling me that I need right now, in this very moment. Maybe I can use this time to work on my own personal goals and get myself whole again.

That's the thing about being with an abuser. You rarely realize it's happening until you are out of the situation and have time to process. Ethan used his charm to hook me and then slowly used manipulation to control me. I was a fool to stay with him as long as I did. But hindsight is twenty-twenty, and I can't keep beating myself up over being duped by his lies. I can only learn from my past mistakes and try not to make the same ones in the future.

Ethan may think his threats over a lawyer scare me, but I know he's bluffing. He is too damn cheap to follow through and swallow those hefty lawyer fees. He just wants to intimidate me.

I pack up my bag, give myself one last glance in the mirror, and then make my way out of the loft.

The drive to HH is an easy one, and I'd be lying if I said I wasn't nervous about going into work today. Once I park, I hang out inside my car for another five minutes, as I mentally walk through all the scenarios that could happen today. I take three deep breaths and then open my door.

A cluster of several employees enters the building. Just the chance of seeing Nic is causing my heart to palpitate.

Stay calm.

I have rehearsed so many times what I would say if approached. How I would carry myself as to not make a scene. I can't repeat what happened at the mixer event at the mansion, and I doubt Graham would ever want that type of drama to be present in his building. He's only recently accepted that I'm a permanent part of Angie's life. I can't ruin the good vibe between us.

I join the group walking in, instantly feeling weird that Nic isn't by my side—like he has been nearly every day for weeks. It feels even weirder walking in with my polished looks. A few employees are doing double takes, and the main security guard almost had a fit when I bypassed some of the scanners until he recognized me. Nic has repositioned or fired nearly half the staff, or so it seems. I'm not surprised. He probably gets off on that type of power trip.

My hair is styled with loose curls, landing just above my shoulders. My makeup is more subdued but done with a new technique the hair stylist showed me on how to implement what he called the "freshly picked" look. The contouring brightens up my face without feeling so made up. I have on a long magenta dress with matching pump heels. In this moment, I feel like I can conquer whatever life has to offer me—the good or the bad.

I refuse to hang my head. I refuse to hide in a corner. I walk to the elevator banks and press the call button. When I get up to the floor that houses Plus None, I'm eager to start the workday. Today is the day our new hires arrive, and it is a momentous occasion because it suggests to the world that we are a legitimate start-up company.

"Hey you," Angie says, entering the office, wearing Graham on her arm like an accessory. She looks blissfully happy. Energized. "Wow, Claire, you look flipping amazing! The cut and the style and the…" She gasps. "Holy cannoli! Are those highlights?"

"Yeah."

"I agree with Angie," Graham comments, "it suits you."

I smile shyly, feeling put on the spot. "Thank you both so much. I donated a ponytail's worth. Needed a change."

"That's wonderful," Angie says, eyeing me closely. "Something else is different, though. It's like you are a new version of yourself."

I rock on my heels. "I also got a very tiny tattoo on my hip."

"What! What did you get? I would have chickened out just from all the needles."

Graham tickles her sides, making her laugh. "Your ears getting done was enough stress."

"Tell us," Angie says between giggles.

"A sunflower."

"Your favorite flower!"

"Yeah," I say with a smile. "Because—"

"They are sun seekers," Angie says proudly.

My eyes fill up with tears. "You remember."

"I love the meaning behind them. Now when I see a sunflower, I can't help but smile and look toward the sun as well."

"Sometimes I need a little reminder to always look toward the light and the things that bring me joy. So this," I say, patting my right hip, "is my little reminder."

"Did it hurt?" Angie asks, wincing at the thought of needles entering her skin.

"Not too bad," I admit. "Blake tagged along and screamed more than I did just as a bystander. At least I was distracted. He kept the staff busy by claiming his blood sugar levels were dangerously low and would request juice every fifteen minutes."

"No doubt I would have done the same."

Angie has a fear of pain that manifested itself from a car accident that occurred prior to her moving to Portland and meeting me. If I'd had that type of traumatic experience, there would be no way I would volunteer to get stuck hundreds of times just for vanity purposes.

"Glad to see the power couple back together," I say cheerfully.

"I took the redeye and got here early this morning," Graham says with a smile. "Big day for you ladies, huh?"

"Yup," I chirp. "I'm really excited."

Angie, too, is about to burst with excitement.

"How did my brother treat you ladies?"

My heart instantly drops at the weight of his words. The question is innocent, and yet my entire throat feels like it is closing.

Graham's eyes study mine, or maybe I'm just paranoid that he knows something that I've been trying to keep hidden for weeks. "Hopefully with the respect you deserve."

I almost choke on my own spit. I really don't want to talk or think about Nic. Not today. Not any day, really. My stomach twists at the realization that Angie and Graham's wedding will be the most awkward event of the century for me. We still have to get through a rehearsal dinner, a wedding ceremony, and a reception.

"Claire, you feeling okay?" Angie asks, her eyes full of concern.

I simply nod. The first bit of acid hits my taste buds and I run out of the office, toward the hallway restroom. I pull open the door, find the first stall, and double over as I retch out of my body the quinoa bowl that I ate this morning. My throat burns, as I have an episode of dry heaves, one after another. My stomach cramps from the force of the heaving, making me moan in pain.

"Claire?"

"It's okay, Angie, I'm fine. Just a nervous stomach."

"You sure? Can I get you anything?"

I think for a moment. "I would love ginger ale," I answer. "With some lemon slices." As soon as the words leave my mouth, I think of Nic and how he cared for me when I had food poisoning. He introduced me to adding citrus, and I never want to have ginger ale any other way.

"I'll send Graham out for some," she says, running out of the restroom.

The door shuts before I can thank her. I flush the toilet and walk over to the sink area. In the reflection of the mirror, I see a pale and broken version of myself. There's not any type of makeover that can mask a shattered heart. I can feel it in my bones, and it hurts to breathe. I am just going through the motions. Maybe to anyone else, I look like I have reinvented myself. I look happy. But I know the truth. I'm barely hanging on. I am trying to forget. I am trying to learn how to live without the one thing I want most in this world —love.

I rinse my mouth out and vow to buy a toothbrush to store in my desk. I feel nasty, like my stomach just went to war and lost. I walk back into the Plus None office and flop down on the couch. I lean forward with my head in my hands.

"I'm here if you ever need to chat," Angie says, sitting down beside me and rubbing my back. "I know you don't want to burden me—with the wedding coming up and all— but you are never that to me."

"I know you understand when I say that I'm at a point in

my life where I wish I could wipe my mind clean of certain memories."

"I do understand."

"That's where I'm at. I just want to clear my mind of the toxicity."

"What can I do to help you? I can sew you up an Ethan voodoo doll and order an economy-sized box of five hundred push pins."

"That does sound like fun," I say half-heartedly. Ironically, Ethan isn't even taking up that much real estate in my brain. On the other hand, Nic Hoffman keeps making unwanted appearances, and shutting him out is next to impossible.

"Really, Claire. How can I help you?"

"Just be your amazing self. Keep showing up in my life. Things will be fine. I will be fine. Sometimes when it storms, we get the best rainbows afterwards."

Angie leans over and hugs me to her. It feels good to be loved by her.

Graham arrives with a twelve pack in one hand and a bag of ice in the other. He places the cans of soda in the fridge, leaving one out. I move to get up to help him, but he motions for me to sit back down. When he turns back around from the break room, he has my glass of ginger ale fixed perfectly with extra ice and perfectly sliced lemon rounds.

"Thank you," I say, accepting the beverage. I take the first sip and moan at how delicious it tastes. "I really appreciate it."

"Anytime," Graham says. "Sorry to hear you and Angie got sick together the other night." He sits down beside her on the couch, pulling her to his side. "I hate being away from my girl when she is ill."

My heart fills with sadness. It is hard being around the lovebirds when I still feel the raw emotion of Nic not reciprocating my feelings. I check my phone for the time and then excuse myself to go sit in the meditation room that I set up for reflection and serenity. Sometimes after Angie leaves for the day, I come in here and sit. I listen to a soundtrack or just enjoy the noise of my own thoughts. Today is no different.

I put on some earthy sounds and allow my shoulders to relax. I sip on my soda and enjoy the taste of the fizzy beverage. My stomach feels so much better, and I think I can have a day of normalcy—which sounds quite refreshing right now.

Out of the corner of my eye, I see several new arrivals enter the main office space. I take a deep breath, fix my hair in the reflection of the glass, and then walk out to greet them with a smile.

"Hi, I'm Claire," I say, shaking each of their hands. I know how daunting it is to start a new job, so I try to keep smiling and not show any of my previous stress through my gestures.

The new employees introduce themselves again to Angie and me, as well as each other. We have a Director of Design, a Vice President of Product, a Head of Human Resources, a Director of Public Relations and Marketing, and a Senior Sales Lead. Each employee we hired is eager to make a splash inside the subscription box industry.

For a start-up, all of the new hires have a title, as well as an equity stake in the company. Vesting periods are set over the course of several years of employment—encouraging loyalty but also fostering the drive for success. If everyone feels like the outcome of the company matters to them on a personal level, then the employees are more inclined to do a stellar job. Plus, who wouldn't want to potentially strike it rich if we take off? I could definitely use the money to pay off my accumulating debt, that's for sure.

While our new hires range in age and experience, it is hard not to feel inadequate when lining my own resume up against theirs. I push down my insecurities and put on my game face as I give a tour of our office space. Each branch will have its own area on the floor, with common conference areas set up for all-hands discussions. The new hires today are essentially in charge of hiring for their teams and building the platform needed with our proposed budget. Angie is definitely not a numbers person, so I handled the hiring of a CFO who is starting tomorrow.

After the tour, Angie and I give a presentation on our vision. I discuss the idea around the subscription box service, while Angie discusses the logistics needed to push us to market. Our new employees take notes and vote on our proposed timeline. Each department branch is given a spending budget, while the Head of HR handles the company credit card distribution. Everything seems to be going smoothly, and by the time I look at the clock, it is already time for our lunch break.

Gourmet Chef delivers a wonderful buffet right here in the office, allowing us to gather as a team to celebrate this milestone. Flowers, balloons, and a photographer arrive for an impromptu photoshoot—all courtesy of Graham.

"Wow," I say to Angie, as she wraps an arm around me, taking in the scene as it unfolds. "We are really doing this."

"I'm thrilled to be starting this chapter with you."

The rest of the afternoon is a blur. I feel energized and on a high that can only be experienced when hard work pays off. At around six o'clock, I call it quits and slump down on the couch to check my phone. I put in a ten-hour day and can barely keep my eyes open, I am that tired.

I check my email and see that one of the studio apartment buildings I applied for wants me to come in for a formal interview tomorrow morning at seven o'clock sharp. They have one unit available and are basically doing me a favor, since I am able to pay weekly instead of monthly. In addition, an advance on rent is not required, because they want to fill the space as soon as possible. I almost want to sign without even seeing the place. It is my only chance to move off of the cheesy-poof couch that Blake has let me borrow. I'm so over smelling like stale cheese every morning and requiring another shower. Plus, Henry keeps trying to catch me in my underwear every time he enters the common area. I am over it.

My eyes grow heavy over the words on my screen, and I promise myself that I am only going to close them for five minutes before I head over to the loft. I yawn and snuggle into the back cushions of the couch and use a throw pillow to rest my head. Everything is so comfy. I feel like I am melting into it.

I must be in a deep dreamlike state, because when I open my eyes, the lights are dimmed and Nic is hovering over me with the absence of an actual expression on his face. I close my eyes again and shake my head at the absurdity of my mind dreaming him up. Turning my face into the pillow, I remember all the good times we had together. Him buying me motion sickness medicine, me wearing his white dress shirt on the plane, him finding ways to feed me pancakes, us enjoying the helicopter tour and gambling in the casino together. I think about the selfie stick, our late-night walks, and the moment he pulled me out of the fountain at Caesars Palace. It is like a montage of memories playing one after another in my head.

My mind drifts and drifts, and when I'm about to go even deeper into my memories, it is the smell of citrus and wood that brings me back to the surface—keeping me afloat. My eyes open, and I blink to adjust to the change of light and my scenery. Where am I? I sit up and notice a soft blanket draped over me. I push it to the side and look around. Shit. I fell asleep in the Plus None office, just like I promised myself I wouldn't. I look for my phone on the end table and do not find it. I get up and turn on a nearby lamp. Then I bend over the sofa and start moving cushions until I find my phone hidden in a crevice of the upholstery.

I glance at the notification screen, seeing a series of texts from Blake and a couple from Angie. There's one missed call from Nic right around the time I decided to lie down. My eyes dart to the clock, and I see that it is currently three in the morning. I count back the hours until I come to the realization that I have slept here for nine hours. Holy hell, I must have been tired.

I move about the office, packing up the bag I brought. When I push through the main doors, I am startled to find Nic camped out on a chair in the hallway, breathing rhythmically. I stand in awe, staring at his form. He looks like he hasn't slept in a month, and his normal calm demeanor has vanished. Even in his sleep, Nic looks visibly stressed. Tense.

I tiptoe past him and hear the sound of his throat clearing. I jump into the air, almost tripping.

"Shit, don't do that!" I snap, holding my hand to my heart. "You're going to give me a heart attack."

"Your hair…"

"What about it?" My words come out harsh. I'm still mad at him for scaring me.

"I like it."

"Okay."

"A lot."

His eyes move over me like melted chocolate, warming me from the inside out. I am taken aback by his compliment. Part of me wants to say, "thank you," while the other part of me wants to say, "suck it." So, I just ignore his comment and instead ask, "What are you doing here?"

"I have to let you out or the alarm will go off, alerting the Portland police of an intruder."

"You knew I was in here sleeping the whole time?" I ask stupidly.

"Yes, Claire. I know everything that happens in this building."

"Then why not wake me up or send someone else to do it?" I huff. "I've been here napping on the couch for over nine hours."

"I know."

"You know…"

He shrugs. "You looked like you needed the sleep, so I didn't want to bother you."

I should have known that Nic would be keeping an eye on everyone in the building. He is the head of security, after all. He probably has cameras spaced throughout the building, monitoring everyone in employment here at HH. He seems anal enough to have thermal cameras to track movement after hours as well.

"I'm leaving now," I say, turning and walking toward the elevators.

Nic follows me. Unlike the times in the past, it is easy to keep my distance from him. I am still so raw over the breakup and his pigheaded ways. I know my worth. I want the man I end up with to be deliriously in love with me. I want him to choose me now and every day thereafter. I'm the idiot for trying to be with a man who put me in a position where I had sex with my boyfriend in front of him. That alone should have been a red flag that neither man valued commitment. They both just wanted to win, while my only option was to lose.

I lost a part of myself and wasted a lot of time pursuing Nic, who was unattainable. Never again will I make that mistake. I am better than the girl he wanted me to be.

I should have listened when he said he would destroy me. But how can he damage a heart that has already been broken?

We enter the elevator, and I stay on my side of the box, looking down at my phone for a distraction.

"Congrats on moving up from a two-person company."

"Thanks." I don't make eye contact. I don't want to get swallowed up by his crystal blues. I don't want to convey any emotion that might make him think he damaged me.

Because he did, so much so that I don't know if I'll ever fully recover.

"I'm sorry."

"So you've said," I gripe.

"I mean it."

"I'm just glad you gave me a reason to hate you. Makes moving on so much easier."

The doors open to the elevator, and I walk out first. Nic catches up to me, types in the pass code, and watches me walk away. I refuse to turn around and see if he is following me. I refuse to let him think he deserves a second look. I unlock my car, hop inside, and drive away toward Blake's loft.

Goodbye, Nic.

3

NIC

I'm starting to think that Claire wants me to snap. For the past three nights, she has gone out on several dates with men from the Entice database. Everything is being done under the table and off the record. This isn't about me getting a cut for the company I no longer want. This is about my limits being pushed to the max. I don't like seeing Claire with other men.

I feel like a stalker keeping tabs on her and obsessing over her whereabouts. I know she isn't doing this for the thrill or for romance. She is simply trying to gather money fast. That is the only logical explanation as to why every waking moment is spent working in some way. It is difficult to watch her walk into HH every morning—often an hour or more before the other workers—and not rush to the lobby to see her face-to-face myself. The TV screens are not enough. I need the fix that only close proximity can bring.

I want to get drunk off her vanilla scent. I want to see

for myself that she is getting enough sleep and nourishing her body well with food.

Claire changed her hair style, got some new makeup, and seems to have found her calling with the subscription box industry. My contacts tell me that Angie and she are making major progress in their company, Plus None. I had no doubts. They both are forces to be reckoned with, but when they join forces—ka pow! Dynamite.

Good luck world, here they come.

I miss her. I want her. I just don't want a commitment. Claire deserves someone better than me. I am damaged. Jaded. But I saw it in her eyes the morning we broke up. She is yearning for a forever love. She wants a once-in-a-lifetime, and that is too much pressure on me to even give her a sliver of that life.

Being with me would be holding her back from her true potential. I've seen Ethan do that to her. I can't be the next guy who limits her from shining as bright as she can.

Yet here I am doing things out of character and against my moral compass—which seems to be completely broken these days. I have to be going crazy if I am following Claire to a reduced-price furniture store on the upper east side, just a couple of miles from River Valley University. There would be no reason to come here unless she is trying to furnish her own place on a budget. I can easily provide for her. Yet, no more lines need to be blurred with the introduction of money. Right now, I need to set clear boundaries for myself, and so far, I suck at this task.

I walk into the store and keep my distance along the outskirts as Claire goes straight for the bedroom furniture. She hovers near the queen-sized bed that has storage drawers built into the base, as well as a headboard made of shelves. It reminds me of one step up from dorm room furniture.

"Can I help you, sir?" a female worker asks me.

"Yes, actually." I nudge my head in the direction of Claire. "I need you to accept some money and convince that woman over there with the beautiful dark hair and flawless skin"—*and smokin' hot body*—"that there is a big sale today."

Her eyes grow like dinner plates. "Wow. This has never happened to me before." Her energy is high and expressed through her bouncing on the balls of her feet. "Swoon. You are the most romantic person I have ever met."

What? No. I shake my head in disagreement. I hand her over one thousand dollars that I just got out of the ATM before coming here. "Don't let her think that this is a charity thing. Make it believable, understood?"

"Consider it done," the worker says, looking down at the wad of cash. Her eyes are dreamy like she is witnessing some grandiose gesture from a romantic film. It's not like that at all. I just want Claire to have a better start at a life away from me. She's pissed off, and although she won't ever know the money came from me, at least I can feel better knowing I did something to help her out—and maybe stop feeling like I'm a total douche. I will settle for just being a partial one.

I turn and leave the store, waiting in my car for Claire to exit. She smiles brightly and talks to the worker who hands her a slip of paper. I hope it's a delivery slip, or we both just wasted forty-five minutes of our lives.

I wait until Claire is safely inside her car and pulling

out of the parking spot before leaving. Not feeling like going home, I drive over to the Entice offices. I go through the motions of parking, riding the elevator, and greeting the receptionist at her desk. It feels weird being back here after avoiding the place for weeks. I check my office for my package arrivals and get to work at replacing all of the security features with better, updated ones. Until I actually take the steps to dissolve the company, I want to tighten up the security and ensure that my privacy is tamper-proof.

I am so in the zone of working that I do not even notice that I skipped dinner and that I have three missed calls from Tyler. I pull up the number and hit call.

"Hey, thought you should know that Claire is on a date with some dude," he says in greeting. "He kinda looks like you too. Less smug though. And a bit more feminine."

I scrunch up my face at his unnecessary descriptions. "It's off the books."

"Wow, I'm shocked you aren't trying to smash something," he teases. "Is this what we should call progress?"

"I will if he touches her."

"Just want me to watch and wait?"

"Yes, and I need a way of wiring money into Claire's account without her growing suspicious. She obviously needs the cash flow if she is this desperate to avoid the protections of the agency and do things off the record. Seems unsafe and careless, if you ask me." I know she has student loans to pay for, and there is no good way to help her out without her noticing.

"Pretty sure no matter what you do, you're going to look like a stalker."

I rub a hand over my face. "Yeah, I know." I just can't keep her out of my head.

Tyler and I barely know each other and yet he is comfortable enough to talk to me this way. It is probably because he is damn good at his job and doesn't really need my money. He really just likes the work. Asher did a great job bringing us together, even though both of them are smart-asses and probably eating all of this up. Asher can put together the pieces, and Tyler was only with me for a day before realizing my level of insanity. I think he may be only sticking around to watch me crash and burn—repeatedly.

Every time I close my eyes at night, I see her face. When I wake in the morning, I reach for her. Even in my dreams, she is with me. I keep slipping further and further into a state of crazy as more time passes. It is only a matter of time until the entire outside world learns about my one weakness. It is Claire Nettles. I just hope I can brace myself in time for any backlash for breaking her heart.

"Anything else, boss?"

Tyler knows I hate when he refers to me as that, because to me we are equals in the field. "Keep eyes on her and inform me if I need to intervene."

"I am proud of you."

I furrow my brow and lean back into my leather chair. "Why?"

"Delaying the war."

"There's not going to be a war," I scoff.

"Let's hope there won't be a war," he corrects.

"Bye, Tyler. Do your job."

It takes several more hours to get everything completely updated at Entice. Losing myself in work is a great coping mechanism for me. The years post-Tara are a bit of a blur because I would drown in overtime hours.

I shake off the feeling that maybe my dedication to work wasn't really worth it in the end. I mean, I have a cushioned bank account that allows me to live a luxurious lifestyle. However, going back to an empty apartment now seems lonely, because I know what it felt like when Claire was basically living there with me. My place that I used for basically just sleeping and working out became a place for watching movies, making food together, and creating memories in just a short amount of time.

That's the power that Claire has. She can change the ordinary to extraordinary. She can make something that seems mundane become a new forever memory.

She is going to make someone very—

I can't even think it.

I check Claire's tracker and see that her designated dot is hovering over an apartment complex a few blocks away from the loft she stayed in with Blake and his roommate. I pack up my stuff, set the necessary security features, and make my way to the parking garage. I start the engine and head over to Claire's new apartment to check out the building.

The sun has already set, and the city of Portland is lit up by the moon and the lights from the buildings. I check my email at a stop light and see that Tyler has sent me the new information on the building and the unit which Claire is renting. From the street, I am able to see which room is hers. Everything seems secure. Quiet. So, at least I can attempt to rest knowing that she is tucked away safely inside the walls of the building.

My phone buzzes with an incoming email alert, and I nearly choke on my spit when I see that the new arrival is from Claire, time stamped one minute ago. I stay parked, trying to imagine what she is doing right now.

I read the email that basically gives me a list of best man duties for the rehearsal night, the wedding, and the reception. I can't help but smile over her need to micromanage me. I need it, though. It's not like I've been in many weddings before, but I don't think she has either. I archive the email and double check that my calendar has the appropriate dates marked.

I glance up at the window that should be hers, wondering how I'm going to get my next fix. Driving away feels like leaving empty-handed. It's as if I'm pining for someone who no longer wants me. I feel conflicted inside and don't know which way to turn. One minute I want to avoid commitment at all costs. The next minute I am secretly paying for used furniture and camping outside of apartment buildings.

When I get back to my place, I hit up the punching bag and then get ready for bed. Every corner of my room reminds me of Claire and how beautiful she looked sprawled out on my dark sheets or pressed up against my wall or leaning against the window as I thrust into her from behind. I hate myself for not being man enough to stay away from her. I hate myself for not being man enough to go to her right now and make her believe that we could be an "us."

When I can't get comfortable, I climb out of bed and raid the kitchen for the ingredients to make some pancakes. Claire's love for them has rubbed off on me, and I now can't walk past a breakfast shop without thinking of her. I pull out the almond flour, sugar, milk, eggs, and butter. I decrease the recipe amounts by a fourth and mix all of the ingredients into a bowl while the skillet heats.

When I plate up my pancakes, I garnish them with fresh fruit and whipped cream. I snap a picture of my plate— something I would never typically do—and send it to Claire with the caption, *Thinking of you...*

It is an impulsive decision to text her, especially this late at night. When the dots appear on the screen indicating that she is responding, I wait eagerly for her to send her message. Except it doesn't happen. Every minute that passes lets me know that it isn't going to happen. I am just wasting my time. What did I want to accomplish anyway?

Claire is better off without me. Even she has come to that conclusion. So, even if I get my head out of my ass and work through my own issues, there would still be no point.

I eat my food and load the dirty dishes into the dishwasher. What am I doing here? I feel like I'm mourning the loss of something that I claimed to have never wanted in the first place. My brain hurts from thinking about her.

I can't sleep without verifying one more time that Claire is still at her new apartment building. If she found out I have been keeping a close eye on her, she would go ballistic. I hope that day never happens.

I get to my office a little late on Friday morning, because I stop at the coffee shop on the way in to grab a to-go cup of coffee. My new personal assistant is arriving midday today, and based on her resume, she should be able to handle anything I throw at her. It'll be our first time meeting. I bypassed the in-person interviews because this is a two-week trial period to see how we mesh. I'm sure she'll learn early on that I'm a picky bastard with some OCD tendencies. The healthy amount, of course.

I touch base in the HH lobby with my security workers. After cleaning house weeks ago, I'm confident that my current staff is top-notch and dedicated to the job. Either that or they are terrified of being let go, which is always a possibility if I see any red flags. The one way to get workers to perform well is to show them that they are replaceable. For as much as I pay my staff members, they can afford to do exactly as I instruct.

I take the elevator up to my floor. I unlock my office door and walk over to the desk. I turn on the wall of televisions and double check that Claire and Angie arrived safely to their office. Graham texted me this morning that the girls were going to meet for an early walk and then go to breakfast prior to coming into work. I placed a camera right outside of Plus None and set a motion detector alert to inform me of any movement.

A knock sounds, and I glance at the door wondering who it is. I rarely have unexpected visitors, so this is definitely out of the norm. My personal assistant, Brenna, isn't scheduled to arrive until later.

"Who is it?"

"It's Dan King, sir. You have several deliveries."

"Deliveries?" I ask. I never scheduled any deliveries. I grab my phone to check for alerts and—

"They've been approved," Dan states, before I have a chance to ask.

He has been trying to prove himself to me ever since the change in power was made public to the building staff. His partner, Eugene, never made the cut. After several weeks of being here as head of security, I am certain that I made the right choice. Dan has been doing great work, and there's a chance I may move him up in rank if he continues to prove to be a valuable asset at HH.

"Fine. Come in," I say, staring at the door in anticipation.

The door opens slowly and three delivery people come in, followed by Dan. One is holding a huge sheet cake in a transparent plastic box. The other is carrying a gift basket full of what appears to be cookies and desserts. The last person is toting a large, wrapped box with a ginormous bow.

"What's all of this?" I ask, staring from one person to the next. "Who is this from?"

"Oh, there's a card attached to the box," the one delivery person answers. His voice comes out almost as a snicker.

My gifts are placed beside each other on my desk. I reach into my suit pocket and pull out some cash to hand to each worker as a tip, except for Dan whose tip is a paycheck. I say the appropriate *thank yous* and then my office clears out again, and I am left with just myself and my packages.

I look through the top of the cake box and—

"Fuck, no," I exhale to myself. "You've got to be kidding me."

On the top of the cake is the image of my dick in full technicolor with the words "Go Fuck Yourself" written in elegant script frosting at the bottom of the picture. I recognize the photo because it is the exact one I sent to Claire as a semi-joke in Vegas. It is mine. All mine. The cake makers had to have laughed their asses off over this odd request that could have only come from my little spitfire. Not to mention how many of my employees must have seen this masterpiece being delivered straight to my office.

I tear open the plastic of the gift basket and am not surprised to find that there are dick-shaped cake pops, cookies, pastries, donuts, and eclairs stashed inside under some tissue paper. There are even lollipops, various chocolate molded dicks, and a dick-shaped fuzzy stuffed animal with cartoonish eyes that wiggle when you shake it. My finger touches the tag, and I see that there is a button that can be pushed.

I take a deep breath and decide to give it a go. It does not disappoint. The entire plush toy vibrates and sings a jingle about dicks. Who the hell comes up with these items?

When I get to the gift box, I pretty much expect the theme to be carried through, and when I rip through the paper and pull off the lid, I am not let down. I pull back the layers of tissue paper to reveal custom-made socks, a tie, and boxer briefs, all made from fabric that has my dick printed repeatedly in tiny images over the entire surface area. It is the same image from the cake and has to be an accumulated two hundred dicks between the three accessories.

I stare at the gifts in awe and don't know whether Claire's message was received as she intended it to be. What may appear as a revenge gift to any outsider, to me shows that she is thinking of me—or a few specific inches of me—

and caring enough to go through the trouble of a thought-out custom gift.

I find the card that just serves as confirmation that she is the sender. I break the seal, pull off the envelope, and open the folded cardboard to see that—

POOF!

Glitter shoots out from the inside in a cloud of sparkly dust ejaculation. I cough as the air in front of me slowly clears. When my eyes adjust to the chaos that now surrounds me, I am able to see that the shiny confetti is really made of glitter and tiny two-dimensional plastic penises. I shake my head as more pieces cascade to the floor. The cleaning crew is going to have a field day with this one.

I'm going to be the topic of discussion in break rooms for weeks to come. I just know it.

Not surprisingly, Claire's name is stamped onto the bottom of the inside of the card. Above it, a message reads —*Feel special...you're the biggest dick of all.*

I stare at the words and then make a call to Dan.

"What can I do for you, sir?"

"Get Miss Nettles in my office."

"What time, sir?"

"Now."

4

CLAIRE

I am in the middle of doing a trial run on the survey that helps to create the custom boxes when there is a shadow passing over my screen. I turn and see a man in a suit hovering behind me, startling me from my work. He looks sort of familiar, and I am sure our paths have crossed between my coming and going from HH.

"Excuse me, Miss Nettles?" he asks.

"Yes?"

"My name is Dan King. I work for Mr. Hoffman."

I smile. "You're going to need to specify."

"Mr. Nic Hoffman."

I eye up Dan. "Is that so?" What is he doing here?

"Mr. Hoffman would like to see you in his office now."

I narrow my eyes at the man and then focus my attention back on my screen. Too bad I don't take orders from that Mr. Hoffman. What does he want anyway? "Tell him"—*to fuck off*—"no, thank you."

"Ma'am, I'm not at liberty to do that."

I turn back to look at Dan. "That's cool. I'll just shoot him an email telling him that I will be there"—a smirk plays on my lips as I think of Nic's reaction—"in a few hours." The dude can wait. Nothing he has to say to me is urgent.

Dan glances around the room, taking inventory of the other workers. Dipping his head down, he whispers, "Please do not make a scene. I value my job."

I frown over his sincerity. He probably is worried about getting fired. Ever since Nic became the head of security, I've noticed a huge shift in the staff. I log out of my computer and push back my chair. I let out a sigh and mentally prepare to see the one and only Nic Hoffman. "Fine."

"Right this way," Dan says, motioning with his hand for guidance—as if I don't know the way out of my office. "Remember, I'm just the middleman."

"This better be quick," I grumble. "Some of us actually work around here."

I follow the suited goon all the way to Nic's Head of Security office. I push open the door and am ushered inside. The door shuts behind me, leaving me alone with Nic, and suddenly the room feels smaller. Stifling.

Nic's back is to me and his attention is elsewhere.

"Why am I being summoned?"

"Because my men do what I tell them to do."

Why won't he look at me? What's the point of this? "Answer the question."

"Why would I do that, when arguing with you is much more fun," he says wryly.

"Something tells me you didn't invite me up here to discuss world news."

"That's correct," he says smoothly, spinning around slowly in his chair.

I am speechless as I take in the scene. Baked items line his desk and lap, while a half-bitten cookie is resting between two of his fingers.

Nic smirks. "I see someone has a fetish for my dick."

I take a step closer. I can't help but stare at the basket and the cake and the clothing accessories. I made the purchases at the beginning of the week and completely forgot that today was the delivery date. If I don't mark things on my calendar, I tend to be forgetful.

Buying items online is one thing, but seeing Nic's penis printed on a cake and on socks is too much. This is probably one of the most creative gifts I've come up with, so for that I have to take a little satisfaction. I did good. I did *really* good.

I look back up at Nic and notice that he has tiny little die-cut penises in his hair. They are on his suit coat, all over his desk, and scattered on the carpet surrounding him. Glitter is sprinkled like snow everywhere within a yard's radius of him.

"Wow," I state. I am nearly speechless over the scene.

"Wow?"

"I wasn't expecting the dick glitter bomb to be that..." I struggle to find the correct word.

"Explosive?" he suggests.

My lips can't help but curl into a smile, which then turns into a giggle, and then it is a full-blown laughfest. Nic just stares at me as I stand in front of his desk, doubling over from laughing so much. Every time I try to stand upright, my eyes connect with his and I lose it all over again. I turn my attention to the back wall behind his desk and try my best to get the words I want to say out. "Yes, that's the"— giggle—"right word." I pause to gather all my verbal strength. "*Explosive.*" As soon as the word escapes my throat, I start the whole laugh cycle again.

"I guess you get what you pay for," he says flatly. "You spared no detail in your message you sent to me."

I shrug, trying to regain my composure. "I mean, who doesn't love glitter?"

"Um, well, probably the guy that now has it permanently stuck in his lungs."

How is he able to maintain a straight face? I can barely keep myself together. I can tell Nic is equally fascinated and confused by my gesture. I didn't think it through, that much is obvious. Maybe he is seeing my gift as a door opening. He left me. Not the other way around. And now we are mutually choosing to keep our distance. Yet here we are, together again. We are playing a dangerous game of tug-of-war where emotions keep getting involved, but there is never a winner. Instead, we stay in limbo. This uneasy feeling of being off-balance is messing with my mental state. I did this for closure purposes, not to rekindle anything.

Except this doesn't feel like closure at all.

This feels like self-inflicted torture.

Every time I'm around Nic, I'm reminded of what I lost. He is right though. He is not the man for me. I need to continue to remind myself to protect my heart. No one else will.

"This is my fault," I say with defeat.

"Obviously," he chuckles, glancing around at the

display. Every time he laughs, more minipenises fall from his hair onto the polished surface of his desk.

I shake my head. "No. That's not what I mean. What I'm trying to say is that I seem to be sending mixed messages and blurring lines that should stay straight. You made it clear that you are a bad fit for me. I will respect that."

"Can I at least keep my gifts? After the shock wore off, I find I don't mind looking at myself."

I smile over his teasing. Nic really does have a good sense of humor, but I can tell he doesn't let it out very often. I can't help but wonder who hurt him so badly in the past. Whoever it was did a lot of damage.

"You can keep them. Wear them to the next security meeting you lead."

"At least have a dick donut or pastry with me," he says softly. He tilts the half-eaten cookie toward me. "As you know, I'm a huge fan of cock cookies."

I almost sense hope in his voice. These little glimmers are messing with my head. Yet the last thing I need is for someone to pick me as a default or as a bed warmer. If I can't be someone's first choice, then I don't want to be that person's anything.

I reach into the basket and pull out a cream filled eclair that is dipped in chocolate. I know this is not vegan, and it sure as hell is not organic. However, it looks divine, and I can't resist. I bite off the mushroom shaped head, and the vanilla pastry cream squeezes out of the side and drips onto my lips. I can feel Nic's eyes on me the whole time as my tongue cleans up the mess. I lick chocolate icing off my fingers and finish the rest of the pastry with two more bites.

"Tasty," I admit.

I expect a sarcastic remark from Nic, but instead I am met with brooding silence. I can tell he has a lot on his mind. I want to scream at him that it is his own fault for not keeping me around long enough to see what I can do with my mouth. We had a good rhythm going with what I thought was a relationship forming, but my inability to keep my emotions in check destroyed every brick in the foundation.

"I'll see you…" *Later*? I want to finish my statement but know that if I do, it implies want. While I know our paths are destined to cross again, I have to maintain this platonic attitude. It's for the best.

I turn to leave, and when my hand touches the doorknob, a knock from the other side causes me to jump. I open the door and see a beautiful woman with sleek, long blonde hair waiting for permission to enter.

"Who are you?" I mouth, staring at her legs that go on for days. I feel extra short in comparison, or maybe that's just the feeling of inferiority slipping in.

"I am Mr. Hoffman's personal assistant that he hired," she says sweetly. "My name is Brenna."

She is so prim and proper that I look like a hoodlum in comparison to her.

"Good luck," I snipe and continue walking down the hall and into the elevator.

As soon as the doors shut and I am left alone to my own thoughts, I let out the breath I didn't know I was holding. My head rests against the wall. It is not even noon and my day is already headed off course. My stomach cramps, causing me to have waves of nausea bubbling up inside. It is not too often that I break form and eat something that is not vegan. It is moments like this that I understand why I'm so dedicated and strict. Dairy products cause me so much discomfort. I feel slightly gross, like my digestive system needs a shower.

When the elevator stops and the doors open, the wave of nausea strikes me hard. I dash into the nearest bathroom and expel the contents of my stomach into the closest toilet. After rinsing my mouth, I fix my hair and smooth out my outfit. I force myself to return to Plus None, despite feeling like crap and wanting to go home and rest.

At about midday, Angie places a glass of ginger ale with lemon slices at my desk and gives me a small smile. "You look like you are dragging today," she says slowly. "How about you start the weekend early and leave?"

I smile up at her and nod. She's right. I'm not being very productive when I am this worn out and exhausted. I sip my soda and pack up my bag. "I have so much organizing to do at my new apartment before I can have you over for a movie night."

"That sounds wonderful. Can I help you with anything? Moving things? Laundry? Shopping trip to a home store?"

I shake my head. "Nah. I just need to spend this weekend getting myself officially moved in and all should be good again."

"Just say the word if you need anything. Other than some last-minute wedding things, I am free."

"Thanks."

"Also, Claire?"

"Hmm?"

"Have you thought about getting your bloodwork run

just to make sure your levels are good? You seem to be not yourself lately, and maybe you just need some B or D vitamins."

I give Angie a weak smile. "Yeah, I'm due for a physical and routine bloodwork. I'll look into it." I can't even remember the last time I was at the doctor's other than the free clinic to update my test results for working at Entice. Part of healthy eating means that my immune system is usually in good shape. However, she is right. I am not myself. Problem is, there is no cure for a broken heart.

It's hard suffering in silence and not being able to run to Angie to share all of my struggles. I would never want her to have to choose sides between me and her future brother-in-law. I should have known better than to get involved with Nic. Even though it feels good to make him the villain, I also made bad choices in this story.

I toss my bag over my shoulder and make my way outside into the hallway. I get on the elevator and slowly walk through the lobby. I am so sluggish. Maybe I just need to spend this weekend sleeping. My new furniture set arrived yesterday, and I couldn't wait to get it set up to avoid another night on the cold floor. However, the directions were not very descriptive and took me way longer than I expected. At least I don't wake up smelling like Doritos. Anything is better than that horrid stench.

The good thing about a studio apartment—besides the cheaper rent—is that the low square footage forces me to stay organized. By nature, I am a bit scattered. I am trying my best to be better though.

The outside air is warm and feels good against my chilled air-conditioned skin. I see Nic's henchman strolling toward me with a to-go cup of coffee in hand. He must be on his lunch break.

"Hey Claire, how are you?" Dan asks.

I guess that since we are not technically at work, he feels it's okay to call me by my first name.

"Did Nic send you?" I ask defensively.

Dan looks genuinely confused. "What? No, no of course not. I'm just on my break," he explains, gesturing toward his cup of coffee. "Sorry I had to basically drag you up to Mr. Hoffman's office. He was very direct, and I felt like I didn't have a choice. Hope it wasn't too awkward being there."

For someone who I assume is in their upper twenties, Dan acts older than his age. He is kind and professional even outside of HH. His brown hair has a bit of a wave to it, and he looks like he has a gym membership and actually uses it.

"It's okay." I shrug. "I'm okay."

"You going out for lunch?"

"No, actually, I'm headed home. Starting the weekend early."

Dan nods and for a brief second allows sadness to creep into his features. He gives me another smile and says, "Have a great weekend. Hope to see you again on Monday." I start to walk again, and I hear him clear his throat and say, "Oh, and Claire?"

"Hmm?"

"I really dig your new haircut."

I turn back to Dan and allow my smile to reach my eyes. "Thank you. I was due for a change."

"It suits you."

"Well, have a good weekend," I say, placing one foot in front of the other.

Dan's comment is oddly similar to Graham's and Nic's in regard to my hair. I am glad people like the change, but I did it for myself. It is my new way that I want to live my life. I can afford to be a tad bit selfish, considering I have wasted too much precious time worrying about what everyone else thinks. It is easy to lose yourself with that type of outlook.

Maybe Dan is not a bad guy after all. He seems very laid-back compared to how I saw him this morning during our first real introduction. Maybe we have crossed more times in the halls than I can remember. He does seem to know me better than I know him. Either that or Nic has done some oversharing. I have wondered what he has told his staff regarding me, especially after I got accosted in the lobby that first day by Tweedledee and Tweedledum.

Angie and Graham's bodyguard, Collins, dropped me off at work today, since we had a girls' breakfast before heading into the office. My new place is just about one and a half miles from Hoffman Headquarters, so the walk isn't horrendous. Plus, I pass by several boutiques and shops along the way, so it's easy for me to sneak into a few and scope out wedding gifts for the happy couple.

My stomach is still uneasy, but the fresh air does wonders. I meander into an eclectic shop that looks like it would sell something unique. Angie has inherited Graham's abundant wealth, so getting her just anything is silly because her fiancé basically would buy her the world if he could. I need something special. Perhaps something that neither would have thought to need or want.

I browse aimlessly, just seeing what catches my eye. Despite having a smallish storefront, the shop stretches way into the back of the building and is multilevel, featuring a stairway to the basement and a stairway up to the second floor.

I travel to the upstairs and am in awe of all of the dresses lined up on racks. Maybe I can find a rehearsal dress here. It is springtime in Portland, so pastel colors are fine to wear, as long as I stay away from bridal white to avoid a major faux pas. Hell, my luck I would get my period wearing white.

As soon as my mind thinks about my period, I start to mentally try to figure out when I had my last one. With my bad luck, I'll probably get it right during the middle of the wedding ceremony where I won't be able to excuse myself to the restroom without the entire guest list noticing. Plus, I bloat like a pufferfish during that time of the month, and the dress that Angie picked out for me to wear as the maid of honor will look horrendous on me if I'm retaining water weight.

I pull out my phone and open up my period tracker app. What the hell? I am thirteen days late. How did I not even notice? My stomach starts to cramp, as a wave of nausea strikes again.

I dart down the steps of the shop and push past a few customers as I get myself out the door I arrived in, sucking in huge gulps of air as I comprehend the possibility that I am...

I can't even think it. No. No freaking way. I'm taking birth control pills. I can't be. I hold my stomach, willing it to settle so I can think. I imagine it bloating up to the size of a balloon that got filled with too much air. Thoughts of crying. Diapers. Being a horrible mom just like the one who raised me. I can't do this. I am not equipped to be a mommy. I can barely take care of myself.

I double over and squat down to the concrete, staring at my polished toenails peeking out through my sandal straps. If what I think is true, there will come a time where I won't be able to see my own feet. I close my eyes as my breathing picks up to an unsafe level.

I'm going to be sick. Yet it all is starting to make sense. I keep getting sick. The nausea, the vomiting, and the revelation that I missed my last period. The timeline is revealing that the possibility that I am—*pregnant*—is more *probably likely* than *probably unlikely*.

I stand up and walk slowly to a storefront bench half a block away. Maybe all of the stress is wreaking havoc on my body. Maybe I have been exercising too much and not getting enough calories. Maybe the breakup with Ethan and then the one with Nic are taking a toll on me. And then it dawns on me.

I put my face into my hands and suck in air through my nose.

If I am pregnant, I may not know who the father of my child is.

5

CLAIRE

As fearful as I am, I still take the Band-Aid approach and walk straight to the convenience store that is just a few minutes' walk from my apartment and pick up four pregnancy tests—each with a slightly different accuracy level and of various brands. I won't be able to shut my brain off from thinking of every what-if scenario until I at least know if I am carrying the child of one of my exes. And if I am, I should look into suing the contraceptive drug company that promised me that I would never be in this situation if I followed the directions. Dammit.

It takes me twice as long to walk back to my apartment because my feet feel like bricks. Maybe I'm already starting to swell up like a jellyfish. Who knows, maybe I am carrying twins. As soon as the thought creeps into my mind, I stop and stare up at the sky. I am driving myself crazy, and I haven't even taken the test…times four.

The apartment building where I reside has been recently renovated and updated on security measures, but just from looking at the outside it is not obvious. Hanging around Nic has given me an eye for working cameras, a twenty-four-hour guard, and locked doors. Before meeting him I never really cared about my safety while in Portland. Despite the trauma Angie endured last year, the city overall seems safe enough—at least for me. The crime I saw living on the outskirts of Washington, DC, pretty much makes everywhere else look like a utopian society.

When money is tight—or basically nonexistent—I can't be too picky. I would have easily accepted less luxurious conditions. How am I going to afford a child? I'm not cut out to be a mom, and I know I am especially not cut out to be a single mom. That's what it will be too. If I am pregnant with Ethan's child, he has made it clear that he doesn't want any more expenses or mouths to feed. He won't accept this child. And since I rejected his offer to be used for sex by him, I doubt he'll suddenly start giving me the respect I deserve. As for Nic, why would he even want a relationship with his baby if he doesn't want to commit to one woman? I doubt kids were even part of any five-year plan. They definitely weren't part of mine.

No matter how I dice it, I am in a losing situation if the little plastic sticks reveal a plus sign. I take the elevator up to my floor and unlock the door to my one-room abode. I don't even know where I would put the crib if I needed one. Maybe I can downsize the queen bed to a twin and then get one of those minicribs. Do they even make mini sizes? I don't even know. In fact, I know nothing about babies, except that they cry a lot and need their moms around the clock for the first year.

Just when I'm making something of my life by growing

a start-up company with my best friend, I am about to have a bomb dropped into my life. I pull out the four boxed tests from the paper bag and line them up on the kitchen counter like soldiers. The directions are basically the same for each one; pee onto each test strip and wait five minutes.

In my twenty-three years of life, never before have I had a pregnancy scare. I have never had to take a home test, yet here I stand about to take four in a row. My stomach feels like it is going to get stuck in my throat. I rip open the first box and pull out the plastic tube device. I read the pamphlet and then go into the bathroom—which is the only room in my apartment with a dividing door.

I pull my pants down and then lower myself onto the seat. With shaking hands, I hold the stick underneath my crotch as I relax enough to let the pee out. Once I know I hit the mark, I quickly stop my flow and save it up for the next test. I wipe and then carry out my used stick to rest on a napkin on the counter. I open the next box and do the same routine.

When I have peed on every stick, I set a timer and then walk over to the window seat that instantly sold me on this place—as if there was even any competition. My window overlooks the street, and between the buildings I am able to get a partial view of the riverfront. Portland is such an enchanting city. It is an easy place to live in to maintain a healthy lifestyle. There are tons of parks, walking paths, and cafes that specialize in a variety of nutritional needs. Cars slow down or stop for pedestrians, and people are friendlier in general. What might have gotten you the middle finger in Northern Virginia gets you a wave and a smile here in Portland.

My timer going off causes me to jump up from my cushioned seat. This is it. It's the moment of truth. I pad across my hardwood floors barefoot and walk into the kitchen. I flip over the first test and see the very distinct plus sign. My heart drops and a flood of tears comes. I then frantically turn over the other three and reveal the exact same results, with the last test spelling it out with a single red word —pregnant.

Seeing the word in print makes me grab hold of the countertop to keep myself from passing out. I am lightheaded and most likely dehydrated. I stumble over to the sink and fill up my reusable water bottle. I gulp the water down like my life depends on it. *Our* lives.

I let the certainty of the moment sink into my reality. I am going to be a mother. And I'll probably suck at it, considering the woman who should be my role model has been MIA from my life since long before I moved to the West Coast.

A knock on my door makes me spill my drink down the side of the bottle.

"Who is it?" I yell toward the door, as I wipe up the mess I just created.

"Angie."

"Be right there," I call back. I open up the junk drawer and sweep all of the boxes and tests inside, careful not to leave any trace.

I am not ready to tell anyone. I'm not even ready to fully accept the results.

I open the door and barely can see Angie over the huge fruit bouquet she is holding in front of her face.

"Angie?"

"I'm behind here," she laughs. "Happy housewarming!"

I welcome her inside and stare at the bright display she got me. There are pineapple pieces, apples, melons, grapes, and strawberries cut into shapes and put on thin wooden skewers to resemble a bouquet of exotic flowers. Some pieces are even dipped in dark and milk chocolate.

"This looks so delicious," I say with a smile. "Thank you so much!"

"I also got you a gift card for *Linens and Lace* so you can pick out whatever you want to make this place your own. It's in the little card that is attached," she says, pointing to the stake sticking out of the fruit with a white envelope stuck on the end of it.

"Wow. I don't know what to say. *Thank you* doesn't seem to be enough to convey my emotions right now."

Angie smiles and glances around my space. "I love this. Cute, cozy, and—"

"Compact," I finish.

"Just like you," Angie quips.

Not for long. "It's small," I admit sadly, while looking around the room. Babies take up space. I can't get the feeling out of my head that my child is going to grow up suffocated in this tiny box. To top it off, my child will also be deprived of a father who wants it and will have a mother who is incompetent.

"Less to clean," Angie says positively.

"This is true." It used to be me that could always see the bright side to bad situations. Now, I can't see anything but gloom. I am poor and going to probably end up having to sell my high-end items from my Doomsday Bin. There's an amazing pair of shoes in it that I could probably get a few hundred bucks for. So, here's to hoping that the world doesn't go to shit, because I'll have nothing to survive on if tragedy really strikes.

Angie turns to me and studies my face. I wonder if she knows something is different about me. I wonder if she can tell that I am carrying cargo that I don't know how to care for.

"Did I wake you up?"

"No," I say softly, although a nap does sound amazing. Maybe I can go to sleep and wake up with all of my reality being just a bad dream. "I took the scenic route home and" —I examine the fruit and feel my stomach start to rumble with hunger—"I'm starving. Let's dig into this yumminess." I start pulling off the cellophane wrapping and pluck the first fruit skewer from the bunch. I bite off a watermelon ball and moan over the taste. "This tastes so amazingly fresh. Try some," I persuade. I continue eating my stick of fruit until it is all gone. Then I grab another one, this time containing a chocolate-dipped strawberry.

I can't stop eating. It's a binge I haven't experienced in years. I just keep plucking skewers and stuffing more fruit into my mouth. I listen to Angie talk about how nice my place is while I eat every one of my feelings.

My attention moves to the front door at the sound of a series of knocks. I glance over to Angie and start to move.

"I may have organized a thing."

"A thing?" I ask, raising my brow.

"Just a little gathering with some friends," she answers innocently. "A housewarming thing."

I shake my head at her for keeping this a secret and answer the door to Blake and a few of my gym coworkers.

"Hey, guys," I greet, hugging each and welcoming them inside.

It doesn't take long for the entire place to feel claustrophobic. Every cushiony surface is taken up, and it makes my apartment feel like it is smaller than a bento box. However, it is cozy. We can all see and hear each other. I just never had this many people relaxing on my bed before. It's not like there are many other choices on where to gather in a studio.

"Time for gifts, my favorite part," Blake announces, about to burst out of his seat.

I watch with fascination as he gallops—yes, gallops—over to the front door and then grabs the huge gift box that he must have left out in the hallway. Just looking at the size, I wonder if he got me a large appliance. I secretly hope not, because my counter space is very limited.

"You didn't have to get me a gift," I say shyly. I hope my confidence isn't gone forever. It feels weird to be vulnerable.

"Only the best for you, Claire Bear."

I rip through the gift wrap and lift the lid of the box to reveal an obscene amount of tissue paper. I laugh as I pull out wads and wads, until I am able to see inside to the bottom. Digging into the box, I pull out a beautiful stone pot that contains a bonsai tree.

"It is a ficus, which can handle a lot of abuse," Blake explains. "But let's not test its limits."

I turn the pot in my hand, examining the beauty of a seemingly simple plant. "Thank you."

I read the little card that shares the care instructions and some fun facts about this type of plant. Blake knows how much I love nature and the feeling of being outside.

"When I saw it, I had to get it for you," Blake says cheerfully.

"How did you know I needed something like this?" I ask, dumbfounded. "I was really wanting to bring some life into this place. This is perfect."

"I just knew. Plus, you can't help but look at it without feeling content."

"Fact," Angie says, helping me clean up the tissue paper.

I move it over to my window seat, which is taken up by a couple of gym friends.

"There's one more thing at the bottom of the box," Blake says, reaching in and handing me a card. "But there is a stipulation on the gift."

"Okay…" I open up the envelope and reveal a certificate for a clean-meals food delivery service.

"That certificate qualifies you for fifteen meals. However, the gym crew all pitched in and got you more. You basically can get one meal a week delivered to you at home if you space it out that way."

"Wow," I say, looking at my name on the slip of paper. "This is so generous." Tears fill my eyes at everyone's kindness. I really could use easy right now, and having meals sent here is as good as it gets for someone flying solo on a meager budget. "Thank you."

Champagne bottles get popped, and I carefully pretend to sip mine without actually consuming any. I am presented with constant reminders that I need to think about the life growing inside of me. Despite not having much hope for myself as a parent, I know at least to not drink during pregnancy.

The gang clears out of the apartment, going their separate ways—except for Angie who hangs around a little longer.

"That was fun," I say softly, tying up the trash bag that is full from the disposable cups and napkins.

"You deserve to be celebrated, Claire. You know that, right?"

I nod and then ask, "What do you still need help with for the wedding?" It is easy for me to change the subject. I want to think about anything else besides myself.

Angie is kind enough not to call me out on the conversational detour. "Graham's mom is in overdrive with this whole rehearsal dinner thing. She is making this into the party of the century, and you know how I feel about crowds and attention on me."

I chuckle. "Wrong emotion to have when you are the *one* getting married." Sadness rushes through me as I realize that having a child will make me unmarriageable material to any guy I ever attempt to date. Heck, dating will be nonexistent for years until I can learn how to juggle a life I tried to prevent from happening. It is not like guys are specifically searching for girls like me on dating apps. *Looking for a single mom, who is struggling with life and is broke.* I mean, what type of guy—even if he does exist—is really looking for that level of baggage? I would be worried over his character too.

"Claire?"

My eyes move to Angie with confusion. "Hmm?" I get

the look of an expected response to a question I didn't even hear. "Sorry. Can you please repeat the question?"

"I was just asking if you were going to bring a date. I know that," she says, pausing to collect her thoughts, "things are over with Ethan, but you've been so distant lately that I just assumed you were pursuing another guy and wanted to make sure it was stable before telling me. Oh, I'm sorry, I'm obviously prying. Just forget I said anything."

"I'm now a plus none."

Angie frowns. "He never deserved you. Had me fooled for a while too. But you are better off single and happy than tied down and miserable."

I want to ask her if being single and miserable trumps everything. I want to tell her that Nic broke my heart and that I went to Ethan's and beat him up. I want to tell her *everything*. But instead, I tell her nothing. "I'm looking forward to your big day. Any guesses on honeymoon location?"

She shakes her head. "Graham is making it his priority to keep me in the dark over these plans. He is even keeping me from packing anything."

"You guys are too cute. Like real-life storybook characters who fall in love."

"Well, I can't wait to have the roles reversed, when I get to watch you fall in love. You know how much of a sap I am for a good romance."

I smile at her. It's true. But I don't need fancy or a fairy tale. I just need forever.

6

NIC

I answer my phone on the second ring from an unknown number. "It's Hoffman." I am still groggy with sleep from all of the tossing and turning I did last night.

"Nic, it's good to hear your voice."

I groan and lean farther into the comfort of my king-sized bed. My eyes close, and I pinch the bridge of my nose to alleviate some of the tension building. "How did you get my number, Tara?"

"Oh, I have my ways," she says cheerily.

"What do you want? It's been a long time. Get to it." I have changed my number three times since moving back from the East Coast. Tara has tried to connect with me numerous times over these years, and it seems that today she is back to her old tricks.

"When will you forgive me?" she asks in such a tiny voice that it makes my head hurt worse.

I never realized it in college, but her voice, when it gets whiny and needy, can cause someone to get a migraine. She played me then, like she is trying to play me now with her false sincerity. At the time I was blinded by the illusion of love—that feeling that another person can make you into a better man.

Unfortunately, it turned me into a worse one.

I went from the sappy hearts-and-flowers type of partner to the kind of partner you would never want to bring home to momma.

I know I'm twisted. I know I'm damaged.

I just don't know how to undo the trauma that this bitch has caused me.

Lies.

Betrayal.

And nearly a destroyed bank account.

Tara didn't just want the cake. She wanted the entire bakery. She wanted to live two lives, stringing me along until she sucked me dry. But I caught her.

"Oh Nic, you still there?" When I don't answer, she sighs. "I can hear you breathing."

"Forgiving implies that I care. And Tara? I don't care. Move on with your life. I did."

"I've tried. I just keep thinking about what we could have been," she says dreamily.

"That ship has sailed. I'm never getting back with you." *You ruined my life and my vision of the future.*

"That's too bad. I just thought—"

"Don't call me again. We are over." I disconnect the call and toss my device onto the pillow beside my head.

I drift back into a lazy weekend sleep, with thoughts of Claire's lush body pressing up against mine. I float to a time when things were easy. Fun. The rush of anticipation leading up to each kiss. The yearning for more. Teasing. Persuading. My lips glide against hers, drawing her body close to mine. It is like two bodies becoming one. Her sweet moans driving me further, pushing me to peel off each article of her clothing—one by one.

It's like her body was made for my eyes, my hands, and my wild fantasies.

Her fingers trail over my shoulders, up my neck, and around to the back of my head. She can't get enough of me and the feeling's mutual. My tongue slips inside her mouth with her inhale. What starts off as slow and sweet quickly turns into urgent and wanton. I nip at her bottom lip and then quickly suck on it to ease the sting. My hands roam over her naked body, enjoying the goose bumps that form from each touch. Every inch of her responds to me.

I roll her so she is on top of me, her weight pinning me to the mattress. I look up into her beautifully expressive eyes and am overcome by an emotion I have claimed to have experienced before but never to this magnitude.

"Claire, I love you."

As soon as the words hit my brain, I thrust my body upward, launching myself out of the daze. My breaths come out in pants and my heart struggles to slow. I hear a buzzing in my ears and feel lightheaded. What is wrong with me? It was just a dream.

A damn good dream, but still a dream.

Sweat beads on my forehead, and I propel myself out of bed and make my way into the ensuite. I turn on the water for the shower and allow it to heat while I am under the spray. I rub at the back of my neck and try to make sense over what I said during my sleep. I'm not one of those people who looks for hidden meanings. There's no reason to psychoanalyze every single thing. Yet, here I am, standing in the shower trying to figure out my feelings.

Despite being someone who gets easily bored, I doubt I ever would with Claire. She is infiltrating both my waking thoughts and my subconscious ones. Even in my sleep, I am aroused and unable to escape her.

Maybe having the conversation with Tara has made everything jumbled in my head. At no point will I ever go back to her. I can't even believe she hasn't moved on already with someone else. While I said I've moved on, in reality, I am very much still single.

That relationship status title never used to bother me. However, in this moment, it feels…

Uncertain?

Sad?

Final.

I lost Claire. And I doubt there will ever be another woman who will make me feel the way she has. I pushed her away and gave her a reason to never trust me again. My plan worked.

Too well.

What my brain wants and what my heart wants are in direct competition with one another. I know I shouldn't get involved with any woman long-term. No one deserves to be with someone who is broken inside like I am. But I also know that I cannot stay away from Claire voluntarily. Everything she does is intriguing. I thought I could have a taste and it would quench my thirst enough to let her go. Instead, it has created a hunger inside of me that has only grown stronger with each passing day.

But do I love her? No. Love implies commitment and that is something I doubt I will ever want again.

I know I need help. That much is obvious.

I finish up in the shower, dry off, and put on a pair of lounge clothes. I have some work I need to catch up on in the home office, but at least I can do it in comfort.

As I am sending my last email, the doorbell rings. I open my app to check the camera and am shocked to see Penny standing with Collins. I jog down the hall and quickly open the door to my sister who is bursting at the seams with excitement.

"Surprise!" she says, jumping into my arms.

I catch her and spin her around once, placing her back on her feet. I give her a once-over and shoot Collins a look that could only be described as *what the hell?*

"She convinced Graham to let her surprise you with her temporary release," he answers carefully.

Collins doesn't answer to me, yet the level of respect is there. He is Graham's right-hand man and has really spent the last year solidifying his loyalty to him.

"Are you surprised, huh? Are you?" Penny asks, pushing me out of the way so she can make her way inside my space. She glances around my abode, looking for I don't know what. "Are you hiding any females?"

"What?" I give my baby sister *the look*.

"You are, aren't you?"

"What the hell, Penny? Intrusive much?"

"It's okay if you are. I wouldn't blame you or anything. But at least warn me in advance so I can brace myself."

"No, Penny," I say with a huff. "There's no one else here."

I give a wave to Collins and send him on his way. He knows I'll get Penny safely back to Hillsboro when it is time for her to go. Every time she gets out of the facility on a short leave, she stays with our parents, so it's a safe assumption she'll return there. In the meantime, we have a lot to catch up on.

"I expected at least to catch you doing something more exciting," she says with a pout. "You can be so"—she pauses and taps a finger to her chin—"boring."

"What did you want to find here? An orgy? A concubine?"

She makes a face and plops down on my sofa, making herself at home in my apartment—despite only being here one other time. "Ew, gross. I just thought by now you would settle down. Sex parties have to get old after a while."

"It was a joke, Pen. Judgmental much? Haven't Graham and Angie fulfilled your excitement-o-meter enough with their upcoming wedding? Surely those lovebirds have maxed you out on the squee factor."

Penny giggles, and it is so good to hear, even if most of it is at my expense. I prefer that any day over the shell she became after an incident that nearly shattered her life. I remember all the years that Penny used to come to my wrestling matches and cheer Graham and me on and how excited she would get. Just seeing her this full of life again gives me hope that she may be okay. This whole past year was a wake-up call for the family to learn not to take people for granted. Getting wrapped up in the wrong type of crowd can do that to someone. Plus, her track record of trusting people who are bad for her blatantly sucks. I'm not sure if Penny will ever be the same after being drugged and wondering if she was raped, but having justice served to those that did her wrong helped her cope. After months and months of intense therapy, she is finally morphing back to the baby sister I grew up with, the one I would pick on and torment in good fun.

Oh, how the tides have turned. Now, she is dishing everything right back at me.

"I don't mean it in a negative way, Nic. I'm just wanting you to find some happiness like Graham. Ever since you moved back here, you haven't really tried to make any efforts with women."

"How do you know I haven't?"

"Because if you had, you wouldn't find the need to micromanage my potential release from the facility. See? I'm doing well again."

I sigh. Penny does appear to be on the path to overcoming her past trauma. However, she is good at putting on a show if it means getting what she wants. Being the baby in the family has trained her for this role. But is it too soon for a release? What if she has a relapse or an emotional breakdown that sends her back to the facility? A backslide may push back her recovery, and I'm not sure Penny would be able to endure getting officially discharged just to go back again.

For the first time in months, I've seen genuine excitement and hope in her eyes that once were so dull I didn't think they would ever come alive again. None of us want to disappoint her. The entire family wants what is best for her.

"C'mon, Nic."

"Penny, it's not that I ever wanted you to stay there forever. I just want to make sure it is safe and healthy for you to get acclimated again to life outside of that place. Less chance of a relapse."

"I swear you and Graham are the same person sometimes."

I quirk a brow at her and sit opposite her on the sofa, bending my knee up onto the cushion. "We both know I am way smarter."

We both laugh—just like old times—and it feels so good. Penny gets up and walks into my kitchen in search of snacks. She rummages around in the pantry and cupboards until she finds a bag of popcorn to pop. Good, because I can't seem to perfect the art of not burning it ninety-five percent of the time. She throws it into the microwave, sets the timer, and hovers nearby until she decides it is done. It still burns.

"How do you mess it up when you are literally standing there watching?" I tease.

"Making popcorn is a fine art."

I laugh as she tosses the burnt bag into the trash and then throws in another one to start the whole process over again. I can't even tell if this one will be better, because the only thing I smell is the horrid stench from the previous attempt.

This is Penny's way of changing the subject off herself. She uses snack detours as a distraction. I fish my phone out of my pocket and check for any messages or email. I sneak a peek at the tracking app, just because I cannot go but a few hours without looking. It isn't until I hear the eruption of laughter that I look back into the kitchen and see Penny hovering her head inside the fridge.

"I cannot unsee this! I cannot," she squeals, backing out

and covering her eyes. "I need to scrub my eyes. Ew, Nic. Ew."

"What's wrong?" I can't tell if Penny is being overly dramatic or is genuinely shocked.

"I just wanted a drink. And now I am traumatized by a freaking cake!"

Oh shit. Claire's gift. I completely forgot the leftover cake was put in the fridge to keep fresh. "Yeah, about that…" I rub the bridge of my nose. There's no way to make this less awkward. "It was a gag gift."

"Eww! Don't say *gag*. Ugh, Nic, really?"

I chuckle. "It's a really good cake. At least cut a slice."

Penny shutters. "I am not going to Lorena Bobbitt you. I can't. I just can't!" She then pulls a glass down from the cupboard and fills it with tap water. "I am just glad you aren't vain enough to order a cake like that for yourself."

"It actually is really good quality cake," I defend.

"Yeah, if you can get past the visual."

"I may order one for myself in the future, without the dick."

Penny makes the most obnoxious face. She returns to the sofa with the bag of popcorn opened and leaking out a billowing mist of steam. She leans it toward me, and I take a handful and throw some into my mouth. I make a face at how salty it is. It is almost inedible. "Who did you screw over to earn that type of culinary creation?" She's referring to the cake again. It really is a showstopper.

"Why do you assume the worst in me?" I scoff.

"Please tell me it isn't Claire. I really like her."

I look at Penny with disbelief. "You met her once, Pen. *Once*," I remind.

It was over Christmas. There was such a sadness to Claire then. I now look back and wonder if she was getting emotionally abused by Ethan Maxwell then. Not spending the holidays with your girlfriend is a huge red flag.

"Well, that is all it takes for me to know when I like someone or not. When you know, you know."

I munch on another handful of popcorn and toss a few pieces at Penny's head. She retaliates by rubbing my head with her knuckles. To many, Penny may seem introverted. However, around family, she comes to life. As the baby in the family, she was always on a short leash when it came to exploring the world. Between me and Graham keeping tabs on her, she never had the chance to really make the mistakes that most teens make. It didn't stop her from making them after high school, though. A part of me still regrets moving away for college and not being there for her to keep her safe. She doesn't see it that way, but it is hard not to feel some sort of responsibility.

I watch as Penny readjusts her green army jacket and matching ball cap. Ever since going to the facility, she's been loving the grunge look and seems the happiest when she is sporting comfortable clothes. I'm sure with nowhere really to go, it doesn't make sense to get fancy while taking up residence there.

"I just wish you would find something other than work to focus on, Nic."

I guess we are back to talking about me. Never before has Penny cared this much about this particular aspect of my personal life.

"Why does happiness have to be equated with a relationship status, Pen?" I challenge.

"It doesn't," Penny mumbles, struggling to chew and talk at the same time. She slinks back into the throw pillow, knocking some popcorn accidentally onto the area rug. "I just know that you have a lot of amazing qualities, and some lucky lady would be stupid to pass up on all you have to offer."

"How are you so sure I am even a good person? Maybe I'm the exact opposite."

She scrunches up her face at me. "That's just what you want others to think so you don't have to actually go through your catalog of emotions and select one that remotely implies that you care."

Wow. Penny sure has a grasp on my typical behavior. Young, wise, and free. That's what she is. Well, almost free. And when she is finally released, I'll have a whole new set of worries.

I don't negate anything she is saying. Plus, seeing the spark back in her personality is worth having her psychoanalyze my life—which seems to be the theme of those close to me.

"Not every female is that bitch, Tara, Nic. Some women really do want to build a life on trust. Not everyone cheats."

I've been miserable since brokenhearted Claire walked out of the guest room at Graham's. I did that to her.

I hate myself for putting her in the middle of a bet. Sure, my motive was to get her away from her abuser Ethan as fast as I could. Creating a scene that she would despise him for forever seemed logical at the time. However, I am no better than he is. I'm the same type of abusing scum.

But Claire trusted me anyway afterwards. That phenomenon right there is the sad part. Why did she? Why did she even give me the time of day after the shit I pulled? Was I the lesser of two evils? All I did was convince her passively to leave one man, just to jump into bed with someone else unworthy of her love.

Claire and I were starting to form something…

Special?

It was temporary in my eyes, granted. But it was still *special.* How could Claire look at me after that hotel room scene without fully grasping the gravity of my fucked-up-ness? It has taken a lot of self-reflection for me to even come to terms with how I got to that place in time.

I may have a type, but apparently so does Claire. I am attracted to women who stray and lack commitment. Claire must prefer assholes who degrade her.

I can continue down this lonely path of self-destruction, or I can make some changes in my life. Maybe it is time for me to stop making excuses and stop living in the past.

From the time I wake up to the time I fall asleep, I think of Claire. I wonder if she thinks of me. If I even cross her brain.

I look over at my innocent little sister, who is too smart for her own good. "You are right."

Penny sits up, knocking even more popcorn onto the floor. Not sure how someone so small can make such a big mess.

"Come again?"

"You heard me."

"I *might* have heard you. Repeat, please."

"You have a point," I chuckle. "About the *not every woman is a cheater* spiel you just said."

"Finally, you have come to your senses!" she cheers, raising her hands into the air in victory.

"Ohhh nooo—"

Penny's words hit my brain a few seconds too late, as I watch the bag of popcorn plummet to the floor.

"I'll get the vacuum," I say, looking down at the mess. "Remind me to never take you to the movies."

"You know my attention span would never make it that long."

"True."

I pull the vacuum out of the supply closet and plug it into the outlet. Within just a minute, all of the mess from the popcorn explosion is cleaned up. That is one thing Penny and Claire have in common—they are both clumsy. I laugh to myself over Claire dumping her drink on herself on the flight to Vegas and needing to wear my shirt. That girl can make my clothes look damn fine. I lost count of how many times I've caught her as she has stumbled. It's a miracle she hasn't really gotten hurt.

"Have you seen Claire lately?"

"I thought we segued out of my personal life, Pen."

"Um, no, but I bet you wish we did." She laughs. "Well, have you?"

"She and Angie have started their own subscription beauty box company at HH. So, yes, I see her almost daily." I also see her in my dreams and on the video footage I may watch in the privacy of my work office when I'm unable to concentrate on business matters until I get my fix.

"That's cool. But have you made any attempt for more?"

"Where is this obsession coming from?" I ask. "Not to mention a whole lot of speculation."

"Your life is better than any reality show I have binged on. Please, give me something, Nic," she begs. "I'm getting really bored and growing antsy, and if you don't throw me a cracker once in a while, I'm going to create my own drama just to feel alive again. Maybe I'll plan my own escape and—"

"Hell, Penny, you better not."

"Oh, I just sprinkled that last part in to make sure you were paying attention to me."

I roll my eyes at her. She really has some nerve joking with her all-about-safety brother about bypassing security at her therapy facility. "Penny, I know you're putting up a good front, but I know you. I know how you love to tuck your feelings inside, and that is no way to actually deal with anything."

"Hold up," she says, raising her hand in front of my face. "Is my brother giving me life coach advice right now?"

"Maybe."

"Does Claire know how amazing you are? Because you can be, when you aren't an ass."

I'm starting to grow exasperated with this interrogation. The only thing I know for certain right now is that I miss Claire, and I want her back in my life in some capacity. The details of the big picture are still blurry in my vision. Plus, I don't even know if she will want to try again. While her closure gift to me of a hundred dick desserts may not have sent the exact message she was intending, that by no means suggests she wants to get back together either.

"I'm tired of missing out on life," Penny answers sadly, tears falling out of her eyes.

"Pen, you aren't missing anything if you aren't healthy enough to enjoy it." Her tears make me so sad. "What is this really about?" I pass her a tissue while she sniffles into it. It guts me to see her this upset.

"Maybe if you had your own love life to entertain yourself with, you would stay out of mine."

Finally, she has shared her point to all of this. "Is that why you wanted to get released early?"

She shrugs. "Partly. But the reason changed when I realized that you or Graham or Dad had threatened my boyfriend—"

"That delivery guy?"

Penny looks off to the side of the room. "He's more than just a delivery guy, Nic. Now, he doesn't even look at me. Was that really necessary?"

"Yes."

"Why?"

I shrug. "Just trust us."

"That's all you have to say?"

"That's all you need to know about the topic."

"You know what, Nic? In case you haven't noticed, I am a grown-ass woman. And you cannot dictate and control whom I date or what I do in my spare time. Got it?"

"This is the consequence of having two older brothers who specialize in privacy and security," I say nonchalantly. I don't have an ounce of guilt for threatening her boy-who-happens-to-be-a-friend to stay away from Penny. Once I realized she was having romantic feelings toward the Tuesday-Thursday delivery guy, I immediately did my research. "Plus, you can do better, Pen. The guy didn't even have a high school diploma. You have better judgment than that."

"Wow, how about *you* being judgmental, Nic? Plus, I didn't even finish college or have a degree."

"Then how about focusing your attention on that?"

"I'm going to start dating again. That's a fact."

I nod. I figured as much. "Just as long as I approve."

"Whatever, Punk."

I laugh over Penny resurrecting an old nickname she gave me growing up. *Punk.* To her, I was always the brooding middle child who only appeared calm on the outside.

I can't stop her from living her life. I can just try to steer the assholes into the opposite direction of her. There's more to Mr. Delivery Boy that I am not sharing with her. He also had a petty theft misdemeanor back when he first turned eighteen. Granted, we all do stupid things in our teens. Hell, I'm still doing stupid things as an adult. But surely Penny can pick someone who can provide for her. She deserves someone to give her the world.

Claire deserves the same. However, the thought of anyone else trying to give to her what I know she needs makes me want to hurl something—correction, *someone*—at the wall. I don't want her to move on with someone else, but I also don't want to equate lust with love. Does that make me an asshole? Of course it does.

Penny clears her throat, jolting me back to the present.

"What are the chances Mom will not pick apart my life when I drop you off at their place?"

"Slim to none," she mutters with a knowing smile.

"Thought so."

"Yeah, you don't stand a chance with that woman. She is ready to marry you off as soon as Graham and Angie tie the knot. Probably already has your tux picked out and everything."

"She needs to find a hobby," I say blankly.

"She has. It's *you*."

"You know you can talk to me about..." Dad starts, probably sensing my turmoil, "stuff." I'm sure I look a bit unkempt—which Penny basically confirmed.

I lean my back against the counter, crossing my ankles. So many times I've stood in this very spot, having chats with my dad—but never about this type of *stuff*. We've never discussed something so heavy, and yet I've always known he'd have amazing listening ears. "So there's this girl..."

"Wait." He puts his hands up to pause me. His eyes study my face, and I can't help but smirk. "We are actually doing this? Right here. Right now?"

I shrug. I get his shock. It's not like I'm an open-book kind of guy in the emotions department. But I'm miserable. I'm not sleeping well. I'm not eating well. And I sure as hell am not coping well.

For someone who initiated the breakup, I'm certainly not feeling the effects of freedom that usually follow. Instead, I'm a walking disaster.

"Only if you promise not to tell Mom."

Dad stifles his laughter. "Son, there's not much that woman doesn't already know."

He's right. Donna has a sixth sense when it comes to interpersonal relationships. It's probably the very reason she's not badgering me right now to tell her why I look like hell.

Cracking open two beers, Dad hands one to me. Tipping it forward, we cheers, then take our first sips. "Please, go on."

Extending my feet out farther in front of me, I relax into my leaning stance. "I honestly don't have much to say, other than I fell hard without realizing it and then broke her heart in the end."

"So fix it."

I huff out a laugh. Gee, why didn't I think of that? "You make it sound so easy."

"It is. Men always act like women are some big mystery and that we have to read between lines to figure out what they really want. But it's really simple. Fight for her. If you want her back, fight. But do it hard and with thoughtful intention."

I take another drink, allowing myself a moment to mull over his words. "Tara messed me up—badly."

"You are using what happened in your past as a safety-net excuse to keep yourself disengaged from anyone new that comes into your life in the present. But aren't you tired of playing the same unemotional game, where you basically lose every time? This isn't about settling down. It's simply about treating yourself with respect, so you in turn can treat women that way."

I sigh. Dammit, he's right. "It's complicated."

"So was your mom. She still is." He glances around the room. "And look what we created together. Sometimes you encounter someone who's worth the risk of getting hurt. But in reality, you already got hurt it seems."

I nod in agreement. Dad is always so wise and level-headed when it comes to these things. He knows the balance between providing too little advice or too much advice.

"Listen, Nic. There's no shame finding someone with better resources to talk with, but know I'm always here to listen, and I know your mother would say the same. You're never too grown to lean on either of us."

"Thanks, Dad."

"Will I like her?"

A smile beams on my lips, unable to be contained. "There's no way you couldn't."

Leaning in, Dad gives me a hug, which I gladly accept. I can't remember the last time we really hugged, and it doesn't matter, because it is occurring at the perfect moment —when I need it most.

He resists asking me who "she" is, and for that I am thankful. When I bring Claire here, I want to do it with her as my girlfriend.

I say my goodbyes to Mom and Penny, who are lounging out on the back deck, and exit the house, silently wishing that my dad's words were true. Is getting Claire back as easy as just fighting for her? It might be if I wasn't so damaged.

When I settle into the driver's side of my car, I press my forehead against the steering wheel. I might be familiar with heartbreak, but I'm definitely not familiar with how to actually heal from it.

Sitting up, I remove my phone from my pocket, open up my contacts, and hover my finger over a number in the list. When Dr. Mitch Saber, a longtime friend and personal physician to both Graham and me, picks up, I suck in a deep breath through my mouth and slowly release it out my nose.

"Hey Mitch, how are you doing?"

"Just fine. But I can't say I was expecting to hear from you. Everything alright?"

Switching the call to hands-free, I start the engine and make my way down the driveway. "I need a favor."

"Let's hear it."

"I would like to, um, chat with someone about..." I don't even know. "Things I've been dealing with in regard to my past."

"Want me to email you a list of my personal recommendations and their qualifications? And when you're ready, you can let me know, and I can set up your first appointment?"

"That would be great."

Maybe this is the first real step in the right direction.

Time will only tell.

7

CLAIRE

It is a solid fifty-one hours that I have known that I am pregnant. I thought sleeping on it would make me feel better, but time is only acting as a ticking bomb for when the truth will be revealed. I can't hide forever. I haven't even decided how I'm going to avoid drinking at the wedding and no one finding out. It would be pretty off-character for me to turn down a glass of free champagne, especially during an epic celebration like Angie's nuptials. Plus, being so close to Nic during the festivities will be a great reason to drink in the first place.

Every time I really think about how my life is going to change, I get nauseous. I'm not ready to be a mother, but the thought of passing my child off to another family or terminating the pregnancy causes me major anxiety. I'm the product of my mom cheating, and she could have gotten rid of me too. I want my child to grow up feeling the love I yearned for from my own family. It's not fair for a child to ever think they are a burden or a mistake. It starts with me and my own attitude.

Time to put my big-girl panties on and start acting like an adult.

I force myself out of bed and kneel down to pull out the drawer from the underneath space-saver storage. I find my fanciest dress that isn't too badly wrinkled and get myself dressed up to go out—by myself. All of this sulking over not having anyone in my life to love me is a pity party I don't need to throw for myself right now.

There are plenty of people in worse off situations than I am, so I need to count my blessings and push forward. Feeling sorry for myself is not very productive. Time to prove that I can rise above.

I do my hair for the first time this weekend and even add some black jewelry to my look. I pull open my bathroom's medicine cabinet and revamp my vision board that is attached to the back of the mirrored door. I grab a magazine that rests on the top of the toilet, and I scan it for images that help to represent some of my current goals.

When I see the image of a house, I rip it out and stick it to my board. *Dream big.* I add to it a picture of a piggy bank for a reminder to save. I also include a picture of my favorite flower and the graphic I got tattooed on my hip. *Always look toward the sun.* I add the clippings for the following words—strong, energized, and decisive.

Feeling empowered and in a good head space, I decide to go out to dinner. I am getting a bigger appetite lately, and eating well helps cut back on some of the nausea. I put on a pair of dressy sandals to go with my silver and black layered chiffon dress. After a dusting of makeup, I grab my handbag and decide to walk to find a place to eat.

I love how close I live to so many cool places. I wander around and explore my options, scanning menus in the windows or on podiums set up in front of entrances to see if I can even afford a fancy meal. There is no living from paycheck to paycheck right now for me. Instead, I am just charging everything and slipping further into debt. It is hard to see the light at the end of the tunnel when the tunnel is about thirty years long. That's how long it's going to take me to pay back those loans—at least.

When the smell whiffing out of *Cutlery*—a Brazilian Steakhouse—makes my mouth water, I must go inside and try it out. I can tell that whatever the price is will be worth it. I am *that* hungry.

Coming from a place of living life to the fullest and not having a financial worry to living life with a weighing fear of not making ends meet feels like whiplash and quite frankly a bit of culture shock. Days of getting my nails professionally done and securing the freshest and most natural foods are over. I need to let this meal be the last hurrah and then start taking my budgeting seriously. It does help that my friends got me a meal delivery subscription. Not having to worry about one dinner a week will cut down on unnecessary stress. Maybe I can even learn to garden and set up pots in the windows or something. Fresh produce at the store always costs more than junk in a box.

I walk inside the restaurant and can't take my eyes off of the polished interior. Everything looks South American from the artwork to the tapestries to the waitstaff.

I am so distracted by my own thoughts that it takes the

clearing of a throat to draw me back to the present. My eyes look up to meet a pair of beautiful green eyes that belong to an ultrathin hostess.

"Are you waiting for your party to arrive?" she asks in a professional tone.

"No," I say softly.

"So just one?" Her smile conveys friendliness, but I can't help but feel slightly judged.

I'm nearly positive I am the only person in Portland that has entered this venue solo. This is a place where business meetings are conducted, birthdays are celebrated, and people gather over wine and delicious food. I am here for none of those things. Other than extreme hunger, I don't really know why I decided to enter. Surely, based on the decor, I could have chosen a cheaper place to dine. Regardless, I'm happy I did. I can already tell by the amazing smell that I'm going to thoroughly enjoy my dinner.

"Just one," I echo. The words do sound sad leaving my lips. It's technically two, but the baby doesn't have much of a say in its food selection.

"Alright."

"Alright," I repeat. I can't even remember the last time I ate alone and actually liked it. Probably never.

"Any preference on seating?"

I furrow my brow. "Umm, I've never been here before. So, I guess just give me the seat that...oh I don't know. Just pick one. I am super hungry and the smell coming out of the restaurant enticed me into entering," I ramble.

Her smile moves from professional to genuine. "I love it here," she says sweetly. "I get to eat during my breaks, and I thought after a few months of working here I'd grow tired of the food. Nope. Just makes me crave it more. It's addicting. I tried replicating the same type of cooking styles in my own kitchen and it never turns out the same. I really hope you enjoy your experience."

"Thank you," I say with a smile.

"I also have the best seat for you next to the water fountain. Follow me."

I allow her to escort me through the restaurant. We pass by a huge salad bar that is bigger than any I have ever seen before. Several chandeliers hang from the rafters, competing for attention with a wall fountain that is absolutely breathtaking. A male waiter takes over the hostess's duties and pulls out a chair for me, pushes me toward the table, and offers me an elaborate drink menu. I scan over it fast and notice that they have four different water options.

"Just spring water for now and some lemon wedges if you have any."

"Are you expecting anyone else?" he asks.

I shake my head. "No. It's just me." *And my unborn baby.*

"Very well. The way Cutlery works is that there are no menu options for dining in. All of our guests are encouraged and welcome to frequent the salad bar as often as they want. Meat will be brought around to your table on skewers by various staff members. If you are wanting more, keep this card up on green." He places a little circular coaster that has two felt sides onto the surface of the table. "And if you want to stop the meat parade, just flip it to red."

"Sounds easy enough," I say cheerfully. I glance around the restaurant and see the men dressed in all black carrying the huge metal skewers of various meats. This is a great way to break my vegan-ness. Might as well keep it classy. My mouth is already watering over that first bite. I turn my card to green and place my cloth napkin on my lap. "Let the meat parade begin."

The waiter motions over one of the staff members holding bacon-wrapped scallops. I nod and watch as my empty plate gets the first offering. Another worker has prime rib. I nod my head eagerly. When the pecan-and-parmesan-crusted chicken arrives, I just motion with my fork to add it to my meat hill, because my mouth is gaping in awe. It isn't until the pork chops and filet mignon top my plate that I decide to turn my card to red.

My leaning tower of meat is huge. I may have overindulged, and I haven't even eaten anything yet. Reaching for my fork, I give it a kiss and then stab it into the stack. I cut my first piece of beef and am just about to place it in my mouth when I hear, "Claire?" from behind me. No!

My head whips around, and I see Nic Hoffman standing in a pair of black trousers and a silver-gray shirt. I roll my eyes over the fact that our outfits match.

"Hi," I say suspiciously. I try to look around him to see who he's with. Maybe he's on a date or with family. I feel slightly embarrassed over gaining another witness to my eating choices. I hate feeling judged.

"Never in a million years would I bet to find you at a Brazilian Steakhouse." One look at my mountain of meat, and he can't hold back a smirk. "May I join you?"

"I'm not sharing," I blurt out, ready to stab any hands with my fork if they move too close. I have a plan of shaving off layers from my pile, and I have already envisioned how I will be savoring every bite. And I definitely don't need help with my appetite.

My eyes follow his every movement as he takes a step closer and hovers over the free chair opposite me. He smiles as he notices the empty glass and still-wrapped silverware. He knows I'm alone.

"May I?"

"Don't you already have a table?" I ask with confusion.

"They were boring company," he mutters. "Plus, watching my favorite vegan eat a plate of meat is way more enjoyable than some stuffy colleagues who want my expertise to solve all their problems."

"Fine. Sit. But I'm not making small talk with you. I came to eat and eating is what I plan to do. And quit looking at me like that, or I'll be the one who chooses another table."

Nic holds his hands up in mock surrender, as he stifles a laugh. He never was good at resisting teasing me. He pulls out the chair across from me and motions with a hand to the waiter.

"What can I get you to drink other than water?" Nic asks, nodding toward my glass.

"I'm fine with water."

"What can I do for you, sir?" the waiter asks.

"I'll take a glass of your house wine. Red."

"Of course," he responds, never questioning why my table for one is now a table for two.

"Oh, and a glass of your finest ginger ale with lemon slices."

"Right away," the waiter responds, with a nod to his head.

"You must be thirsty," I mumble.

"You must be hungry."

I fork a piece of steak into my mouth and close my eyes over the taste. I can't even remember the last time I ate something so juicy. When I am done with my moment of surrender, I open my eyes and find Nic's steel-blue ones staring back at me. There's no point getting shy around him while I pig out. He has seen me in so many more vulnerable positions that I lost count.

"I know you are mad at me but—"

"Do you know that?" I ask bluntly, moving my eyes to my meat mountain.

"One can assume…"

I hold my fork and knife up, crossing them. "Shh! Let me have this moment to enjoy my food and not get upset over something so menial, like your ever-changing moods."

"I just—"

I pull back my chair to leave and Nic sighs.

"Fine," he surrenders.

I focus on my food, avoiding eye contact and ignoring every movement that Nic makes on the opposite side of the table. It's like he's not even there, except I feel his penetrating gaze and his silent judgment.

We fill up our plates with another round of meat. This time I pair it with the mashed plantains that the waiter brought for the center of the table. They are deliciously caramelized with just enough color to bring out their sweetness. Maybe I need to find a job working here so I can eat during my breaks. Pretty sure after a few weeks, I'll be pregnant with a food baby alongside the real baby.

"Talk to me, please," Nic begs.

I look over at his sad demeanor. This meal was not supposed to be like this. I am supposed to be picking myself up, not getting more and more depressed. I swallow hard and collect my thoughts.

"We live in two different worlds, Nic. You know that. And I was finally able to see that. You probably helped me from a bigger heartache later on. So, for that I'm thankful."

A veil of regret washes over his features. He rubs at the smoothness of his freshly shaven face, never taking his eyes from mine. "What happens if I tell you I made a mistake?"

I shove more meat into my mouth. Once I'm done chewing it, I stuff more in. And more. I keep my eyes on my dwindling tower, and when I finally can see the white of the plate, I excuse myself and head to the salad bar, leaving Nic alone at the table.

The salad bar is not the kind that you would find at the Country Buffet. Nope, this one is upscale and features the best imported cheeses, cold meats, and marinated vegetables. Every item is fresh and of high quality. I grab a plate and take a little from each section, which adds up to being a crazy amount of food.

I join Nic back at the table and feel his eyes bore into my forehead, mainly because I keep my attention focused on my prize. The arugula is so good. I need to figure out the recipe for the lemon citrus honey dressing. And the marinated mushrooms? Divine.

"Are you going to ignore me for the entire meal?" he asks. In my periphery I can see him lean back in his chair and examine me while he eats his scallop.

"Yup."

"Why?"

I stop midbite, chew what is in my mouth, and then drop my fork onto the table. "Because what's the point of addressing such a ludicrous, hypothetical, nonsensical question? Yet, here I am drawing more attention to it…"

"I'm sorry I hurt you." When I don't say anything, he continues. "Hurt people hurt people. I'm working on my own issues, Claire. I'm done with the cycle of pain I seem to cause the women who choose to get involved with me. You helped me see that I was so wrong." He lets out a sigh, and I can tell his frustration by the rigidness of his posture. "Don't you see that I'm trying?"

"I'm not asking you to try, Nic. I'm not asking anything of you."

"I'm not used to—"

"Jacking things up so badly?" I ask bluntly.

"Yes," Nic admits. "I'm sorry for pushing you away that morning at Graham and Angie's penthouse. I am sorry for not explaining from the very start that I was only looking for a sexual relationship and not an emotional one."

I grind my teeth together, my jaw clenching tighter until the ache is too hard to endure. I huff out a breath, no longer worrying if I am being too aggressive. I don't want the other neighboring patrons to hear us, but he just cannot stop making this turn into a scene.

His eyes. The way he plays with the ring on his finger. His chest rising and falling with each breath. Everything about him is driving me wild. Making me want to climb the walls just to get away from the air he takes up. "I need to pee." There. I did it. I said something monumentally stupid —just like I knew I would.

A smile breaks out on his lips. Even when we are in a

tense conversation, Nic always seems to find a way to see the humor. I start to push back my chair, but he is up and helping me out before I can even protest.

He bends at the waist and brings his lips to my ears. "Every hair on my body is standing on end over your exquisite beauty. You are stunning, Claire. Glowing. And I think I am falling in l—"

"No," I snap. "Don't say it." I can't hear it now. Not now. I have waited so long to hear his words of adoration, and right now, in this moment, hearing them would be a punishment to my soul. Maybe in another life, I would have welcomed them with open arms. But his words now are daggers to my heart. I want to tell him I am pregnant. I want to tell him it could be his. However, the last thing I need right now is one more disappointment.

The less he knows, the less of a chance he has to shatter my heart again.

Nic only thinks he wants to be with me, but that's because he doesn't know the full truth of the situation. He doesn't realize I'm carrying a child that might not be his. Sure, he might do the noble thing and say it doesn't matter. But then all too soon the actual existence of a full-time commitment will seep into the reality of even the strongest relationships, and *happy together* gives way to what? Friendship, if you're lucky, or if you're unlucky, then...

Sacrifice.

Indifference.

And the ultimate worst—resentment.

Nic won't realize it now, but hopefully with time, he'll understand that breaking up with me was the best thing for him and his future. He made the right choice for himself, and it'll be best if I maintain that solid break—regardless of how much he tries to get me to cave.

I feel Nic's eyes on me as I force one foot in front of the other and I make my way to the other side of the restaurant in search of the restroom. I stare at myself in the mirror. There's a swell to my belly, most likely from my carnivorous food choices. I may have consumed an entire animal, and the more I think about it, the more disturbed I feel.

I place my hands over the small bump, imagining what it would look like if it grew significantly bigger. I'll have to buy new clothes, change some of my routines, and start going for check-ups. Going out for drinks will be a thing of the past, and I'll need to start on some kind of vitamin regimen. There is so much to think about that the more I try to think about all of these changes, the more freaked out I get in return.

I'm not prepared to be a mother. I don't have the knowledge or financial means necessary to give my child a good life. I want better for my baby than I had growing up. Isn't that what all parents strive for when raising a kid? At least the nonshitty ones do. I'm not quite sure what my parents were thinking when I was born.

I can't turn away from my own reflection. There are bags under my eyes that no amount of foundation can conceal. Even though I've been sleeping for longer periods of time than I typically do, it's just surface-level sleep. It's not a deep, restful sleep. I could stay in bed all day and still feel like I lack energy. Maybe all my energy is going into growing this baby.

I pivot and enter a free stall. I just can't keep my thoughts at bay. Every single thing that passes through my brain is in regard to the new life developing inside me. I need to find an obstetrician. I need to find out why my birth control failed. I need to stay on as an Entice employee so I can reap the benefits of having decent health coverage.

I wash my hands and exit the restroom. On my way back to the table, I catch the waiter's attention and ask for my bill. He kindly pulls a receipt out of his pocket, double checks that it is mine, and then passes it over to me.

"Thank you," I mutter, scanning my eyes over the bold amount printed at the bottom. I blink and try to clear my vision. Seventy dollars and fifty-three cents? Shit. "Here's my credit card."

I walk back to the table, feeling Nic's eyes all over my body. I slump down into the chair opposite him. The food was delicious, but pangs of guilt erupt over the wastefulness of money that could easily go toward the baby. I definitely need to start cutting back on eating out and figure out ways to pack my food for workdays.

"Ma'am," the waiter says, hovering over my seat. He leans in toward me and whispers, "Your card was declined."

I snatch the piece of plastic from his hands and shove it into my handbag. "That's fine, I'll pay cash," I mumble out of reflex. I don't even know if I have enough. I dig through my handbag and pull out every loose bill I have stuffed inside. The waiter goes about his work, while I am left alone with Nic. I can't make eye contact with him. He has to know by my frantic pile of ones and fives I keep adding to the table that I am struggling.

"Claire?" he asks, drawing my attention to him, as he places his hand over my shaking one. "I got you covered, okay? I interrupted your dinner, so let me take care of this."

I wad up my cash in disproportioned balls, handing it over to him in fistfuls. "Here's my contribution. Take it. I'm going to be short, but take it anyway."

He smiles warmly at me, but not in the pitying kind of way—at least that is how I would like to interpret the curvature of his lips. "Save it for a bakery purchase for the future. I am craving a cream-filled cock. Bigger, though. More life-sized and proportionate to mine."

My eyes grow wide and then I burst out laughing. "They were good, huh?"

"The best I've had, but not like I have much to compare it to."

We continue laughing with each other, and it makes me wish our circumstances were different. I want things to be easy again.

"Claire?"

"Hmm?"

"I'm going to fight for you."

My eyes dart up to his. "What?" He looks sure of himself—maybe even smug.

"You heard me, baby. I'm going to win you back."

"Why?" I ask stupidly.

"Because I've been miserable since I let you walk out of my life. What I thought I wanted and what I thought I didn't deserve were competing with one another. I"—he clears his throat—"want a chance to try."

"Try what?" My head is spinning, and I can't keep up.

"Try to get you to love me again."

8

NIC

There are few things in this world cuter than when Claire puts out her bottom lip in a pout. I can tell she is allowing my words to marinate in her brain. She is caught off guard; I get it. But once she has time to really think about what I am proposing, then she will be on board. She has to be. I let her walk out on me once, and I am not allowing history to repeat itself. Penny and my dad are right. Not everyone is Tara. It is just easier going through life acting like they are.

I have work to do on myself, I know. But I also don't want to filter my feelings in the moment.

Sadness fills up her features, and I want to grab her from across the table and hug her to me. I miss her sass and her impulsive zest for life. So, why do I keep catching these little glimmers of melancholy from her? Why is she holding back so much?

"I have to go," she whispers.

I reach for her handbag and place her bills that are scattered about the table back inside, straightening them as I go.

"When you are with me"—I look directly in her eyes, so there is no misinterpretation—"you never have to worry about money."

Claire winces over my words and it makes me frown. She breaks eye contact. Why is she being so timid and shy?

As she stands up from the table, I rise as well. I move over to help her slide out of her seat and place a hand on her bent elbow to keep her from tripping over the leg of her chair. I find it endearing how she seems to be clumsy around me. Maybe I get under her skin the way she gets under mine. Maybe I make her a little bit nervous and on edge.

"When can I see you again?" I ask.

She purses her lips, and her eyes get a little sparkle. I brace myself for what words are to come—most likely some smart mouth response. It's about time. I thought she was losing her spark.

"Probably on your security footage when you see me walking into work tomorrow."

A smile breaks out on her lips, and she knows just how much I like the bite to her words. I much prefer her wicked tongue over her sadness. I can handle my girl and all her fluctuating moods.

My girl.

I'm not much for labels, but that seems to be the best description for what Claire is to me.

"I look forward to it," I say with the tip of my head. "Just make sure you walk extra slow, so I can savor it." I reach into my pocket for my wallet and toss several big bills onto the table that will cover our meals and service. "Let me walk you to your car."

Claire turns to me, and before she can say it, I know she walked here. It's not too far from her place of residence, but I don't like that she is walking around the city in a gorgeous dress alone. Even though we have been apart and never were in a committed relationship, I've seen no one, and I very much consider her still mine. I always have, even though it has taken me time to figure it out.

Everything is different with Claire. More intense. More real. She makes me feel alive and has awoken parts of my heart that I only reserved for her. She is walking through uncharted territory. Even Tara never entered those spaces. It took losing Claire to be able to separate the past from the present. It took losing her to realize how lonely it's been living my life, while never looking toward a future.

I reach for her hand out of reflex when we walk outside, and she lets me take it. We are halfway down the block when she slips her hand out of mine. I don't frown. I don't ask for hers back. I know that this is progress. She is slowly melting the wall of ice she built around herself, to protect herself from me. It is only a matter of time when she will let me have full access to her again. Her submission is a gift I never thought I needed, so even the slightest lean toward me is welcome. Time. All I need is more time to make her see clearly again.

When we arrive at her apartment building, I expect her to go in the main entrance, but instead she takes me around the building to the back street. I'm about to ask her what we are doing—despite enjoying more time spent with her in any capacity—but then she smacks the hood of her street-parked car with her hand and hops her butt up onto the hood. It is candy-apple-red and suits her fiery personality perfectly.

"Here's my car that you said you wanted to walk me to," Claire says proudly. Her smile is so bright that it competes with the setting sun that is equally blinding.

I chuckle. "Funny." It takes everything in me not to pull her to me and demand her to be a part of my life. "Do you want to grab breakfast in the morning? I can pick you up before work."

And just like that the smile that I proudly thought I helped to create vanishes. I reach for a piece of her hair and tuck it behind her ear. She slides down off the car and takes a step back away from me.

"I know you don't believe me when I say I'm sorry and that I want to have another chance, but I hope with time my actions can match my words and you gain back some confidence in what we could be."

Her head shakes, as if she is trying to keep my words from entering it. I know with time I can prove to her that I am serious about pursuing her. For far too long, I feared commitment and avoided it at all costs. Claire changed my views on it, and it took losing her to help me to see what really matters. It is her. It has always been her.

"You want a cookie-cutter bad girl. I am just a number to you. Some tally mark on your score sheet of women. I may not have had much self-respect for myself when I permitted Ethan to involve me in your betting game, but I do now. I am better than the girl you wanted to mold me into being."

"Don't you know by now that you broke the mold? Who

I was then and who I am at this very moment are different. You changed my mindset. You helped me to see that—"

"Hey you guys!"

Claire and I turn to see Angie power walking up the street with a garment bag in her hand.

"What are you guys doing here together?" she asks, eyeing us.

"Just confirming calendars for the wedding," Claire answers for the both of us, getting me off the hook from lying to my soon-to-be sister-in-law.

I can see the suspicion on Angie's face. I glance behind her and see Collins not far away. He gives a tilt to his head and then stays in the shadows. Part of the arrangement that Graham and Angie agreed upon was that she would have a security detail when out in public, as long as they remained unobtrusive. I don't blame my brother for wanting to keep his girl safe. I would be doing the same if the roles were reversed. Angie went through a hell of a year last year and had too many near-death experiences. To some, Graham may look paranoid. To me, he looks smart.

When you find someone worth holding on to, you would be an idiot to let them go. I'm done being an idiot.

"I have your dress for the last fitting, if that's okay. Otherwise I can just drop it off and come back another time."

Claire plasters a smile on her face. The girls have been best friends for years, so I would be surprised if Angie is buying this fake behavior from her. I know I'm not.

That's the thing with Claire—she is good at putting on a facade, using humor and her bubbly personality to deflect from her underlying sadness. Sometimes the happiest people on the outside are hurting the most on the inside.

I will forever feel sorry for hurting my girl like I did.

If I wasn't such a selfish fuck, I'd leave her alone and let her try to find someone who can give her the world. I just am incapable of letting her go. She's mine. I just need her to come to terms with it.

"I'll leave you girls to it," I say reluctantly. I don't want to leave Claire. I want to hold her to me and demand she empty her soul out so I can understand what is bothering her. I need to know why she is so wishy-washy with her emotions toward me. One minute she looks hopeful, the next she is sad.

Claire lifts her hand and flutters her fingers in the air to wave goodbye to me. I can tell she would like to say something, but from the look on her face, I know her words are trapped in the knot forming in her throat.

"See you, Nic," Angie says.

"Bye. Catch you later."

I pass by Collins and ask, "What's Graham up to at the moment?"

"He's at his home finalizing honeymoon plans."

I nod.

"And Penny?"

"She has made it clear to Graham that his security guard is not needed, appreciated, or welcome in her life."

Oh boy.

I groan and rub at the tension building in my forehead region. "Any more to that?"

"Penny decided to go on a shopping spree and test the

guard's limits by deliberately trying to lose him—four times."

"Hell," I sigh.

"Graham was made aware of everything. He's not happy, though."

I nod. I am glad my brother is handling our baby sister. I can already tell from our last meeting that she is raring to go out into the world again and make up for lost time—which translates to poor decisions and reckless behavior almost ninety percent of the time.

"So, I take it she discovered the guard relatively easily?"

"Within the first three minutes on the job," Collins informs.

I stifle my snicker. "Maybe he was just a bad candidate."

"Sure, we'll go with that," Collins says with a smirk. "I'm sure the two decades of field experience never prepared him for your sister."

I burst out laughing. "True. So true." Not many people get to see this side to Collins. He is usually in full-on professional mode, never letting any real feelings break through. We both actually have more in common than I originally thought. We like to keep our emotion cards close to our chests. "Next time you have a real day off, let's go grab a beer together or shoot some pool."

"Sounds good," he responds with a half smile. "In the meantime, I can keep an extra eye on Penny. Angie keeps me busy enough, but I can still keep tabs on Penny if that helps."

"Thanks, man," I say, shaking hands with Collins, "for your loyalty and top-notch work ethic." I am not a man who hands out compliments often, but when I do, they are warranted. "When does my sister go back to Seattle?"

"Tomorrow morning."

I nod. "I hope she enjoyed her freedom while it lasted. Is Graham taking her back?"

"Your father."

"Okay, good. I don't think either Graham or I are ready for the stress of Penny getting released early. I know she's eager to get out, but a part of me worries over a relapse."

Collins nods, understanding my fears. He's been a huge help at monitoring Penny whenever Graham and I are unable to make it up to Seattle.

We say our goodbyes, and I head back to Cutlery to grab my car. Settling into the driver's seat, I shoot Mitch a text to give him the green light on setting up an appointment with Dr. Zimmerman, who seems suitable for handling whatever it is I'm willing to throw at her. I try not to overthink it, and I vow that I won't cancel the session prior to it occurring.

Despite working in the same building, Graham and I rarely cross paths unintentionally, so I decide to pay him a visit. While we keep in close contact via text or email, sometimes face-to-face interaction is necessary.

I call Graham ahead of time to grant me access without having to go through the added security features. Like my own place, he lives in a fortress. It is how we both operate and choose to live our lives.

On my way up on the elevator, I think of my vegan-meat-loving girl with her stack of meat she refused to share with me. I can't stop smiling while thinking about her dedication to conquering the mountain. That girl never stops surprising me.

When the doors to the elevator open, I quickly wipe what must be a cheesy-ass grin from my face.

"How's your weekend going?" Graham asks, greeting me in the foyer.

I follow Graham inside and we head into the kitchen, where he pours me a tumbler of bourbon without even asking.

"Ha, do I look that stressed?"

He sips his own and smirks. "Maybe."

I am. I can't get my sassy and smart girl out of my head.

"How's the honeymoon planning going? Do you think Angie is catching on to where you are headed?"

"No, she is trying to figure it out, as I would expect she would. But as of now, she is clueless. I love being able to surprise her with something."

"I'm sure she will love it."

"Something's wrong with Claire," he says, doing a one-eighty on subject matter.

"What? Why do you say that?" I just saw her twenty minutes ago. I haven't gotten any reports from my guy Tyler on her, other than that she and Angie are safely inside her residence.

Graham brushes hair off his forehead and takes a deep breath. "Angie is obsessing over her, and as much as I have encouraged her to give Claire her space, she is losing sleep over her at night. You know how close the two of them are. I need you to keep a close eye on Claire when we go away. I need Angie to not worry about her friend while we are gone."

"I've been keeping a watch on Claire," I mutter, my thoughts racing over what could be wrong with her. I have noticed the sadness, but I just attributed it to how she is when she is around me. However, if Angie is noticing some red flags, then maybe it is more than just her reaction to my close proximity. "Outside of bugging her phone or placing a listening device inside her apartment, how would we be able to figure out what is going on?"

"Yeah, none of those options will work. I promised Angie I would never be that intrusive on her or those she cares about—no matter what the circumstances. Trust me, I've been tempted. We both know how I snap when my girl is distraught."

I get it. It's exactly how I feel when *my girl* is upset. "I can only promise to watch over Claire while you guys are away. But if she won't talk with Angie about her feelings, I doubt she will talk to anyone else."

Graham nods and throws back the rest of the amber liquid, placing his empty tumbler on the counter. My empty glass joins his with a clink. "And then to add to everything else on my plate, Penny has only been home for a day and is already causing havoc with the security staff I had Collins hire to drive her around and accompany her on her short stay in Hillsboro."

I sigh. "Yes, I ran into Collins and he filled me in. What a mess. I don't understand why she is so difficult all of a sudden."

"I think she is trying to make a point with us and let us know that she will be doing life on her own terms soon."

"I just hope it isn't sooner than she is capable of handling."

"I hear you. Trust me, I've been going through all of the scenarios in my head in regard to Penny's official release."

He glances at his watch. "Want to watch the pay-per-view fight with me that starts in ten minutes?"

I smile. "Just like old times?"

"Yeah, just like old times."

Even though Claire rejected my offer to pick her up for breakfast, I decided to bring the meal to her at the office. I am the first to arrive to HH. The only employees here are the nightshift guards who are about to leave with the turnover of the next set of employees. It has taken me some time to fine tune the circuit of schedules. However, after several adjustments, I think I have everyone placed correctly and the job descriptions ironed out appropriately.

My personal assistant, Brenna, arrives shortly after me. I have instituted "on call" hours for her each morning that I pay her for, even if I do not need her that early. I just like to have the flexibility of having her assistance if need be. Despite just starting, Brenna appears to value professionalism, and I can respect that. On paper, she is marked down as being my personal assistant. However, with her security and bodyguard background, I pay her extra to perform duties that go outside her on-paper job title.

"I need you to keep tabs on Claire Nettles who works in the Plus None office space. Anything that looks *off* with her behavior, I need to know."

"Okay, sir," she says slowly, making sure she heard me correctly.

"Obviously do not give her any insight on my orders."

"Alright. Can I ask a question?"

"Sure."

"What should I do if she catches on? I mean, I don't work on her floor, so how would I be able to explain why I am there?"

I think about the question for a few seconds. Brenna does have a point. "You're right. And if she found out, I think she would try to hurt me."

Brenna smirks and tries to hide her giggle. She has seen the results of Claire's penis-obsessed bakery purchases, so she knows firsthand how impulsive and free-spirited she can be. I've been on the receiving end of her wrath, and as sexy as it is to see her worked up, I don't need to add additional stress to her plate.

"If I notice anything in just passing, I will share it with you, sir."

"Sounds good, Brenna, thank you. I'll be back here in a bit. I have a mission to complete."

9

CLAIRE

I shouldn't be surprised to find Nic in the meditation room sitting on the floor with a breakfast buffet laid out on a large black-and-white checkered picnic blanket. I arrived at the office an hour before the others, as I often do. I have so much work to do, and seeing him taking up not only physical space but also mental space is frustrating. When our eyes meet, I huff out a breath and stomp into the room where I go for peace and to think. Clearly, neither of those things are happening today.

Nic brings about chaotic thoughts and increased blood pressure—the exact opposite of tranquility. He is getting under my skin, and the more he notices that his antics are working, the harder he pushes. I hate to admit that he is stripping some of my layers off. It is flattering to be pursued. However, no one actively pursues a pregnant woman with the excessive amount of baggage I have. As soon as he finds out, he'll bolt.

It will be the fastest magic trick known to man.

If Mr. Commitment Phobe is scared of a relationship, he sure as hell will be scared of possible fatherhood. Who wouldn't be? It's not like any of us expected to be a parent while actively using birth control.

"Good morning," he chirps cheerfully.

"You are extra chipper this morning," I grumble, scanning over his setup.

"I am."

"Why?"

"Just happy to be alive."

"Is that so?" I ask slowly.

"Come eat with me."

My morning sickness has moved out of the a.m. time slot today, but I expect it to flare up by lunch time if I do not eat on schedule. Having an empty stomach seems to set me off and into a dry-heaving fit. So, seeing all of the pastries, juices, and fruit does make my stomach growl.

"Why are you doing this?" I whisper. I wish he would stop being so cute. All of his attention is simply reminding me of all that I am losing because I managed to get pregnant by one of two men. "Angie is going to be here soon."

"She doesn't leave the penthouse until 7:53 a.m."

"That is oddly specific. And creepy."

Nic shrugs, not the least bit fazed by my remarks. "I work in the security field, Claire. We are all creepy."

"Or just you," I quip.

He rolls up his sleeve to glance at his watch. "We have forty-three minutes until Angie has the opportunity to see us. So let's start eating."

"There is no *us*," I remind him.

His brows lift. "Then come up with a better pronoun."

When I have nothing to add, he motions for me to sit down on the blanket, holding up a variety plate for me to take, already loaded up with food. He is playing dirty. Food is my love language right now, and I can't get enough when I'm not doubling over a toilet throwing up. Ask my clothes. They will tell you. All of the salt I've been consuming and the extra carbs are making me bloat. This morning, I had to switch outfits three times because of fear I would look as pregnant as I feel. I know it's irrational, as I'm less than two months along, but I can't shake the paranoia. The wrap dress I settled on is forgiving enough and allows for extra stretch in the waistline area. However, I give it a couple more months, and I won't be able to just use "extra carbs" as an excuse as to why I'm packing on weight in record speed.

I sit down on the other side of the blanket and break off a piece of pastry from my plate. I close my eyes as I welcome the buttery taste to overwhelm my senses. The smell, the taste, the look of the flaky layers, all make me continue biting and chewing until there's nothing left. So good.

The only thing that would make this meal better is bacon. Greasy, no-nutritional-value bacon. That is what I'm craving right now. The baby wants meat.

I can feel Nic's eyes on me while I eat in silence. I don't need to look over to see that they are on me. I can feel them.

He is wearing me down. And the smug smirk playing against his lips is enough evidence to know that he knows it too.

"What do I have to do to get you to go on a date with me?" he asks boldly.

I look at the food scattered about the blanket. Pretty sure I would call this current situation a date, but who am I to make these types of judgments?

And then I smell it. Bacon. I look over at Nic as he pulls open the take-out bag and lifts out a container of freshly cooked sugar-maple glazed bacon. He is playing dirty. Despite being heavily saturated with nitrates, I want it more than I want anything else at this moment.

"It's organic."

"What?" I burst out.

"I said"—he pauses to look at me—"it's organic."

"Give me," I say, motioning with my fingers. "Give me the bacon, now."

Nic laughs at me. *Laughs.*

My mouth salivates as I watch Nic pop the container lid open—slowly. He is taking his time and enjoying himself by teasing me. He dangles a piece of bacon above his mouth, and I watch, entranced, as he tilts his head back and allows it to disappear between his parted lips. When he goes to do the same stunt with a second piece, I lean over and snatch it from his fingers before it can make contact with his mouth.

"Excuse me?" he scoffs, faking being offended.

I accordion the strip of meat into my mouth and chew it all up before speaking. "What?" I shrug. "Bacon is my weakness."

His smirk makes me smirk. He leans in closer, making sure to keep the bacon out of reach. "I thought the thing I do with my tongue is your weakness."

My eyes widen, as I think about all the things his magnificent tongue has done to my body. I fake indifference. "I probably did think that, at one point. But then I discovered bacon. And there's no competition." I look off to the side of the room as I bite my bottom lip, and then I feel the tickling sensation at my sides. "Stop!" I laugh. "Stopppp!"

Nic finally releases me, leaving me panting. His smile is the biggest I've seen in days. He's enjoying himself. And so am I. I hold out my hand for more bacon. It's that good.

"You are the weirdest vegan I have ever met."

"I keep you on your toes, don't I?"

"You definitely have a way of making life interesting," he says with mirth.

We manage to clean up the entire indoor picnic display and remove all evidence that we just spent the last twenty-nine minutes together. I enjoy spending time with Nic—there's no denying that. Lining the periphery of my thoughts, however, is the constant reminder that I'm pregnant. I am carrying a baby whose father is not known. I also know that neither candidate wants to be a fresh or repeat father. I mean, who would with someone they have already booted out of their life? Nic may seem interested in me again now, but as soon as he figures out I'm pregnant, he'll see me less as a thrill and more as extra baggage. I know the weight is too much for anyone to carry.

I don't think my heart can handle another loss. Us breaking up the first time was hard enough.

I throw away the last napkin and turn around to come body to body with Nic's rock hard one. "Excuse me, sorry," I mutter, obviously frazzled at his close proximity. I glance around the office space and see no sign of life. I expect Nic to take a step back, but he doesn't budge. I can smell his aftershave and feel the heat radiating off his body.

"What could I do to get just one kiss?" His words come out like a throat-growl, full of pent-up need.

His question catches me off guard. My eyes move up to his lips, and I suck in air through my closed teeth. My heart pounds in my chest, and my eyes stay fixated on his mouth.

My shoulders shrug in a nonchalant manner. "Just ask," I answer simply, without thinking of the—

Nic's eyes change with the impact of my words, stopping my thoughts. His mouth swoops in and captures mine; at the same time he grips my hips with hurried need. He does not ask. He just takes. I open for him and allow his tongue to explore. I moan breathlessly, savoring the taste of his mouth and reacquainting myself to his touch. I stand on my tiptoes to allow him better access, tipping my head back in sweet surrender.

Slowly and methodically, his feet walk me back until I am stopped only by a wall. Nic breaks the kiss, just to lick down my chin and suckle at the sensitive spot at the base of my neck, all while his hands roam and feel along my sides. Making a wet trail, he slides his mouth along my jawline and settles against the shell of my ear.

"Beg me for it," he whispers, tickling my highly charged skin.

"Never," I grind out.

I can hear his snicker as he jerks his hips forward and lifts me at the same time. My core grinds against him, and I throw my head back as I resist giving in. Like a delicate butterfly, I am mounted to the wall, helpless prey to my own toxic desires. And I'm addicted to that euphoric feeling of knowing I am Nic's to do with as he pleases.

"Submit to me," he coaxes. "Say the words I need to hear."

"Never."

I can feel the vibration of his laughter. He is having too much fun. It's as if he already thinks he won. My eyes close as his hands grip at the fleshy globes of my ass cheeks. Squeezing.

"Ahh," I pant. My legs wrap around him tighter. I bounce a little in his hold, only adding to the friction.

He is not even trying to hide his desire to break me down. The way he looks at me, his eyes taunting me—beckoning me to relinquish control over to him.

"This doesn't mean anything," I choke out, my breaths coming in staccato intervals. "You hear me? It means *nothing*."

"Sure, keep telling yourself that. I'm not convinced. And you don't sound to be either."

"I'll stop then if you think this means more," I threaten.

"No, you won't. I'll call your bluff."

"What?"

"There's no way in hell you are going to voluntarily stop my dick from sliding in between your soft folds on your own. I think you crave me like I crave you. We both know we are bad for one another and yet our bodies were designed for this level of sin."

I bite down on my lip at the clarity of his words. I swallow, but the moisture pooling in my mouth has a difficult time going down. I adamantly shake my head *no*. I can't do this right now.

"You want me with the same magnitude I want you. Lie to yourself? *Fine*. You do that. But this thing we have between us?" He motions between us with the nod of his head. "It ain't going away, baby. It's just making it clearer to me that everything I thought I feared is precisely what I need. And that is you. All of you, Claire. Body and soul. You are my cure."

"Nic, you don't know what you're saying."

"Expect me to pursue you. Expect me to not give up. Expect me to be relentless. You are mine."

I bite my tongue. There is no way I am giving in, despite feeling like I am gushing just from the way his hips hold mine in place. Every breath he breathes vibrates me just enough to feel the rub of his pants against my center.

"Come on, Claire," Nic eggs me on. "Show me how mad you are at me. I can take it. I can handle all of your emotions. Your fire. Don't hold back."

I push at his chest, at first lightly. Then harder. And harder. I thrash in his arms at the pent-up aggression I have toward him and how he broke up with me and how he is pulling me back to him like he did our entire trip to Vegas.

"I hate you for involving me in your bet!"

"Keep going," he persuades.

"I hate you for showing me kindness and then making me feel like shit when I fell for you!"

"Give me more, Claire."

"I hate you for fucking with my mind!"

I slide down Nic's body as he releases his hold on me slowly. I think it is his way of giving up but quickly realize it is actually his way of reminding me how good we feel when we are together.

My whole life I have had men try to tame me, not encourage me.

Claire, you're too much.

Claire, you're too loud.

Claire, you're too sexual.

And here I stand before a man who seems to appreciate the spontaneity I can bring to a situation. It is refreshing and new. And that fact, combined with how delicious he is looking, makes me want to jump his bones.

Without giving myself more time to change my mind, I do just that.

I lunge at Nic and he catches me midair, turning me so he is the one with his back to the wall.

"You have no fucking clue how badly you control me," he bites out, taking my hands and placing them over his, above his head. He looks anything but submissive.

"How can you even say that?" I snap back. "*You* are the one who seems to be calling all these shots."

"Because you are being so difficult."

I huff out a breath and bring my hands back down to my hips. "Really?" My simple question oozes with sarcasm. "You're really going to blame all of this on me?"

"Yes."

"Oh, the nerve of you!"

I go to turn around and leave, but Nic's hand is on mine, pulling me back to him like a boomerang. Our mouths collide, and between our squeezed bodies, he starts to undo his pants. This is happening, and no matter how much I know I should deny myself this pleasure, I am going to savor every moment. I want this. He knows it. I know it.

"Tell me to stop, Claire, and I will."

When I have no words to contradict what I know will happen, my dress is pulled up over my hips. Hands run up my spine as my neck gets bitten.

"Ouch," I wince. I can feel Nic's smile on my sore skin. He licks and kisses the spot, knowing just what to do to soothe my pain. I'm sure he left a mark—one I will look at often.

"You like it," Nic teases.

I nod. "I do. How much time do we have? I have some papers I need to file," I tease. "Emails to check."

One glance at his watch has me being pulled from the room, through the main part of the office space, into the hallway, and entering the elevator car in under a minute. He punches the number for his floor and walks me back to the wall of the elevator with just the push of his hips. My head flies back as he devours my lips, my neck, my ears. It is like he is dying of thirst, and I'm the only source of fulfillment.

The dinging sound alerts us that we have arrived. When the doors start to open, Nic reaches for my hand and pulls me from my trance. He leads me down the hall and into his office space. It isn't until I see his pants sliding down over his boxer brief-covered ass cheeks from the hurried movement that I remember that he already started undoing them in my office.

"Say the words," he demands, holding the sash of my wrap dress between white-knuckled fingers. I can tell he is struggling to maintain control. I am too.

"I want you, Nic."

His eyes darken, and my dress is undone with ease from a few flicks of his fingers. It pools at my feet on the floor of his office. I watch as he discards all of his clothes, while I stay in my panties and bra. Nic slides to the floor on his knees and presses his lips to my new tattoo, licking the image with the flick of his tongue. He then kisses my belly so sweetly that I swear he knows my little secret. I melt under his attention, feeling vulnerable and open to whatever he has to give to me.

I spread my legs a little more and brace my hands on his head as he rips my panties in half and shoves his face into my crotch.

"Ahhh!" I scream, trying to get my legs to close over the extreme pleasure. It is too intense.

Nic's hands grip my thighs, holding me apart for his skilled tongue to snake through my folds and enter me. A shriek fills the silence, and when I realize that it is me who produced the sound, I cover my mouth with my hands.

Nic slurps and sucks and in record time, I am writhing with the force of an orgasm. My eyes roll into the back of my head and for a moment I think I black out, because when I come back to earth, I'm straddling Nic who is resting in his office chair. His dick is hard against my stomach, and I can't resist the urge anymore to lift up to allow him access.

I see my bra hanging off a tv monitor on the wall and bite back a laugh over the absurdity of it. Like a flag of surrender, it stares back at me—taunting me—reminding me that my body belongs to this man below me. That despite being on top of him and dominating the movement, he is the one in control of my body.

Nic Hoffman owns me.

His fingers scale up the vertebrae of my spine, inch by inch. "You are the most beautiful thing I have ever seen."

His eyes lock on to mine. No matter how much I try to look away, he draws me back to his crystal blues.

I feel sweaty, undesirable. Yet, Nic seems to be attracted to the imperfect makeup, the messy hair, and the rumpled clothes thrown about his office space. It's the *real* side of me.

My hands wrap around Nic's neck as I leverage myself upward and back down again. When I think we have both had enough, I squeeze the inner walls of my pussy so tight that they milk him and bring me to climax. I flop my body onto his like a doll that's lost its spine. I feel boneless and content. Nic hugs me close, enveloping me in his arms. With his fingers, he draws lazy circles and patterns on my back in the most soothing motion. I feel safe. Desired.

It is in this moment of the afterglow that I come to terms with just how much I missed Nic.

I shift in his lap, feeling my inner walls tighten over the soreness from the unexpected office romp. I should be used to him by now, but every time seems like the first with him. Nic has opened up my world to how good things can be, and these glimmers are only messing with my head. Every time we blur the lines, I am only making it harder on myself.

I melt as Nic combs his fingers through my hair, sending goose bumps racing all over my body. Both my heart and mind know not to attach themselves to any more illusions, yet no part of me wants to move out of the comfortable position that Nic offers.

I'm in a dream-like state when the creaking sound of the door startles me, and a shrill voice slices through the air. I know that sound. It is unmistakable. My head whips around in shock. Nic's and my own voice merge as we both spit out the same two-syllable word in unison. "Tara?"

"What are you doing here?" I ask stupidly, shielding my breasts with my arm. She has probably seen them before, so there's not much point to hiding.

Her hands rest at her waist as she cocks a hip out. "I've come to take back my man," she says with certainty.

10

NIC

I stare at Tara and then back at Claire as my mind tries to connect the puzzle pieces together. "You two know each other?" I ask, dumbfounded. "And what the hell are you doing here, Tara?"

Her eyes glare at Claire, and I pull her closer to shield her from Tara's view. Every instinct inside me says to protect my girl.

"Give us a minute," I snap at my ex. When Tara doesn't budge, I scream out, "Give us a damn minute!" I wait until the door closes and huff more to myself than to Claire. "Who the fuck let her into this building?" I think of all the ways she could have gotten in and managed to get up to my office undetected. Something happened, and when I find out, there better be a good explanation or I'll be going on a firing spree.

I look down at my girl who is trembling—maybe from the situation or maybe from being cold after coming down from her high. I want to cuddle her, wipe her clean, and give her the aftercare she deserves. However, I have an urgent situation to take care of and remedy before Claire gets some illusion that Tara and I still have a thing together. Because we most certainly don't.

I gently lift my girl off my lap and scan the room for her clothes, finding her bra draped over a television. I grab it and hand it over to her. "Here." Her eyes avoid mine. She is refusing to talk to me, and that alone is making me want to smash something. "She's my ex, Claire. There's nothing between us anymore. Just a history that I never want to repeat."

Tara's tinny voice calls out from the other side of the door. "Nic?"

"A minute!" I yell back. *Impatient bitch.*

I try to help Claire with her bra but get shooed away angrily with her hands. "I can do it myself."

Tara pounds on the door. "Nic?"

"For fuck's sake, give us a minute!"

"You still in there?"

No, I somehow managed to get absorbed into the walls and vanished. "Wait one fucking minute!" I yell back even louder. Maybe I need to invest in more soundproofing insulation. Just the fact that I can hear her nails-on-the-chalkboard screech is enough to be alarming. I stomp toward the door and click the lock into place. I'm head of the entire security department here, and somehow my cheating ex-fiancée got in without me having a clue. I grab my clothes and start putting them on as Claire finishes up with hers. She crosses her arms over her chest as if she is trying to conceal herself from my eyes entirely. "Will you at least say something? Anything? Be mad at me, fine, but we need to talk this out so you can see—"

"Listen." She sounds so defeated that I want to pull her to me and make her see reason. I can already tell that the light that I started to see again in her eyes is about to be turned off. Our relationship is very fragile right now, and this developing situation is not helping it.

"Baby, I'm listening," I plead. "Don't shut me out. Please."

"I have no clue what has you so jaded and hating on any human with a vagina, but ten bucks says it has something to do with Tara Lonsinger—who I might add used to cheer with me when we attended the same high school. She was three grades above me."

"Damn."

"Anyway, I digress. My point is, I can't keep being your emotional support animal. You obviously have some shit to deal with, and I voluntarily will give you the space you need to work through it all."

"Claire—"

"It's nothing to be ashamed of, and I'm not trying to punish you. I have things to work through too, like how I allow two men to emotionally abuse me and not see the signs ahead of time and walk out before I get hurt more. But Nic? This is me walking out and this is me doing some self-care."

"Claire, please don't leave. Tara is nothing to me."

There are a series of knocks at the door. "Let me in! I am tired of waiting!"

A string of curse words spills out of my mouth. I rub at the back of my neck. I know now that the girls have had some past history together, but the last thing I need is for both of them to be sharing the same space. I walk over to the door and wrench it open, coming face-to-face with Tara. I glance at her appearance as if seeing it for the first time. What the hell is she wearing—a prom dress? From head to toe, she is dolled up in a floor-length silk dress. It is in my favorite color—green. Yet, somehow, at this moment, I hate the shade. If I didn't know what desperation looked like, I do now. What is she thinking? I want no part of this. Everything about Tara is drama with a capital D.

"Oh, hi, love bug."

"Don't call me that," I sneer. In my periphery I can see Claire flinch over the nickname. I move to shield her from Tara. We both have histories with her. I just never thought mine would crash into my present when I least expected it.

"Fine," she pouts. "I just thought we could have a little chat." She looks behind me to see Claire, who she gives a fluttery wave to. She literally just saw her speared by my dick and yet she is acting like Claire is nothing more than a fling.

"What do you want, Tara?" I ask directly.

"I flew here to see you and prove to you that I'm serious about starting over again with you. I am ready for you to forgive me, just like I told you on the phone."

I'm sure my jaw just hit the floor. She can't be serious. She flew all the way here to get me to change my mind?

"So, Tara and you had a thing?" Claire asks from the sidelines.

I'm glad she decided to stay, but I'm distraught over why.

"Yes and it was"—Tara pauses with a grin—"*is* very serious."

"Biggest mistake I made was trusting you," I say, looking Tara directly in the eyes. "You just wasted a trip coming here. We had a past that will never be a future."

"Not really," she says with a shrug. "It was worth it to see my old cheering buddy. You still get around with all the boys, don't you, Claire? Loving the sloppy seconds."

I cringe over the comment about Claire's sexual experience. I know I have not been her first, but I would like to think I snuffed out the other memories from her past involving her lineup of men.

"Whatever, Tara. Our friendship ended," Claire interjects, "when you tampered with my shoes during a state competition. You kept me from my chance at nationals." She swallows hard and glances away only to return her focus to be dead point on Tara. "I try my best to no longer surround myself with toxic people who have a skewed view on what the truth means."

"Oh dear, you need to get over that. Freshmen don't win championships. They just hang out as backup plans."

"Jealousy still doesn't look good on you," Claire snickers. "How does it feel to be rejected yet again?"

"Rejected?" she echoes. "Nah, Nic likes a little spice in his life that only I can give him. Plus, we would make the cutest babies. That's a fact."

"I don't want kids, Tara, nor you." I sigh and watch as Claire frowns and starts to gather her belongings.

"But we have so much to talk about." Tara pouts.

"On that note, I'm out," Claire says, opening my office door and slamming it shut.

I start to chase after her, but Tara moves in front of the exit, doing a little twirl for attention. She looks at me expectantly, hoping I give her some forced compliment over her Barbie doll appearance. Her makeup is caked on, and she is the epitome of someone who is trying way too hard to get attention. It is a bit unnatural and definitely not something I'm attracted to. What did I ever see in her? At one time I thought she was the most beautiful girl in the world, but now I can't look at her without seeing her ruining what I thought was our future. I shake my head over her craziness and walk over to my wall of windows overlooking the city. When I turn back around, Tara is sitting at my desk, spinning the chair side to side, with her feet propped on top. I literally just had Claire sitting on my cock in that chair, yet here Tara is dirtying up the memory with my girl that I want to last forever.

"Let's order in breakfast and chat about our future."

"No."

"No?"

"No!"

"Why not?"

"There is no future. We will never get back together. Ever. Get out of my office. This stunt you pulled today is crazy—even for you. What were you thinking flying across the country? Did you honestly think I would come running back to you after you cheated on me? If you did, you are delusional."

"Have you told your little sidepiece how you came about that knowledge?" she asks, making me growl deep within my throat. "Because it would serve her right to know the full extent of your stalking capabilities. Have you perfected them over the years, Nic? I doubt you are doing everything on the straight and narrow." She looks down at her fake nails. "Not your style."

"Shut up, Tara."

"I'm just saying that you better hope I don't share these valuable tidbits with your dear Claire. Or maybe she is that type of girl who likes to be watched and followed and managed."

Tara is goading me. She wants me to feel indebted to her, and I refuse to relinquish any power over to her—even if just to give her an illusion of control. I'm done with her games. "Why are you really here?"

"Yeah, I totally don't miss your dry personality, but your dick is a nice bonus. Anyhoo, I heard through the grapevine that you are working with your brother again. And I wanted to—"

"Milk me for more money?" I interrupt.

She shrugs. "Nice suggestion."

Back when we were still engaged, Tara had full access to our joint bank account. I trusted her implicitly, never thinking she would ever betray me. When I found out the truth, I hired the best lawyer in town, but Tara had already been withdrawing money and putting it in her own secret personal account. Her scheme cost me thousands before my detective work led me to the truth.

"Get out." I talk so slowly that surely she cannot misunderstand my words or derive an alternate meaning. "Never come back here." While I want to tell her that I am jaded now about all other women, and that her infidelity caused me irreparable damage, I refuse to give her any satisfaction that she still affects me. Instead, I just let her walk out of my office the same way she arrived.

I fish my phone out of my suit pocket and call Brenna who should be at her desk waiting for her morning orders. "Make sure the blonde girl who just left my office dressed like a prom queen gets out of the building. And get Dan King up here now."

I pace in front of my desk until the soft knocks draw my attention to the door.

"It's Dan, sir."

"Come in." I grab the remote and flick on every television, pulling up the security footage replay of Tara entering the building. I point to the main screen. "Who authorized this? She is not even an employee and yet she was allowed access to my floor and my office. Unacceptable. Whoever gave her permission past the lobby checkpoint can go ahead and resign or get fired."

Dan swallows hard and looks like he is about to shit his pants. He should be used to me by now and my I-don't-sugar-coat-anything attitude. He doesn't get paid the salary he does to make these types of rookie mistakes.

"I'm working on it, sir. She had to have access to a badge."

I run a hand down the side of my face, as I switch over to the live feed showing Tara exiting through the lobby. I want to hit something—or someone. I close my eyes and tilt my head upward toward the ceiling. I feel a migraine starting.

My eyes open at the sound of another series of knocks at my door. What the hell is this—Grand Central Station?

"What!" I yell at the continuous knocking. "What is it?"

Graham peeks his head through the door. "Hey Dan, can you give us a minute?"

Dan nods and leaves, allowing Graham to enter.

"What's up?" I ask, half expecting him to drop some form of truth-bomb on me.

"Let's get out of here. I already am starting to get a headache," he says, but I know he is lying by the lack of a tick to his jaw. He probably is just trying to get me to talk. "C'mon."

"Fine," I cave. "Where are we going?"

"The ring."

"Why?"

Graham narrows his eyes as he studies my face. "Because it looks like you need to hit someone and it isn't even noon yet."

I nod. "Accurate."

"Turns out, so do I."

The cool thing about having an influx of money is that special privileges are granted freely. Just the name *Hoffman* holds a lot of power in the city of Portland. Our name implies influence and opportunity. It is easy to walk into the converted warehouse boxing gym and get access to all of the equipment without being on the schedule. The owner knows us and clears out the venue for our own private use. It helps that Graham owns a percentage of the chain and often contributes financially to the upgrades. To him, it is charity. The owner allots time each day for usage of the rings for underprivileged kids, almost as an after-school type program. Angsty teens need a place to expel their pent-up aggression. So, what better place than the ring?

Ironically, it is the same facility where Graham and I often practiced our skills during our high school days. Mom or Dad would take time out of their schedules to drop us off and pick us back up. If it wasn't for them believing in us, we would have never been the athletes we became. Championships cannot be won without hard work and dedication. It was on these mats where we learned discipline and resilience—life skills that have carried over into our current work ethic.

"What are you in the mood for?" Graham asks me. He knows I am not ready to talk yet. He knows that he needs to coax my emotions out of me in order for me to open up.

"I'm up for whatever."

"Let's go old school," he says with a smirk.

I nod and hit up the locker room to change into a pair of spandex pants and headgear. Graham and I have a stash of equipment here, and the owner hired a worker to handle the laundry in the industrial machines he invested in.

I stretch in the middle of the rubber cushioned ring, making sure my joints and muscles are limber and ready to be challenged. Graham and I are each other's most worthy opponents because we think alike. This will be fun.

We smack hands with each other and get into position. Hired refs are on standby to facilitate any pickup matches. I wave one over and wait for the whistle to be blown to signify the start.

Graham and I circle each other, looking for an opening.

He infiltrates my defensive stance first and does a take down, from which I escape. We scurry about the mat until I can take him down with a trip move and then use an arm bar move to pin him—which he escapes.

After several rounds and no actual score being kept, we call off the referee and really get our sweat on by going freestyle. No points are kept. We just have fun and try to pin each other as our ultimate goal.

"Now are you ready to talk?" Graham asks, tossing me a towel and a bottle of water.

"Tara showed up in my office today."

"Damn. How did she get through security?"

"That's a problem I am handling. And trust me, when I find out who let her through, they will pay the price of losing their job and being blacklisted from the industry. It is unacceptable. I thought I made myself clear to every worker who managed to not get fired thus far that I do not piss around."

"Yeah, you've made quite the name for yourself at HH," Graham says with a slight edge of humor to his tone. "You even earned a new nickname."

"Oh really?"

"Yeah. It's all hearsay though."

"Do share," I chuckle. "I'm sure it's a good one."

"Oh, it is. Rumor has it that you are basically known as The Nictator."

"That's cute," I deadpan. I wonder who orchestrated that development?

"Jokes aside, I'm relieved that I have one less worry with you taking up the lead on all of this."

"Not sure how good of a job I'm doing when there are still people sneaking into the building in broad daylight," I mutter, clearly annoyed. I run the clean white towel over my face and neck, gathering up my sweat. It feels great to work out. Already I can tell my mood is less hostile.

"I have confidence that you will figure this all out."

I nod, taking a big sip from my water bottle. "And when I do, those who have double-crossed me will pay."

"I have zero doubt."

Because we are both in the same relative location, Tyler and I decide to meet face-to-face. I just never thought he would have chosen a frilly tea shop to be the venue.

"Remind me the logic behind this particular choice," I say, glancing around the space. For it still being the morning, I'd expect to find more patrons, but we are the only ones present.

"No one will ever expect to find us here. Plus, their butter toffee scones are"—he does a chef's kiss—"divine."

"I need a favor."

"As long as I get my future Christmas bonus, I'll try my best to grant it."

Ignoring his lame-ass commentary, I proceed. "I need a vagina cookie delivered to HH."

"I, um,"—Tyler scratches the back of his neck—"was not expecting those words to come out of your mouth. Do you have any graphic images so I can know exactly what to tell the baker?"

"What? No. Can you just get me one?"

"Are we still talking about cookies?"

I give him a blank stare. "Yes."

"Sounds super tasty for a substitute for the real deal. I'm getting myself one as well."

"Whatever."

11

CLAIRE

I am only alone in the Plus None office for a few minutes before Angie arrives, followed by our employees. Since it's Monday, we have our weekly round-up meeting where we discuss our goals and plan for progress. Due dates are reiterated and marked on the company's huge vision board that is on display in the common area.

I embrace my jam-packed morning schedule but cannot seem to push Nic into the back of my head where he can commingle with Tara alone.

I never let anyone think Tara did anything wrong. We were friends and everyone in the school knew it. No one would have believed me anyway.

There was a certain stigma surrounding me then, and while at first I tried to convince others to see me for who I was on the inside, it became a comfort when I just submitted to their ignorant views and played the role.

Sometimes the lies are easier to believe than the truth.

Despite growing up in a nice neighborhood that was

affluent, I was very much treated like the girl from the wrong side of the tracks. Everyone thought they had me pegged as the troubled girl who spread her legs for anyone who was willing. Truth of the matter was, I barely had any sexual experience, and the memories I did have from the experiences were uneventful. It wasn't until I went to college that I started to take things seriously and stopped using men as a way to feel less lonely. I obviously resorted back to my old habits, because once the agency work for Entice basically fell into my lap, I jumped on the opportunity and turned it into my self-fulfilling prophecy.

A tiger can't change its stripes.

And no matter how hard I try, I can't change my past.

Sure, I can sit and sulk over how unseen I felt back then. However, those moments in my past helped me to spread my wings and transform into the person I am today—flaws and all. Growing up financially affluent but emotionally deprived helped me to learn what I wanted for myself when I moved to Portland and met Angie. Unfortunately the consequences of having two uninvolved parents didn't help me be able to find stable relationships—no matter how hopeful I am when I meet men.

Unless he's wearing a diaper, you cannot change him.

And the cycle of finding the wrong men for me—ones who cause me emotional harm—may never stop. Unless I stop.

Maybe I'm destined to be single. Maybe I deserve to be single. Maybe my life would be better if I was single.

This baby deserves to have a mommy who doesn't cry all the time. This baby deserves everything that I never had growing up.

Love.

Stability.

And to go through life never thinking it's a mistake.

Even though Nic and Tara seem very much done from what I witnessed earlier, I know that there is more to their breakup that I do not know. I can't blame Nic for keeping his personal life hidden. I also am carrying around the burden of a secret that will end things between us for good. Maybe I'm scared to lose the one man who seems to accept me for me. Maybe I want to preserve the last fraying thread holding him to me before my entire life implodes.

I have perfected the coping strategy of avoidance since I was a teen, so I bury myself in my daily tasks. I pop in my earbuds and take a break in the meditation room—which is easily my favorite place in the whole building. The air still smells of greasy bacon, and while I savored that scent just an hour ago, right now it makes me hold my nose and exit as fast as I can. Ugh. My hypersensitive sense of smell is what really spikes my nausea. Even smells that most people would agree smell good can make me double over with disgust.

If I was at any other job, I would look like a slacker relaxing on a sofa with a laptop propped up on my legs. However, this is not a normal job. I am thrilled over the work climate that Angie and I have created here. Taking breaks is encouraged. Socializing between departments is almost mandatory. I've never felt this safe in a career to be exactly who I am.

I am enough.

I can think freely, brain dump ideas, and never fear that I'm being *too much*.

Maybe all of my struggles growing up have helped me to appreciate the joys that I have in my life now. You can't get a rainbow without any rain. I'm excited to see where Angie and I take this adventure. We have some future team-building activities and outings planned to nurture the inclusive environment that we strive to maintain. Happy workers almost always breed organic success.

Around lunchtime, Brenna stops over and drops off a mystery take-out bag on my desk. Without a word of confirmation from her mouth, I know who sent her. Can he be any more transparent?

"What's this?" I ask, eyeing the paper bag.

"Just thought you would like this," she says sweetly.

Guilt flows through me that maybe I misjudged her when we first ran into each other on her first day. She may not be so bad. I walk Brenna out of Plus None and am about to head for the restroom when I catch movement from the side hallway.

"Hi Claire," Dan greets with a huge smile.

"Hey Dan."

Brenna rocks on her heels while twisting her fingers in front of her. "Hi Dan."

"Hey." He turns his attention back to me, and I see Brenna deflate. "I was just about to take my lunch break and wanted to know if you wanted to join me. We can try out the new restaurant in the parallel tower that just opened or go somewhere outside. Whichever you prefer."

My eyes float down to my toes that are peeking through the straps of my sandals.

"I'll see you both later," Brenna says quietly. Her voice is shaky and agitated.

I wave at her and then look into Dan's hopeful eyes. He has sandy-brown hair and dark brown eyes. To most women, he would be considered hot. It's not that I am immune to his good looks, because I'm not. He's attractive. It's just that I know that there is zero point even trying to have a relationship with anyone when I'm toting around a fatherless child. Being a single mom is going to consume my life. I'm not going to have free time, and in my current state, I'm not looking for anything that even resembles a relationship.

He'd have better luck trying to get to know Brenna more. It already appears that she has some natural interest anyway.

"C'mon, Claire. It's just lunch," he coaxes. "I won't even try to hold your hand."

Just the way he says the last sentence makes me inwardly cringe. Dan chuckles and puts both of his hands in his suit pockets, while leaning against the wall. My stomach growls. I am hungry. However, I don't need to string someone along just to fulfill a physical need for food. Plus, Brenna just dropped off some type of takeout bag that I assume is from Nic.

"Give me a second," I mutter, walking back into the office. I open up the paper bag and find a cookie inside that is shaped like lady bits. The pink frosting with the candy pearl embellishment is a detail I would never have thought of if my job was to replicate a vagina using edible ingredients. "Damn." I guess I deserve this surprise from all the edible cocks I sent him last week. I place the cookie back inside the bag and decide that I will eat the pussy for my dessert. It will be a first. My eyes catch notice of a note at the bottom, and I pull it out to read—"Without doubt, yours tastes better."

I feel my cheeks heat over the five simple words. Even floors apart, Nic can still make me blush. I get up from my desk and look around the office space. Outside in the hall, I no longer see Dan and figure he got bored waiting for me and left. At least I can avoid some awkwardness of sharing a meal with someone who seems borderline too forward. My stomach growls demanding food, so I have learned to not ignore those signals.

I grab my purse from my desk drawer and exit Plus None. When the elevator arrives, I hop on and make my descent.

The main lobby of HH is full of the hustle and bustle of employees exiting for their lunch break. It is a beautiful spring day in the city. The fresh air is warm and smelling of—

Ugh. Flowers. As soon as the smell hits my nostrils, I instantly feel like the pollen and scent are permanently stuck inside my nose, becoming stronger with each inhale. My stomach churns from the potency of the scent. I walk faster to get away from the bushes that are blooming, and when I finally clear them, I see Dan smiling brightly on the sidewalk just a couple of yards in front of me. Shit.

"Perfect timing," he says, hope evident in his tone.

His persistence went from being charming to being annoying. I don't have time to tiptoe around my rejection speech. For someone older than me, he doesn't really catch on to social etiquette or even cues. I'm either oblivious to my own body language or his special talent is being pushy. I don't know how to get out of sharing a meal with him without it turning awkward. By the way he is looking at me, I know this is going to feel weird no matter what the outcome.

"Oh hi," I say, glancing at my phone to appear busy. I inwardly groan when I realize it is upside down. "I was just going to grab a smoothie and then get back to work."

"I'll join you." He follows me into the shop, leaving me no time to protest. He leans in closer to my body and whispers into my ear, "What's good here?"

I keep my attention forward at the menu and answer with a simple, "Everything."

"Are you seeing anyone?"

Seriously? My eyes shut and then open again. "Yes." I shake my head. "I mean, no." How do I tell someone *it's complicated* without sounding like a checkbox on a dating app?

"Well, what do you know?" he says, as if having a light-bulb moment. "I'm not seeing anyone either."

Shocker. I move up in line and rock on my feet to the instrumental music playing throughout the sound system in the shop. I can hear Dan mumbling something behind me that I'm sure is inappropriate, but I just act like I do not hear him. When I am next in line, I sigh in relief.

"Can I please get the strawberry antioxidant blend with added protein? Oh, and with oat milk, please."

"Make that two," Dan says, leaning in closer and then tilting his head at me with a wink.

Whatever hotness I originally saw in him has dwindled to nothing. He is a frat boy stuck in an out-of-college body.

We work in the same building, otherwise I would tell him where to put his twitchy eye.

When my name is called out from the pick-up window, I grab my beverage and am about to head out to the street when my phone vibrates with an incoming call. I scan the screen and see it is my mom calling. No matter what she has to say, I'm relieved to hear her say it—if just to get away from Dan's unwanted attention.

"It's important," I say, gesturing toward my phone. "I'll see you later."

"Oh, umm, okay," he stutters, taking his drink off the counter and finding a seat in the cafe alone.

I quickly head out the door and answer the call before it heads to voicemail. "Hey Mom."

"Claire, I need you to come home and get your stuff out of the bedroom and garage."

"Oh, um, okay?"

"The house sold and it needs to be gone."

"Can you just send it?" I ask, trying to think of how I would be able to get to the East Coast easily.

"No."

"Okay."

"It would cost a fortune, and I already lost enough in this damn divorce. Plus, it is more than what would fit in a suitcase. Just drive and load up your car."

"Let me look at my calend—"

"Don't look too hard, it's not like I have all the time in the world." Mom's voice is gruff from years of smoking. Based on how hoarse it is at the moment, I imagine she picked it back up again after years of quitting. "It needs to be out by this week, or I'm just trashing it. Storage units are so overpriced."

"Got it," I mutter. I don't even know what I left at her house. Maybe some jewelry or birthday gifts? I can only hope I have forgotten some valuables that can be pawned for quick cash.

"Okay, good. Got to go," she says, disconnecting the call.

Bye, Mom. *Looking forward to seeing you.*

I'm not sure if I am more upset over no longer having a home I can go back to or the way my mom is basically erasing all the memories of me from her life. Maybe I'm the main reason for the divorce. Maybe her cheating on my stepdad would have ironed itself out if there hadn't been a constant reminder—*me*—of her infidelity.

My mom hasn't exactly used the words "ruined her life" but that is basically what she is implying. If only she would realize how difficult it is going through life carrying the dominant genes of a man I don't even know. I don't look anything like the rest of my family members. It's not like I can even pretend I belong. I am the only interracial member for multiple generations. Despite being mixed, I was very much raised to ignore my father's culture. I was raised to be white, although I check a different box on all my health forms.

My mom did this. She made the choice to have relations with someone who was not her husband. She had sex with a stranger and got pregnant by that stranger. So, no matter how much guilt she tries to press onto my conscience, it is all in vain.

As soon as I get back to the office, I open up the search

engine and remind myself that if there is no traffic, it would take me forty-two hours—without stopping—to drive back home on the East Coast. If I have too many possessions that can't fit inside some empty pieces of luggage, it is not worth it to me to keep them. Flying is my only doable option, if I don't intend to miss very many days of work.

I pull open the flight listings with a departure out of Portland for this week and scan through the options. Ouch, the price is steeper than I was expecting. I shouldn't be surprised at this, considering this is a last-minute trip.

"Hey you," Angie greets, while coming into the office from our lunch break. "Can we please go back to eating together? I'm starting to stress eat, and I'm afraid my dress will no longer fit."

I look up at my best friend with concern. She is rocking on her heels and biting her bottom lip—two telltale signs she is anxious. "What has you all stressed out?" I ask.

"I love her dearly, but Graham's mom needs to take it down a notch or two. She is missing some of the low-key elements I am striving to achieve with the festivities. You know how understated I like things. Simple beauty. I could recruit Penny indirectly for some help, but she is still in Seattle. Plus, I'd rather keep her duties easy. I know she is a bridesmaid and all, but—"

"Want me to—"

"Yes!"

"I didn't even finish my statement," I chuckle.

"Whatever it is you are offering, the answer is one hundred percent *yes*."

"Okay. I will intervene but still make it appear to be Donna's idea. Does that sound good?"

"Oh my goodness, yes," Angie exhales, leaning her backside against the surface of my desk. "The last thing I need is to make waves with my almost mother-in-law. She has impeccable taste, but I prefer the whole less-is-more concept."

I nod. Angie has always liked the simpler, less extravagant things in life. She leans over and gives me a hug. I didn't know how badly I needed one until she squeezes me a little more, and I start to tremble.

"Claire?" she asks, pulling back hesitantly and examining my face. I'm sure I am a mess. I can already feel the dampness seeping out of my eyes. "What's wrong?"

"I'm fine."

"No. No, you're not. And that line only works on men, so don't pull that shit with me."

I sigh, allowing my shoulders to slump forward from the emotional exhaustion so far from this day. "I have to go back home for a night or so. I know this is last minute but—"

"Of course," she says, soothingly running her hand over my back. "Take as much time as you need."

"What about work? I didn't even give advance notice or warning."

"If you need to handle something then handle it. We are business partners. You don't need permission to visit family."

"My parents are divorcing."

"Oh, wow."

"It is messy. I'm basically going back to say goodbye to my childhood home and get whatever crap I still have stored there. This isn't a joyful trip." I can't even remember the last time the emotion of joyfulness was even held in a memory while there. "Just going to get some closure, hopefully."

"I'm so sorry. I know what it is like saying goodbye to a home that holds so many memories."

Even though there weren't a ton of amazing memories created, it is still sad to say farewell to a place that was a solid part of my developmental years. It was *home*, albeit a bit dysfunctional.

My current situation on the West Coast feels more like what a nomad creates. I went from living in a townhouse with Angie, to cohabitating with Ethan, to living with Nic, to camping out on Blake and Henry's cheesy-puff futon, before currently struggling to make ends meet in a studio apartment.

"Thanks for being understanding about the last-minute trip. I'll try to continue doing work virtually while I'm gone."

"Claire," Angie says, looking me in the eyes. "Just take care of you."

"I'm trying."

12

NIC

"Why am I being informed about this now?" I snap at Tyler. Dammit!

"It had to be a last-minute decision. There's no other explanation. I got the flight information, seat number, cost of the ticket, and sent someone to verify Miss Nettles made it safely to the airport."

I take a deep breath in through my nose. At least Tyler has given me enough information to help settle my anxiety. I just do not like Claire traveling alone—especially cross-country.

What if something happens to her?

What if she needs help or runs out of money?

So many things could go wrong, and she would be all alone as she tried to figure things out.

I lean back in my office chair and rub at the tension building in the back of my neck. Tyler and I are meeting—for the second time today—in my office at HH. Most of my day has been putting out fires, so I was completely unaware that Claire even left the office early, let alone decided to take a spur of the moment trip back to Virginia. We had breakfast together in her favorite room, enjoyed each other at my desk until Tara surprised us, and then I bought her a bakery-made cookie after hitting up the ring with Graham.

Tyler did well with his hunt for the perfect pussy. I'll give him that.

No one has come forward as to how my ex was able to roam around the building unaccompanied. Ironically, the security footage held only partial information due to a power glitch in the cameras. What are the chances that right as Tara stepped foot in the lobby, the recordings all stopped? I don't believe in coincidences. I believe in sabotage.

There are only so many security staff members who would have had access to the recording. Yet, no one stands out in my head as an obvious culprit.

"I may need you to do some investigating on how my ex got inside HH without it being detected by my staff. Something is not right with that whole situation."

Tyler nods and continues listening to me ramble about Claire flying to Virginia. I have typed out at least six different text messages to her, resisting sending each at the last minute. According to Angie, she had a few things to take care of that required her in-person presence. I don't like it, though. She never gave a time frame on her return, so not knowing when she will be back into the city is eating me up inside. I don't like being this on edge. It's not a good addition to my already pissed-off mood.

"Oh damn," Tyler says, looking at his cell, while swiping the screen a few times.

"What? Tell me," I demand.

"Just when I thought things couldn't get worse…"

"Quit delaying and tell me!" I'm on the verge of hitting the wall, I'm that anxious.

"Tara Lonsinger is confirmed to have bought a ticket for the same flight back to Virginia."

"What are the freaking chances?" I snap. I figured Tara would go back east, but I never contemplated the odds of Claire selecting the same flight as her. I can only hope their seats are on opposite ends of the plane. "What's her seat?"

"Not near Miss Nettles."

"See if you can upgrade Claire to first class. Keep those two even farther apart."

Tyler nods and works at getting the airline to make the accommodation. I hope Claire remembered to bring her motion sickness medication so she is comfortable on her flight back home. I know how scattered she can be when she has a lot on her mind. I wish she was mine—in all senses of the word—just so I could insist on traveling with her. I don't know much about her family—she never really brings them up even in casual conversation—but the fact that she spent last Christmas with mine tells me that she was not itching to go back home. Maybe there is tension there. I want to know these things. All of these memories and experiences help to sculpt a person. I would never be the man I am today without the love and devotion from my parents. It is easy for a boy to veer off path and into the wrong crowds growing up. I'm just fortunate to have had Graham and my dad always looking out for what is best for me.

I have to remind myself that I value Claire's self-confidence and independence during times like these where she drives me to insanity. She is capable of handling so much and is very strong. While her stubbornness heightens all of my protective instincts, I know deep down that she needs someone to walk beside her and not someone always looking to be the lead. It is hard to relinquish that level of control. However, I never want to dull her sparkle or make her feel like what she needs is secondary to my own selfish ones.

I want to put Claire first. If this is what a healthy relationship looks like, then sign me up. While I have had my fair share of conquests, I have yet to have a relationship that resembles what I would call healthy. Once again, I am in new, uncharted territory. Worst part is, I don't even think Claire considers what I'm doing as a relationship. Maybe with time, she will see that my words match my actions. Then, she'll be able to start trusting me again with pieces of her heart.

Time. All I need is more time with her.

"Miss Nettles just got through security and made it to her gate. No sighting of Miss Lonsinger yet."

I nod and relax a bit of the strain I am holding in the muscles of my upper body. Maybe, just maybe, this flight will be successful—and not a disaster. I hope someone is around to help her with her bags. She will probably give herself a concussion trying to avoid asking for assistance when she obviously needs it. That woman. I smile to myself thinking of her stubbornness during the flights to and from Vegas. She would rather strain a muscle than admit she could use a hand.

"Keep me updated. I'm going to need it done often."

"Understood."

Tyler exits my office and nearly runs into Dan who is waiting to enter.

"Mr. Hoffman, I have a lead on what went wrong this morning," he says, eyeing Tyler. It's Dan's job to know who is in the building, so the exchange between the men is not shocking.

I wave Tyler off and welcome Dan inside my space. He is carrying a folder under his arm. I wasn't expecting him, but any insight into the mix-up this morning is welcome.

"Let's hear it."

He takes the seat Tyler just vacated and places his hands on his lap as he collects his thoughts. "I did a little investigating and discovered that there was an electrical malfunction in the control room with the breaker. I hired an electrician to come look over the cables and make sure all of the voltages are up to code."

"So it was a completely random thing that happened?" I inquire further.

"Not necessarily. At the same time the cameras stopped recording, there was someone trying to access the back door to the building and set off an alarm that went silent from the internal power outage. All of the lights and computer systems were on a different circuit. However, the security system was able to trip with the glitch."

"How do you know someone was trying to break in then?" I ask, sitting up farther in my seat. This is all news to me. The back doors are set to deadbolt during any type of malfunction. This is probably why no one was able to get through the back door at that time. It was an added feature I enabled last minute when I updated the overall system.

"I was able to get access to some of the neighboring

buildings' feeds. Took me some time to get permission, but I managed to get some still images. They are blurry though, and you can only see the back of the intruder's head."

My pulse races at the thought of someone trying to get inside the building unannounced and through the back door. Whoever it is will pay. "I would like to see them."

Dan nods and opens up his folder, pulling out a series of enlarged images. He passes me the stack, and I glance at the photos. Shit. The person who appears to be trying to get into the building undetected looks just like Tyler from the back. I feel my heart sneak up into my throat. He was just here in my office delivering me information. We met earlier at the tea shop. But the time stamp on these images don't coincide with those meetings.

Could it be that the man I have been assigning to look out for Claire is someone who may have an ulterior motive? I look down at the image again and the striking resemblance to my hired investigator. Dammit. I have no way of really knowing this is him, but now that the doubt is in my head, I'm not sure I can fully trust him.

Maybe that is why Dan was eyeing him weirdly today when they were passing through the door. Maybe he saw the resemblance, despite meeting Tyler for the first time.

"This is good work, Dan. You are really solidifying your position on the team. Keep it up."

"Thank you, sir."

Dan's face lights up from the personal praise. He leaves the images with me and exits my office space. I follow him out and grab a bottle of water from the snack area down the hall. Brenna is at her desk typing up an email when I clear my throat, bringing her gaze up to meet mine.

"I know we briefly discussed this before, but I need you to find a way to be on Claire's floor more often without it being awkward. She is not here at the moment, but when she returns, I need more frequent updates on her so I know she is safe."

Brenna nods and waits for me to walk away before going back to her typing. I head back to my office and shoot Graham a text.

> **Nic: I may need to borrow Collins for some work. Can he be spared at all this week?**

> **Graham: Yes. I will send him to you. He's in the building.**

> **Nic: Thank you**

> **Graham: Everything ok?**

> **Nic: I'll discuss it with you later. There may be a mole.**

> **Graham: Need my help?**

> **Nic: You focus on getting ready to end your single life. I got this.**

> **Graham: My single life ended as soon as Angie and I first met.**

It is true. As soon as Graham met Angie for the first time, he knew that his life would forever change. We may be brothers, but we are very different in how we pursue and accept love. Maybe this whole time I've been expecting my feelings to be fireworks worthy in regard to the opposite sex. Things with Claire never were like that. She was a part of the bigger picture long before I actually saw her. Sure, she was always beautiful to me. However, it took getting to know her and seeing her different sides that caused me to fall, and when I finally did, I fell hard.

It might have taken me longer to come to terms with my feelings, but that doesn't mean they aren't real or intense. I have grown up in the shadow of my brother, and while we are similar in many ways, we still go through life walking in vastly different shoes.

Where Graham is open to expressing his love verbally, I've always been more reserved. No one ever questions what Graham is thinking because he wears all of his emotions on his sleeve. I, on the other hand, am more mysterious with how I let others know what I'm feeling.

Maybe this feeling I am having makes me edgy because I have never felt it before—not until Claire walked out. Sometimes it takes losing someone precious to realize how important that someone really is. Yeah, it's cliché but it's the truth.

It takes Collins approximately four minutes to make his way to my office. He has been working for Graham for years, so asking him for a favor is not new or outside of his job description. He is paid well for his years of service and loyalty. I thought Tyler was going to hold a similar title and rank. However, if he is trying to double-cross me, then he will have to be dealt with. He has ample opportunity to see into my life and what I value. If someone is going to cause me damage, Tyler would have enough ammo to inflict the most pain.

He knows my biggest weakness—Claire.

"What can I do for you?" Collins asks, walking slowly into my office.

The entire day has been a circus of visitors walking in and out of my door. Some were welcome, some were not.

"I hate to ask this of you, but I need a huge favor."

"Name it."

"I need someone discreetly followed. The person works in the industry and would be naturally paranoid and in tune with these types of shadows, so it has to be well done."

"Understood."

"I also need all bank records and any knowledge of offshore accounts retrieved. I am hoping my suspicion is false, but I am running out of people I can trust. You are one of those people I can count on."

Collins nods. "Appreciate it. Can I ask one thing?"

"Of course."

"Does Graham know?"

"No details yet. I will have a chat with him soon. This is time sensitive and extremely important that I get accurate information before I make my next move."

"Understood."

"Thanks, Collins."

I hand him Tyler's full name on a Post-it note and watch as he reads it and hands it back to me. I send it through the shredder. Tyler has access to a lot of my security features, and the last thing I need is for him to change his methods if he is in fact doing nefarious things. If I am going to catch the mole, they cannot see me gunning for them.

I walk Collins out and head down to the neighboring tower's food court to grab a sandwich and drink. Graham recently leased out the space to a variety of food vendors, with the hope to keep employees happy by not having to venture out far to get a snack or meal.

Sitting down at a circular table, I pull up my tracking app and see that Claire is still located at the airport. Her flight will be taking off in the next thirty minutes, assuming there are no delays.

I want to text her. I want to book a flight and travel with her, but I resist. I can only hope that this time apart helps her to miss me, because I already miss her.

Virginia may be for lovers, but I hope Portland still pulls at her heartstrings.

———

After the work shift ends, I drive back to my place and take that first step into doing something outside my comfort zone by logging onto the online portal for my session that Mitch set up for me.

Do I want to do this? No.

Do I think it will help? Who the hell knows.

But here I sit, waiting for the psychologist to enter the virtual meeting and pick apart all my flaws. Hell, that should be a session in and of itself—I'd assume.

I think the unknown is the hardest for me. I love having a clear plan and yet there's nothing predictable about how I'll win Claire back—or if it will even work. I just know that everything I've done post-Tara has been self-destructive behavior, and there comes a time when it's best to stop the cycle.

She should have never come to Portland. I don't need her tainting this state with bad memories. She's the reason I left the East Coast when I could have easily settled there instead.

The ding sound alerts me that the professional has entered the room and turned the webcam and microphone on.

"It's a pleasure to meet you, Nic. Welcome."

I nod, struggling with what to say. I knew this would be uncomfortable but we haven't even started yet.

She provides a warm smile. "My name is Dr. Zimmerman. Can you tell me why you decided to reach out for therapy and what you hope to achieve from it?"

I shrug. "I'm trying to win back the woman who stole my heart." I watch as she jots down what I assume are notes.

"Please continue."

"That's basically it."

"I highly doubt that. Please do not read into anything I'm doing on my end with my note keeping. I will periodically jot things down so I can loop back around to topics, while still allowing you to fully open up to me. I hope we can build trust during our time together and come up with healthy ways to move forward. So…please continue."

"I think"—*I know*—"there's something wrong with me."

"And why do you say that?"

"I damage everyone who comes in my path."

Dr. Zimmerman glances at a file folder. "Actually, based on your intake form you filled out and submitted, you have plenty of people who haven't experienced the damage from you that you've claimed. Your mother, your sister, and your soon to be sister-in-law all have experienced your compassion and mercy. So the question is, why do you punish the women who you seek sexual gratification from? And more importantly, how do we channel that toxic energy over to something that can morph into a positive end goal?"

"I don't know," I answer honestly.

"And that's where I think we should begin."

13

CLAIRE

I take my window seat in the front of the plane and relax into the leather seat. It was a surprise to hear my name announced over the intercom to come to the boarding station and get informed that I was eligible for a free upgrade for today's flight. No one in their right mind would turn such a gift down, so I graciously accepted. Despite having a rough start to the day, maybe things are finally looking up for me.

I pull out my journal and jot down some of the things I want to accomplish while at home. Besides the obvious, I would like to visit a few of my favorite spots in town and maybe even head into DC to visit a museum or two. The cool thing about being so close to a metropolitan area is the rich exposure to a vast amount of cultures and ethnicities all at once. Maybe it's time to learn about my Filipino roots, even if just in the general sense. Plus, it would be nice to make a good memory to counterbalance the bad memories that I'm sure will take place around my parents. There is too much toxicity when they are in the picture.

I can't stay long in Virginia because I am anxious to get back to work on the subscription boxes for Plus None, but I also don't need to rush. Angie has made it clear that time away from work is healthy. I would just prefer if this trip was better planned and not a last-minute thing. Besides the flight costing more than normal, I'm not exactly sure what the dynamics will be between my parents. The uncertainty gives me a bit of anxiety. Even though my dad is really a stepdad, he is the only thing I had growing up filling that role. Now that I'm an adult, however, he doesn't have to censor his true emotions toward me. In simplest terms, I am the catalyst in why his marriage has crumbled. Maybe he would still be with my mom if he didn't have the concrete proof that she cheated.

I am strong.

I can handle whatever gets thrown my way.

While I may be the catalyst in the divorce, I am not the reason. This is one hundred percent on my mom. I never asked to be born. I didn't have a choice.

I take a few deep breaths as I finish my journaling and move on to people watching. As seats get filled, I can't help but watch and admire the couples who board the aircraft. Love is a beautiful thing, and to travel with your partner seems so fun.

It is the metallic sound of fake laughter that signifies the new arrival. I look over the seat in front of me to find Tara Lonsinger walking onto the plane. You have got to be kidding me. What are the flipping chances? I guess I should be relieved she is not planning on lingering in Portland any longer than is necessary. I wouldn't put it past her to break into Nic's apartment and accidentally find herself nude under his sheets. I used to think the over-the-top stereotypes for the desperate girls in movies were fake. Then I encountered Tara. She has fulfilled every one of the mean girls' characteristics. I may have what people label as "daddy issues," but Tara has "human decency issues" which no amount of therapy can fix. She is rotten to the core, and until she comes face-to-face with how she treats people, then there's no cure. When someone refuses to take responsibility for their actions, then I lump them into the box I labeled *Hopeless*.

I look at the empty seat beside me and start tossing my purse, sweater, and carry-on onto it. I am about as graceful about it as a baby giraffe learning to walk. *Avoid eye contact. Avoid it at all costs.* I pull out the pamphlet from the pocket of the seat in front of me and start to read about what to do if I feel the need to throw up while in the air. What the hell? I turn the paper over and see the insulated bag attached with the bendable metal clip at the top. Lovely.

Maybe Tara is in another section, and I don't have anything to worry about. I am not even sure how seating arrangements work on this flight. Is it too late for a sliver of hope?

"This is my seat."

The tinny tone causes goose bumps to creep up my skin. It is almost an unnatural sound, like the ones mechanically produced using digital sound technology. I know she has a future career in doing voice-overs for animated movies—the ones featuring obnoxious female dogs. She would be perfect.

I glance up to see Tara tapping her foot with one hand on her hip and the other hand waving her boarding pass in the air. I clear out the seat and pop my buds into my ears. I just need to zone her out. There is no point rehashing the past. There is also no point making small talk about the present with someone I never want to be a part of my future. Our so-called friendship ended the day she sabotaged me during a competition and then proceeded to lie to the entire school about it.

My phone buzzes with an incoming text, and I open the app to see that it is from Nic. He really has a way of catching me off guard.

Nic: Heard you are taking a trip back home. Hope you took your meds.

Claire: I did. Thx.

Nic: Have a safe flight.

I want to text back but also don't know what to say. There is so much that can be misconstrued during this nonverbal way of communicating, and the last thing I need right now is the stress of erasing boundary lines that I have spent the past week drawing. Although, allowing Nic to get me into his office pretty much destroyed everything. I told myself I would not give in to him. I promised myself that I had more self-control than that. Like magnets, we get pulled together even in the murkiest of situations that life brings. I just can't keep punishing myself like this and then expect different results. What I am doing to my heart is insane.

I feel Tara shift in her seat and announce, "Smile."

"What?" I ask, looking over just in time for her to snap an unflattering picture of me and her.

"Sending this to Nic. It's a great way for him to compare us side by side and see what he is missing out on by not choosing me. You definitely do not age like merlot." She makes a face at me and then holds her nose with her two fingers. "More like milk," she snickers.

I shake my head at her and go back to looking out the window. Pretty soon I will have to put my phone in airplane mode and rely on old-fashioned methods to pass the time for the almost five-hour flight. I cannot afford the luxury of in-air Wi-Fi. However, I also cannot afford to shed layers off my eardrum while listening to Tara being a bitch. A message pops up on my screen alerting me to a new text message. I click on the notification and see that it is Nic again.

Nic: Hell, Tara is seated right beside you?

Claire: Yup.

Nic: This is a fucking disaster. I'm sorry.

Claire: Get the bail money ready. If she doesn't keep herself in line, we may break out into a fight. Who do you think will win?

Nic: You are not helping my anxiety. Just ignore her. She is toxic.

Claire: She is not making it easy…

Nic: Just remember that I am on Team Claire. :)

There is something oddly comforting having Nic to chat with, even though I am sitting beside his ex-fiancée and my ex-friend. I know he wants to pursue me. Nic has made himself very clear on that subject, but he also doesn't know the secret I am hiding. Part of me wants to pretend for a little while longer that nothing has changed. I am just me. I don't have any added responsibilities. It is fun to flirt and have that level of anticipation bubbling inside over the start of something fresh. I allow myself to believe—just for a moment—that I am carefree.

In another time, in another world…maybe we could have been perfect for one another.

"Bubbly?" the flight attendant asks, cutting right through my serenity.

I shake my head, declining the complimentary champagne. So much for trying to forget. The flight attendant finishes taking orders, formally introduces himself to our section, and then goes through the routine speech of all the safety protocols. Switching my phone to airplane mode, I lean my weight toward the window as we taxi to the runway.

I have flown more times this year than I have in previous years. I never really had a reason to travel before now. While this trip is not an elective one, at least I can get away from the hustle and bustle of my day-to-day life and adapt to another type of chaos that will most likely ensue at my childhood home.

I can use this time to reflect and rejuvenate my mind. How I proceed through life is almost always a choice. I can choose to be happy or choose to hold on to the past.

I grip my seat as the pilot turns the plane, announces departure, and speeds down the runway. After a few minutes of being in the air and reaching our required altitude, the flight attendant delivers Tara a tall glass of champagne, which she eagerly accepts.

"Not used to you refusing free alcohol. Are your wasted days over?" she asks, looking at me with an evil eye.

"I never used to get wasted in high school, Tara."

"Riggght."

"That's just what you'd tell everyone I was into."

She gives me a once-over, trailing her eyes over my body until she settles them back on my eyes. "Look at you being so self-righteous. You've come a long way."

I shrug and try to find anything else to do with my hands so they don't accidentally end up in her face. "Whatever," I sigh.

"You were always an attention whore, who never cared if the rumors were true or not anyway. It's not like you really tried to deny anything."

"Maybe I was just doing you a favor by playing along with your narrative."

"What did Nic ever see in you?" she asks, her tone serious. "You are an obvious downgrade from me. But we ended years ago, so I'm sure he has a huge list of women he bagged. You weren't the first and you definitely won't be the last."

Ew. I feel like I need to wash Tara's nastiness from my body. She is that gross. "Listen," I say, sitting up straighter in my seat, "this is not a short flight. I really just want to avoid talking to you. So let's make that happen."

"You know why Nic can't commit?" She doesn't even give me a chance to ignore her, before answering her own question. "Because I am it for him. I will forever be the girl who slipped through his fingers. I am the woman he compares all others to. How does it feel to never live up to my own standard? I set the bar that all of his flings will never reach."

I would be lying if I said Tara's words were not causing me some internal damage. She is so confident that it is easy to believe them. Maybe that has been it all this time. Maybe no woman will ever hold a candle to his beloved first love.

I dig through the bag at my feet and pull out my journal. If I am going to avoid Tara's damaging words, I need to get my mind to focus elsewhere.

I was afraid to fall asleep on the flight, so when we land at Reagan National Airport just before eleven at night, I am exhausted and barely able to keep my eyes open. I stumble off the plane, unceremoniously part ways with Tara, and trudge to baggage claim.

With a nearly empty airport and being one of the last arrivals for the night, it doesn't take long for my empty pink-and-white-striped suitcase to make its way along the conveyor belt. All of my clothes and toiletries are stuffed in my carry-on bag, leaving my bigger piece of luggage free for bringing anything back from home. Mom didn't make it very clear how much space I need, so I am basically winging it.

After using the restroom, I take my phone off Airplane mode and see that Nic has sent me a series of texts.

Nic: Hope you are able to rest on your long flight.

Nic: Let me know when you land.

Nic: Did you arrive safely?

Nic: I can't settle my mind until I know you are safe.

I quickly shoot him a text confirming that I am fine and on stable ground again. Even I am surprised I survived the flight with Tara gunning for me from just the adjacent seat. I polished up on my self-control skills, and at least that is something positive from the trip so far.

I glance around at some of the reunions happening with family members and spouses holding signs for some of the passengers on my flight. I can't help but wonder what that feels like to be embraced and welcomed like that. It almost feels intrusive to witness these intimate moments, but I can't keep myself from looking. Women are being spun around by their lovers and handed bouquets of flowers. Maybe they are doing long-distance relationships. Maybe a spouse is in training for the army. Regardless, it is super romantic, and I yearn for that type of love story.

I don't even look around for anyone I might recognize. I know that no one showed up for me. Back in high school, I would get dropped off at the school dances and often had to catch rides home with friends, because no one would show up for me. It was a sobering feeling as a teenager to realize that during the chorus concerts and homecoming games that no one was in the audience to watch me perform. Granted, I was not the best by any means—especially with singing— but it felt good to be a part of something that was bigger than just me.

I wheel my bags outside and look around to get my bearings. The air has a bit of a bite to it, and I hope I have enough variety of clothes to keep myself comfortable while here. I get in line for a cab. The good thing about being at a busy airport is that there is always transportation readily available. I don't need to hunt.

The driver helps me with my bags and opens the back-seat door for me to enter. I strap in, give the address, and relax my neck against the headrest. I shoot my mom a text, letting her know I'm on my way, to which I get no response.

I thought being back would be more nostalgic. However, in a place that is heavily saturated with negative memories, it is no wonder I am struggling to see anything that brings me joy.

I lose track of time and doze off. It isn't until I hear my door opening that I realize I have arrived at my destination. I pay the driver, drag my bags up the eight concrete steps, and come face to face with the home where I grew up. The lights are off in the house, except for the outdoor one right near the entrance. I text my mom again and after a few minutes, I give the door a try.

Knock. Knock. Knock.

When there is no response, I try the doorbell. Silence. I look back on the street and see no sign of a vehicle belonging to this house. I no longer know any of the neighbors on the street. Many moved when their kids got out of school. While this doesn't appear to be a young family area, there are still some telltale signs that children are around. The playground that I could walk to is still in the same location, but it has gotten a facelift.

I walk over to the garage and jump up as high as I can to see if I can look inside. I remember shoveling the inclined driveway some winters when we would get a dumping of snow. The repetitive nature of the task was soothing for me as a kid. I wasn't into nutrition and fitness then like I am now, but I still had a decent grasp on what healthy habits looked like.

To have a single family home in the city means that you are wealthy. My parents have done well for themselves with the restaurant. While the house is overall on the smaller side, what is presented outwardly to the rest of the world is really nice.

What a shame that it is getting sold.

I fish my phone out of my pocket and find my mom's number in the contacts list. I hit the call button and wait for her to pick up. It goes to voicemail, so I try again. When I hear the sound of someone picking up on the fourth ring, I sigh in relief. I'm not even sure what I would have done if she didn't answer. I guess look for a hotel closer to the city.

"Hey Mom, it's me. I just arrived at the house but no one is opening the door."

"I wasn't expecting you to come the day of, Claire."

"You made it seem urgent, so I—"

"Well, it is. The closing is a time sensitive matter," she says defensively.

"Well, then I'm glad I didn't delay." A car drives down the street, and the headlights shine on me. I hope they don't call the cops. I do look like an intruder.

"Okay, that's fine. I'm staying somewhere else tonight. Just get the spare key taped to the backside of the garage light."

"Okay…"

"I'm going back to bed, if I still can. I'll come see you tomorrow."

I frown into the phone as she disconnects and then stare up at the light mounted to the siding of the garage. I look around for a flowerpot and slide it over underneath the light. I climb carefully on top of it and reach up. Still too short. I wheel my luggage over and put the pot on top. I just need a few more inches, so this should do the trick. I teeter on top and detach the key that is duct taped to the metal trim, just like Mom said. Jumping down, I frown over the sad appearance of my now crushed-in luggage. I hope the dent pops out or I'll be in the market for a new set.

Once inside the house, I notice the emptiness. It is like no one has been living here for years. It is the same feeling I had coming home from school and walking into a lifeless house. It always felt like a holding cell. I hit the light switch in the foyer and say a silent thank you that there is even power. Dust is settling on the floors, and the few pieces of furniture still arranged in the living room are covered with once-white sheets. I wonder when is the last time my mom or dad stepped foot into this house. It's not like they tried too hard to stage it to sell, or maybe they did and I am just seeing the aftermath of everything being given back to the rental company. I really don't have personal knowledge on the process; I've just watched a few of those house hunting shows.

My stomach growls with hunger and I walk over to the fridge to find it empty, except for a few bottled waters and a partially opened bottle of wine. A sticky residue is dried on the shelves. When I grab a bottle of water, I have to pull it hard to get it to unstick, ripping the label off on accident in the process.

The pantry has a few packaged soups and a box of dry pasta. From the numbers stamped in black lettering across the top, it appears to be a year past the sell-by date. I open up the cupboard and find one of the only bowls inside. I remove it, wash it heavily with some hand soap I find under the sink, then set it on the counter to dry. The can of soup has a pop top, which makes it easy to open and pour.

I glance around the kitchen for the microwave and am surprised to find none exists. I see where it should be located, but it is just not there. Moving over to the stove, I push several buttons but nothing makes it come to life. It probably is disconnected. Ugh. Beggars can't be choosers. I pick up the bowl and lean over to take a sip from the room temperature soup. It could be worse. It can always be worse.

I sit on a haggard-looking bar stool and devour the heavily processed, sodium-enriched soup. It is pretty gross, yet weirdly nostalgic. I am seated in the same location where I would do my homework after school, usually while eating a bowl of cereal. One day—probably between Thanksgiving and Christmas—I accidentally had my first real taste of soured milk. It wasn't long after that my stomach rejected the spoiled food from my body. Now, as a result of that incident, I smell milk before I ever pour it, and because I mostly consume a vegan diet, I stick with almond or oat milk as my main source of calcium.

Similar to now, I usually had the whole place to myself while here. It was easy to invite friends over or whatever boyfriend I was seeing at the time and have it all go undetected. It should have been a teenager's dream to have that much leeway and slack for their actions, but I was always crying out in a figurative way to be seen. To be heard. To be noticed. Getting punished would have been welcomed. At least then I would know that someone cared enough to try to steer me in the right direction.

The guys I would associate with told me I was pretty. They would attend the games where I would cheer. At lunch, I had someone to eat with me. I soaked up the fact I was no longer left alone and equated someone "showing up" as love, when in fact they just didn't have anything better to do. So they did me. I had low self-esteem and that made me an easy victim. The littlest attention would make me soar. I was easy to take advantage of.

I wish I created better memories with the freedom I was allotted, but I don't have that many. I lacked the structure that was needed for me to successfully establish boundaries with my relationships. The years in high school were not the best ones of my life. It was a time of competition. Competing for my parents' attention and trying to seek validation of my self-worth with every guy I would "date."

I am sure word got out fast that I liked the bad boys. I was simply looking for any type of connection with someone who just happened to be equally as damaged.

Shit.

That's it.

Damaged people attract other damaged people.

That's how I stuck around with Ethan for as long as I did, and that's how I allowed Nic to infiltrate my heart and take up residence there.

We are just damaged souls, stumbling around in life trying to heal our past wounds.

Glancing around the empty house, I know that my healing process must start and end with myself. No one else cares about my welfare more than I do.

14

CLAIRE

I eat about half the soup. It is just enough to calm my hunger and keep my nausea at bay. If I was smart, I would have taken a chance on the airplane food. But hindsight is always twenty-twenty. I was never expecting to come here and find it deserted. The ability to give people the benefit of the doubt or multiple chances must be a deeply rooted character flaw, because no matter how many times I let my guard down, I always wind up getting hurt.

I meander about the main floor, walking from room to room, desperately trying to remember holidays and birthdays and any type of goodness. So much has tainted the good that it is hard to even see through the haze. I walk to the place I used to put up the Christmas tree. I would decorate it while jamming out to holiday music and munching on homemade cookies. I was one of those people who would make my own fun. I had a hefty allowance and would buy whatever I thought would help me achieve superficial happiness.

It is ironic that now that I have less, I feel like I am finally on the right road of figuring out what I really want in life. I want a job that excites me. Plus None checks all of the boxes. I want friends who are there for me—even when I am at a low point. I lacked that while living here. People wanted to be around me for what I could do for their social status. When I got into River Valley and met Angie and Blake, it was clear to see that I never had friends here. They taught me so much about myself and what I deserved. I want a man who wants me beyond sex. Someone who will fight for me. Defend me. I don't want to be the option until something better comes along. I want certainty that what I have to offer is enough.

I've never had that type of connection with a man until I met Nic. Then he turned out to be just like the rest. I am past those days. I have moved on from this house and my old mindset. I want better for myself. I deserve better. I cannot keep repeating the same pattern of behaviors and expect anything to change. It starts with me. I have some control over my destiny.

I fish out my journal from my carry-on bag and write some encouraging phrases for the entry I started on the plane.

Always look toward the sun and what brings you joy.

You are not the same girl you were yesterday.

It is okay to make mistakes, but learn from them.

I carry my bags upstairs and find the door to my former bedroom. It creaks when I open it. I look around the room and see defeat. Boxes border the wall with the windows. With a black marker, my name is labeled with scribbles on the sides. The curtains look like they haven't been washed in years. My bed? Gone. Dresser? Draped with dusty sheets. I can't help but question why I even needed to come back in the first place. What is between these walls that I want to hold on to or remember? Nothing is really sacred or of value.

I wheel my luggage inside and instantly feel claustrophobic, so I open up the windows to let in some fresh air. With the breeze comes the outside noise of sirens and horns honking. Even in the wee hours of the morning, there are still signs of chaos. I used to embrace the noise. Now, I look for the quiet. I leave the windows open long enough to set up a makeshift bed on the floor using a few folded blankets from the closet and a rolled-up hoodie from my carry-on. Without the air conditioning running, I won't need to worry about getting too cold on the floor. I just need a few hours of rest and tomorrow I can start packing up a few things.

Laying my head on my lumpy improvised pillow, I drift off to sleep thinking about how far I have come. I now realize how unacceptable my welcome home really is from someone who claimed to love me.

The sound of the front door opening startles me. I roll to my back and feel like I aged a decade overnight. My neck is sore, and my spine feels like it got slammed by a ton of bricks. I feel anything but rested.

I am wearing the same clothes I wore on the plane yesterday and feel another layer of grossness because of it. I really need to shower and get into something clean.

I hoist myself off the floor and walk downstairs to greet Mom in the foyer. She looks good. Her hands are full, holding two coffees, and she has her purse draped over her shoulder.

"Hi, Claire," she says softly.

When I get to the bottom step, I hesitantly move toward her and embrace her in a hug. Her body stiffens as she tries not to dump coffee on my back.

"Oh my goodness, Claire, you smell rank."

I pull back immediately and wipe at the tears in my eyes. There's no point hiding them. My mom has seen me cry plenty of times. How can I earn the nickname Cry Baby any other way?

"I have to shower," I mutter.

"Yeah. Yeah, you do."

I want to ask her if one of the coffees is for me, but figure by now she would have offered one up. Maybe Dad is coming too, and she is trying to be nice.

"Anyway," she says, "I'm sure you saw your boxes in your room. There's a few more in the garage labeled with your name on them."

I swallow hard and try to keep my composure. My mom brings out a level of vulnerability in me that I would rather keep concealed. "Okay. I'll go through them and take what I want."

"I can't believe this place got sold as fast as it did. I hope the new owners create better memories here than I did," she says with sadness.

Me too.

"How are you doing, Mom?" I ask, rocking on my heels.

She looks over at me, shocked that I even bother to ask her. "Some days I struggle more than others. Some days I search for some meaning in all of this."

I nod. I imagine that she is not completely oblivious to her bad choices in life. I can only hope she will someday learn from them.

When the conversation lulls, I excuse myself to go back upstairs and shower. I'm not sure how much it actually helps though. Between the sight of the rusty water and the mildew stench billowing from the shower head, I know that my bodywash can only mask so much.

I dry off, twist my hair into a loose ponytail, and get dressed into fresh clothes from my luggage.

When I make my way downstairs, Mom is exactly where I left her.

"Is Dad around for me to see him?"

"He decided to take a vacation during this time and leave me and the lawyers to handle all of the legal stuff. He is something else. What did I ever see in him?"

I frown over her description of the only man I could call Dad. She decided to cheat on him. I hate that all throughout my childhood, I was manipulated by her negativity toward him. This was never my fault. I am just a product of her bad choices.

"Is there anything I can do to help you out while I am here, Mom?"

She flinches over my offer. Maybe she is confused why I am willing to help. "No. Ivan has been great at distracting me from this bad chapter in my life. He's been a real blessing."

I want to tell my mom that it is more than a bad chapter. Pretty sure she has starred as the main character in a bad book.

"Who is Ivan?"

"Just someone…"

I inwardly groan. "Okay." I am not sure I need to know who Ivan is right now.

"Don't worry, he is picking me up in a bit. I'm letting him use my car. Here, let's go to the garage, and I can show you the boxes."

I follow my mom and get a chance to actually see her. Her long hair looks to be created with extensions and dyed tips. She looks great for her age and is wearing clothes I would have worn at one time. Actually, her black skirt looks exactly like something I did own.

We carry some boxes into the kitchen and start pulling out old assignments, school pictures, and a few trophies. Another box contains some of my cheer uniforms, a prom dress, and my cap and gown.

Mom starts giggling over one of my pictures where I just hit puberty and was battling some bad acne. "Sometimes even makeup can't fix that mess."

Her words sting. She was always like that. She loved taking cheap shots at my confidence. I had plenty of my own negative thoughts, so she didn't need to add more. It was hard enough fitting into my own skin—when my skin looked so vastly different than everyone else's. Now, I embrace my differences. I overcame the acne through a better diet, and my complexion is admired by most people who know me now. I always look like I have a glowing tan. People actually pay salons to get what I have naturally.

If only my mom would see me now as something other than a stain on her porcelain reputation. I'm an adult, but maybe in her eyes I never grew up.

I hear more giggling, and I know it is over another hideous prepubescent picture. I excuse myself to the bathroom to avoid any more damage. The wall mirror is dirty, but it just adds to my already less-than-stellar appearance. My eyes have bags under them, my mascara from yesterday is smeared from not washing it off well enough, and my clothes are rumpled.

When I was a teen, I would slather on layers of makeup to try to hide everything different about me. I would try to buy foundation three shades lighter and then struggle to get the rest of my body to match. I hid behind bad relationships and slutty clothes and the stigma of being a latchkey kid.

I don't have much to freshen up with, so I just use the toilet then wash my hands. When I make my way back to the kitchen, I hear a masculine voice and know that I am about to meet my mom's boyfriend for the first time.

I round the corner, and as soon as my eyes meet his, I feel an odd feeling of déjà vu. "Ivan Burk?"

"Clarinet?"

I flinch at my old nickname that was awarded to me because my name is Claire Nettles. Oh, and because the star quarterback for the football team told everyone that when I came, I sounded like a woodwind instrument. We never had sex. I'm sure he wanted to, but even with low self-esteem, I still had my bar set higher than him. I despised him and guys like him. But the rumor stuck and so did my nickname.

I turn to my mom. "You are dating someone I went to school with?" My tone is very judgey. What is she thinking?

"We are both adults," Ivan says, giving me the once-over.

"With a huge age gap," I point out.

"Tell me you guys did not date," Mom says, turning to Ivan as if she is just now realizing the difference in age. Is she this oblivious?

"Oh no, I had standards," he says, chuckling, making my mom smile. She smacks his arm playfully and their casual interaction makes me want to scream. I can't tell if Mom is relieved about our lack of history or because Ivan made a joke at my expense.

"What does the nickname Clarinet mean?" Mom asks, alternating her attention between the both of us. Her eyes twinkle with curiosity.

"Don't," I warn Ivan who just smirks. He whispers something to my mom who melts at his closeness.

Between the shock of finding that Tara and Nic were once engaged, then finding out my mom is dating someone I went to high school with, I'm not sure how many more surprises I can endure. None have been positive.

"Oh, come on, Claire, quit being so sensitive. You've always had such thin skin," she teases. She reaches behind her to hand Ivan a to-go cup of coffee, standing up on her tiptoes to kiss him before he takes his first sip.

I swallow hard. "Do you even want me here, Mom?"

Her sigh is exaggerated. "Buckle up for the ride, Ivan. Here comes the drama."

My lower jaw relaxes, and I impulsively scowl over her comment. "Really? Is this really happening?"

"Just get to the point, dear."

"Since I've arrived, I have been met with snappy comments, snide remarks, and a welcome fit for a stranger. You have spent most of my life trying to avoid taking care of me—except financially. Shoving money at me was the easy part. You know what I needed during that time?"

Mom mumbles something, making Ivan snicker.

"Love. I needed love, Mom. I searched everywhere else to fill the void, oftentimes making horrible choices. But at the end of the day, I took responsibility for my mistakes. Sorry I was one of yours."

I don't wait for her to respond, because I know she won't without saying something hurtful. What can she possibly have to say anyway? How can you expect someone to say sorry when they never think they do anything wrong?

"I forgive you," I say with emotion in my voice. "I'm doing it for me. Not for you. I need to move on from here."

"Good luck with that, Claire!" she yells at my back, as I walk up to my room to gather my belongings.

I shove whatever fits inside my luggage, while still being able to zip it closed. I can sort it at my apartment when I get back to my real home. In order to accept love, I need to love myself. Staying here for a minute longer is not loving myself. This is fucking torture.

Sometimes the hardest part about moving on is letting go of the guilt. Maybe my mom and I can have a healthy relationship again in the future. It's not like I'm completely shutting the door to the possibility. However, I know that she has to get her shit together and go through some counseling in order to allow that to happen. I can't force someone to change. I can only choose how I react.

I empty the boxes we brought in from the garage into my carry-on and push down on the top layer in order to get the zipper to close. I use my phone to call for a taxi and wait outside on the cement stairs alone. I've sat on these same steps many times waiting for rides to arrive. I was a naive young girl then. I know I am not the same girl now.

The sun shines down on me, warming my skin. I roll down the waistband of my pants and allow my tiny little sunflower to be exposed to the UV rays. *Always look toward the sun.*

The taxi driver takes me to Reagan National Airport. It has not even been twelve hours that I've been here and I'm already coming back, this time without a physical ticket or any hope to ever return. I came here to get closure, and despite being met with opposition, I got exactly what I needed to end this chapter and start a new one.

I walk up to the luggage drop-off for the biggest airline available and ask, "Can I please get a flight back to Portland?"

The worker types on the keyboard for a few seconds and then smiles. "We have one seat left and the flight is leaving in about forty minutes. Do you want it?"

"Yes, please."

I need to go home.

15

NIC

My girl is coming back to Portland and expected to land in the next ten minutes. I have been unable to think, constantly wondering if she is having fun, if she is warm, or if she is taking good care of herself. I never worried about anyone as much as I have worried about Claire. Something has been bothering her lately, and I want to do everything I can to protect her.

The thoughts of Claire hailing a cab or relying on mass transit don't sit well with me, so I decide to surprise her by picking her up myself. At least I'll be able to see for myself that she is all right and not rely on her minimal usage of words via text. Her strength is admirable, but it has to be exhausting trying to be everything for everybody. Maybe she went back east because someone was sick. Perhaps it was a family reunion. Whatever the case, it was urgent and didn't require her to be there long. I can't shake the feeling of trepidation over just how short her stay really was.

I make it to baggage claim just as the luggage is dropped down the slide for the circular conveyor belt. I scan the area for Claire and pray I didn't miss her. I look at the row of monitors and see that her plane is just unloading now. I didn't have a chance to try to upgrade her ticket, so I can only hope she was comfortable on the long flight back here. Being in the middle seat, squished between two people, does not sound fun at all. She has to be so tired.

I watch as people greet one another from the various flights and wait for my girl to arrive. I made her a sign, so there is no mistaking that I am here for her. After about twenty minutes, I grow anxious and start pacing the area. And then I spot her on the escalator coming down.

Claire is staring at her feet, toting her carry-on over her shoulder, and looking like she hasn't slept in over a week. My poor girl looks like she has been crying, and it takes everything in me not to make a scene. I hold up my sign—which basically is an enlarged cutout photo of her face on a stick handle—and wait for her to notice me.

It isn't until she steps off the escalator that she looks up and does a double take. When she sees me holding her head, a smile brightens up all of her sad features, and in this moment, I know that it is all worth it. I will do anything I can to bring her joy. She is my sun.

Claire lets her bag slide off her shoulder and starts walking fast toward me. And then she breaks out into a jog. I meet her halfway and scoop her up into my arms, dropping the sign as I do it. I hold her, my fingers tangling in her hair.

"You showed up," she mumbles into my shoulder. I can feel the dampness from what I assume are tears seeping through the fabric of my shirt.

"I will always show up for you, baby." I kiss her neck and her hair, but she doesn't smell like my Claire. What the hell happened to her in Virginia?

Her sniffles cut me. I give her a chance to calm herself down before I set her on her feet and get a good look at her. For someone who always looks put together, I'm surprised to find Claire so disheveled. Don't get me wrong, she is still beautiful. I just hate to see her so broken.

Picking up the sign that is resting on the floor, I give her another once-over. Something is off. "Let's get your bags. I'm taking you home."

She nods and looks back to the location where she dropped her stuff when she came barreling toward me. I walk her over and toss the strap around my shoulder. I don't care that it is pink and striped. I will carry any of her burdens if I can. By now, the checked bag has made it to the circuit, and I pull it from the belt and extend the handle so I can wheel it along.

"Is this everything?" I ask, looking down at my girl who is trembling and biting her bottom lip. What the fuck? I bend down to be eye level with her. "Claire? Are you hurt? Sick from your flight? What's wrong?"

She glances away and I want to hit something. What happened in Virginia that has her this traumatized? "Just my heart," she says softly.

I hug her to me and guide her out of the terminal and into the first shuttle I can find. We sit together and get taken to the short-term parking lot where I have my car waiting to escort her back to the life she has here. I thought her going back to Virginia would have done her some good. By the looks of it, it seems like it has caused her pain and heartbreak.

I help her into the passenger seat, secure her belt, and hand her a bottle of chilled ginger ale I had waiting for her to drink. I unscrew the cap and let her sip from the opening. I shut the door and walk around the back of the car, counting to ten to keep my mood in check. Claire doesn't need me to go into caveman mode right now. What she needs is a safe spot to open up to me.

I start the engine and back out of the spot, keeping an arm draped around the backside of her seat. I see her shiver and quickly turn down the air conditioning. She is wearing a hoodie, and it is warm out for being late afternoon, yet here she is fidgeting and looking cold. At a red light, I reach into the backseat and hand her a fleece blanket. Penny left it by accident, but I know she won't mind Claire using it.

"Nic?"

I look over at Claire, trying not to wince at her fragile appearance. She looks seconds away from breaking down. "Yeah, baby?"

"Can you go through a drive-thru and get me a hot chocolate?"

"Have any particular place in mind?"

She shakes her head. "Any will do."

I nod and pull through the closest chain coffee shop on the way back to get her a large hot chocolate made with her favorite almond milk. She gives me a smile when asked about the whipped cream add-on, and when I place the cardboard cup into her hands, she wraps both around it and takes the first sip.

"Good?"

"Yes, thank you."

I pull out of the parking lot and drive in a silence so deafening that my inner thoughts are screaming at me to say something to break it. I settle a hand on Claire's blanket-covered thigh and watch as she cries even more, all while sipping her warm beverage. What the hell? Everything I am doing is causing her to break down. I feel helpless.

"You can just take me to my place," Claire says slowly, when she realizes I passed her street.

"No. And I won't bend on this. You are coming back with me. I'm a selfish man, Claire, but I will respect your boundaries. Promise. I just need you to be safely in my space or I won't be able to function."

I glance over at her as she slinks down farther into the seat. It is like she is giving up, and her defeat doesn't feel like a victory at all. I want her whole again. I want her snappy comments to bite and tempt me. I want her spirit back.

This version of Claire makes me anxious, and seeing her this way makes me want to make all of her pain go away. My girl is hurting, and my mind is racing at how I can help her.

I pull the car into the parking garage and find my numbered space. I cut the engine and jog over to the passenger side to help Claire out.

"I'm sorry."

I look at her with confusion. "Sorry? For what?"

She glances away as more tears fall down her cheeks. I stop a few with my thumbs and then cup her face in my hands. I kiss her forehead.

"I'm sorry"—she pauses and clears her throat—"for being so needy."

"Oh, baby girl," I say, pulling back so she can see my eyes. "You never have to be sorry for anything out of your control. Let's get you inside and you can decide whether or not you want to talk about what happened in Virginia." I silently pray she will talk though. I can't help her if I don't know what she went through while there. If someone touched her, I will go there myself and break them.

What the fuck happened to her?

I sense relief in her eyes. Maybe having the permission to talk or not talk is what she needs to feel comfortable. I want Claire to let her walls down, but I can't force her to let me inside her world. She has to be willing and open to the possibility that I can change.

I have changed.

I am still changing.

Some women think that a man is incapable of change, and that just isn't true. It just takes an amazing woman to show him how big of an ass he's been. And I've been the biggest.

I will forever regret how I helped to facilitate Claire's abuse with her ex-boyfriend. Sure, my intentions were noble in that I knew Ethan was horrible for her. I knew that she would have stayed with the bastard unless he did something monumental to help her see the light. However, my intentions were also nefarious because my ultimate goal was to lure her away from him, just to be with me in the physical sense.

Except nothing has ever been just physical with Claire.

It was impossible for me not to fall for her—and fall

hard. She brings out a nurturing side to me that I buried under years of hatred for women who cheat. I tried to control every woman I ever slept with post-Tara by making them into the villain, when in reality I only set myself up for the emptiness I thought I craved.

I wanted no-strings-attached, but in return found Claire. She makes me want to give her the world, tie every string around the gift that she is to me, and never let her go.

If me going to therapy helps to achieve my end goal, then so be it. I'll submit myself to Dr. Zimmerman's probing questions if it brings me closer to Claire.

I won't let her go.

She is mine. She just has to accept that fact.

I leave Claire's bags inside the car. I have whatever she needs at my place, and I don't want any bad memory from her trip to taint her growth when she finally shares what happened. I am trying to be patient. I just need her to open up to me.

As soon as we get off the elevator and into the foyer, I help Claire out of her shoes and hoodie. They are so dusty and dirty that I just toss them onto the floor in a pile, with the plan to get them into the wash or simply buy her new ones. I lead her into my master bedroom and watch as her feet start to move like they weigh a ton.

"Trust me to take care of you," I say soothingly. "I'm going to give you some privacy, but I want to draw you a bath and get you something warm to eat. Does that sound okay?"

Claire nods and fidgets with her fingernails. "I'm so hungry."

"What are you in the mood for?"

"Anything that isn't an outdated lukewarm can of salty soup," she grumbles.

I am half-confused and half-disgusted by her response, but sense that it has some layer of meaning and is not just a flippant expression. I fill up the huge bathtub with hot water and add some vanilla-scented soap to make it bubbly. Ever since I have gotten close with Claire, I have developed her love of vanilla. I have converted many of my soap products over to that scent, so when I use them, I can think of her.

Hell, I don't even need something tangible to remind me of Claire. All of my waking and subconscious thoughts lead to her.

The bathroom warms with the steam from the bath, and the smell inside is incredible. I hand her a robe. "Make yourself comfortable. There's a sound system installed so feel free to use it."

I meander back into the bedroom to search for something for Claire to wear. During the time where we couldn't get enough of each other, but were still too afraid to actually talk about our feelings, I bought a few items for her to wear while here to feel comfortable. Sadly, she never got a chance to see them or use them. Several arrived via online delivery after we already ended things. It was a punch to the gut every time a new box arrived. I just didn't have it in me to return them. Maybe it was my own heart's way of not officially letting go.

When Claire declared her love for me at Graham's penthouse, I shut down. I thought I was unlovable, and while I'm still managing those feelings, Dr. Zimmerman is convinced I'm already making progress. I allowed a person from my past to control how I proceeded into the present. It was unfair for Claire, but also unfair for me. I stayed stagnant for years, never pushing forward. Then Claire came along and changed everything. She was the one who let me start living again. She wasn't the game changer. She made it so there was no need for any games.

With Claire, I could take her words at face value. There are never any ulterior motives or hidden messages. It took me some time, but I learned that I can trust her. And for me, trust is everything.

I lay a pair of bright purple fuzzy pajamas on the bed, along with a soft cotton bra and panty set in an aqua-blue shade. My girl likes to be bold. Even though she appears rough and ragged right now, I know that her spirit will shine through again, and she'll learn to cope with whatever happened to her during her trip.

"Nic? Are you out there?" she asks from the crack in the door.

"You done already?"

"No." She hesitates and then clears her throat. "My hair is really knotty and I thought…" Her eyes cast downwards, as a shyness coats over her features.

"I will help you," I say softly.

I'm not used to seeing my girl this solemn, and a part of me wonders what she went through when I shattered her heart.

After a few seconds, I walk carefully into the bathroom and find Claire resting under a sea of bubbles. I clean up the water that she dripped on the floor and grab the hair brush I bought specifically for her from the drawer. I grab a folded towel to sit on and lean forward to gather up her wet hair. I run my fingers gently through it and notice right away the nest that must have been created over the course of days.

I section off the hair and glide the brush through it until it comes to a halt with the first tangle. I squirt some conditioner into my palm and massage it into the knot. It takes a lot of patience and a slow methodical pace to untangle everything from her hair, but I have success.

"All done, baby."

"Thank you," she says, giving me a small smile while tilting her head back to look at me.

"I would do anything for you, Claire. Please know that." She nods and I continue. "Even when I was stupidly pushing you away, I never stopped wanting the best for you." I watch as she glances away.

Claire may not be responding with words, but I can tell my declaration is marinating inside her brain. My girl is a deep thinker. I imagine that her bubbly personality is confusing to those who don't really know her at her core. People like her mask their emotions with a positive outward appearance. I just hope she continues to let me know the real her, because what I have seen so far is unique and beautiful.

Claire allows me to help her out of the bathtub, dry her off, and get her dressed into her warm clothes. She looks small and fragile, as if one wrong move could cause her to break down.

Her shoulders round forward, as she wraps her arms around her midsection. "Thank you," she whispers.

I help her into the living room, where I wrap a blanket around her and prop up pillows for her to rest her back. I move into the kitchen to prepare hot tea to be steeped on the stove. I call in an order to be delivered of a bunch of comfort foods from a local restaurant that I think Claire would like.

I will be happy if my girl starts to look less pale and fragile. The way she looks off into the room—at nothing in particular—is scaring me a bit. If she doesn't start telling me what's wrong, then I may have to call Mitch to come evaluate her.

I pour some tea into the ceramic mug I ordered with my dick pic printed all over it. I add some honey and a few lemon rounds. Stirring it, I walk into the living room and hand it over to Claire.

She lets out a half giggle at the sight of my member in glossy paint all over the side of the steaming mug.

"Buy yourself a gift to go with the others I got you?"

I shrug, try to act cool. "What can I say? I was inspired."

Claire laughs. Really laughs. Even in her sadness, she has an aura of strength and resilience about her that I can't help but find beautiful.

"Aren't you worried about a family member finding your cock on a mug in the cupboard whenever they visit?"

I take a seat on the opposite side of the sofa. I pick up Claire's legs, draping them over mine, and work my fingers into her feet to help her relax. She melts into the sofa cushions, as I continue my massage.

"Can't be worse than being harassed by Penny when she discovered the sheet cake in the fridge on her quest to find something to drink."

Claire covers her mouth with her hands. "Damn." Her words come out mumbled as she giggles. "Oops."

"You don't look that sorry," I tease.

"Oh, I'm not sorry at all. You deserved everything you got."

"I did. I really did. And I'm really sorry for my part in helping to orchestrate your breakup with Maxwell." I watch as her eyes shift from humor to seriousness. "I'm not sorry you left that asshole. However, I'm sorry for the ways in which I influenced the decision. I convinced myself that you would be better off without him, and that if he didn't do something monumentally stupid, he would have just manipulated and guilted you to stay."

A trail of tears travels down Claire's cheeks. "Sometimes when you're in the thick of abuse, it takes getting out for you to realize just how bad it was."

"Something tells me you are referring to more than just Maxwell."

Quiet fills the room, and I continue rubbing Claire's feet while she floats to another place. Her eyes darken, and I can tell that her breathing changes. For several minutes, we just sit. Sometimes in the calmness, things start to become clearer. Whatever she decides to share with me will be a gift. It has obviously devastated her.

Claire's throat clearing breaks the silence of the room. "I know you want me to talk about Virginia..."

"I do," I admit.

"I honestly just want to forget I even went."

I need to be patient. I need to get her to open up on her own time.

The doorbell rings, and I excuse myself to retrieve the food. Returning to the living room, I place the bag down on the coffee table and pull out several containers of food. The restaurant included paper products and serving spoons, so I dish up a variety plate for each of us.

I take Claire's mug from her hand and place it on a coaster. "There's plenty of food, so eat up," I encourage, handing her the plate I made.

Claire is munching on macaroni and cheese made with bacon and savoring every bite as if she hasn't eaten in days. She made an odd soup comment earlier and maybe she really is starving. That thought alone causes my insides to twist with—

Anger?

Pain?

Heartbreak?

"Sometimes talking about the pain makes it easier to move past it," I suggest, desperately wanting to know what is bothering her so I can try to help. I am a fixer—a problem solver by nature—but right now I am grasping at straws.

"I know I put on a smile and try to always be positive, but I just can't do it anymore. I'm tired of going through life acting like everything is alright."

I squeeze her feet and run my hands up her calves in a soothing manner. "I'm here to listen."

Claire clears her throat, while her eyes droop from the weight of the words I pray she'll share.

"Growing up, everyone thought I was privileged based solely on the designers I would wear and the house I lived in, and to some extent I probably was in comparison. I grew up with a silver spoon in my mouth, but no one to feed me with it. I was always on my own. I didn't have much reason to go back to Virginia, but my mom is going through a divorce.

The house I grew up in has sold, and I needed to go back to clean out all of my shit. I just never expected to get there and be alone. She made it sound so urgent, so I booked the first flight I could find out of Portland. I wasn't looking forward to going back, but I never expected to find my childhood house as deserted as it was. My mom wasn't even staying there anymore. When I arrived, I had to find the spare key hidden outside and let myself in. Everything was dusty and drab."

"I'm sorry, baby," I whisper, trying to avoid losing control over her information dump. I keep listening and rubbing at her feet, trying to relax her enough to keep talking. I need her to talk and tell me everything. Every detail.

"It was like my mom didn't even care that I was visiting. Never bothered to come stay with me. I shouldn't be surprised because looking back that is basically how I grew up my whole life. But I guess as a kid, until you start visiting other family's houses and seeing how the rest of the world lives, you think that what you are thrown into at birth is how life is supposed to be. I just thought it was all normal, until I learned what could have been. And the cruel realization that you have been neglected and unloved and treated like a burden is a lot for any child to endure." Claire looks off into the other side of the room. "No child"—she sniffles—"deserves to ever feel like they are unwanted."

I lean forward and wipe a tear from Claire's cheek that keeps falling. Who procreates and then does this to a child? I want to go to Virginia and raise hell. How can someone be so oblivious to the damage they can cause another life?

"So, I was all alone for the night, which I guess is better than being with someone who has no respect for me. I slept on the floor, since I no longer had a bed. It was so late when I arrived, and I didn't have transportation, so I sucked it up and ate nasty soup out of a can—" Her words come out choked, as she shudders at the memory.

I try my best not to react. I want to fucking react. But I keep myself in check. I reach for Claire's hand and rub gently, trying to get her to keep talking. The more she shares, the more she can hopefully let go.

"Anyway, this morning my mom shows up and then the real fun begins," she responds sarcastically. "Bored yet?"

I want to tell her not to do that. I don't want her to use humor or act like this whole situation isn't a big deal. Because it is a big fucking deal, and I feel murderous inside over it.

"I want to know about your life, Claire. Even if what you are sharing with me is very disturbing and not how anyone should grow up."

She swallows and glances away. When her eyes return back to mine, I can see just how difficult it is to hold herself together. I am finding it hard to keep from joining her in the emotional spiral.

"This next part gets really awkward, so brace yourself. I come to find out my mom is dating a guy I used to go to high school with. It was humiliating to see. Yet not nearly as embarrassing as to how she treated me in front of him. Throughout my childhood, I was treated like a *mistake*. I was conceived via a one-night stand with a guy visiting from the Philippines on vacation. I've never met him. He probably doesn't know I exist. The man who helped raise me—the man my mom was married to—probably couldn't stand knowing that I was a product of my mom's infidelity.

I don't even look like anyone in my family, so it is super obvious. There's really no way to hide it."

I continue massaging my girl while she cries and shudders over the memories she just had to freshly endure. Sounds horrid.

No wonder why when I look at Claire, I see a strong woman who knows what she wants. She's spent the majority of her life learning through bad examples what she didn't want.

"Part of me wishes I would have just been put up for adoption. That way I would have known I was unwanted and not just have to assume."

"Oh, baby," I say, sliding her to my lap. I hug her and let her break down some walls in my arms. I don't want to let her go. I want to shield her from all the pain of her past and—

Plan a future?

I was never interested in such an idea after getting my own heart broken. But now, I want something more than just a moment. I want to make memories—better ones. I want to erase these bad ones and promise her that she can move forward with her life.

"I thought it would get better," Claire starts. "I thought that with time and maybe being here in Portland, I would give my parents a chance to miss me. Nope. And it is a hard pill to swallow to realize that the only thing I was—the only thing I am—is a burden. I am like a persistent stain that could never be washed off. I'm a constant reminder to the man I called Dad that I am not his."

I sit up straighter over Claire acting like this is somehow her fault. "He had a choice to love you, baby. This is on him. You never asked for your arrival into the world to be met with such controversy. As for your mom, maybe one day she will realize that her love had conditions and that she missed out on getting to know an awesome human being. Her loss."

"Thank you," she mumbles into my shoulder.

"I take it your dad was not around during your trip?"

"No. And maybe in a way it was better like that. I already had my mom and her new boyfriend to contend with. Maybe she is having some type of midlife crisis. The nastiness spewing from their mouths was horrid."

"Did anything positive come out of this trip at all?" I ask.

"I definitely got closure," she says between sniffles. "I never want or need to go back again."

Good. I kiss her forehead, relaxing a bit when she doesn't pull away.

Claire shifts to look at me. "Thank you for showing up at the airport. I wasn't expecting that and it really means a lot."

"Like I said before, I will always show up for you, baby."

We spend the next few hours watching movies, eating snacks, and even hitting up the home gym for a little kick-boxing. It is like everything that has happened before now was made to occur so we could both get to this pivotal point in time.

I used to equate intimacy with sex. Claire helped me to see that the deeper connection between couples is found by being content doing the everyday things, like brushing our teeth together or deciding which side of the bed to sleep on.

While there are no more heavy discussions on feelings or status or expectations, it is the first time since we have really hung out that I feel like we are moving in the right direction.

I fall asleep with Claire wrapped around my body, her soft hair tickling my shoulder and her warm breaths blowing against my neck. Things are exactly as they should be.

And for that I am genuinely happy.

16

CLAIRE

I am without doubt still in love with Nic Hoffman. Maybe it was how he brushed my hair the night that I came back from Virginia. Maybe it was the way he would cheer me on when I was kicking the punching bag. Or maybe it is how, even in his sleep, his arms search for me.

Regardless, I am head over heels for the man.

It has been almost a week since I got back from the horrid trip, where Nic greeted me by surprise in the airport with an obnoxious 2D monument of my face. No one has ever done that for me, let alone put my head up on a stick—but in the cutest way possible. No one has ever been that excited to see me. It is in these seemingly insignificant moments that I have found what really matters.

I can see Nic trying—like *really* trying. He is also making changes within himself. I notice how open he is being with his feelings, and the transformation has been wonderful—albeit a bit surprising.

Nic's arms represent the comfort I so desperately crave

after the realization that the life I once lived is no longer worth going back to. There is nothing left of me in Virginia. No, the childhood memories I wanted to hold on to are now just the hollowed-out shell from a lifetime of trauma that I mentally packaged to appear better than it really was.

I deserve what my parents couldn't give to me…

Love and attention.

Sense of security.

A place to call home.

However, I'm carrying a big secret that is going to explode in my face. I'm not going to be able to hide it much longer. I am going to have to figure out how to handle this head-on with the least amount of heartbreak. There are too many feelings involved, and the guilt I'm feeling is excruciating.

I am wrapped up in the scent that is proprietarily Nic Hoffman. I could get used to sharing his bed and his space again. So many of my day-to-day routines are now part of Nic's. We work out together, try out new recipes, and enjoy talking about our days. He has shown me that someone can change and be better. I would like to believe I had some influence in his progress—but I know it is something bigger.

I roll to my side and start to climb out of bed, when I am pulled back and pinned under a very sexy Nic.

"Eeek," I squeak, from being caught off guard. I look up into his eyes as I wiggle my hips underneath the weight of his. "Hello, mister." I look down between our bodies and lift my hips up to grind against his. "And hello down below."

"Time to pay your ransom."

"My ransom? For what?"

"For your own release," he says coolly.

"What happens if I like to be your captive?"

Nic's eyes darken. "Then it's time to pay for your keep."

I pout. "That doesn't seem fair. Either way you slice it, I have to pay."

"My bed, my rules."

"My body, my bounty," I counter with a smirk.

He chuckles. "You better not be putting a bounty on my head. Either one," he says, making his penis twitch. "You scare us both when you get mad."

"Good." I giggle and then stretch up to kiss his lips, which he leans down to meet halfway. We are both naked, and it is easy to get lost in the moment. And we do.

I open my legs to allow Nic to slide into my pussy. I will never get bored of the moment of anticipation of him first entering. He pulls back and sinks in. We keep this rhythm up and then when I think I'm about to come, he pulls out.

"Hey!" I whine. "I was close."

"You'll get there again," Nic promises. "I need to see more of you."

I yelp as he scoops me up and carries me into the bathroom, where he sets me on a towel spread out over the top of the vanity.

"Better?" I ask, turning around and looking at my body from various angles in the mirror. I'm not sure I like how soft I'm starting to look. When I glance back up at Nic, I can see hunger in his eyes. The inner walls of my pussy clench with the knowledge that he is going to be back to take what is his.

"You look so hot like this perched up on my counter,

waiting for me to fuck you, deep and hard. You like it rough, don't you, baby?"

"Yes," I exhale, right as he thrusts into me.

His fingers slide under my ass and hoist me up to accept every inch of his length. I don't last long, and as soon as I start to moan and throw my head back in ecstasy, Nic lets out a roar and releases so deep inside me that I think I will be leaking him out the rest of the day.

We stumble into the shower and come down from our highs. I run the soap over his pecs and down his stomach. I am squatting down, cleaning his legs when I get an idea in my head.

With the water pelting on my back, I suck Nic's cock into my mouth and slide him in and out until he hardens from my attention.

"Fuck, Claire, your mouth is perfect. Suck harder. I like a little bit of bite."

I follow the instructions, as his hands twist my wet hair into a rope. I have sucked on him before, but not like this. Right now, I am taking my time, and he isn't going to stop me from getting everything I want.

I use my hands to wrap around his base, twisting and pulling to the same rhythm as my mouth at the tip. I look up at him as I pull him all the way out and remove my hands entirely from his shaft. Then I push forward until he hits the back of my throat. I can only do that a couple of times without feeling like my gag reflex will go off, and just those few times is enough.

"I'm close," he warns, giving me a chance to back down.

I keep my rhythm until I feel him harden a fraction

more, hear him let out a groan, and then taste the salty liquid hit my tonsils. He slides out, and I lick my lips.

"You are full of surprises today," Nic says, picking me up and wrapping me in his arms. "That was incredible."

I never expected us to ever be like this. I am content. Nic treats me like an equal partner, and I feel cherished.

We dry off and get dressed for the day. I glance at my phone to see that I'm going to be late. I throw on my power heels and dress in a pink chiffon layer dress—all before Nic is even into his boxers.

"What's the hurry?" he asks with satisfaction still present in his voice.

"I don't want to keep your mother waiting."

"My mom? What? Why are you seeing my mom? I mean, of course, go see her, but what is this over?"

"You are rambling."

"I know."

"I promised Angie I would help her navigate some of the last-minute details for the wedding," I say slowly, reading between the lines as I evaluate his expression. Apparently Angie's future MIL is quite the planner. She is a walking Pinterest post with all of her ideas. While classy is the goal, Angie definitely appreciates understated beauty. I know what her vision is, so I just need to guide the choices in that direction—through gentle persuasion.

"Can I come too?"

"What?" *No.* "Why?"

"So I can introduce her to you."

"Nic, we have met before. I'd assume she remembers me."

"As my *girlfriend*."

I turn away from his penetrating gaze and throw a few items from my nightstand into my purse. Is that what we are? Boyfriend and girlfriend? It doesn't seem right making that type of commitment without sharing with him that I am carrying a baby. *And oh yeah, it may or may not be yours.*

"Right now, the focus is all on Angie. I made a promise to my bestie that I would handle this crossroad for her. She has enough on her plate, and I owe her this much. Do you mind if I navigate this solo?"

Nic wraps his arms around my midsection from behind and kisses the sensitive skin at the bottom of my neck. I melt into his hold like I always do. He melts my protective layer of ice. With him, I feel safe. With him, I also feel an insurmountable amount of guilt. The tug-of-war going on within my head is exhausting. Should I follow my heart and hope that love is enough to cope with my secret? Or will I always wonder if I am just an obligation?

I tote my mini vision board under my arm, which serves as a backup to my already practiced speech. The entire car ride here has been used to rehearse what I plan to say if I am met with resistance.

Donna has been nothing but nice to me, every encounter we've ever had, so I'm not expecting anything hostile. However, I still need to tiptoe around getting her to see what I think is Angie's vision. This is her wedding, so she deserves to have things the way she likes them.

I walk along the stone path toward the beautiful restaurant called On The River and take a few cleansing breaths to settle my nerves. Most people think I like confrontation, when in reality I just like a good discussion. I enjoy seeing both sides, and it isn't unheard of for me to change my views on the spot. I love the challenge and learning other people's thought processes. However, this meetup is primarily to persuade Mrs. Hoffman that less is more.

You can do this, Claire.

The hostess welcomes me inside and leads me down to the private section that is made of glass and is overlooking the water.

"Hello, Claire," Mrs. Hoffman greets, getting up from her seat to envelop me in a hug.

"Hi, Mrs. Hoffman," I respond, taken aback at how welcoming her arms feel.

"Oh dear, please call me Donna," she reminds me.

Back over Christmas, I spent time in her home so I wouldn't be alone. Ethan didn't want to get together and had other obligations that didn't involve me. Now looking back, I know that I was never in his long-term plan. It wouldn't surprise me if he was with Deena the whole time.

When I met Ethan through the Entice database, he was looking to even the score as Deena started dating again. Looking back, I was a pawn in his game all along. He was using me to make her jealous. Either way, I didn't mean to him what I thought he meant to me.

"Thanks for meeting me here today," I say softly. "Angie is so excited to marry Graham, and I doubt she is able to sleep well from all of the excitement. She is going to make a lovely bride."

"That is for sure," Donna agrees. "So, the rehearsal dinner is the job of the groom's family to throw, and as maid of honor, I thought we could make sure we are on the same page with all of the selections I need to finalize."

Relief rushes over me that Donna thinks this is primarily her idea. This meeting may go easier than I thought.

"Angie has given me some ideas on what she is looking for. I think her style is very understated but elegant, if that makes sense. She is not an over-the-top person and dislikes being center stage. I am excited she is even having a wedding and not running off to elope on some island."

Donna nods and smiles as I talk. She is going to be the best mother-in-law for my bestie. Angie lost her mom at a young age and later lost her brother to a tragic car accident that almost claimed her life too. Maybe we have bonded all of these years over not having a mom. Granted, my mom is alive but needs reminders that I even exist. We are two very different people, from very different backgrounds, who somehow have been heartbroken enough to know our friendship is special.

The waitress brings us out samples of food and dessert to try out so that it is easier to make the final decisions on what menu will be offered.

"You look beautiful, by the way," Donna says, catching me off guard. "A girl as exquisite as you can wear any shade on the color palette, especially with your perfect complexion."

Tears well up in my eyes over her compliment.

"Oh dear, what did I say?" she quickly asks, handing me a cloth napkin to dab at my eyes. "I'm so sorry. I really shouldn't—"

"No, no," I say, blowing my nose into the fabric. "It's just that I had a really shitty month and"—I furrow my brow as I think of the right words to say—"hearing anything that isn't an insult has been hard for me. I think I just got used to others who should love me seeing me as less. So, when someone who is basically a stranger tells me I am pretty, it just brings all of these emotions up like a volcano. I'm sorry."

"Hey," Donna says, grabbing my hand and giving it a squeeze. "Always look toward the sun."

My eyes smile with my mouth, and I nod my head. "That's *my* motto."

"It's a good one. I've heard Angie use it a few times and asked her about the origin."

I clear my throat and tuck my emotions into the back of my heart. I need to push through and do what I came here to do. "Okay, back to business. Let's give Angie the best damn wedding on the planet."

"Now that deserves a toast. Two mimosas, please," Donna announces to a waitress who is not even assigned to us.

"Oh, I'm on a strict diet if I want any dress to fit," I mutter, trying to come across as bummed.

"One extra-large mimosa, please!" She leans into me and whispers, "I bought my dresses bigger just so I can indulge on an occasion like this."

I laugh as I relax into my role. I can tell that Donna's heart is good and her intentions are pure when it comes to Angie. She isn't trying to steal the spotlight. She is just trying to give Angie the dream wedding. Thing is, though, with Angie *less is more*.

I glance out at the boats floating down the river. This venue is amazing, but I am not sure it is quite what Angie is looking for, and with the event date approaching, we don't have much room for making adjustments to the original plan.

"You have something on your mind," Donna says, drawing my attention back to her.

I shrug.

"Say it, please," she coaxes.

"I know Angie. She isn't into the crazily priced cost-per-head that this place probably is."

"Money is no object when it comes to Graham and his fiancée. If it ends up being too pricey, he will cover any added expense. He has made that clear, multiple times."

I nod. "Yeah, I get that and all. But I think Angie's vision is more elegant but simple." I open up my mini vision board and show Donna some of the ideas that I have. "I know it isn't really my place to make this type of suggestion, but I think Angie would prefer to have this final dinner before the big wedding day at some place more intimate."

"Like where?" Donna asks, intrigued.

"Maybe in Hillsboro, where Graham grew up. Perhaps your home? We could get it catered by some place locally and hire wait staff to help with the serving of the food."

Donna mulls the idea around in her head, and then the biggest smile breaks out across her entire face. "It's the perfect idea. Let's do it."

With all of the planning with Donna taking up the majority of my morning, I arrive at work just before lunch. Nic has left me multiple text messages to come see him in his office, if I need to get away from my desk. Ever since I broke down on his sofa after Virginia, he has softened up toward me and my needs.

I am seeing Nic in a different light, a more vulnerable and nurturing light. It is refreshing to see someone as rugged as he is being so tender and loving. When we are together, it's easy to forget about my troubles.

I greet my workers, touch base with Angie, and am not even at my desk for a few minutes before I get an ominous text message from someone I don't know.

Unknown: You are being watched by someone you think is your friend

Claire: Who are you?

Unknown: I will reveal my identity outside of work

Claire: You work here?

Unknown: Yes

Claire: So you are watching me?

Unknown: No, but I know who is

My heart races over the exchange of text messages. What is this person trying to say? Am I being spied on? Watched? Is this a male or female texting me? Who is watching me? What does that even mean?

My phone buzzes, and I look down to see the message.

Unknown: Let's meet at the corner coffee shop at noon. I will tell you everything.

Claire: How can I trust you?

Unknown: Because I haven't given you any reason not to trust me. Public place. Broad daylight. You are safe.

Claire: Fine

I glance at the time and see that I have twenty minutes before I need to leave to get to the shop. I can't concentrate, and being productive right now is unrealistic. I leave the office and use the restroom. My hands fidget at the sink, and I can already tell I am getting myself worked up over whatever I am about to learn.

My phone vibrates again, and I pull it out of my bag to see it is Nic.

Nic: Want to eat lunch together?

Claire: Oh, not today. I am still full from breakfast with your mom. I have to run a couple of wedding errands during my break but maybe we can do dinner.

There is a long pause and I scold myself for sending out warning signs to Nic with the word "maybe." For the past dozen meals, we have been enjoying them together. There is no "maybe." There's just the expectation that we will be spending that time together.

I type out another message.

Claire: I'm starting to feel the pressure to make sure Angie and Graham have the perfect celebration. Time is ticking down.

Nic: Anything I can help out with? I'm the best man after all...

Claire: This is all girly stuff but thanks.

I quickly make it back to my desk to make sure I shut off my computer and gather anything I think I would need for my bag. I rip off a Post-it note and write the name of the corner cafe Ground Floor on the top. I add the time and date to the little square piece of paper and slip it into my drawer as a backup plan in case something happens.

The person I am meeting obviously wants to keep their identity concealed. I know there are security cameras everywhere, so leaving the premises seems to be the logical solution for this mystery to be revealed.

I take the elevator down to the main floor lobby and look around at everyone exiting and entering through the security metal detectors. I'm not even sure I can guess who I am meeting. I literally know nothing about the person on the other end of the phone.

I keep my head held high and am careful not to send off any warning bells to anyone watching. I need to have the illusion of confidence, just in case this whole thing ends up going south.

Adrenaline runs through me as I walk at a fast pace to

Ground Floor and scan the tables once inside for any sign of someone I recognize. My phone buzzes in my hand, and I glance down to see the message.

Unknown: Walk to the right and I am at the back near the window

I follow the directions, and within a few steps, I see the person I thought I would never see again.

"You?" I ask softly, trying to remember his name. Our paths crossed what seems like months ago, but maybe it isn't that long at all. "I thought you got fired."

"Yeah, thanks to you. And it's Kevin."

He seems to be insulted by my lack of remembering his name. It's not like he made a super big impact on my life, and the only real experiences I've had with him have all been negative.

He motions for me to take a seat, and I only do so I don't feel any more awkward in this intimate coffee shop setting.

"What's the point of this meeting if you aren't even part of HH?"

"Like I said in the text messages, you are being watched."

"By you? Should I call the cops?" I ask with a flare to my tone.

I imagine he and his security guard friend are both just butt sore from getting fired for accosting me when I first started working at HH. Neither seemed like the brightest crayons in the box, so maybe their time would have eventually come to an end on its own without the incident propelling Nic's decision.

"You can do whatever you want with the information I'm about to present to you. Just promise me you won't let it be known I shared it with you."

"Just get on with it," I huff. I feel uncomfortable as it is in front of him, even in a public setting. There is something about the way he looks at me that makes me feel dirty or that I need to take a shower. He is basically dangling some type of secret over me like it is a carrot, and I am the rabbit. I don't want to chase the truth. Nobody has time for that.

"Here," Kevin says, passing me a large envelope.

"Why are you even caring to share this with me?" I ask, as I peel the sticky flap off the back, half expecting it to be nothing.

His eyes darken. "This is my version of revenge."

I empty the contents onto the table and see tiny still images of me in black and white. They look to be taken from HH, which I guess I should not be surprised about. Kevin could have gotten these from any worker still hired to run the control room, I am sure.

I sift through the stack until I see more sheets of stills, but this time they are of me outside of HH. Images of me walking at the river, ones of me running into my apartment, some of me teaching yoga, and a few leaving Blake's loft.

I don't need to ask who took these. I already know.

My stomach feels sick when I get to the last picture. It is of me being intimate with Nic while in the elevator. I am so stressed out that I can't even remember which elevator or what date it was taken on. It doesn't matter though.

"He has a tracker on you."

"What?" I ask, glancing at my body. "Where? What are you talking about?"

He gestures toward my purse. "I imagine it is on your phone, but he probably has one on your car too."

"Is that even legal?" I ask under my breath, trying to think about how this is possible.

"The tracking devices? Or the fact that you are being stalked in general?"

"I don't—" I cut off my sentence and shake my head over all of this newly acquired information.

I know Graham keeps a close eye on Angie, but that is because she had a horrible run-in with danger last year. Plus, she knows that he hired guards for her. It's no secret. Collins has been watching over her almost from the beginning. Is he watching me too? Does he even have time to do both jobs simultaneously?

"Does it even matter?" Kevin asks. "Pretty sure your love interest thinks the law doesn't apply to him."

"How do you—" I pause, as I try to think of the right words.

"It's obvious to anyone paying half attention that you mean something to him."

"Not anymore. Not after this." I am tired of the mistrust. I am tired of handing over my heart, just to get it stomped on.

This is not how you build a foundation...

This is how you wreck one.

"You seem nice enough," Kevin assesses, "so just be careful. Nic Hoffman seems to not accept rejection well."

It feels like the floor got blown up underneath my feet. Just when I think I am finally having a breakthrough with him, he proves to me yet again that we are horrible for one another.

I grab my purse and tuck the photo sheets back into the envelope. If I am going to confront Nic, I need to have my evidence. "I have to go."

I head toward the front of the coffee shop. My heart is racing and my stomach feels like I could be sick at any moment. I need to eat or drink something. I feel light-headed from hunger and the sobering fact that Nic Hoffman is exactly the man he warned me about. He is the bad guy.

I reach for my phone and quickly shut it off. Whatever tracking he has on me, he already knows my whereabouts. He knows when I get home and everywhere I go in between. The amount he has invaded into my privacy is unspeakable. He crossed a line I never even knew existed. We have been playing on uneven fields since the beginning, with him always having the upper hand.

I think about all of the times our paths have crossed on what I assumed was fate or a crazy coincidence, when it was probably just Nic following me. I feel violated, and now that a new level of paranoia has been unleashed, I'm not sure I can be in my apartment without wondering if he planted a listening device or a camera. He has been inside before, and he is an expert on these types of things, so I wouldn't put it past him.

When I get to the front of the line, I order a strawberry smoothie drink to go and walk back to my apartment—the one I haven't visited in days—to drop off my phone and look where a tracker might be hiding. Where do trackers hide? I scan over anything that I wear on a daily basis and place it on my end table. I am done being followed. I am done being Nic Hoffman's little entertainment.

I take the stairs down and push open the back door to the building. The sugar from my smoothie is helping my nausea, making me feel energized. It is time to tell Nic-fucking-Hoffman where to put his obnoxious trackers.

I step out onto the street, take another sip of my drink, and start huffing my way in anger toward HH. By the time I arrive, I will be extra fired up from the workout. I rehearse my speech in my head at how I will tell Nic exactly where I stand. I will leave nothing up to his imagination. We are beyond the sugarcoating stage.

When I am about halfway there, I can feel my pulse pumping in my neck. There is sweat forming on my fore-head, and my feet hurt from some exercise-induced swelling. I turn at the corner and my foot hits the—

CRASH.

17

CLAIRE

My hands fly out to catch my fall, but it is too late. My stomach collides with the cement, and I cry out in agony as my drink splashes all around me. I roll to my side and hold my belly.

"Are you okay?" a passerby asks, reaching for my arms to pull me upright.

"I think so," I lie. I can feel the cramps forming as tears rush out of my eyes.

Another onlooker hands me my purse and mutters a few words about how hard I fell.

"Claire? What happened?"

I turn to see Dan rushing down the street, a take-out bag from lunch in his hand.

"Are you okay?" he asks, looking me over for any noticeable damage. He runs his hands down my arms and my side, turning me to evaluate my appearance.

"I must have tripped," I sniffle, looking down at all the

pink drink splatters on the sidewalk. "I look like a hot mess, don't I?"

"How you managed to get nothing on you or break a bone is a sheer miracle," Dan answers in awe.

The cramps increase in intensity, and I reach for my phone that I no longer have. It is in the apartment.

"My apartment is nearby if you want to come back and get cleaned up," he offers with a genuine smile.

"I'm just going to go to the restroom," I say, pointing to the diner that he must have just walked out of prior to finding me. "Don't worry about me. I think it is my ego that got bruised. I'll see you back at HH."

Dan hesitantly waves and allows me to walk into the cafe without any more discussion. I find the ladies' room in the back corner. I walk in and sit down at the toilet. In the crotch of my white lace panties, I see the damp spot of fresh blood. My heart races and my breathing increases. My baby. I pee and wipe my crotch. When I get up and look inside the toilet bowl, I see the crimson color. It is so bright and a sign that something is wrong.

I grab a pad out of the little basket of feminine items at the sink and wash my hands.

I stumble out of the restroom and ask one of the workers to call for a taxi.

When I step out onto the street, I find Dan leaning against a light post. My heart sinks at how I am going to get away and get some help without drawing any attention to my situation. My emotions are all mixed up, and I just need the space to think clearly again.

"I am going to go home," I lie to Dan. "I just need to get more sleep."

He seems to buy it, and when I see him retreat back down the street toward HH, I sigh in relief. I get into the ride and tell the driver, "Please take me to Portland General."

I check in inside the waiting room of the ER and wait for my turn. It takes roughly twenty minutes for my name to be called by a nurse wearing blue scrubs. She has braided hair and smiles at me, making me want to cry even more.

"I am sorry," I sniffle, walking toward her. I dab my nose with the balled-up tissue I have squeezed into the palm of my hand.

"You are in good hands here," she says sweetly. She grabs a wheelchair from the side closet and opens it up for me to sit in. "You are going to be transferred to Labor and Delivery since you have indicated that you think you are pregnant on the admittance form."

"Okay…"

"Just sit and try to relax," she comforts. "We're going to take a little tour."

I slide into the chair and allow her to push me through the hallway, into an elevator, and through a series of automatic doors and corridors. Based on the sign above the unit, I am in the triage section.

"Think you can give me a urine sample?" the nurse asks. When I nod, she hands me two square packages and a plastic cup that has a tamper-proof seal on it.

She helps me out of the wheelchair, and I walk into the bathroom with my supplies to give my sample. My hands shake as I follow the steps. As soon as I pull the cup away and see the blood-polluted pee, I start to cry again. I seal the lid, scribble my name, and then wash up.

"All done?"

I nod and bite my bottom lip between my teeth. I follow the nurse down the row of triage rooms, stopping at the one toward the end of the hall.

"Your new nurse and the doctor will be in shortly. Get undressed and put on the gown that is in the protective plastic on the bed. Take off your panties, but you can leave your bra on. I put some absorbent pads on the bed so you should be fine."

"Thank you," I mumble, staring at my little cubicle, made mostly of hung fabric.

I get naked and put on the blue geometric patterned gown that has too many snaps and ties. I toss my clothes into a pile on the chair and climb up on the cold bed using a footstool, pulling the disposable paper blanket up to my neck.

Thin cotton curtains separate me from the patients adjacent to me, so it is not shocking that I can hear the doctor in with the woman to my left. No matter how much effort I take to not listen, to just focus on my own steady breathing, I will never be able to forget his words—"I am so sorry."

I flop back down on the lumpy temporary bed and listen to the quiet sobs from the mother-to-be. I want to pull the curtain back and give her a hug. She is by herself, except for a nurse who joins her. How awful.

My hands rest on my belly, and I pray that the baby is okay after my fall. I brace myself for the verdict as the doctor pulls back the panel of curtain and enters my open-air holding cell.

"Hi, Miss Nettles?"

I lift one corner of my lip and nod. I am fighting back

the tears that want to desperately escape. *Keep it together, Claire.*

"I am Dr. Blackstone." He adjusts his wire rim glasses on his pointy nose and glances down at the clipboard. "I see in your chart that you took some home pregnancy tests and discovered that you are pregnant."

"Yes," I confirm, my voice quivery.

Dr. Blackstone steps behind the curtain and comes back in with a cart on wheels with what appears to be an ultrasound machine on it. He places a condom over a long wand-like device, then squirts a clear gel over the tip. At this moment, I wish I would have ordered some type of baby book and brushed up on these types of procedures prior to today, because I haven't seen one of those gadgets on any of the shows I have watched on TV with pregnant women.

"The first thing we need to do is confirm the pregnancy and then get an estimate on the number of weeks you are along." He readjusts his glasses and looks down at my chart. "You know the date of your last period, I see, so that helps with the measurements."

"But I fell and am bleeding," I sniffle, a solo tear falling down my cheek.

The middle-aged doctor nods and clears his throat. "There can be many reasons why you are bleeding. Try to stay calm and not stress. Many things are out of your control during the first trimester. What you can control is your lifestyle choices and how you react to these little speed bumps in the road. Before we get ahead of ourselves, let's first see if we see the sack. And the number of sacks."

I completely forgot that having multiples is always a possibility. There is motion at the side curtain panel, and a young nurse enters to stand beside me. She is beautiful and has the most angelic eyes. She holds my hand as the doctor gives me instructions to lie back and spread my legs. And to relax. I must not forget to relax.

"I'm going to insert the transvaginal ultrasound wand since you are early along in your pregnancy. It may feel a bit cold but try to relax."

I look at the monitor where a cone-like image appears. Dr. Blackstone moves the wand a bit and then smiles when he sees the little white kidney bean figure appear into view.

"I see it," I sigh. My sweet baby.

"You are indeed pregnant, Miss Nettles. A singleton."

I let out a breath in relief. *Just one.* I watch as he draws some lines and hits a button on the keyboard that captures the images. He does this several times from various angles. Then he clicks onto the screen, and a muffled thump-thump sound fills the room.

"Is that the heartbeat?"

"Sure is. Healthy and strong. I am measuring you at seven to eight weeks, which puts the date of conception about five to six weeks ago. I saw in your chart that you left the box unchecked for known father."

My eyes droop despite the doctor not seeming judgmental. Maybe this is a common occurrence. Or perhaps I am in the minority. Regardless, it makes me extremely anxious that I do not know who fathered this child.

Nic told Tara the morning she surprised us in his office that he doesn't want kids. That alone should have made it clear to me that he is not the one. Because if this child is his, then he would just be going through the motions to not look like an asshole, when deep down he will be harboring resentment toward me or the baby. I don't need negative feelings toward this baby, and no matter how I run through each scenario in my flowchart of thoughts, the result is always the same.

A small part of me wishes Nic and I never blurred the lines again this week by cohabitating and acting like we are a couple. I can't keep doing this to my heart. All of this uncertainty is fucking with my head.

Ethan, on the other hand, would be pissed off that it was his or maybe just angry it is mine. One can't be sure with him and his moods. Plus, he is so impulsive that I have no idea what he would say or do in reaction to the news. Just the lack of respect he showed toward me over the apartment and storage unit lets me know that he would be a horrible coparent. I know it's not fair to keep a secret this big, but I don't think I can handle his reaction.

The doctor removes the wand and fixes the sheet I have draped over my legs. The nurse steps out of the room, and I watch fixated as the doctor peels back the used condom and disposes of it into the trash. It is ironic that the only thing penetrating me while using protection for the past couple of months is the inanimate object officially letting me know I am indeed pregnant.

"I was taking the pill," I defend, despite the doctor not giving me any reason to feel defensive.

"Oral contraceptives are only about ninety percent effective, with the assumption that it was taken correctly, which means on time and without antibiotics."

I nod. I know this. Well, I know how to take it correctly. I guess I just never expected to be part of the less than ten percent that it fails for. I am not an idiot, and yet I acted stupidly for not insisting on a double form of protection. At the very least, I should have been watching the calendar to decrease the odds of this happening.

My hands rest over my lower abdomen, directly over where the baby is growing and developing. While the news of its existence is shocking, I want this baby. I want to try to be a good mother and break the cycle of bad parenting that I was subjected to. I never want my child to wish I put them up for adoption rather than to raise them. A tear slides down my cheek and I wipe it away.

I look over at the doctor who is typing out some notes on the computer. "Why do you think I am bleeding? Did the fall hurt the baby?"

"There's no way of knowing with certainty that the fall didn't hurt the baby. However, everything from the scan today looked good. This is your first pregnancy, right?"

"Yes."

"I know everything is new for you and can be a bit scary. Your body is going to change to accommodate this new life. However, please know that your hormones are going to shift and your mental clarity is just as important as your physical health. So many things are outside your control right now and especially this first trimester, which you are only halfway through. While it is too soon to know for sure, you could have a condition called Placenta Previa. If this is the case, we will handle it. I will give you a pamphlet on the condition to proactively prepare you. It is not too serious to worry about, and I won't be able to confirm until you are further along. But knowledge is power."

"Okay," I say with a shaky voice.

"When was the last time you had sex?" he asks in a professional tone.

"Umm," I hum, looking to the side of the room, "about five hours ago."

"Miss Nettles?"

"Yeah?"

"I'm not here to judge you or make you feel uncomfortable in any way. I just want to point out that your cervix and all of the surrounding area is increasing with blood volume, as well as sensitivity. The act of sex alone can cause bleeding. This all may seem alarming, but it is basically normal. Right now, I need you to stay hydrated and to start taking a prenatal vitamin if you haven't already. You are now considered high-risk due to the unexplained bleeding, so you'll need to be monitored closely. Therefore, I'll see you in two weeks."

"Okay."

"However, if you are bleeding more than a pad, you have to go straight to the hospital, just like you did today. Spotty vision or sharp pain on the right side, you come straight here. Otherwise, I can see you at my office complex where I do routine checkups."

"Thank you, Dr. Blackstone."

Once the doctor exits, I get dressed in the clothes I arrived in and get pushed along to the nurse at the big circular desk, where they watch all of the patients' monitors.

"You are free to go, as soon as you sign this discharge document," the nurse states, pointing to the line where I'm supposed to write my signature.

I expect a hefty bill to be sent to my residence, even though I do have health insurance. I know I have a deductible to meet, plus all of these appointments are going to add up with copays and facility charges.

I exit out of the double doors when the nurse hits her button to open them. I glance around for the elevator but find an information display instead full of pregnancy-related resources. I gather a few brochures that look helpful, knowing that I need all the support I can get.

After exiting the hospital, I slide into the backseat of an idling taxi and get dropped off at HH where my car is parked. Nic and I drove separately today due to meeting his mom for breakfast. I've been gone so long that it feels like the day has been going on forever. I am exhausted, and I just want to lie down and sleep away my worries.

I slip inside my parked car and start the engine. It feels good to be someplace that is solely mine, but I can't help but think about what Kevin shared. Maybe there is a GPS device in my car somewhere, alerting Nic of my where-abouts. I don't have the first clue about where to look for it. What does a tracking device look like? Can I hold it in my hand?

I glance in my rearview mirror and groan at the situation. I am sandwiched in rather tightly between an SUV and a smaller sedan. Using my mirror, I back up a little and then turn my wheel to pull out a bit. I then back up a little more. After strug-gling to not hit two parked vehicles, I finally get out of my side and walk around to the rear to evaluate how much space I have.

"Claire?"

I turn and see Angie and Graham walking toward me. I am going to scream. I just need to get back to my apartment so I can think about my next steps regarding my baby.

"Oh, hi," I stutter, surprised to be caught on the street after work hours. I will have to use tomorrow to catch up on all that I missed today with the distractions.

Angie narrows her eyes at me. "You were gone all afternoon."

She doesn't look angry. She looks deeply concerned. I glance down at my pink layered dress and frown at how rumpled I appear. I look like I got stuck in a windstorm. I imagine my hair looks that way as well.

"Sorry, I had a thing I had to take care of. I know I should have explained more, but I just had to take care of something, and I..." I take a couple of deep breaths. "Well, now it is taken care of so that is that."

The lies.

The deceit.

The facade.

I am a fraud. I feel an overwhelming amount of pressure to be perfect and to give off this illusion that I have my life together, despite everything falling apart.

Angie's eyes follow my every fidget, and I know she knows I am spinning in circles—a telltale sign I am hiding something. She gives me the common courtesy not to grill me on the street.

"Sweetheart," Graham says, looking down at her, "please let Collins take you back home. I would like to have a chat with Claire alone."

My eyes grow wide as Angie reluctantly slides into the backseat of the SUV that is parked directly behind my street parked car. How did I not notice it was theirs despite how many times I have ridden in it in the past? I turn around and wave to Collins, trying to figure out how I can be this oblivious.

I rock on my heels as Graham gives me a half smile. He knows he makes me nervous, probably from having several face-to-face verbal confrontations in the past. So much has happened since the days where I was trying to protect Angie from him. With time, it was very obvious to me that he would risk his own life to save hers.

"Where, um, do you want to talk?" I ask nervously. I really have no idea what he would like to discuss that cannot wait for tomorrow when I am back in the office. Maybe a wedding gift for his fiancée? Maybe the Plus None business? He is a key investor after all. None of these things seem urgent.

He points to the cafe across the street. "You okay with going there?" I nod and start to cross the street, but he clears his throat and asks, "Are you going to shut off your car?"

I turn to look at my idling car and realize that I was in the process of backing up when I ran into him and Angie. Shit. "Ah, yeah. Give me a second." I open my driver's side door and slide in. I straighten out my wheels and get my front bumper off the road. Then I kill the engine and hop out again. I walk beside Graham at the crosswalk and enter the little cafe. We move toward the back of the dining area, searching for a free spot. "What's on your mind?" I ask, settling into the booth at a corner table.

"Do you want something to eat or drink?" Graham asks politely.

I feel like I just ate, but as soon as I see the soups listed on the chalkboard menu, my stomach instantly growls. "Some baked potato soup, please. Extra bacon bits."

Graham nods and leaves the table to place the order. When he comes back, he passes me a bottle of unsweetened tea. I scan the label and see that it does have caffeine. I think I am supposed to limit it, so I just take a couple of sips to quench my thirst, saving the rest for later. I have so much to learn when it comes to being a mommy.

"Figure I'll just cut to the chase"—he sinks down into the bench seat on his side—"and not waste your time."

"Okay?" My nerves heighten at the directness of his words. I am not naive enough to think that this meeting is just for fun. I expect him to have something worthwhile to say. However, with the stress over the baby and who the daddy is, my anxiety has skyrocketed.

"I know what you are hiding," he says bluntly, sitting tall and watching me for a reaction.

And I give him one.

My eyes widen, and I slouch into my seat. My hands instinctively slide up toward my belly, under the protection of the tabletop. I am so exhausted that I just want to get this over with.

"Are you going to tell Angie? Especially right before the wedding? The last thing she needs to be doing is fussing over me. How did you even find out?"

"My brother has made it clear to anyone in employment at HH to stay the hell away from you. That coupled with how he couldn't stay away from you in Vegas was easy for me to make my own conclusions. Even our sister noticed his change in demeanor, and she isn't even around him regularly. Nic and I went sparring today while you were meeting with our mom, and while he would not admit that he is pursuing you, I can read between the lines. But, Claire?"

"Yeah?" I am still trying to figure out if he knows I am pregnant. Maybe my secret is still concealed, at least until I can figure out what the hell I am doing.

"I need to warn you about a few things." Graham moves hair off his forehead and runs his hand down the side of his face. "My brother is scarred from his past relationship where his fiancée was caught cheating on him. He has made it clear to our entire family that he is a commitment-phobe. He is not the type of man who wants to settle down and have a family."

"I'm sure you know that said ex visited your building last week to try to win Nic back?"

"I am very aware."

"So then why are you telling me this?" I ask, my tone serious. "Do you think I am oblivious to the risk of dating your brother?"

"Because the last thing you need is to look for a *forever* with a guy who just wants a *for now*."

I nod. Graham is right, except for the fact that Nic has changed. It is understandable for other people close to him to have a hard time believing the change, but that doesn't mean it didn't happen. Even though Nic is trying to start a relationship with me, he doesn't know that I am pregnant. No one knows.

"You know that Nic is the one making all the moves, right? I am not chasing after a *for now*." Like my tattoo represents, I am looking toward the sun and the things that bring me joy. Right now, I am focusing on my growing baby who needs me more than anyone else does.

"I love my brother; I swear I do. But I also love my

soon-to-be-wife. If you get hurt, she gets hurt. Please just be wise if you want to pursue him."

I take a few bites of my soup and a sip from my tea. I need to cut my ties and focus on this baby. When the truth finally comes out, I'll have a whole lot of explaining to do to Angie. Hopefully she'll be back from her honeymoon and still living in marital bliss and won't allow my drama to stress her out.

I clear my throat and try to keep my emotions at bay. "Now that you have gotten that off your chest," I say, "then how about I get something off mine?"

Graham leans back in his chair and crosses his arms over his chest. "Let's hear it."

"The tracking of me needs to stop." My words come out of my mouth as blunt as I intended.

His eyes narrow at me, testing my expression for truth. "It's for safety purposes."

"It's intrusive, illegal, and inappropriate."

Graham gives me a single nod. "You missed the one thing in your list that makes this all okay, though."

"Oh, yeah?" I challenge.

"It's *necessary*."

I scoff over his casual reaction. "Have either of you Hoffman boys learned the definition of *consent*? I am not Angie. I am not anybody's."

"But anyone close to my future wife needs to know the score when it comes to being around her. Her safety is my utmost priority. So the protective measures I instituted for her, trickle down to you."

"*Consent*, Graham. That's all it would have taken and

this would not be a discussion. Surely, you have learned something over the last year."

"I did learn a lot," he says blankly. "I refuse to take anything for granted. But take this complaint up with Nic. He's in charge of this."

"Oh, I plan to."

"I just want you to be careful about your romantic choices when it comes to my brother. You deserve someone who can give you everything you need. I can't help but look out for you, too, Claire. I have known you for as long as I have known Angie. Despite what my past actions have been toward you, I do care a great deal about you."

I give a weak smile. I know he cares. We wouldn't be here now if he didn't care. "I'll make it clear to Nic tomorrow that we can't ever be. We want two different things."

Graham nods and presses his lips together. "Believe it or not, your happiness matters to me."

His words make me sad. They are another reminder of how tough life can be. But it is in the direst of conditions that something beautiful can grow.

18

NIC

"I can't keep doing this," I tell Asher. I run my hands through my hair and let them rest at the back of my neck. "I'm going nuts with the doubt and second-guessing."

I am still at HH after Claire insisted on having a night off. She said she needed some space and to sleep in her own bed. I wanted to push back. I wanted to demand that I stay with her or move that bed of hers over to my place. However, I know how fragile she is right now, and if she asks for time, I better damn well give her time or risk scaring her off.

Dr. Zimmerman's voice haunts my thoughts. *Focus on what you can control.* And my girl cannot be controlled— even with my best intentions.

Everything changed for me when Claire came back from Virginia. I saw someone go from being so spirited and vibrant to being defeated and broken. I can only hope to have a run-in with her family, just to have the chance to tell them that they missed an opportunity to get to know an amazing girl.

Asher clears his throat and looks directly at me via video chat. "He has zero reason to double-cross you, man. Tyler's references have checked out. He has a clean record. Plus, I have personal experience with him."

"Anyone can be bribed," I add, leaning back. "Maybe you can help me set one up to see if he reports back to me. We can call it a test."

"No, no, no. There is a code men like us live by. If he happened to turn to the darkness, it will be for other reasons besides money. But for the record, I don't see that ever happening."

"If he has an interest in my brother's business ventures, then I need to know why. Maybe he got to see the value or got some insider information."

If Tyler is the mole, he will never get a job working privacy and security in this country. I will make sure his name gets spread to everyone I know, and if I can get a lawyer to take him to court for something-or-another, I will. A heavy-handed cash flow can cause evidence to just pop up out of thin air.

"You are paranoid, man."

It's true. I am.

Tyler has been watching Claire, keeping tabs on her happenings, and has been an excellent resource for when I need jobs handled. Up until recently, I have trusted him implicitly, and he has given me zero reason to question where his loyalty lies. However, someone was trying to get into HH and the resemblance is striking to Tyler's features.

"I cannot concentrate if I don't have someone watching my girl."

"Whoa, wait a minute."

"What?" I cross my arms over my chest defensively.

"Mr. Hit-Em-And-Quit-Em has upgraded from playing softball to hardball, eh? Let me savor this moment."

"Shut your face," I huff at the screen. "You always were so dramatic."

"But there is a chance you will eventually settle down, right?" he probes.

"I already am settled down, Asher. I have a stable job, a place to live, and no real chance of leaving Portland anytime soon. How much more settled can I get?"

"Put some bling on the fing."

"Don't ever say that again," I deadpan, and when I can't keep a straight face any longer, I laugh along with Asher. "What's wrong with you, dude?"

"It's okay to go slow, Nic."

"Thanks, Mom."

"No really, man. If you shut yourself off from being open to the possibility of building a future with someone, then that's where there's a problem."

I sigh. "I'm trying."

"That's good," he encourages. "Trying is good."

"I just need to know who I can trust and not trust."

"I'll do a little digging. If you need me to fly up, I have some vacation time that I must take this quarter and"—his eyes get goofy and a big smile breaks out—"I need to meet this magical princess who has stolen your heart and made you turn into a huge sap."

I shake my head at him. "Whatever."

"Oh, and for an unsolicited pro-tip, the ladies love original poetry."

I burst out laughing. "Chat later. Thanks, man."

I end the call and check my tracking device to find Claire's dot hovering at a cell phone shop in the Pearl District. I try texting her to see what's going on. She's been acting weird all day, and my instincts tell me that something is not right.

I check my email and find one from Tyler, asking me if there's any work for him to do. I have abruptly taken him off Claire duty until I can figure out who tried to sneak into HH during an electrical fluke. I keep giving him bogus fake work to keep him busy, but I doubt it is fulfilling for him—and probably is confusing. I am running out of excuses as to why I have shifted his focus. The last thing I need is for him —if he is the mole—to veer from his original plans. If he plays it too safe, I won't be able to catch him and take him down.

I clean up my office space, log out of all of my devices, and make my way to the lobby to check in with the night shift guards. It is getting dark out, and I hate that Claire is wandering the city with what might be a broken cell phone. I need her device to work if I am going to keep notice of her whereabouts.

I am about to step outside when my phone buzzes with a text from Dan.

Dan: One of your ex-employees is seeking revenge.

Nic: How do you know?

My heart races as I try to figure out who Dan is talking about. Since taking on the title of Head of Security, I have let go over half of the workers who were originally hired. The structure of the entire department changed when I came on board. I can imagine that I pissed off a lot of people with my no-nonsense type of leadership.

I wait for Dan to text back, and when I don't get anything in response, I text him again.

Nic: How do you know? And who is it?

Dan: Are you free to meet? I am only a couple of blocks away from HH.

Nic: I'll come to you. Where are you?

Dan gives me the street address, and I quickly exit HH and take a left onto the sidewalk. I set a brisk pace, and within minutes, I find Dan sitting on a bench outside of an apartment complex.

"Hey," he says, almost shyly. "I figured you would want to know this information."

"Of course, share it." I sit down next to him on the opposite end and brace myself for whatever he has to give. I watch anxiously as Dan retrieves an envelope from his inner breast pocket and hands it over. "You are being very secretive."

"Open it and see for yourself," he presses.

I pull open the flap of the envelope and see the bank records for my former employee Kevin. I see the exact moment where his savings doubled. I look at the next document and see a picture of Kevin accepting an undisclosed amount of money from someone who has their back turned. I analyze the photo, and when I see the wrist tattoo on the mystery man, I know that Tyler also has one strikingly similar. Dammit.

Fuckers!

"Looks like Kevin is accepting bribes," I grind out. "But what for?"

"Probably to try to taunt you or blackmail you in some way by gaining information that you would prefer to keep concealed? I'm not quite sure."

"How did you figure this all out?" I ask.

"As soon as I realized someone was trying to break into HH, I took it upon myself to dig a little into the previous employee records and find out who got fired and what they were doing now. I saw Kevin never got another job. And—"

"With limited funds, he could easily get involved in accepting money for doing favors."

"Exactly," Dan agrees.

"But who is pulling the strings? And why?" I point to the photo of the man with his back turned. "Him or Kevin?"

"I'm not sure."

"Thanks once again for bringing this all to my attention. Meet with me tomorrow morning in my office so I can discuss moving you up in rank. You are proving to be a valuable employee. But with the new rank will come added responsibilities."

Dan reaches his hand out for me to shake. "Thank you, sir. I'm up for the challenge."

I walk back to my car and call up Asher again. "Your boy Tyler looks to be getting involved in something nefarious."

"Do you have proof?" Asher asks, sounding exhausted from my constant probing.

"Not exactly."

He sighs. "That much is obvious."

"I have a picture of the back of his body. But he has a very distinct tattoo, and this photo has it located on the same part of the wrist."

"Things can be Photoshopped," he adds.

"Yeah, sure, but I have already been suspecting him of double-crossing me. Now this just adds to my suspicion."

"Seems careless on Tyler's part to be associated with something that he could easily get caught doing. Men like us don't get caught, Nic. Tyler is not an idiot. If he wanted to do something, he sure as hell wouldn't get himself filmed doing it."

I sigh. I am starting to get a migraine. "You're right. This all seems weird."

"I can help you get to the bottom of all of this, but I need time to line up my resources."

"Thanks, man."

"Just take care of yourself. I know how much you love to be a hero."

"I'll try. Bye."

I toss my phone into the cup holder and rub my fingers over the bridge of my nose. This whole thing is one mess after another mess.

As if I don't have any more free will, I drive north

toward the Pearl District and park my car on the street near the cell phone store. Through the tall glass windows, I see Claire talking with a worker. She looks so beautiful and pure—even from a distance. I know she is struggling financially to make ends meet. With me, there is no reason to continue to push as hard as she does to make money. I can take care of her. I *want* to take care of her.

If Claire thinks she can use Entice to moonlight, then she doesn't know me well enough to think I wouldn't put a stop to it. There is zero chance of me sitting back and allowing her to entertain any man's company. I've been toying with the idea of dismantling the company for weeks now. If she shows interest again, I will just speed up my timeline. It serves no positive purpose anymore for me.

My phone vibrates with an incoming call, and I look at the caller ID to see it is Collins.

"What's up?" I ask in greeting.

"I've been watching Tyler's actions and nothing seems off. I hired a close buddy of mine to follow him, check through his trash, and gather any type of information he can on his hobbies and interests. Nothing. He's clean."

"I should be relieved, but if it isn't Tyler trying to double-cross me, then who? And I just got more evidence pointing toward him being the mole."

"I don't know, sir. But just because we haven't found anything yet, doesn't mean we won't. Want me to keep my man at his post and do some more digging of my own?"

"Yeah. I think Graham would approve as well. He has a lot on his plate, and this is not something he needs to fret about."

"Understood," Collins answers.

"And if you can keep an eye on Claire, that would be great. I had Tyler doing that job as a favor for Graham. My brother doesn't want anyone to harm Angie through her friends. After all the shit that happened last year, neither of us are taking any chances."

"I'll do what I can."

"Appreciate it."

I watch as Claire exits the shop with a little bag in her hand. She searches the parked cars. Does she know I am here? Her attention goes to the store bag, and she pulls out what looks to be a new phone.

"Graham is calling me now, so I need to take this," Collins says, cutting through the silence.

"Keep me posted."

I end the call and watch as she gets into her vehicle and starts the engine. I wait a few minutes for her to pull away before deciding to follow her back to her place to make sure she is safe. We have been spending so much time together lately that being apart for just one night will feel lonely. I am going to miss her.

I pull open my tracker and only find the dot that indicates that her car is parked. Without access to her new phone, I no longer have the ability to know where she is if she moves away from her vehicle. I can't imagine Claire wanting to upgrade her device right now, with how tight her budget seems to be. It was easy gaining access to her device prior to us engaging in a physical and emotional relationship. However, I'm not so sure she will freely give it over to me with the way her mood seems to fluctuate. I will just have to convince her to spend the night with me so I can add on the hidden app.

I'm not proud of myself for the things I do to make sure she is safe. I am very aware of my obsession and my inability to accept that she is strong enough to take care of herself. I have seen too many women in my life get taken advantage of, and I refuse to allow Claire to be added to that list.

I hang out in a street spot, waiting for Claire's lights to turn on in her place. I need to know she is safely inside her room before I can tear myself away. Time hasn't made my compulsion die down, and I doubt anything will.

I start to worry when I see zero movement from Claire's window. She has a routine of turning on lights and opening her curtains once she is home. I am about to hop out of my car and go check for myself when I see an SUV pull up and Collins walks around to the back passenger side to let Angie out. He walks her to the door, and Claire greets her with a weak smile.

I quickly pull out my phone and shoot him a text.

Nic: I'm here making sure Claire got back safe and I see you are bringing Angie?

Collins: Graham isn't happy. But she insisted on seeing her tonight.

Nic: Couldn't wait for morning?

Collins: Apparently not. And she refused to let him come. Said she had to handle this on her own.

I curse under my breath, and my mind races to figure out what this meeting is about and why my brother has to stay out of it. Dammit. This isn't good. All the warning bells are going off in my head. I already lost Claire once—due to my own fault—but I can't lose her again.

19

CLAIRE

I can feel a tic forming under my right eye as I usher Angie inside, followed by an extra quiet Collins. His calm and rigid personality puts me on edge. Seeing him with Angie, who looks like she is going to throw up, just adds to my already building anxiety. Something tells me whatever she has to say has nothing to do with the wedding and everything to do with our friendship.

"I wasn't expecting this tonight," I say, trying to make small talk. We aren't those types of friends who have to fill the silence with unnecessary words. Yet at this moment, I am twitching with nerves to figure out what is going on with her—with us.

"Couldn't wait," she says methodically. Her whole demeanor seems off. Angie didn't come over to paint nails or to talk about work. No, she came over to discuss something personal, and I fear that everything I have been doing to try to cause her less stress is going to blow up in my face —just like basically everything else in my life.

I unlock my apartment door and start to turn on the lights. I watch as Angie turns back to Collins who is texting on his phone and asks him to stay outside the door or go back to the SUV to wait.

"Want a drink?" I ask, watching her shut the door and walk into my tiny space. It feels even more claustrophobic all of a sudden. "I wasn't planning for a visitor tonight, so I didn't stock the fridge or buy any drinks other than water."

"I'm fine," she says blankly.

I study her face. She has a wrinkle forming on her forehead that appears to be stress lines. "You obviously aren't," I point out. "What's going on?" My heart races at her silence. She is eerily quiet, and every second she doesn't speak makes me even more paranoid. "Please, don't keep making me wait. Something is obviously bothering you and it has to do with me or you wouldn't be here at night unexpectedly." My voice trembles in fear that all this time I have shut Angie out, I just put a hole in the foundation of our friendship. Guilt floods through me at the sight of her standing before me looking destroyed.

"I thought we were friends," Angie says sadly, a quiver vibrating her words. She has always been a warrior of strength, so seeing her this agitated is alarming.

"We are." Tears well up in my eyes. I did this to her. I had so many opportunities to come to her with the truth that I was secretly pursuing an on-again-off-again relationship with her future brother-in-law and at no point did I trust her with the information. I treated her like a fragile flower that would wilt from the stress that this could cause to the dynamics of her soon-to-be family if we were to break up. And I never considered the alternative of what not telling her would cause. Sure, I told her that we kissed while in Vegas, but Nic and I have always been more than a kiss. I am a selfish friend. She would never do this to me. "We are best friends."

"Then why all the lies, Claire? Obviously you don't trust me or respect me enough to tell me the truth. And after all we have been through over the years? I have shared a part of my life with you that I don't share with just anybody. Why can't I get the same courtesy?"

I sigh and sit on the edge of my bed, while Angie paces. "I thought I was protecting you."

She stops and glares at me. "Protecting me? From what? I am tired of being treated like some chronic victim. Yeah, last year was a hell of a year, but quit downplaying how far I have come with my methods of coping with stress. I am not going to relapse. Quite frankly, it is insulting how I am being treated by someone I thought always had my back."

I lean forward and put my head in my hands. This is one disaster after another. I can't handle any more disappointment. "I'm sorry." I mean, what else can I possibly say to make this any better? "I suck at being a good friend."

"In a few days I am supposed to get married with my best friend by my side, and it is like you don't want me to be part of your life. You don't trust me, and I already have anxiety that as soon as I say 'I do,' you will say, 'I don't.'"

"That's absurd, Angie."

"Is it? I mean, you are basically treating me differently and I am not even married yet. You think that tying myself forever with Graham will somehow diminish our friendship, so you are pulling back now to protect yourself from what you assume is going to happen. This isn't about protecting me. It is about protecting *you*."

I let her words marinate in my head, and when I process what she is saying, I realize how true they are. I do worry about Married Angie being different from Single Angie. We have had so much fun together that her tying the knot is essentially saying that she doesn't need me anymore. I hate feeling left behind, and maybe subconsciously I didn't trust her to handle all of my bombshells with grace.

And right now, I need some grace.

"You are the very best friend I could ever ask for. I fucked up. Majorly. And I have been so in over my head for months that I can't even recognize the person I used to be from the person I am now. I'm sorry. I mean it."

"What changed?" she asks, taking a seat next to me on the bed.

We bend our legs and prop one up on the mattress so we can look at one another. If I'm going to make this better, I have to face her head-on and be vulnerable. The bullshit stops today.

"Somewhere between the Vegas trip and now, I fell in love with Nic Hoffman."

"Took you long enough to admit it," Angie says.

"You already knew?"

"I had my suspicions. I mean, you guys did kiss. But I also know that Nic has some issues."

"I didn't want to fall in love with him, but some things are just out of our control. Nic has all the qualities I should have tried to avoid, and trust me, I tried. He is controlling, frustrating, overprotective, and so wonderfully attentive. He understands me and encourages me to be myself. I have always been not enough for any man I associated with. I finally found the one man who makes me feel alive, but he is a commitment-phobe."

"He's been hurt in the past," Angie explains.

I nod. "That is an understatement. Nic turned my life upside down. He made me see that Ethan is a horrible match for me. He pursued me relentlessly, and when I finally gave in and allowed myself to fall, he decided not to catch me."

"You guys broke up?" Angie inquires with sadness in her voice.

"Yeah."

"When?"

"When I was staying at your place while Graham went to New York. I've been having a secret relationship with Nic almost since we returned from Vegas. Ethan kicked me out of the apartment we shared. He has several secret properties, and then decided he wanted to go back with Deena. Having Ethan and Nic in Vegas made it easy for me to compare how each made me feel. Ethan made me feel like a gold digger who didn't have a brain. Actually, he goes out of his way now to tell me that. Nic made me feel like I am smart and that my opinion matters. I thought I was choosing between good and bad, but what happens if both are bad?"

Angie frowns, which is exactly what I didn't want to have happen. This should be the most exciting time of her life, and now I'm dumping cold water all over her happiness.

"Why not tell me? Why keep this all to yourself? I could've helped."

"Because you are planning a wedding of your dreams, and the last thing you need is the maid of honor and the best man to have any animosity toward each other while we celebrate you and Graham tying the knot."

"But you obviously do have negative feelings. So how did keeping it all to yourself help in any way?"

"It didn't help; it just made things worse," I admit.

"Keep going. You guys got back together?"

"Yeah. And when I took the trip back home to Virginia, where I learned my mom basically regretted having me and started dating a guy I went to high school with, I came back to Portland with Nic opening more than just his arms for me. He shared a part of his heart with me and has painted a vision of hope inside my head that I want even more than I could have dreamed."

"What was it?" Angie probes.

"He showed me glimpses of what life with him could be like. How we could mold to one another and share our aspirations. He let me know that it was safe again to fall. He apologized for our breakup. We connected on a soul level, and I thought he was the one for me."

"But he's not?"

I sigh. "He can't be."

"Why the hell not?" she probes, looking at me like I am dense.

"Because I'm pregnant," I blurt out.

Angie shakes her head as if something is stuck in her ears. "You're what?"

"Pregnant." I haven't said the word much out loud, and hearing my own voice proclaim it makes it seem more real.

"Holy cannoli."

"And to top it all off, I don't know who the father is." I sound defeated. I turn away to avoid Angie's reaction, and then I feel her arms wrap around me and hug me close to her body, and I weep with the ugliest tears. "I have cried more in the past weeks than I have in years. Maybe the anxiety of everything is getting to me. Maybe I am being forced to mature overnight."

"It's going to be alright," she soothes. "You wait and see."

I pull back just to lean over and grab a tissue to wipe my nose. I am a blubbering mess. "You don't know that."

"You're right, I don't," Angie agrees. "But I know you. You are resilient and strong and fierce. Whatever you encounter, you will do it with the grace you always seem to muster up."

"Stop being so nice to me."

"Why, Claire?"

"Because you are just making me feel worse for lying to you. I just never thought Nic kissing me for the first time in Vegas would turn into a big triangle. Those are the two potential sperm donors, you know."

"Things can always be worse," she comforts.

"I just found out Nic has been tapping my phone and put a tracer thing on my car without telling me. He violated so many unspoken privacy rules that I have no idea how I can possibly trust him again. Plus, he doesn't want kids. He told his ex, Tara, those very words when she surprise visited us in his office. Oh and to make matters worse, Tara is the same girl who I went to high school with back home. She tormented me in school and is still a jealous bully. She also sabotaged me during a cheer competition and then made my teenage years a living hell. So even if Nic is the father, why would he want to even be involved?"

"Whoa, there's so much to unpack there. First off, about the privacy. He's a Hoffman and they—"

I huff. "That's no excuse. I can't ever trust him."

"So it's over?"

"Yes. There's more to it than that, but this is a pattern of behavior I refuse to tolerate. I would rather parent my child alone than be forced to parent with a man who thinks he does nothing wrong."

"Nic doesn't know you're pregnant?"

I turn away. "No."

"Why not tell him?"

"I told you. He doesn't want kids."

"Claire, some men can't see themselves having kids until they can visualize a life with a solid partner. Maybe he said he didn't want kids because at the time, he knew having them was not a real possibility. Shouldn't you give him a chance to alter his view? Or at the very least see if it has changed?"

I shrug. "I don't see why I should put him through all of this. I never envisioned myself in this mommy role, prior to discovering I was expecting, and I'm not even sure I won't fail at it."

"Claire, you are going to be the best mommy for this baby."

"Again, you don't know that," I respond.

"But what I do know is that you are a go-getter. Nothing stops you. You're a perfectionist by nature, and you have a wonderful spirit and zest for life. Sure, this is not the way you wanted things to play out, but it is what it is. Do you think learning who the father is will make this any easier to swallow?"

"No. Because no matter how I cut the rotten fruit, it is still bad on the inside."

"Surely you would prefer one man over the other to procreate with?" she challenges.

I allow her question to mull around in my head, and then I remember the kicker. "Oh, and Ethan has been propositioning me for sex."

Angie tosses her hands up in the air. "What a freaking animal. Who does he think he is?"

"I beat the shit out of him when I was tired of his harassment. But the universe keeps having us cross paths. I can't imagine what it would be like to coparent with a monster. The doctor doesn't want me under that level of stress."

"You saw a doctor already? How far along are you?"

"I fell and was bleeding."

"What? No…"

"I went in and got seen in triage. The baby seems fine. Heartbeat is strong. I'm about seven or eight weeks along. I just feel like I'm being thrown repeatedly under a moving train but surviving each time—barely."

"You have been carrying so much on your own. It's time to accept some support. I also think you need to tell Nic— sooner rather than later. You keep predicting his reaction without actually knowing."

"Baby might not be his," I remind her.

"He still deserves to know that it could be his, Claire. He has the means to take care of you. I have seen how he looks at you when he doesn't think I am watching."

"And how is that?"

"He looks at you like you are his sun, and he is just happy to be part of your orbit."

"That's ludicrous. Angie, you're a hopeless romantic. But not every story has a happy ending."

"But yours will. Happiness is a choice, Claire. You are lumping Nic into a box with all the other jerks you dated. You're doing the exact same thing to him that he does to women. Stop the cycle. I saw how Ethan treated you in Vegas, and it took everything inside me to resist stepping in. Trust me, I nearly tried. But Graham warned me that if I tried to sway you away from him, it might push you closer together. And I wanted to smack the shit out of that narcissistic asshole."

"He would have deserved it."

"But I know that Nic got a few swings in on him while in Vegas."

"Really? I didn't know. I mean, I suspected something happened. Before going to the airport, Nic claimed he had to go do an errand. And when I ran into Ethan at the Parkhouse Plaza and saw the way his face was bruised, I made assumptions. But it wasn't like Nic and I ever discussed it."

"Yup. And as expected, Nic came out the victor. He did what we all wanted to do. Ethan is plain gross."

I frown over her words. "Ethan may be the father."

"If he is, you will figure out a way to coparent then. You won't have much choice."

"Do you see my dilemma? You see how much this is eating me up inside? Now you are involved, and you are going to go home tonight and you are going to think about this, when you should be thinking about the beginning of the rest of your life. You are about to marry your soulmate. How freaking awesome is that?" I exclaim.

"I just wish my mom was here to witness me taking this huge step."

"Angie, your mom hasn't left your side."

Tears roll down her cheeks. "I feel her with me all the time. More so now than ever. I think she would like Graham."

I lean over and give her a hug. Despite my reluctance to share these parts of my life with Angie for fear she would stress out, I am glad everything got said tonight. "I vow that when you are officially married, nothing between us will change. That is my promise."

"Good. Because despite what you might think about yourself, you are my rock. I don't enjoy life without you in it."

"Feeling's mutual."

"I better get going before a search team gets sent out for my recovery," Angie teases.

"Can you apologize to Graham for me?"

"What on earth for?"

"For complicating things with his brother. But first wait until I tell Nic I am pregnant. I know Graham doesn't approve of the relationship," I explain. "He basically warned me that Nic would break my heart. But I think I'll be doing the breaking this go around."

"Graham will forever put me first, and as much as that sounds romantic, I need to lose sometimes so I can stay grounded. He was probably worried about me finding out that Nic did you wrong, and that I would go completely ballistic over it. I mean," she says, pausing, "I am naturally a passionate activist for women. So, Nic better keep himself in check or face the wrath of Angie. But Graham has no say in who you decide to pursue or not pursue. He is a boundary pusher and thinks he can get away with it. Nope. I will tell him exactly how it is."

"No more tension. Please. Let me just get through your wedding without any more incidents. This is about you, not me. I can put all of this on hold until you guys are on your honeymoon."

"Speaking of which, where is Graham taking me?"

I giggle. "Like he would ever tell me that."

"We aren't leaving until a couple of days after the wedding. I will take a few days off work to relax and acquaint myself with married life, but I can still check in."

"No worries. I can handle it."

"That's why we are partners," she says, blowing me a kiss.

"For life."

20

NIC

"Holy shit!" Angie expresses, clasping her hands over her heart.

"Sorry," I answer sheepishly. "Didn't mean to startle you. I'm here to ask Claire a couple of last-minute questions about the wedding stuff."

"Sure, right." Her eyes give me a knowing look, and I can tell she knows more than she is letting on. Her hand isn't swinging back to hit me, so at least there is that.

"I'll walk you to Collins who is waiting for you down in the lobby."

"I'm sure I can figure out how to get to the lobby, Nic," she almost whines.

I grab my phone out of my pants pocket and dial Collins's number while Angie gawks at me. She knows me well enough by now to realize I work with the same code as Graham does. We take care of those we love, and while it will never be romantic between us, there is no shortage of emotion I feel toward her. She was family long before she ever got engaged to my brother. I look out for her as if she is my sister.

"Angie is ready and refusing for me to walk her down," I say into the speaker of the phone.

"You take your role very seriously," she goads, huffing under her breath.

"On my way," Collins says before disconnecting the call.

"You better not hurt her," Angie warns.

I narrow my eyes but remain silent. I want to ask how much she knows but bite my tongue. Now is not the time to hash out my relationship status with my soon-to-be sister-in-law.

The arrival of Collins ends the stare down. I wait until they are safely in the elevator before knocking on Claire's door. She may not even know I am here. Or perhaps she is avoiding me, which I have been suspecting she has been doing most of the evening.

"I didn't order any pizza," she yells from the other side, an edge of anger to her voice.

"I ain't got a pizza," I echo back. "Let me in, Claire. Whatever it is you are pissed at me about, we can discuss it and move forward."

I wait anxiously until the door cracks open just enough for her hand to fly out and launch a cell phone toward my face. I duck just in time and hiss over the sound it makes as the screen shatters from the impact of it being thrown against the wall.

"There's your parting gift. Shove it up your ass if you want or put it up on a shelf as a trophy for fooling me for as long as you did."

I dart toward the open door, but Claire slams it shut before I can wedge myself into her apartment. "Claire?" I knock gently on the door. I refuse to apologize for keeping a tracker on her phone—if that's what this is even about—but I will apologize for not telling her I was doing it. "Open the door, baby."

"Don't you *baby* me!" she bellows.

"We can discuss this. Just open the door."

"No!"

"Need me to contact the landlord and get a key to open this place up? I can make up some story and—"

The door flies open and my girl is standing in all her glory, fuming from head to toe. Between the time Angie left and now, she must have changed into her soft cotton pajama set. She looks cute yet tough, and her ability to pull both off makes her even more desirable.

"You wouldn't." Her words come out more as a dare, rather than a sneer.

"I most definitely would," I say, trying my best not to break out into a smile. "You want to keep testing me?" As much as I love when we are getting along, a sliver of me misses this vibrant and passionate version of Claire. When my girl is mad, she doesn't hold back. While I don't particularly like being on the receiving end of her wrath, I will take her explosive reactions over her silent treatment any day. I can catch whatever she wants to throw my way.

"Oh, how I wish I could smack your stupid smirk off your stupid face."

"Come here and try," I goad.

"No."

"No?"

"No. You want me to go crazy, so you will be the one who looks normal," she bites out.

I can't stop my smirk any longer, and I can feel it break out over my lips. "Invite me inside. C'mon."

She props her hands on her hips and gawks at me as if I lost my mind. "You drive me absolutely insane."

"Not any more than you drive me."

"Me?" she scoffs. "I drive you insane?"

"Yeah. And I think you like making me go crazy, so you can feel alive."

"You are out of your mind, Nic Hoffman! You have moved from the unhealthy amount of crazy to certifiable pretty quickly."

Claire stomps toward me, and I brace myself for her spirited arrival. With a finger poking toward me, I back up as she takes a step closer and closer and only stop when I am pressed up against the wall. I allow her this illusion of victory and stay pinned, but I have no intention of backing down from her. I just need to get her to see reason and logic. With as fiery as her temper seems to currently be, it may take me all night to get through to her.

"Let's talk."

"I am done canoodling with liars."

"Is that so?"

I bite my bottom lip to keep from laughing. It is just that Claire is so dang cute when she is this heated. It does something to me inside that makes me want to turn the tables on her, press her lush body against the wall, and kiss the hell out of her. I haven't heard the word "canoodling" outside of an old movie, and the way she surprises me with these little moments in time only makes it clearer to me that she is the one.

"I don't need your smirks or your ill-placed kindness. Just go."

"Well, I don't need your attitude," I counter. "But here I am, being graced with it and still not running away."

"You should run away."

"I'm not some weak boy, Claire. I can handle you and your mood swings and help you find your Midol and heating pad."

By the fire in her eyes, I know I've hit a nerve.

"Oh, fuck you! I'm not on my r—" I can almost see the steam coming out of her ears, as she angrily taps her foot. "Just stop!"

"I really hope you can heal from the events in your life that no one has yet apologized for. But here I am, standing before you, saying sorry."

Her eyes dart away, as they fill up with moisture. "This is all just too much."

"Did you eat dinner?" I ask, completely changing the subject.

"No." She pauses and narrows her eyes at me. "I'm supposed to be mad at you."

"Be mad, but let's at least eat so you can regain your strength and continue fighting with me over more nonsensical things." Her eyes flare, and I hold my hand up for her to wait until I finish. "Let's call this an intermission. What are you in the mood for?"

"Nic, no. I can't keep doing this."

I frown over the sad edge to her words. "We can talk

about everything on your mind. But how about I order some soup for us and a salad? Fresh bread?"

She thinks about my offer and I can tell she wants to accept, but her stubbornness is also helping to sway her mind. "I can't keep going down this road with you. We aren't compatible."

"And why is that?"

"You think relationship rules don't apply to you and that you can just do whatever the hell you want and lump your actions under the 'I'm protecting you' arbitrary category you made up."

The elevator door dings, and I don't even have to look to know the peace treaty has arrived from the shocked look on Claire's face.

"You are something else," she mutters under her breath. "I swear you make every nerve in my body cranky."

"Here's your delivery," the worker says, passing me a huge bag from the cafe just a block away.

I hand over the money and sheepishly smile at Claire. I don't know how I can get into her good graces again, but I know it starts on a full stomach. Nothing good can come from this if she is hungry.

"You are so presumptuous," she grinds out.

"You are giving me way too much credit."

"Am I?"

"I am simply hungry, and I hate eating alone," I say with a smile. "Should we eat out here in the hall or inside your place?"

"You are beyond any words I can even come up with," she huffs.

"So, will you eat dinner with me?" I ask like a teenager waiting to hear back a response to prom.

"Not like I have a choice."

"You really don't." I mean for my words to come out like a joke to lighten the mood, but just from Claire's stance, I know she is fuming and still ready to fight.

I manage to get us through the door of her apartment so we aren't continuing to share our dirty laundry with the entire hallway of tenants to hear. I serve up the food, and we eat at her kitchen counter because her place is too small to really enjoy it elsewhere.

I want to talk and ask her about her day, but I know she is going through the motions just to appease me. I feel like I'm not even in the room. We eat in silence, and I sneak glances at her to see if her reaction has changed with some food in her belly. Nope.

"Tell me why you're mad," I challenge. "Say the words."

"How can you be this obtuse?"

"I just want you to be real with me."

"You bugged my phone and my car," she says bluntly.

"I did," I admit, causing her to openly gawk at me. "Were you expecting me to deny it?"

"I braced myself for you to lie some more about it, yes."

"You saw what happened with Angie last year. You are her best friend. How could you not expect me to make sure you were safe and that if something were to happen, I would be able to find you? It started out being a favor to Graham to make sure both you and she were safe. Then it became my number one priority for my own personal reasons."

"Why not tell me? You violated my privacy and made it

impossible to trust you again. Sure, we can be civil. I mean, we work together, my best friend is now going to be your family, and we both have wedding traditions to adhere to. I won't *not* talk to you, but the truth is we are lousy for each other. I can't do toxic right now."

"I'm sorry for not telling you. I'm not sorry for actually doing it. If I had asked for your permission months ago to keep a tracker on you, would you have agreed?"

"Hell, no."

"This is my exact point, Claire." I sigh. "When you surround yourself with someone as lucrative and influential as my brother is, then you need to accept the added protective measures we push on those we care about. It's a part of the whole picture."

"You had ample opportunity to share this information with me, yet you took it upon yourself to do whatever you want. You think rules don't apply to you. That code may work for Angie and Graham, but I am different."

"I was wrong. But you are wrong too." I watch as Claire frowns, and I can tell I hit a sore spot. I didn't come here to make her sad. Instead, I came here to see why she is sad. "You are holding something back from me, and no matter how hard I try at giving you space, I need to know what it is so we can move past it. Please. Trust me enough to confide in me."

"I…"

"Oh, baby girl, don't cry." I move closer to her and wipe away her tears. Claire's swollen eyes look up at me, and they are so stained with redness that I break a little inside. She seems emotionally battered and torn, and there isn't anything I want to do right now other than hold her to me.

"Come here. Tell me what you need right now, at this very moment."

"Just hold me," she says with a quivering voice.

"Okay," I easily comply, wrapping my arms around her slender waist.

It feels so good to be this close to her after an entire day of not knowing where we stand. I breathe in the vanilla scent of her hair and relish this moment before the inevitable storm rolls in.

I move us over to cuddle in her bed, which barely has room for the two of us. My hands alternate between rubbing her back and soothingly playing with her silky hair. We lie in silence and just enjoy the simple touching that I have missed most of the day.

"Whatever it is, Claire, it'll be alright."

"No!" she shouts, detaching herself from me. She scoots off my legs and bends hers along the end of the bed. "Everyone keeps telling me that, but it is not a guarantee. You don't know that it is going to be okay. I feel like the walls are closing in on me, and I am tired of keeping this secret. I'm going to go insane if I wait any longer."

I swallow hard and brace myself for whatever she is about to drop on me. "What is it?" I demand, my voice gruff.

Flinging herself off the bed, she stomps to her little kitchen, yanks open a drawer, and whips out what appears to be some plastic sticks. Spinning around, she waves them at me as if they are on fire, as tears cascade in angry rivers down her cheeks. "I am pregnant," she wails.

I flinch at Claire's declaration and allow the realization to soak into my brain. How can it be that three little words can cause my life to implode in the short length of time it takes to breathe them into existence?

I couldn't have heard her correctly. There is no way. I obviously got this all wrong.

My eyes alternate between every affirmative test and Claire, silently hoping this is all some colossal prank. But when the only thing reflected back to me is fear, I know I'm living out the one scenario I just didn't see coming.

"I'm pregnant, Nic," she repeats, probably alarmed over my utter silence.

"Isn't that theoretically impossible?" I challenge, watching her toss the test sticks onto the counter. "You're on the pill. You've been taking it, right? All this time I've been trusting you to take it, Claire."

"It's not one hundred percent effective."

Dammit, I know this. I'm not an idiot, yet right now I feel so stupid for allowing this to happen. I take a deep breath and put my head into my hands as I come to terms with her declaration. I don't know what I was expecting, but I was not expecting this.

"You're sure?"

"Yes," she weeps. "I'm sure. And it gets worse."

Oh, hell no. "Well, quit delaying," I snap.

"I don't know who the father is..."

KNOCK.

KNOCK.

"Let me in, Claire!" a voice bellows from the other side of the door.

21

CLAIRE

"Go away, Ethan!" I yell back, only making him pound harder. He's going to break my door, or Nic is going to break him.

"What does he want?" Nic asks, staring at me over this turn of events. "And how does he know you live here?"

"I don't know." My voice quivers. "I'm sure it's not hard to figure out."

"Open this door or I'll show the police every second of video footage of you entering my property and assaulting me! And I will, dammit. I'm also done with you stalking Deena. She told me all about it!"

Nic's imploring eyes lock in on mine. "You hit him?"

"He has been harassing me for weeks," I say quickly in defense—mainly to myself but also to Nic. "And I never stalked Deena. She was at The Shack, but I didn't know she was going to be there." My voice is frantic.

I never considered Ethan had any proof of me at his property. I'm so stupid; of course he would record it.

Anyone as financially loaded as he seems would savor that level of protection for his assets. In fact, he basically encouraged me to come after him. He wanted concrete blackmail material—that asshole! I think back to when we ran into each other at the hair salon. Deena mentioned a lawyer. Was this their ultimate plan for revenge?

"You should have fucking told me he was harassing you."

I quiver over his snapping words. Everyone is angry with me tonight, and I'm not sure how much more I can take.

KNOCK.

I stomp to the door before someone decides to call for security. I don't even want to know what my neighbors think of me. It's not like we really chat, other than when our paths cross in the hall on the way to our residences.

I open the door a few inches to see Ethan's angry face glaring back at me.

"Open the fucking door," he grinds out, pushing it open only to be stopped by Nic's strong arm.

"What do you want, Maxwell? I've warned you already with my fists to leave her the hell alone."

"Oh, she didn't tell you that she trespassed on my personal property? I have all the proof on my security system and will use it to bring you both down. I'll do every-thing I can to protect Deena. She's carrying my child."

His snarling words freeze me to my core, causing the once warm blood to ice over in my veins. How? Why?

Fuck.

If my stumbling reaction doesn't serve as its own truth serum, with the layers of my heart peeled back for examination, then the evidence sprawled out on the kitchen counter will do it.

"You've got to be fucking kidding me," Ethan barks, pointing to the test sticks. "You're carrying my offspring too?"

I feel my body sway, as every vulnerable cell in my body ignites into a fiery ball of despair. "I…"

"Dammit, Claire," Nic hisses.

My legs turn to Jell-O and my knees buckle. I fold like an exhausted accordion, plummeting toward the floor of my toaster-sized apartment, too weak to handle the realization of how a few bad choices can culminate into this one pivotal moment in time.

"Claire!"

Strong arms brace me, lifting me and carrying me to a sea of pillows.

"Stay the fuck away from her."

I try to lift my head, but it is anchored to my bed, unable to be moved. I curl awkwardly into a ball, as the chaos around me ensues.

"She could be carrying my child."

"She could be carrying *my* child."

I force my eyes to open, only to see the two potential fathers for my child squaring off in some testosterone-filled showdown. Guilt shakes through my system.

"I'm sorry," I mouth but the sound doesn't make it out of my throat. I feel like I could throw up. Just seeing the two men together again brings up a lot of emotions that I was feeling in Vegas. Knowing that they both are mad at me for different reasons makes me want to just move away and forget that I even shook up their lives this drastically. I feel responsible for getting pregnant—even though logically I know it takes two. And in this case, there are three people involved—and an innocent one who has yet to be born.

"Little whore is a freaking sperm receptacle. She'll spread her legs for anyone with a pulse. If I was smart, I would've—"

I hear Nic hiss and then watch as he darts toward my ex in a fit of rage. His body collides with Ethan's, sending him to the floor. I roll off the bed and join the scene, letting out a yelp as I dodge the men and their swinging fists.

"Stay back, Claire," Nic warns, as he punches Ethan in the face.

I wince as I watch his lip open up. "Please stop, you both are going to get hurt." According to Angie, they've been in this situation before in Vegas, but this round I have a front-row view.

"You are going to pay," Ethan snarls.

Nic hits him again, shutting him up. He jerks him up by his shirt collar, making Ethan's eyes pop open. "You threaten Claire again, and I'll break you. Stay the fuck away from her. Don't look at her. Don't even think about her. Your role right now in this whole situation is to just shut your mouth before I shut it for you. Do you understand?"

"There's not a judge in this country that will see your little bitch as a fit mother." He wipes at the blood dribbling down his chin. "So you better hope I'm not the father, because I guarantee I'll fight to have both of my babies under my roof. And I'll win. Siblings belong together— even if they have different mommies. You'd have to be crazy to think I'd share any custody with someone as unfit as"—he points my way—"Claire."

I refuse to look into his beady eyes and give away any of my emotions. He is an exploiter, a manipulator, and a narcissistic pig—and that is putting it mildly.

"I'll get us a paternity test scheduled," Nic says with defeat.

I can feel him pulling back. I can sense the utter shock he once harbored now shifting to the logistical nightmare being with me will now cost him.

And deep down inside, I know I'm not worth it.

"May the best man win," Ethan snickers, making me want to hurl my fist at his face. "Chat later, Claire. Just let me know when to show up for my test. Oh, are there any other candidates? I know how much you like men."

Picking Ethan up, Nic tosses him out into the hallway, growls out some unintelligible words of another warning, and then slams my door shut. Shaking off his hand, he rests his back against the frame.

"Any more surprises I should know about?"

I look up at a broken Nic and shake my head no. "I wanted to tell you, but I just—"

"Didn't think I would make a good father?" he probes.

"What? No," I yell back. "You made it clear to me that you never wanted kids. I was pulling away from you because I didn't want us to get more involved, but you are relentless and kept pursuing me."

"Yeah, before I had all the information."

I frown. "Yeah. But now you know everything."

"I'm going to go," he says sadly. "I have too much on my mind right now to think clearly. Last thing I need to do is something I'll regret in the morning."

"Okay..."

I move toward my door and watch the best man I have ever met walk through it, and something tells me he won't be back any time soon.

I wake up to the sound of my own heart breaking as I cry out from a nasty nightmare. I sit up in bed and pant for air, as I make sense of my reality and the dream. Problem is that my reality could easily turn into a living nightmare if Ethan is the father—and he pretty much confirmed it hours ago. I can't tell if Ethan really wants to father my child or just wants to punish me. Regardless, I trust his threats. He will stop at nothing to strip me of my rights if he has any say about it.

After a little searching on the Internet last night, I was able to determine that a paternity test could be done at any of the local hospitals. I just need the potential fathers to show up and get an oral swab test done—while I am subjected to the blood test. It is a small price to pay for peace of mind throughout the rest of the pregnancy, but I need to get through this wedding first. I have enough on my plate as is, and avoidance seems like self-care right now.

From my nightstand, I grab my phone and open it to find a group text from Nic's mom requesting that all bridal party members arrive at her house the day before the rehearsal dinner for an overnight stay. When Donna and I sat down to finalize plans for the rehearsal dinner, it was a lack in judgment for me to suggest doing it at her house in Hillsboro. This was me setting this whole thing into motion. I just didn't think ahead about my heart's reaction to seeing

Nic's childhood home again, but this time—knowing that our relationship is damaged—is another reminder of all that I have lost.

I didn't just lose the man. I also lost the chance of a brighter tomorrow.

I roll out of bed and bump into my nightstand on the way to the bathroom. My apartment feels smaller and smaller these days, and I haven't even purchased anything for the baby yet. After having Ethan visit last night, I know now that having him as the father is the absolute worst nightmare scenario out of my two options. Even if Nic and I don't end up together, he is by far the better choice. At the very least, I won't have to fight to be in my child's life. How it took me this long to realize that is yet another bad judgment on my part. It wouldn't surprise me if Ethan is happy I'm pregnant just to hold it over me for leverage.

Warming up the shower, I get undressed and look into the slowly steaming mirror. I have a barely-there bump forming in my lower tummy that stands out because my frame is so small. It is hard to imagine what it'll look like when I can't see my feet. I should be thankful that I'll have someone to love me without conditions. What I lacked growing up, I promise to never withhold from my child— even if I can't get along with their father. I want this baby to know it is loved and cherished, and despite being conceived with less than ideal circumstances, I will spend forever proving to it that it is wanted.

Getting ready in the morning takes more time these days, as I struggle to keep on top of the nausea. I have found that if I eat some crackers and drink my lemon-wedged ginger ale, I can diminish the morning sickness. With all of the drama that went down last night, I am dreading going into work today and possibly running into Nic. I promised Angie that there would be no drama for her wedding, and if I see him and burst into tears, that isn't exactly keeping everything civil. I'm not sure I can do chill right now. I have to keep my emotions in check, but it feels like I am one harsh look away from a breakdown.

Aside from the bleeding after the fall, I have not had any more spotting. I know it can happen again, but for now I am glad everything seems back to normal.

In a bin under my bed, I find a red strapless sundress, which has a little silver butterfly embellishment under the decorative elastic band of my chest. I pair it with white slip-on sandals that are flat enough to hopefully keep me from falling down.

When I am ready, I text Angie to see if she wants to meet up at the coffee shop that is in the parallel tower at HH.

I make it through security and head up to the office to drop off my bag before heading over to meet Angie. At my desk, I find a little envelope addressed to me with the most beautiful calligraphy handwriting. I open up the back flap and remove a little card. I read the message—*Sometimes a surprise is better than the expected.*

Turning the card over, I look for a sender. Nothing. I'm not surprised by the lack of signature. Nic has been known to put surprises in my office in the past and not take credit.

I put the card back into the envelope and tuck it inside the drawer of my desk. Maybe Nic left this for me yesterday when the secrets were still concealed between the two of us. Maybe he put it there this morning after learning about the surprise baby. Regardless, it doesn't prove anything has gotten better between us. We are as rocky as we have been from the start. Just because you know the avalanche is going to hit you doesn't make the pain of it any more bearable. I can brace myself all I want for the paternity test results, but I already know that I'm going to have to work overtime to prove to this baby that it is not a mistake.

Angie is waiting for me when I get down to the other building's lobby.

"Hey you."

"Hi," I say softly.

"How did last night go?"

I suck in air through my teeth, weighing with myself how much to divulge. Keeping secrets from her hasn't worked out in my favor thus far, so I opt for the abridged version. "As awkwardly as you could imagine. Nic was unhappy I kept the pregnancy from him, Ethan showed up to threaten me and announce he got Deena pregnant, and then Nic punched him in the face, yada yada."

"Dang. Deena is pregnant? Holy hell."

"Yup. Oh, and Ethan is going to use the video footage he gathered of me trespassing at his house to prove I'm unfit—if he's the father. He wants sole custody."

The color drains from Angie's face. I need to change the subject.

"But at least both men know the truth. Ethan could be bluffing." He's not. But I can pretend. "I just ask that you keep Graham in the dark until I get through my wedding duties. Then, I promise to put on my big-girl panties and face him head-on. I hate asking you to do this, but the wedding is days away."

Angie nods. "No, this makes sense. I think you aren't giving Graham enough credit, but I know your past history with him is hard to forget. So I get it. I can keep quiet for a few days."

"Thank you." I sigh with relief. I look up at the menu and see a whole list of drinks and breakfast items to meet a variety of dietary restrictions. "What's good here?"

"Rumor has it, everything. Which could get dangerous just being a few minutes' walk from our office. You know my weakness is food."

"Ha," I respond, moving up in line to get a decaf iced latte with oat milk. "Pretty sure all of my food hang-ups got thrown out the window with this"—I lean in closer to only allow Angie to hear—"*pregnancy*."

"How are you feeling?" Angie asks, after she orders her blended mocha drink with extra whipped cream.

"A little better than I did two weeks ago. I think knowing what is causing all of the nausea has helped me stay on top of it."

"Well, that's good."

"I still can't believe my pill failed. The shock has not worn off entirely."

"Sometimes surprises are not always bad," she says softly, with a smile.

"You didn't leave a note on my desk, did you?"

Angie shakes her head. "No. Was it a love note?"

"Nope. Just an odd thing about a surprise being better than the expected. No signature."

"Have you received these notes in the past?"

"Yeah, but they have always been from Nic. Must be him too. Although, I don't really know where we stand. He didn't exactly take the multiple truth bombs as gracefully as I would have hoped. Actually," I say, shaking my head, "maybe he did. I am just so mixed up in my emotions, and I am ready for my life to get back to a healthy rhythm."

"Hi, Claire," a voice from behind us greets.

I pivot and see Dan approaching from the drink pickup area. Brenna is beside him and smiles. "Oh, hi." The wheels in my head turn over the possibility of them dating. Nothing like a little office romance. Plus, she seems to have just the right amount of social awkwardness to blend with his.

"Good seeing you, Miss McFee," he says to Angie who smiles and waves. He gestures toward his to-go cup of coffee. "Looks like great minds think alike."

"Yeah," I say and then wave bye to them as they leave.

I continue walking with Angie back to our office space. We have a lot of delegating to do today, since we are both taking a couple of days off this week to prepare for the weekend's festivities.

"What was that about with Dan King?" she asks, her tone serious.

"He was just saying hi."

She turns toward me and tilts her head. "You don't honestly believe that, right? He looked at you like"—she pauses to think of the right words—"you were single."

"To him I am, Angie. No one really knows I was ever with Nic unless they were paying me any type of real attention."

"Yeah, I guess that is true. I haven't heard any rumors, and you know how my ears perk up for drama."

I laugh. "I hope our show renews for the summer. I miss our Monday night rituals."

"Same, girl, same."

"The girl walking with Dan is Nic's assistant, Brenna. Maybe a little office romance is what we need to spice up the drama around here."

Angie laughs. "Yeah, because we don't have anything else to focus our minds on."

I take a sip of my latte. "We both know a little drama never hurt anybody."

But then I think about Brenna being Nic's personal assistant and Dan King being Nic's second-in-command. They keep popping up in the building around me, and it is starting to make sense to me as to how Nic is getting so much of his information about me. He is probably using one or both of them as spies.

I am not Nic's pet project to worry about, and I sure as hell am not having a shadow. This craziness stops today.

22

NIC

"You have proven to me that you are ready for the next level," I tell Dan, who arrived right on time to my office for an in-person meeting. He shared with me last night that Kevin was showing signs of retaliation, but more importantly, he had enough evidence that will help with my investigation into whether or not Tyler is helping.

"Thank you, sir. I will do my best."

With my uncertainness with Tyler, I need to have full confidence in the decisions I make and the people I trust. Right now, I have less than a handful of men I'd consider in that category. Unfortunately, Asher is in California and working remotely to help me figure out my hang-ups with Tyler. Something just seems very off.

"I'll be gone on Thursday and Friday of this week. I will be heading out of town for a family wedding."

"Mr. Hoffman and Miss McFee's, correct?" Dan asks.

"That's correct." I lean back into my leather chair and tap my finger along my jawline. "I need you to keep this place running smoothly without us here. You have already shown great potential and leadership skills. I trust that you will conduct business as professionally as you can, while being the interim boss to all of the security staff until I am available again on Monday."

"You can count on me."

"If there are any issues, contact me—not Graham," I explain.

"Understood," Dan says with a nod of his head.

"If you can handle this with us gone, then there may be more opportunities and a bigger bump in your salary."

"I'm up for the challenge."

As soon as Dan exits my office, I pull up all of the video footage from the various cameras I have around the building, just hoping to get a glimpse of Claire. She frequented my dreams last night, and as much as I am frustrated with the whole situation, I still need to see her. Not being able to adequately track her has caused me some anxiety, especially now that I know she is pregnant with what could be my child.

I haven't had a lot of time to process all of the information she dropped on me all at once, but my feelings for her have not gone away. Sure, things are less than ideal, but I still care about her and want what is best for her—even if what is best may not be me. I'm just protective of my own heart and not sure I want to go down the road of imagining every worst-case scenario prior to knowing all of the facts.

I'm about to leave my office for a trip to the break room when my phone buzzes with an incoming text. I glance down at the screen and see that it is from Collins.

Collins: Can I meet with you to discuss the wedding logistics?

Nic: Yes. My office?

Collins: I can be there in ten minutes.

Nic: Sounds good

I fill up my ceramic mug with the fresh coffee that Brenna has brewed and touch base with her at her desk.

"Everything seem up to par here?" I ask her, while she stops typing at her computer to give me her full attention.

"Yes, sir."

"And the overall employee climate?" I probe.

"Seems positive from what I've been noticing," she says with a smile. "I saw on the calendar that you are taking off an extra day this week, in addition to Friday. Anything I need to do while you are gone?"

"Just keep doing what you are doing, Brenna. You are doing a great job."

Her face beams with pride. "Thank you, sir."

When Collins steps off the elevator, I escort him into my office and we sit on the couches instead of at my actual desk.

"We will be heading to Hillsboro a day early, as you saw in the group text from my mom."

Collins nods and pulls out his phone to what I assume is the calendar. The bridal party for the wedding is small. Collins and I are the groomsmen, while Claire and Penny are bridesmaids.

"Graham said that Penny is released from the facility and is staying with your parents?"

"Yes, that's correct. She actually got awarded an extended release. This is the biggest one yet. But she's itching for a full discharge."

Collins nods. "I just hope it isn't too soon."

He has been with Graham and me through all of Penny's recovery. On many occasions, Collins has visited the facility in Seattle and provided updates on Penny's progress. Granted, it's in her best interest that she isn't made privy to these details.

"I agree. She wants to be on her own. Graham and I will have to sit down and discuss how we can make sure she stays safe while still having independence once everything is official. Penny has always been a free spirit. Anyway, we need to make sure all news outlets are far away from the mansion where the ceremony and reception will take place. I have hired a few men to pose as waiters to make sure that nothing goes wrong and no paparazzi ruin the intimacy that Graham and Angie want."

"I can definitely be on the lookout as well. I'm sure the photographers will be lined up at the gate, trying to sneak a glance."

"Yeah," I say with a sigh. "We can only do so much without actually making a scene. I made some promises about being on my best behavior, but if you see something that needs handled, by all means, *handle* it."

"Here's to hoping that there is no drama," Collins says with a sigh.

Knock.

Knock, knock.

We turn to the sound coming from behind the door.

"Mr. Hoffman?"

"Come in, Brenna," I direct.

"Sorry to interrupt." She pauses and rocks on her heels. "But can I—"

Collins gives me a wave and walks toward the door. "I'll chat with you later."

"Sounds good." Once he leaves, I get up from the couch and make my way over to my desk, before turning my attention back to Brenna. "What's up?"

"I think Miss Nettles suspects me of watching her."

Sitting down, I tap my fingers along the polished surface. "Why do you say that?"

She takes a deep breath. I'm not mad, so I don't know why she is so nervous around me. Well, actually I do know why. I have a bit of a reputation.

"It's just a feeling. And from the movement I see on the cameras, Claire is the only one on the elevator and she pressed the button for the Security floor."

"If that's the case, send her in." It's not like I've gotten any work done today thus far. Might as well be graced by Claire's temper on top of everything else. I can bet that she is pissed off over something and ready to brawl.

Brenna nods and leaves. She is very good at her job, so I imagine if she thinks Claire knows, then she knows. It was only a matter of time before my girl caught on. She already figured out the trackers.

Leaning back in my chair, I wait for my girl to make her way through the—

BAM.

The door slams behind Claire as she saunters closer to me and flops down into the cushioned chair.

I prop my hands up behind my head and relax even more. She hates it when I am cool and confident. Drives her mad. I would be fooling myself if I said I didn't like to toy with her on occasion. I know I shouldn't, but any emotion I can pull from her—even if it is a negative one—is better than being ignored by her. I cannot stand when she refuses to talk to me. By the sparkle in her eyes, I can tell she has a lot to say.

Seeing her so fragile yesterday caused me to plummet toward my breaking point. Sure, the entire situation sucks, but no matter what happens, I will always try to protect Claire.

"We need to talk," she announces, eyeing up the monitors behind me. I had enough sense to turn off all of the video footage. She doesn't need to know the real extent of my obsession.

"Something tells me it doesn't involve the stock market."

"You are correct," she answers tersely.

"Then what brings you here, Claire? Want to share breakfast together?"

"No."

"Revisit the top of my desk while I eat you out?" I can't help but meet her glare with a smirk.

"No."

"Bend you over the chair, while I pump into you from behind?"

"I'm pregnant, Nic."

"You told me last night," I say matter-of-factly. While I

still need time to process the situation, I haven't stopped thinking about her. There's no eradicating this feisty ball of sass from my mind.

"You can't pretend the baby doesn't exist."

"I don't pretend."

"Then quit flirting with me."

"Why? You think being pregnant somehow is making you less attractive? Nope. Quite the opposite."

How did I miss the glow before now? She is radiant.

Claire tosses her hands into the air, but it doesn't distract me from seeing the hints of pink warming her cheeks. "That's the problem with you! You think this whole thing is some joke. There are lives involved, Nic. Real lives. You act like you own the place. Stomping around the building and summoning me and then when I do show up freely, you make it so impossible for me to even want to stay. You and your, your…"

"My?"

"Your broody emo self," she blurts out. "You need to find a new hobby because it ain't me! Quit having me followed. Quit keeping tabs. And for the love of every techno nerd in the universe, quit tracking me! I can feel eyes watching me, and it is making me crazy. Everywhere I look I think I see someone who works for you."

I shrug. "Umm, they probably do work for me."

It takes everything in me not to burst out into a full-blown smile. Claire is so freaking cute when she is irritated and stuttering about all the little things that piss her off.

"But can we back up to the 'techno nerd' part?" I add air quotes just for fun. "What is that? You have piqued my interest."

"Someone who gets excited over technology and then uses it against people for shits and giggles."

"Is that what I'm doing, Claire?"

"Nic, if I knew what you were doing, I wouldn't be here now."

"Just to clarify, you don't want me to order breakfast?"

She lets out a sigh, and if she had something in her hand to throw, it probably would be aimed directly at me. "We can't keep doing this. Graham and Angie know. We can't do this to them days before their wedding. K'bye." She gets up to leave but I beat her to the door.

"Hold up," I say, lifting my hands to mimic a peaceful surrender. "How does Graham have anything to do with this? Keep him out of our business."

"He's protecting Angie from any fallout that may occur from us. We need to stop. Cut ties and just learn to coexist. It's not like our paths really have to cross while I work here. So just stay out of my way and I will stay out of yours."

"Is that what you really want?"

Her eyes dim and she tucks her bottom lip under her top row of teeth, while she nods.

I smack the door with my curled-up fist, startling her unintentionally. I inwardly scold myself. I would never hit her. Why is she so timid all of a sudden? "Dammit, Claire. When are you going to stop doing what everyone expects you to do and follow your own path? What has you so afraid right now?"

"You don't get it, Nic. People like you just don't."

"What do you mean *people like me*?"

She turns away from me and paces, brushing her hair back over her shoulder in a nervous gesture. "I can't find a new job. This is all I have. And I need the money. You probably don't understand what it is like to live from paycheck to paycheck, but that is where I'm at right now. I have no safety net to fall into—*none*. So please do not push me so much that I am forced to leave the job I have and love right now. *Please*. Just let me work, and stop showing special interest in me by hiring workers in-house to spy."

"If you need money, I can—"

"No," she says with finality. "I am an adult. Adults handle their own problems. Right now I need to focus on working and getting through the rehearsal dinner and wedding without Angie noticing any of this tension that we keep building between us."

"It's called chemistry," I add.

"You are insane."

"I like to refer to myself as spirited."

Claire stops pacing to look at me. Then her lips curve into the most beautiful smile. She looks so pretty with her face slightly flushed from all of the movement that I want to scoop her up into my arms and make all of her troubles disappear.

I don't have all the answers—no one does—but everything inside me is screaming for me to not let her slip away.

"I've got to go," she mumbles, allowing the smile to fade.

I watch as she exits my office, and the void is almost unbearable. I have so much to process but one thing is for certain—my feelings for Claire are not going away. If anything, they are just getting stronger.

I cut out early from work for the first time since becoming the head. I just can't do my job efficiently with the amount on my mind. Tyler requested to meet up, so I take him up on the offer and join him near the waterfront, where we will have some privacy to hash things out.

"I have a gnawing suspicion that you don't trust me anymore," he says solemnly. He kicks up some stones with the toe of his shoe. "And I wanted to meet to discuss things man-to-man."

"Have you been completely honest with me?" I ask bluntly.

"Yes, sir. I have."

Tyler doesn't answer too quickly but he also doesn't hesitate with his response. From his eyes, I can tell that he is genuinely concerned that I don't believe in his integrity.

"Good. Because if you ever think about crossing over and becoming disloyal, then there will be hell to pay."

"I have no idea why there is any controversy between us. You hired me to watch Miss Nettles, and so far, I have done just that. I report to you every finding. I follow your orders. I'm in shock that there is anything wrong, except there is, isn't there?"

I clear my throat. "Yeah."

"I know you have taken me off my typical duties," he says softly. "I'm not an idiot."

"The day that there was a power glitch at HH, I found some stills of someone who looked like you trying to enter through the back door without permission."

"I would love to look at the photos. Whoever it was, wasn't me. I swear it. I'd never do that. You've been more to me than just an employer, and while I wouldn't go as far as saying we're friends, I felt like it was moving in that direction."

I nod. He's right. But I have to have trust in order to move past this, and right now, no matter who tells me otherwise, I have an eerie feeling that something is just not right.

"Even if you aren't the mole, I don't know how I can get my mind to trust you again."

"So you are firing me?"

"You will get a decent severance package."

Tyler stops and rubs his hair at the back of his neck, looking out at the boats floating down the river. "You know I have never done any of this for the money. All of my references should have checked out, and I have a stellar record of doing good work. Yet, whoever is trying to make you doubt me is the real winner. Because it obviously worked."

"Sometimes it's easier to doubt someone than to trust someone."

"Isn't that the truth."

Tyler shakes my hand but doesn't say goodbye as his eyes connect with mine. I feel the paper in my palm but discreetly keep it concealed. As he retreats back to where he parked his car, I carefully slide my hands into my pockets.

I have a growing pit in my stomach that tells me I may have done the wrong thing. Someone is out to get to either Graham or me, and I will find out who it is. I just need to get my head on straight. Claire's news last night is not helping me think clearly. It feels like the answer is right in front of my face and I just can't see it.

When I'm safely back inside my car, I pull out the note from my pocket and unfold it.

I'll do anything to prove my innocence. -Tyler

Just seeing Tyler's note has me more confused than ever. And why is he being so secretive about passing it to me? Unless...

He knew we were followed and being watched. He staged this meeting publicly to try to dispel doubt from himself and warn me that he's working alongside me but in a parallel universe.

Scrolling through my contacts, I click on the call button for Asher.

"I think Tyler's innocent," I say with confidence.

"Well, that's fucking obvious."

"But that still leaves the issue of figuring out who is trying to frame him."

I end the call and pull out of the parking lot. When I get back to my apartment, I am mentally drained and feeling like the wind has left my sails. If I'm going to eliminate the mole from HH, I have to play my cards right and learn about motives first.

Opening up my laptop, I start my own database search. I type in the name of my previously fired employee, Eugene Whitacker, and continue down the list of other people fired. If someone is going to try to take me down, they probably have some axe to grind.

While there was so much doubt cast on Tyler, I have to put my trust in Asher who introduced us to each other.

Looking at my screen, my eyes glaze over as I scan through lists upon lists of documents and photos—all featuring Eugene. Except he's not alone in some of his photos...

He's with my personal assistant, Brenna.

Now what are the odds that my ex-employee and my current assistant would be in a relationship?

Opening up my phone, I send off a text to Collins.

Nic: I need my personal assistant Brenna investigated as well as Eugene and Dan

Collins: On it

Nic: It appears from the time stamps of some photos I've found on a search that Brenna's dating my ex-employee who was vying for my current lead position

Collins: I'll see what I can find out from my own digging

Nic: Thanks, man. I appreciate it

When my mind can't handle any more bombshells, I send a message out to Brenna to take a few days off and move to my bedroom to pack my bag for Hillsboro. With the wedding coming up, it isn't that farfetched that I wouldn't need my personal assistant in the office.

My mind wanders to how Tara was let into my office. It would make sense that Brenna allowed her access to that floor. As my assistant, she definitely has special privileges.

Dammit.

But why would she risk the chance of experiencing the repercussions from her betrayal—unless it was for love?

Was Brenna trying to get hired at HH just to serve as an instrument for Eugene to execute his rage for getting fired?

Opening up the closet in the bathroom, I find my bottle of ibuprofen and toss back three. I guzzle some water from the tap just to get the pills down. The headache forming in the back of my head is already moving toward my temple.

When the pain has seemed to settle, I finalize the arrangement for my wedding gift to Graham and Angie. I decided that for someone who really has everything—or can buy anything—that the best gift to give is a legacy rather than a trinket or houseware appliance. Thus, I've created a scholarship fund for students who lost their mothers to cancer, in honor of Angie's mom who passed away when she was just a young girl. I have hired a banker and manager to handle the funds and a committee to handle the entries they will receive each spring for potential students wanting to enter college. I hope that Angie will be able to appreciate the memory of her mom and the opportunity to help other students get through a time in their life that is a huge milestone.

I hit up my home gym and punch the hell out of my weighted bag, growing fatigued faster than normal even with my headache gone. After my shower, I do some work from my office and end up crashing into bed at the earliest time that I can ever remember.

23

CLAIRE

When the limo arrives at the curb outside of my apartment building, I swallow the knot in my throat and tell myself that I can get through the next few days unscathed. I just need to keep any focus off myself and put it on the bride-to-be, who cannot look any happier than when I see her as I enter the car.

"You look incredible," she says cheerfully, her eyes full of love and admiration. "You seriously can wear any color."

The one thing about being around Angie is that she makes you feel good, and it goes way beyond the surface level. She gives me hope for a brighter future because I see how she has turned her life around, despite getting knocked on her ass repeatedly. Therapy has done wonders for her addiction and her ability to cope with stress. Her strength radiates with how she talks to people and builds them up. Once Plus None gets some traction, I can see her volunteering at a clinic to help with group therapy sessions. She is a giver at heart.

I slide into the leather seat beside Nic and smooth down my long emerald-green maxi dress. It is made of a stretchy material and designed to be fitted around my chest and loose around my ribcage and down. Just a few of us in this vehicle know of the truth I am hiding underneath the cottony fabric, but after this weekend, the whole world will eventually know.

Graham pops a bottle of champagne, and I hold my breath as he passes around flutes.

"None for me," I say meekly. "Still watching everything I eat until after this wedding."

No one gives me a hard time. I guess the only person other than Collins—who is behind the wheel—who doesn't know I'm pregnant is Graham. With a history of being a finicky eater, no one should be surprised that I am turning down the empty calories.

"I can't believe I am going to be yours in a couple of days," Angie says to Graham, snuggling in closer to his side.

"Sweetheart, you have been mine since I first saw you out by that pool."

I melt over their epic love story and feel myself blushing from being a witness to their cuteness. Their love is so pure that anyone who is part of their world would easily be able to find hope in the possibility of finding it themselves. I thought I had it with Nic, but in order for things to work, it has to be mutual. With the addition of the baby, things are complicated. Maybe his love is dependent on the baby being his. We haven't had a real chance to chat about it, and using avoidance seems to be the best coping mechanism until we get through this weekend.

I am watching the scenery pass by out the window when I feel a gentle hand on top of mine. I look down and see Nic's. When my eyes meet his, I am shocked by his PDA in front of his brother, but when I glance over at Graham, he is consumed with all things Angie. Can that man be any more smitten?

"Here's some ginger ale," he says, handing me a glass with his other hand. He pulls the one that is on top of mine away, and I instantly miss the physical touch, although it is the epitome of innocence and friendship.

I accept the drink and take my first sip. "Thank you."

"You're not getting motion sick, are you?"

I shake my head. "I'm good actually."

He gives me a weak smile, and my insides twist at how platonic his expression is. I don't know what I am to him anymore, but I know that things are different and will never be the same. While I can't see into the future, it is at this moment that I know I will regret ever getting involved with Nic if things never work out between us. I can't be *just friends* with him. I can't even be in his presence without comparing what we were to what we are now, and the difference is enough to make me nauseous.

"That's good."

I turn my attention back to him. "Hmm?"

He gives me a lopsided smile. "It's good that you aren't sick," he explains.

"Oh...thanks."

"You look exquisite."

I cough a little as the ginger ale tickles my throat. "Thank you."

"Angie's right. You can wear any color and always look amazing."

"You are full of compliments today," I say with a smirk.

"Just being honest."

"Too bad you weren't honest with me about the trackers." I'm not as angry as I was the night Nic showed up at my apartment with a peace offering of food. However, I'm still rather sulky. It's pointless to imagine going through life with that level of surveillance because everything that I thought of prebaby will never be part of my vision for the future.

The baby changes everything.

"Too bad you weren't honest with me over the—" His eyes drift to my belly.

I swallow hard. He's right. But so am I. I settle into my seat and continue to sip my ginger ale. The only thing missing is the lemon slices I've learned to love; now I don't want to drink it any other way.

It is an easy ride out of the city and to the smaller town of Hillsboro, where Donna and Germain Hoffman reside. I haven't been to their house since Christmas, when Ethan was too busy to spend the holiday with me. In fact, he never wanted to spend any special occasions together. How I kept him around for as long as I did is a true indication of my own lack of self-worth. Pretty sure there was a red flag the size of Oregon waving to let me know that he wasn't *the one*. And I still pushed my gut feeling away.

When we arrive at the house, Donna is waiting in the driveway in her slippers, looking to bum rush the limo in excitement. Penny joins her, probably coming out to see what the high-pitched screams are all about. I know I would be curious at what type of creature could make such a sound.

I'm waiting for the day that the Hoffman brothers react to a scene like their mother does. She definitely has enough excitement bubbling inside her for everyone.

We all embrace, and it isn't until I step away from the group that I notice Germain approaching with a huge smile on his face.

"It's so good to see you again, Claire," he greets. He skips my extended hand and envelops me in a hug. I didn't realize how much I needed one until we let go.

"Thank you for having me."

He pulls back to study my face. "You are always welcome here. Any time," he says with a gentleness to his tone. If he knows something, it's only because of my paranoia, and not because he gives any indication.

Tears well up in my eyes, but luckily I can keep them hidden until I collect my thoughts. Nic's parents sure know how to express their love and appreciation—through both words and their actions. I'm not used to it, so being receptive to their affection takes a bit of work on my part. I wonder how I would have turned out if my parents loved me with an ounce of what the Hoffman parents love their children. It's impossible for me not to compare.

Despite calling the Hoffman boys barbarians on more than one occasion, I can see where they get their gentle-giant vibe, just by looking at Germain's eyes. He is calm and collected, yet staid and proud. As he should be—he has raised a wonderful family.

Penny approaches me after Germain lets me go. "So

glad you are here to help balance out my mom," she whispers.

Penny is in loose-fitting, nondescript clothes. However, her angelic face, with her broody expression, hints at her story. Penny has been through some things, and while I know some of the story from Angie, I also know that there is more that neither of them are sharing.

"Oh yeah?" I ask, unsure what she means.

"Yup, she basically has been running around here all morning making sure she has everything perfect. And for some reason you calm her down."

"What? Me?" I cannot possibly have heard her correctly. I usually have the opposite of a calming effect. Hell, Nic pretty much tells me I drive him insane on the daily.

"Yeah, she holds your opinion up on a pedestal, so if you find approval in what she did inside, then she will relax the rest of the evening knowing that she accomplished the vision you tried to get across for Angie."

"Oh," I say, more to myself than to Penny. "I didn't realize she cared about what I thought, at least not to this magnitude."

Penny grabs my elbows and gives me a shake. "Um, yeah, she totally does. You are so creative with your style, and Angie has been talking so much about your endeavors with Plus None and all you have contributed thus far. Anyway, I digress. What I'm trying to say is, my mom values your opinion."

I smile back at Penny who is a bundle of nervous energy. While still rocking the more laid-back tomboyish look, she is always so elegant and thoughtful in her clothing choices. In fact, her aura is giving me an idea for another lifestyle box idea to bring up to Angie after the wedding. We can totally create a subscription box that caters to those who want that understated, confident look.

That is what Penny represents to me, or at least what she should. The girl is gorgeous with flawless skin and the most enchanting blue eyes. She appears shy, but I can see her coming out of her shell when given a safe opportunity. I'm not sure how the old Penny acted, but I'm hoping with time, she will learn how to fly again.

Already, Penny is a different person than when I met her for the first time over Christmas break. I know she has been through a lot, and getting back to normal is sometimes a struggle.

And then it dawns on me. I have been through hell too, and look at how I am still standing. We women are all warriors. I am definitely not the same person I was when I still lived in Virginia, and I am not even the same woman I was a couple of weeks ago. Life changes a person and helps mold us into hopefully better versions of ourselves. I don't want to regress. I don't want my past to be a roadblock for a better future.

"Come inside, everyone," Donna announces, linking arms with both me and Angie. She ushers us through the foyer and into the main living area, where she has decorated the entire room in white flowers. Huge glass lanterns rest on end tables and shelves, casting a warm glow. A pianist sits in the corner, playing instrumental love songs for us to enjoy. "I know this is just the night before the rehearsal, but I wanted it to be elegant and special, nonetheless. Even if we just order in some grub and play some rounds of family games."

I swallow hard over the announcement of games. I know how competitive the Hoffmans are, and I can already predict whose team I will be placed on. How am I going to survive the rest of this week when I still haven't had a good chance to make sense of it all?

"It is perfect," Angie announces, looking over all of the details that Donna put together. "You captured the essence of what I was looking for."

"You did a great job," I agree. "You really have an eye for making things pretty."

Donna beams from my praise and shows us all up to our rooms. On each door, she has custom-made name plaques, and I can't help but laugh when I see who is next door to me.

"Really Mom?" Graham says with a huff. "You are making Angie and me sleep in separate rooms?"

She makes a face at him. "Traditions, son."

I look over as Germain whispers to Nic, "Hundred bucks says that ain't gonna happen."

I resist smirking over their exchange, just in case Donna notices.

"Did you not read any of the wedding books I sent to you?" she asks him.

"Not a single page, Ma."

"Well, now that your evening is freed up,"—she chuckles—"maybe you can catch up on your leisure reading. I put a couple in your room on your nightstand."

We all laugh and then head back downstairs, congregating in the kitchen. Germain pulls open his liquor cabinet, and the men chat while serving themselves up some drinks.

"So, ladies, would you like to have tea with me?" Donna offers.

Penny and I nod.

"Sounds great," Angie says, speaking for all of us. She appears so thrilled with how things have turned out for the celebration.

We follow Donna into the living room where a tea cart is already set up. She serves up the tea, and we all add in our own sweeteners. Through my research, I have found that a little caffeine is fine for the baby, as long as it is consumed in moderation. I forgo the artificial sweeteners and just use a bit of honey and lemon slices. Angie pours in some flavored whiskey to spice her cup up a bit, and I laugh at Donna as she moves Angie's hand so more falls in.

"You guys want to get me drunk so I can lose at these epic family games," she fake whines. "You all see me as fierce competition."

I laugh. "We are all a bit competitive, aren't we?"

"And I would say I am the least competitive of the group," Penny snickers. "For me, it isn't about always winning. I just hate to lose."

"Don't we all," Donna agrees.

We relax on the sofas and chat about the plan for tomorrow. I sip my tea and sink into the cushions. It feels good to be in Hillsboro. The town is beautiful and quaint, which seems perfectly suited for Donna and Germain's personalities.

The guys join us as our conversation shifts to being less wedding business-y and more casual. I cross and uncross my legs as I feel Nic's gaze centered on me. I don't need to look. I know he is staring, just like he did at the cafe when I attempted to plan the bachelor and bachelorette parties.

"How about I go order some high-calorie takeout, and we can all relax? Tomorrow is a fancier dinner, but I thought tonight could be pajamas and games. How does that sound?"

"It sounds perfect," Angie says with excitement. "And I've been practicing my skills so I can be a better competitor."

"How did you know what to practice?" Germain asks.

"Oh, I just got better at bossing Graham around. So if it comes to any game requiring listening, he better nail it."

Everyone laughs, and we head to our individual rooms. Donna and Germain have done amazing upgrades to their house, and the modern features are beautiful, yet cozy and warm. Collins already delivered my suitcase, so when I enter my room, I find it resting on the window seat. I imagine that despite being a groomsman to Graham, he probably is forever in work mode and can't really shut it off. Maybe once the alcohol he consumed in the kitchen kicks in he will be able to unwind and have a good time. Even in a relaxed setting, he always looks ready to pounce.

I change into my soft velour pajama set with little hearts all over the fabric and freshen up in the ensuite bathroom. My room overlooks the back garden, which I am itching to explore whenever there is down time, and has a partial view of the pool. This trip already feels like a retreat, so maybe I will be able to relax and find some mental and emotional clarity.

When I arrive downstairs, Germain is already situating the score board. I am the first to arrive and notice that the teams are as I expected them to be. Angie is paired with Graham, Donna is with Germain, Penny partners with Collins, and I am teamed up with Nic.

Donna answers the doorbell and sets up a buffet between the living room and dining room. Three different types of salads, pizza, wings, and stuffed mushrooms are set out on the table, followed by a huge tray of miniature desserts. Everything looks amazing, and my stomach growls in anticipation of chowing down.

When everyone arrives downstairs, Germain silences the room with a whistling sound. "I'd like to make a toast," he says, holding up his glass. "To friends, to family, and to the future. Let love guide your ways and hope bring the spark of new possibilities."

"Cheers," everyone says in unison.

"And to Angie and Graham," Nic says, keeping his glass raised in the air. "Thank you for being a great example of taking a chance and having it pay off. Let those who are skeptics bear witness to your love and forever find hope."

"Here, here," Germain says, kissing Donna on the forehead.

I look around the room and see all of the smiling faces. The entire atmosphere is vibrant but calming. I could get used to this. Growing up, I never had a stable home. It was just a house. A lonely house without a heart.

I thought I would miss Virginia after I got back to Oregon and had a chance to decompress. Nope. I barely have any good memories there, so the emotional attachment is lacking. Thus, I don't miss it at all. What's to miss? Feeling like I am a burden and would have been better off if I were given up for adoption? It's not healthy to dwell on a dysfunctional past, so I push all of my ill thoughts into the back caverns of my mind. I can unpack them later or keep them buried forever.

I don't even realize that everyone is eating until Nic hands me a plate full of a little of everything. "I wasn't sure what you wanted. So I just kept adding stuff to it."

"Oh, thanks," I say, taking it from his hands. Nic just nods and takes a seat on the couch next to Penny. "You didn't have to do that." My words come out as an airy whisper. He really didn't have to serve me. And I wish he hadn't. Every nice gesture is blurring the lines between us, making it hard to see where I stand. If his mom wasn't so wrapped up in snapping photos of Angie and Graham, she might have noticed Nic's special treatment toward me. Does he want his family to notice? All of this uncertainty is messing with my head and causing me to question what I really want. There's no closure. There's no clean break. What I am in the middle of right now is a jumbled mess of emotions, what-ifs, and societal obligations.

I wait until everyone else finds their place and then sit on the armchair in the corner, alternating my time between eating and observing. It is interesting watching the Hoffman family dynamics unfold. Penny is an instigator and likes to add her two cents in wherever she can—if only for a reaction. Her personality is quirky, and I bet if we spent more time together, we could really have fun.

For the first time since meeting him, I notice that Collins can be normal. He and the guys are discussing spring sports and enjoying some beer. Just from the way he is sitting, I can tell he is unwinding. I am so used to seeing him being rigidly formal that being a witness to any other behavior seems a bit bizarre. He is not dressed in pajamas, but he definitely is more laid-back in his khakis and collared shirt. His sleeves are rolled up at his elbows, and the top two buttons are undone. From the little bit of skin that he has exposed, I can tell he is built. Shouldn't be surprising since he is basically Graham's bodyguard and right-hand man.

"Can you believe you will be getting married in just two days?" Donna asks Angie, who is beaming with happiness.

"It all seems so surreal," she admits. "Like I'm being awarded everything I've ever wanted."

I want that feeling of euphoria that Angie is currently basking in right now. Who wouldn't want to be worshipped and adored by a man who can provide a life for you better than any you could ever dream up? That is what Graham does for Angie. He basically has painted her gray world with a fresh palette of colors.

"I'm just glad that my Graham didn't mess this relationship up and let you slip through his fingers. Heaven knows my boys are not the easiest to love."

I glance over at Nic who seems to have his attention on the happy couple. How will I ever be able to truly let him go when he has already captured such a deep place in my heart?

"It is worth it though," Angie says with a smile. "You definitely have raised three amazing people. So thank you, Donna and Germain, for your hand in sculpting Graham into a wonderful man."

Graham scoops Angie up and kisses her so passionately that I start to sweat. Sometimes their love is so intense that I need to look away. It is like I don't want to diminish it by staring.

I used to think that the chance of finding love is worth the challenging journey to get there. However, right now, I'm not so sure. Seeing the happiness of my best friend, coupled with the looming fact that I am pregnant, makes it impossible for me to get out of this situation without being heartbroken. If I had kept things platonic with Nic from the start, I would not be in this mess today. He seduced me into his orbit. He got me away from Ethan.

While I should be thankful that he helped me to see that Ethan was a horrible fit for me, I am also a bit resentful that he gave me the illusion of happiness. I know what I want, but I have no clear path to actually getting it. Makes me wonder if any of this was worth it— knowing that everything I have ever wanted could be flushed down the drain by a single throat swab.

My phone buzzes with an incoming text, and I fish it out of my pajama pants pocket to see that Nic is texting me. I glance up and see his smirk as he opens his mouth for his fork to enter. How can that man make eating such a stimulating experience for my senses?

I click on the notification.

Nic: Quit daydreaming.

Claire: Stalker

Nic: Eat your food.

Claire: Quit staring at me.

Nic: Quit looking pretty.

Claire: Your family will figure it out.

Nic: What don't you want them to figure out, Claire?

I think about the question, and when I have no good response, I tuck my device back into my pocket.

I eat my food despite having a heavy heart. I just keep pushing my feelings back and back and back, until I can't feel anything but numbness. Today is not the day to be emotional. I need to let this all be about Angie and Graham.

I chew my food, while enjoying the conversing and overlapping of topics. Angie is very fortunate to be joining such a wonderful family. They are lovely. When everyone finishes their plates, we do a quick cleanup and put away the leftovers.

"Let the games begin," Donna announces, her words a bit slurred from her wine. Bottles have been passed around and glasses have been filled. "Honey, get the game board."

"It's literally right behind you," Germain says with a chuckle.

Donna turns around, comes face-to-face with the scoreboard, and bursts out laughing. "So much for utilizing my strategy of getting everyone else drunk so I can take home the trophy."

"You seriously did not get trophies, did you?" Penny inquires, her eyes dancing with humor.

"You bet your overpriced designer socks we did," Donna says.

"Hey, half the proceeds go to charity," Penny huffs.

"They are still overpriced. And that's a fact." Donna is

teasing. I know just from listening in on conversations that she is big into charities.

"But don't expect much with the trophies," Germain chimes in, making Donna smack his arm.

"Fine," she sighs heavily. "I bought them online, and the description of gold-plated should have been described more like *painted yellow*."

"Way to keep it classy," Nic razzes.

We all laugh as Germain stands up and rearranges some of the furniture to give us more room. "The first game is called Eyes and Ears," he says. "Each team needs to select one person to be the *eyes* and the other person to be the *ears*."

"We know which person is going to be the ears," Graham whisper-yells to Angie across the room.

"Oh yeah, who?" she calls back.

"Me," he says proudly.

"Why?"

"Because you don't listen to anything I say."

Angie bursts out laughing. "It's a scientific fact."

After we all settle, Germain continues with the rules. "Both members stand back to belly. The person situated at the back is the ears and must place their arms around their partner to conquer a specific task while blindfolded. The team member in front is the eyes and must tell their partner what to do by describing the location of objects and the details needed to get the job done."

"Who the hell comes up with this stuff?" Nic asks, shaking his head at his parents.

I love the relationship the Hoffmans have with each other. They can share their thoughts without the fear of someone running off in tears from being offended. They can harass each other, but still take a joke themselves. My kind of people.

"What's the task?" I ask, trying to figure out who should be the eyes and who should be the ears.

"Oh, you will soon find out," Donna says slyly, "but you have to decide first on your position."

With a little help from Graham, Collins moves a huge folding table into the center of the room and raises up the legs to allow the teams to stand around it and still have easy access to the surface.

I smell Nic's manly citrus scent before I see him stand beside me. "Do you have a preference on what you'd like to be?"

I shrug. "Hard to decide when I don't know what the task is. So, I guess I'll be the eyes?"

"Sounds good," he says slowly, moving behind me as Donna and Germain demonstrate the stance. Nic places his arms around mine and lays them flat against the surface of the table. Donna blindfolds all of the members standing in back and then places a baby doll in front of each team on the table, along with a diaper.

"You have one task," she says with mirth in her tone, fluttering about the room. "Undress the baby, put the diaper on, and then get the baby dressed again. Fastest team wins."

"Hold up," Graham interjects. "You're being serious?"

"Yes, son," Germain says, pretending to be annoyed. "You should know your mother's ways by now. Quit being so dramatic."

We all laugh as Donna continues with the supplies and blindfolding. "The members who are in front and are acting as the eyes must use descriptors and directions to get your partner to accomplish the task. Good luck."

"Really, Mom?" Nic asks, a look of pure shock on his face before Donna ties on his blindfold. She shushes him and ties the knot extra tight, making him chuckle.

"It'll be good practice for the future," Germain teases and takes his position behind Donna. He slides a blindfold over his own eyes and tightens it. "And just for the record, I didn't know what the task was going to be."

I swallow hard as I look at the baby doll in front of me. Nic is so close that I can feel his breath on my neck. We are all ironically in the same male in the back and female in the front position.

Donna clears her throat and announces, "Go."

"Find the baby," I tell Nic, watching him search the table with his fingers splayed out. Surely this won't be the hardest part of the task.

"Where is it?"

"Lean in closer. Reach." I watch as Nic grabs the baby's leg. "Okay, now unzip the sleeper." He fumbles with the zipper but manages to pull the outfit off the baby. "Undo the onesie."

His hands stop moving, and I can feel his stance shift behind me. "The what? Did you just make that word up?"

"I think they are called *onesies*? I don't know, but the thing that is like a bodysuit."

"How do I do it?"

"There are snaps under the crotch." I watch as he rips apart the pieces of fabric, jostling the baby onto the floor. "Oh shit. The baby! You have to go get it. It's on the floor."

We shimmy down to the rug and Nic is able to grab the

poor plastic doll. He picks me up off the floor, and I nearly stumble into the table.

"Now what?" he asks, acting like we even have a chance of winning. I look over at the other teams and find that Graham is surprisingly very good at following orders from Angie. They have been practicing, like she said.

"Get the diaper and put the baby on top of it and Velcro it on."

"Oh, okay," he says sarcastically.

"We have a winner," Donna announces, making us all stop the game. "Team Almost Newlyweds. Congrats!"

I am glad we can move to the next game, because this whole thing was a bit stressful. Maybe it is the fact that in just over half a year, I will be struggling to take care of a baby, with or without any support.

Nic removes his blindfold and looks at the hot-mess baby. I know he wants to say something, but he resists. Maybe he realizes just how unprepared we both are for this. He very well could be praying it is not his child.

I excuse myself to the bathroom and forestall having a panic attack. It is just a silly game. I freshen up my lip gloss and head back out to discover that everyone has left the room.

"We are going out back."

Nic's voice startles me, and I nearly jump at the sound of it. "Outside?"

"Just on the patio. Apparently Mom thought having a piñata shaped like a wedding cake would be a fun idea."

"A piñata? Like people have at kid birthday parties?"

Nic shakes his head, as if he cannot figure out how his

mom even comes up with these ideas. "Something like that."

I allow Nic to lead me out and we gather around a huge cake piñata, as Donna goes over the instructions.

"It's simple," she explains. "The winning team who can break it open wins the points for the scoreboard. However, inside are little bingo balls and a bunch of other goodies. Whoever finds the one marked *Angie and Graham* wins bonus points for their team."

We draw names and Collins is up first. Germain blindfolds him and allows him to swing twice. Next up is me. I hold the baseball bat firmly and aim blindly at where I think my target is. Winding it back, I swing hard and hear the crack of the cardboard, but not the sound of prizes falling. I do it one more time but have no luck. We go through the names in the dish and then circle around again. It is Nic who manages to shred the tissue papered cake apart, scattering bills, mini alcohol bottles, condoms, and coins for everyone to gather.

I laugh as I scoop up as much as I can and put my loot in a bag that was passed out before we started. It is fun, and everyone's carefree happiness is contagious. I can't help but relax and enjoy the moment.

After another hour of games, Nic and I manage to take the victory and cheesy trophies. I place mine on my nightstand and tuck myself into bed. It feels weird being a physical wall away from Nic and yet feeling worlds away emotionally.

No matter what happens, nothing will ever be the same again.

24

NIC

No matter what I do, I can't stop thinking about Claire. I have lied to myself and acted like her being pregnant changes things, but in reality, it only makes me want her more. I don't need a paternity test to keep me from already envisioning my life with her and this child. Sure, if Maxwell is the father, things will be vastly complicated. I believe his threats—as in he'll try to take the baby away—but he is underestimating the invisible reach I have in this city. I'll probably end up in prison myself for beating the shit out of him, but my feelings for Claire will still be there. I can't shut them off. I can't make them disappear.

The more she resists me, the more I want to throw her over my shoulder and take her away until she sees reason. There's a connection there. I see it every time she looks at me and then looks away, as if staring at me causes her pain. I'll do everything in my power to help her see that I'm a better man because of her. She has irrevocably changed me.

With Claire's permission, I scheduled the test for after the wedding, hopefully when our schedules are less chaotic due to all the festivities.

I don't want the test results to dictate my next moves, however. I love Claire. I need to tell her how I feel, and she needs to know that she is my priority—she and the baby—regardless of whether or not I am the father. But knowing my girl, I have to approach this with an actual strategy. Claire has been heartbroken too many times by the people who should have loved her unconditionally. I am guilty of hurting her too. I am a gambling man, though, and I am willing to bet that with some patience and perseverance, I can get her to see that we belong together.

I rest against my pillows and turn out my end table light. I am about to drift off to sleep when I hear a high-pitched shriek break through the silence of the house.

It's Claire.

I fly out of bed and rush into the room beside mine where I know she is located.

"Baby?" I ask in the dark, feeling my way through the room until I reach her bed. "What's wrong?"

I turn on the lamp and find my girl with tears dripping down her cheeks and her breath coming out in pants.

"I...I had a"—she pants—"bad dream."

I sit on the side of her bed and open up my arms for her to climb into them. I scoot back so I can rest against the headboard and wrap us in the blanket that is at the foot of her bed. Her breathing is so erratic that I worry she is going to hyperventilate. I rub my hands up and down her back, pausing my rhythm to play with some locks of her hair.

"Do you want to tell me what you dreamed about?"

She shakes her head no and continues to sob into my neck. "It was horrible," she gasped.

I play with the skin exposed from her sleep shirt slinking down over her shoulder. She is so soft and delicate, like the petals of a newly blossomed flower. I breathe in her vanilla scent and close my eyes as I wait for her breathing to calm and slow.

She clears her throat, and I wait for her to collect her thoughts. I resist kissing her neck, even though that is exactly what I want to do.

"I dreamed that the baby was ripped out of me," she chokes out.

I hold her tight and run my hands over her back. I don't know what to say, but I can totally see why she would be freaked out. I want to ask questions but I also don't want her to have to relive her nightmare.

We scoot down and lie next to each other until her breathing returns to normal. Glancing down at her, I see her eyes are still open. "Try to go back to sleep," I encourage. "You and the baby need your rest."

Claire shakes her head. "I can't. When I have such a vivid nightmare, it's hard to fall back asleep."

I kiss her forehead and start to sit us both up. "Throw on something warmer and grab your shoes." I roll out of bed, smiling at Claire's confused look.

"What? Why? Where are we going?"

"You'll see."

After Claire tosses on a sweatshirt and sneakers, I drag her by her hand out of the bedroom and next door to my room. I throw on a hoodie and slip on a pair of my Chucks. In my closet, I reach on top for a blanket, tugging it down from the shelf.

"What's going on?" Claire asks again, watching from the doorway.

I smirk. "Patience."

"Pretty sure I got that tested recently. I'm negative."

I laugh over her cheesiness. I do prefer this over her indifference. Anything is better than being ignored.

Claire glances around my room, taking it all in. This is where I spent my childhood and teenage years sleeping. While the decor has changed some with the upgrades, the structure of the room is pretty much the same.

"You seem deep in thought," I point out.

"Just wondering what stories these walls could tell."

I huff out a laugh. "Not nearly as interesting as I'm sure your mind is cooking up."

Claire shrugs. "How many women have you brought here?"

I take a slight step back, as I get a better look at her face. Is she being serious? I'd be lying if I said her question didn't catch me off guard. Do I see a streak of jealousy? And over what—my past? My past doesn't matter, when my future is with her.

"Should I round to the nearest hundred?"

"Damn."

"I'm teasing, Claire." I think women give men too much credit to think that we are organized enough to count things like this. "Have you met my mother, Donna Hoffman?"

"I have."

"Then you would understand how intrusive she would be if I brought home a girl back in high school. Graham and I were both smarter than to add fuel to her already stifling personality."

"Do you feel deprived of that missed opportunity?"

I think about the question. "No. Not when I can make better memories now at my current stage of life."

She seems to accept that answer, as a shyness coats her body. Arms cross around her midsection, and her gaze drops toward the floor. I can only hope she is imagining what it would be like for us to be together. Really together.

The house is completely hushed with everyone already in bed. It is just after midnight and even though I haven't gotten any rest yet, I feel a new sense of rejuvenation and energy. That is what Claire does for me and doesn't even realize it. She lights a fire inside me that only she has the power to do.

Once I get everything I need, we exit my room and head downstairs. I lead Claire through the back door and onto the patio. We pass by the flower garden on our way to the field of grass on top of the hillside. As we get farther and farther away from the house, it gets harder to see. I pull out my phone from my pants pocket and shine the flashlight so we can avoid tripping.

When I get to the perfect spot, I lay out the blanket and invite Claire to join me on it. She hesitates but eventually settles into my arms, as we lie back and look at the stars. I check the time and then relax, as we wait.

"I just saw something," she says, sitting up to look at me. "You saw it, right? Like a shooting star."

I smile at her in the moonlight. "Tonight is a meteor

shower. I wasn't sure if we would have too much light pollution to see anything. But the sky is clear and we are far enough away from the house."

More beams shoot across the sky and Claire bursts with excitement as she points out every meteor she sees, as if I somehow am not watching myself.

"Wow," she gasps, wiggling around on the blanket and trying to see in all directions. "I've never seen anything like this before."

"Then I am glad I could give you this," I say softly.

"Do you ever wonder if we would have been attracted to each other if we didn't have so many hang-ups? I mean, we are pretty much on opposite ends of the personality spectrum."

I roll so I can look at Claire's eyes. That's where I see her truth and vulnerability, even in the darkness. "I was attracted to you long before you walked in with Angie for her first meeting at Entice. I knew all of my employees, even if I didn't have a lot of direct contact with them. I remember when I saw your profile and your picture for the first time too."

"You actually remember that?" she asks, narrowing her eyes in disbelief.

"Damn straight, I do. You had a sunflower in your hair and a denim dress on. You were a mix between a sex goddess and an innocent hummingbird."

"But you never acted like you even noticed me. As a boss, you were pretty boring."

"I was living a hermit life then and was balls deep into the FBI's inner workings. I had a job to do, and I would have stopped at nothing to get it done. Plus, I didn't date."

"Just fuck and forget, right?"

I swallow. "Before you? Yes. After you? I don't think I will ever be the same man I was. You aren't a game changer, Claire. You are a game ender."

Claire doesn't say another word. I know she wants to argue or say something witty back at me, but she resists. My words are marinating in her head. It's the only time she is ever this quiet.

We lie here until our fingers and toes start to go numb from the cooler night's temperatures. I stand and pull Claire up toward me. I want to hold her face and kiss the hell out of her. I want to scream at her to let me back in. I also want to make sure that my next move is profound enough to make it impossible for her to say no to me.

I fold up the blanket and place a hand over the small of Claire's back as we walk toward the house. We don't say a word, yet so much is being communicated with just our breaths. We are in sync.

When we get back inside, Claire shivers from being outside for so long, and I inwardly scold myself for potentially putting her at risk of getting a cold. I get her back up to her room and walk into the bathroom, where she follows me.

"Let me draw you a bath," I explain, filling the tub with warm water.

"Not too hot," she says sadly.

I nod to her comment and then add some scented soap to make bubbles. I know she is referring to the baby growing inside her. I already feel like it is mine, yet I don't want to get ahead of myself before the proof. I need to keep a clear head for a potential battle with fucking Maxwell, and not let the hope that is stirring inside keep me from letting my guard down where he's concerned.

"Will you be okay?" I ask, walking backwards toward the door.

She nods and then waits for me to exit. I lie on top of her mattress, while I wait for her to finish in the tub. I must drift off because it isn't until the line of artificial light from the bathroom passes over my eyes that I stir. I sit up and see Claire enter with a towel wrapped around her hair and one around her body.

"Oh," she says shyly. "I thought you went back to your room."

"Didn't mean to startle you. Just thought you may want company or someone to hang out with if you are afraid to go back to sleep."

Claire nods and gives me a faint smile. "Thank you," she mouths.

She grabs her hoodie and slips it over her head. It is so oversized that it covers her down to midthigh. Pulling the towel out from underneath, she tosses it over the armchair. She slips on a pair of sweats, forgoing any undergarments underneath. Damn. How can someone so utterly casual be so fucking sexy?

"Pretty soon I will be so huge that this hoodie will look like a crop top," she says as a joke, but I can tell it is bothering her.

"You will still be the most beautiful thing I have ever seen," I say with confidence and reverence, imagining all the ways her body is going to change to accommodate the growing baby.

"Ha, doubtful. I mean, if you have a penguin fetish, then

you may be in luck." She waddles around the room with exaggerated movements, all while puffing out her belly. "Oompa Loompa is heading your way."

"I'd put every single cent I own on that."

A smirk plays at the corner of her lips. "I've seen you gamble before and"—she picks at her nail polish—"I'm not impressed."

I shake my head at her sass. It takes everything in me not to pounce on her and take what every cell in my body wants. I want all the Claires.

Snarky Claire.

Quiet Claire.

Spontaneous Claire.

Cranky Claire.

Made-for-me Claire.

She takes a seat on the bed, and I kneel on the floor at her feet. "It is as if every inch of you, every curve of your body, was made for my eyes and hands to worship. You are beautiful now. And you will be even more beautiful tomorrow, and every day thereafter. I'm not scared of it anymore either. Bring on the mood swings and the stretch marks and the sight-unseen feet." When I am met with silence and her glancing away, I continue, "You can't wrap your head around the fact that no matter what, I will still find you desirable."

Claire blinks hard. "You're delusional."

"I'm simply being honest." When my face doesn't show any sign of humor, I can finally see my words sinking into her brain. My poor girl has been hardened by the nastiness of this world, and I will forever regret ever being a part of her burden. However, I refuse to be sad over the winding path that got me to where we are today. While not all of the stops along the way were happy or something to be proud of, I am thankful that I am a few steps closer to getting everything I thought I didn't want in this lifetime. Right now, I just need to be patient and wait for Claire to see the light.

Claire's eyes soften as my words settle in her head. "Why does everything have to be so complicated?"

I stand up and situate us both against a mountain of pillows on the bed. Bending down, I kiss her forehead while tucking her to my side. "Not everything has to be."

"But it is," she says on a sigh. "Just when I think I have things figured out, life throws me another curveball."

"I'm trying here, Claire. I'm really, really trying."

"What exactly are you trying, Nic?"

"I'm trying to be okay with even the worst-case scenario," I explain. "I'm trying to be patient and give you space. But it is hard to go through these watered-down motions when all I want to do is pull you toward me and make you stay." Her eyes grow as she listens to every one of my words. Is she finally understanding it?

She shakes her head. "I can't handle any more heartbreak. You think you want me because you think I am carrying your child. But there is still a solid chance I'm not. Your feelings will change if this baby," she says looking down at her belly, "is Ethan's. And gaining you just to lose you again will be way worse than never getting you back at all."

"So that's it?" I ask, looking away from her. "You're allowing this test result to dictate what you *think* my feelings are?"

"Yes," she says with certainty. "I need to know who the father is. It is all I can think about."

"What if I said it doesn't matter to me?"

"I'd say you are fooling more than just me." Claire looks at me and then lets out a long, drawn-out exhale. She shifts her weight so she can see me better. "Do you think this isn't gutting me? Do you think that I don't see all I am missing out on? You live a charmed life." She glances around the room and swings her arm out to encompass the space in a sweeping gesture. "You have the perfect family, with the perfect love story of your parents to look up to. I don't have an iconic model of a marriage and family structure to try to imitate. I have a mom who cheated on her husband and got pregnant by a man I never met. I am unwanted, Nic."

"Not by me."

"You say that now. But I bet my mom thought that the man that I call Dad would come to terms with the fact that he was not my biological father. And well, we both know how that turned out. The fact that I would have been better off if I was put up for adoption is a sobering feeling that no one should go through life thinking. So, you say that the test results don't matter, but how am I supposed to believe that, huh? I cannot put my child in a situation that will later cause them potential harm. I refuse to let this baby ever think it is unwanted by anyone. I am living proof of how a person can be affected by neglect. All a child wants is to be loved. If that means parenting on my own, so be it. I'm sure it will be hard at first, but I'll adapt."

"Baby—"

"How would your parents feel if you are with me and

the child is not yours? I can't have my baby be a stain to your storybook plot. But don't you ever think for a second that I won't be wondering what we could have been if Ethan ends up being the father and makes the rest of my life a living hell with his threats at resisting coparenting."

I wrap Claire in my arms and tug a blanket around us at the first tear that falls from her eyes. I know she may not believe me or see it now, but we belong together and I will fight for us. When doors always close in your face, it is hard to ever expect any to open on their own—without having to pry. She was wrapped around my heart long before I was aware of it. Now I just need her to see that this baby changes nothing as to how I feel about her.

"I am waiting for the moment," I say, "when you start to realize that my feelings toward you are not dependent on the outcome of a paternity test."

"They are for me," she says flatly, which I know is a lie. It is what she wants me to believe, so she can protect her own heart. "And one day you might see that me letting you go is a gift."

I shake my head but resist arguing. Claire doesn't need me to make a case right now for all of my points. I just keep holding her and enjoying this quiet moment of stillness. I play with her hair and rub her back. I know she is crying by the erratic pattern of her breaths, but I do not draw attention to it.

When Claire's sobs stop, I look down and see that she has fallen asleep. I move her so she is lying on a pillow and tuck her under the two layers of blankets. Then, I crawl in beside her and mold my body to hers.

Claire is the rarest, most beautifully broken butterfly,

who just needs a little mending in order to soar. I refuse to allow her to cut me out of her life. I needed time to make sense of my intense feelings for her. She now needs time to know that she doesn't have to walk her path alone.

I might be a masochist, but I can only hope that it is all worth it in the end.

25

CLAIRE

"Can you believe that at this time tomorrow, you will be married?" I ask Angie, as I put the last minute touches on her makeup.

"It really is crazy to think that I found my person when I least expected it."

"That's how all the good love stories happen." I smile. "And you should know from all of those sappy books you read with the half-naked men on the covers."

"*Man*. Singular," she corrects with a giggle. "Although I'm not against multiple naked men, so I like how you think. If there is a fantasy, there's definitely hundreds of books for it."

I join Angie in laughter. We are using a guest room at the mansion to get dressed and primped for the wedding rehearsal. All of the people participating in the ceremony are downstairs waiting for us. I am going to miss her being single and free to have girls' nights. However, a lot has changed for both of us recently and our priorities have shifted. Perhaps we have both matured.

"Now you have your own love story to add to those epic ones you like so much." I lift Angie's hair and fix some strands over her shoulders. "You, my beautiful friend, are getting married. So, let's go practice so you don't make a fool out of yourself tomorrow in front of everyone." I look in the mirror as Angie's face turns to horror. "I'm teasing. You're going to do great. You always do."

"We'll see," she mutters. "You know how I hate to be center stage."

"Ha, pretty sure you are the least bridezilla person I know."

"I still have some time to start making all of my demands," she says with a straight face.

There's a knock at the door and a soft voice calls out from the other side. "Can I come in? It's Penny."

"Yes, of course," Angie says, turning in her seat to watch as Penny enters.

"Sorry I'm late. I was just doing the last-minute touches to the practice aisle outside in the courtyard. We are all set."

While Penny hasn't had much to do in regard to the wedding plans, what she has helped with has been done with a smile. She has worked behind the scenes to make sure everything is running smoothly today, as well as coordinated a few of the deliveries set to arrive tomorrow for the actual day. The thing about Angie is that she would be happy with anything. It is everyone around her that is nervous about making her day amazing. She has told us numerous times that the only thing that matters tomorrow is her and Graham sharing their vows in front of their family and friends. Everything else is just sauce.

"You guys look amazing," she says, moving closer to Angie to rave about her layered bright pink dress.

Penny and I have on simple pastel pink sundresses, in the same color family as Angie's—except less vibrant.

"I got us daisy bouquets to practice with for the rehearsal. But I think your mom put them in the fridge downstairs," I say, digging for my phone to text her.

"Oh, fun," Angie says. I can tell she is getting nervous as her fingers start to pick at her freshly done nail polish.

I extend my hand for her to grab. "Let's go." *Before you undo some of your pampering.*

"I wish the wedding was now and we could skip this whole practice thing," Angie says with a pout.

"Don't tell your soon-to-be husband that," I tease. "He'll pay off the officiant and all of the hard work preparing for your epic ceremony will be wasted."

"Okay, fine. Let's do the damn thing."

"Now, that's the spirit," Penny whoops.

We link arms with Angie and walk with her out of the room, through the hall, and down the stairs. Donna is waiting for us down below with the small flower bouquets in hand.

"Wow, you ladies look exquisite," she gasps, holding one hand over her mouth as she watches us descend the staircase.

"Thank you," we say in unison.

When we make it outside, groups of family and friends are standing around chatting with Graham. When we join the festivities, Angie finds her father and gives him a hug.

He arrived earlier in the day from Baker City, and for someone who is still dealing with his addiction, he is doing remarkably well. The two of them together are inspirations to anyone dealing with feeling out of control and how the power of therapy can change a person's life.

Zander, a good friend from college, waves to me as he sits down to play the piano, while a local female singer stands beside him. According to Angie, she is a rising star and is trying to get her name out there. Well, this will be career-altering, for sure.

The event planner leads us to the chairs set up in the beautiful garden, surrounded by the canopy of trees draped in lights. The fountains are turned on and the sound of fresh water flowing causes a relaxing feeling to ease my nerves. Despite many of the decorations being reserved for tomorrow's actual ceremony, the setup right now is still breathtaking. The whole scene looks like a page ripped out of a fairy tale.

Everyone lines up and takes their place. The parents of the groom take a seat in the front row. Graham waits next to the officiant under a trellis of what appears to be hundreds of roses. Zander is situated behind a huge piano that must have taken a dozen men to carry. Collins links arms with Penny and when directed by the planner, they walk in a rhythm down the aisle. Zander plays Pachelbel's Canon in D and a cello player that I did not notice until now follows along seamlessly.

I am so enthralled watching the musicians play that I don't even feel the hand on me until it gently squeezes my arm. My eyes look down and then up into Nic's crystal-blue pair. I wonder if I will ever tire of looking at him. His eyes are so expressive, and his warm smile makes me want to melt into him.

"Ready to go?" he asks, removing his hand to link arms with me.

"I think so," I whisper.

"Claire, you look beautiful."

"Thank you," I mutter.

"One day, this is going to be you living out your own fairy tale."

Before I have a chance to think of a response, the event planner motions for us to go, and I start off with a big step. It is way too big for my shorter legs and I stumble. Nic pulls me gently back, helping me to balance. "We can't run," he teases.

I slow down and focus on not dropping my bouquet. Once we get to the end of the aisle runner, we part ways and I stand with Penny, turning to look for Angie's arrival.

Walking beside her dad, Angie moves with purpose down the aisle. We all laugh as she ignores the officiant and stands up on her tiptoes to kiss Graham on the lips. I glance around the audience, half expecting the wedding planner to blow a whistle or throw a flag in objection. I take Angie's bouquet from her, pretend to fix her imaginary wedding dress, and then take my place next to Penny. The photographer snaps pictures during the practice run, while setting up a tripod for the video feed.

The event planner gives us all a few suggestions and pointers on how to look our best tomorrow. Once we do one more walk-through, we all depart the mansion to head on back to the Hoffman's house for a dinner party.

Nic helps me into the back of the limo and clicks me

into my seatbelt, since my fingers apparently are as clumsy as my feet. It is just the two of us. I can't help but think of the statement he made to me right before walking down the aisle. Will I be able to live out my own fairy tale? Right now, the only thing I see in front of me is the looming paternity test, which will change my life forever. I am not ready for more change. I just want consistency and stability. I want to be confident in my choices and have the calming feeling like I am doing the right thing.

"What am I going to do when I am a huge puffer fish and can't do much of anything for myself?" I ask, not really expecting a response.

Nic takes my hand in his and massages my palm. "I will take care of you, baby. Whatever you need. If I have to hire someone to help take some stress off of you, I will. If you need to be on a special diet, I will hire you a personal chef. Whatever you need, I can provide it."

I shake my head, fully regretting even asking the question in the first place. "How can you just say that? I am giving you a way out of all of this."

"You think my way out is if Ethan is the father. I don't know how many times I have to tell you this, but those results don't matter to me."

I sit in silence as the door opens and more people shuffle inside. Under the concealment of his suit coat, Nic manages to hold my hand without anyone noticing. It feels good to be wanted—even if I know the moment will be fleeting.

Collins drives us back into Hillsboro, and the catering staff is in full swing, meeting us in the driveway with a celebratory beverage.

Nic grabs two flutes off of the tray and hands me one

that has two berries in the bottom. "This one is virgin," he states simply, nodding toward my drink. "I had them specially made with you in mind."

Why is he being so sweet to me? "Thanks," I mutter, missing the opportunity to get a little buzzed. I push my emotions and feelings into the back of my head as I gear up mentally to celebrate my best friend on the night before her big day. It is easy to be happy for her. It is also easy to want to live vicariously through everything she is experiencing.

Inside, we all sit at a huge rectangular table. The cello player starts playing, while the singer starts to perform. After the first song, Germain clinks his glass with a polished silver fork, silencing the room.

"Donna and I thank you all for joining us today to prepare for the nuptials of our son, Graham Xavier Hoffman, and his lovely fiancée, Angela Renee McFee. Please raise your glass while we toast to a lifetime of happiness and good health. May you both grow together in love and harmony."

"Here, here!"

"Cheers!"

"Salut."

The musicians start to perform again as huge trays of food are brought out and plates are placed in front of us. We all dig in and enjoy the food and light conversation. Most of the time, I sit back and enjoy watching everyone interact. It feels like I am a part of this amazing network of people, and the thought of losing any of them causes me major grief and anxiety.

Donna wheels out the cake and everyone laughs over the chocolate volcano erupting from the center. Angie sure loves chocolate, and this dessert is almost too spectacular to eat. A staff member slices up the cake, serving it on porcelain plates with some of the ganache drizzled over it. Every plate is then garnished with a chocolate dipped strawberry and passed out to each guest. It is decadent and sinfully delicious.

I am so focused on eating my berry that I don't even realize that another one has been added to my plate. I refuse to look over at Nic, who I am positive put it there. Instead, I take a giant bite of it and savor the taste of sweetness with the bitter bite of the chocolate. I grab my napkin and wipe my lips. I take a sip of my sparkling beverage, and when I place my fork back on my plate, it bumps into another strawberry. I quickly glance over at Nic and he is busy chatting with his sister. I look to my other side and see Zander taking a break from playing the piano to eat with us.

I take the fruit between my two fingers and bite the tip off and then the rest of it, discarding the stem onto my plate.

"Ma'am," I hear behind me and look back to see a waiter holding a huge bowl of fruit on a tray. "Would you like more?"

I shake my head and slink back into my chair, feeling slightly embarrassed from my overindulgence. When he is about to turn around, Nic takes the bowl off the tray and places it down in front of him. I glare over at him, but he deliberately avoids making eye contact.

"Hungry?" I ask, trying to get him to engage. I smile at the smirk forming on his lips. He can't hide it because his eyes give it away.

Nic turns and stares at my lips and then trails them down my body to what is hidden underneath the table. "Always."

"Stop," I mouth.

"Stop what?" he asks innocently.

"You know what."

He leans in closer, making my eyes grow big as I glance around the room. No one is paying us any attention. Drinks are being consumed, food is being enjoyed, and laughter is filling up the gaps in conversations.

"I wonder if your pussy is as sweet as this bowl of fruit," he says smoothly, picking up a piece to plop in his mouth. "I bet it is even sweeter."

I open my mouth and then snap it shut. I want to turn away. I want to act like his words don't affect me. But they do. They always do. I want him. More than I have ever wanted anyone else in my life. I just don't know if I have the willpower to give in now, just to say no later. It isn't fair to either of us. None of this is fair.

In the middle of my mental pity party, I feel the lightest brush of Nic's fingers on my thigh. It tickles as he trails them up over the fabric of my dress, teasing me and taunting me with everything I have ever wanted. He knows my weaknesses, and from the gleam in his eyes, I know he will be exploiting them and playing me like a finely tuned piano.

"Not here," I mutter, so only he can hear.

"Why not?"

I look at him like he has five heads. "Isn't it obvious? Someone will see."

"Adds to the excitement, doesn't it?"

"No. And stop doing that thing with your eyes."

"What thing?" he asks, as if he doesn't know what he's doing.

"Don't be coy."

"Don't be cute."

"Hush."

"You hush."

"Good comeback. Are we five?" I ask, snorting.

"You find me hot, don't you?"

I adamantly shake my head. Not because I'm not attracted to him, but because I need to clear my brain space if I am going to survive the rest of the evening.

Nic smiles big. "Pretty sure you are lying to me. I will call your bluff. Spread those pretty little thighs for me and I will find out who is telling the truth." His words are a whisper and in the noise of the room, I doubt anyone would hear. However, anyone paying us a bit of attention will easily see the way we are looking at each other.

Feeling frisky, I start to open my legs to which he responds with a deep growl, and as soon as his hand starts to slide under the hem of my dress, I clamp them shut while sliding back my chair.

"Where are you going?" he asks, narrowing his eyes at me.

I stand up, push my chair back in, and lean over to whisper, "Just to the bathroom, so I can masturbate to the thought of you." And then I walk away. Solo.

Nic is hot on my tail and I pick up my pace, dodging a few waitstaff in the process. When I almost run into Collins, I quickly apologize and then use him as a roadblock for my developing impulsive plan. "I think Nic needs you," I say vaguely. "Seems important."

"Okay, I'll go find him," Collins responds in a professional tone.

I skip off to the main floor's bathroom and lock the door. Looking in the mirror, I have some sweat beading on my forehead. There's a glow and warmth to my skin. I feel alive. That's what Nic's attention does to me, and no matter how many times I resist, we always find each other. I place my hands on the vanity and lean over, bracing myself on extended hands as I contemplate how I am going to survive the night.

There's a round of knocks on the door and I already know who they belong to—Nic Hoffman.

"Just a second," I call back.

I sit on the toilet, flush, and wash my hands. From a container, I pump out some vanilla hand lotion and rub it into my palms and all around my fingers. I bring my hands up to my nose and inhale the scent. It's my favorite. When I open the door and notice no one is waiting, I relax and start back to the dining room. I take a few steps down the hall when I am grabbed from behind and pulled back to a wall of hard muscle.

"Think you could get away that easily?" Nic asks, making my insides turn to mush. His breath tickles my neck and makes a tingle run up my spine. He is so close to me that I can smell his cologne.

"Someone's going to see," I say softly, looking around for anyone else.

"Good."

"Good?" I ask with a flare to my tone. I turn my head so I can get a look at his face. "Is that really what you want?"

"What I want is to fuck you into next week."

I open and close my mouth. What's left to say? Nic has

obviously made his point clear. I should have known that taunting him would bring me to this very situation.

There is something extremely sexy about being pursued and wanted to the magnitude that Nic shows me. I know our lives are complicated right now, but there is no denying our sexual chemistry and desire for one another. I shouldn't give in. I should keep the line drawn with confidence. However, when the two of us are in close proximity, there always seems to be a way to blur that line that neither of us should really cross.

"We shouldn't do this," I say, as he pulls me into the bathroom and locks the door. I can stop him, but I am being selfish with my desires, and as much as I can deny it, I want him with the same voracity as he seems to want me.

"You shouldn't make promises you can't keep."

"What promise?"

"The show I'm expecting to see," he explains.

"Show?"

"It's starring me, isn't it? You know, the whole reason you left the table to use the bathroom."

"Oh. That. Silly me, I was just playing," I say sweetly, smiling up at him in the mirror. He is directly behind me, pressed so close to me that I can feel the outline of his cock against my back. Nic rakes his eyes over me in the reflection. He is slow and methodical, like he is trying to study me for some sort of test.

"You are such a bad girl."

Before I can come up with a snappy comeback, Nic spins me around, lifts me up by my hips, and places me on the smooth surface of the vanity. He pivots me so I can see him and the mirror with just the slight turn of my head. He hikes up my skirt, while bending my knees at the same time. I am so enthralled with his fluidity that I don't even have a chance to think, let alone stop him. With his hands over mine, he places them over the crotch of my lace panties and cups my hand to my mound.

"I can't—"

"Yes, you can," he encourages. Controlling my hand, he moves his up and down, dragging mine over my sensitive parts. "I want to watch you get yourself off."

I'm not sure I can do that with the amount of pressure I feel to perform. I close my eyes and focus on just how my body feels. When I begin to relax, I start moving my hand of my own volition. Moisture seeps from my pussy and when I have teased myself enough, I slip my hand into my panties and slide one finger inside my warmth.

"You're doing great, baby," Nic says, cheering me on. His hands rub at my back, soothing me with his gentle—but urgent—movements. "You're such a good girl." He makes me forget my troubles and helps me block out the rest of the world. Bending, he peppers kisses along the side of my exposed neck, making chills run up my arms.

I let out a moan when I am close, and before I have a chance to finish myself off, Nic turns me so my legs now surround him as he stands between them. His hands grab at my ass and push me into him as he lifts and lowers his hips to imitate the movements of sex. The friction of his pants against the softness of my panties gives me the perfect amount of pressure to finish myself off.

"Ah," I call out, throwing my head backwards as I allow the intense orgasm to flood through my core. Before I can finish riding the wave, Nic undoes his pants and pulls my panties aside.

"Tell me you want this."

I nod and scoot forward to try to get him inside me. I may not be sure about the future, but I know I'm sure about the present. I want him. I have always wanted him. And if life would just dish me a fair set of cards to play with, I might even be able to gamble with the odds that we could be something more.

"I need your words."

"I want this."

He smiles down at me and slides himself inside my pulsing canal. It doesn't take but a few thrusts to send me skyrocketing to another realm outside of the present space.

"You can give me more," Nic says with confidence, as his lips suck and nip at mine.

His hands squeeze my ass cheeks in a punishing grip. He knows I like it a bit rough. A little raw. I push forward, throw my head back, and succumb to the pleasure that only Nic Hoffman knows how to elicit from my body.

"Fuck!" I bellow. "Mmph!" I breathe through my nose as Nic's lips capture mine, holding my scream prisoner.

I can feel the vibration of his laughter as he thrusts a few more times before releasing into me.

If I die in this moment from pleasure, it will be worth it.

26

NIC

"I can do that," Claire says, trying to get me to stop wiping her clean.

Maybe she is vulnerable and a bit shy after coming down from her high. Perhaps she realizes that the more she blurs the lines, the clearer her feelings are to me. She's scared. Regardless, I want to take care of her and make sure she is safe.

"Let me," I state, continuing to run a warm washcloth over her folds, collecting the product of our arousal. There's nothing I want more than to have a reminder of where I've been on the forefront of Claire's mind. I would love to let her feel my seed leaking out of her for the rest of the evening. However, I also want her to feel comfortable and unashamed of our relationship—even if she has yet to acknowledge that she is very much mine. Also, I don't want to put her at extra risk for a urinary tract infection. In the research I've done about pregnancy, I know those can cause issues.

I can be a patient man, but I only have a short amount of time to prove to Claire that the paternity test results are irrelevant to how I feel toward her. I need her to understand my feelings prior to the actual test, and my girl is stubborn at best. I know she is using this baby as a way to distance herself from me emotionally—despite not being able to keep me at arm's length physically. She has already proven to me that she can't resist me when I pursue her relentlessly. Good. Because I don't plan on stopping.

Being without Claire would be like living without the sun. I would be coldhearted and just trying to survive in the darkness.

"We can't keep blurring the lines."

"There are no more lines, baby. Boundaries are no longer being stretched. My feelings for you are limitless."

Maybe in the beginning there were, when we were both convinced that getting involved with each other would be awkward for the family-friendship dynamics. Claire and Angie are best friends, so things would get messy if we started dating and it didn't work out. I never planned on dating anyone after Tara. However, when Claire entered my orbit, I couldn't resist. I had to have her. Now, I don't want to let her go. I did that once and saw what life would be like without her, and I refuse to go to that place again.

She shakes her head and looks away. What do I have to do to prove to her that I am not going to leave her ever again? Never.

I help her down off the vanity and straighten out her dress.

"You are so fucking beautiful. You know that?"

"Please stop."

"Stop what?"

"Being nice to me. Stop being the perfect boyfriend I would have wanted in another time in my life. You are saying all the right things and yet I keep stabbing myself in the heart every time I allow myself to engage with you. I can't keep doing this to myself. Things are different now. I am *pregnant*. I have to stop being selfish and think about what is best for this child and not just me."

I pull her to me and kiss her forehead. My hands cup her cheeks, and I stare into her solemn eyes wishing with every part of me that I could remove her sadness and promise her that everything will be alright. I know when we leave this room, Claire will force herself to avoid me, and even though I know her reasons, I don't agree with them or like them. "What if I am best for you and for this child?"

"C'mon, Nic. Do you know the first thing about raising a child? Because I barely do. It's not like I have had that much experience with babies. Do you know how my body is going to change and how I am not going to have time anymore for the things I used to love? Quit making this harder for me. It is what it is. It has to be easier ending this now than ending it after the baby is born, when you come to the realization that life will forever be different. The last thing I need is for you to one day wake up and start treating the baby like my dad treated me."

I swallow hard as I recall witnessing her broken heart when I picked her up at the airport from her trip to Virginia. I never want to see that degree of pain in her eyes again.

Sighing, I rub both hands at the back of my neck. "Claire, I grew up in a family where love was easily shown. Sure, I lack the personal experience, but don't all first-time parents? I very much see this child as mine because it is a part of you. You are the only one complicating matters, while I fully plan to show that I am in this for the long haul. If I need to fight Ethan for custody, I can do that. If bashing his face in again will help, sign me up. If we're going to figure out coparenting, I can do that. If you need vitamins or health insurance or maternity clothes, I can do that. But you have to let go of this idea that I am like your dad and that you have to walk this journey alone." I fix a piece of her hair behind her ear and run my hands down her arms. "And if therapy has taught me anything, both of us need to stop using our loneliness as a crutch. I get that you were hurt in the past by those who should have loved you. We can work through our past trauma together, baby. Just give me a chance."

Her sad eyes connect with mine. "You went to therapy?"

I nod slowly. I guess she knows now. "I'm still going."

"Why? I just never thought…"

"To work through all my insecurities."

Claire looks away, and as soon as her eyes blink, tears drip out of her eyes. She stays motionless for some time; the only sound is her sniffling. "I'm scared," she whispers, finally breaking the silence.

"What are you afraid of?"

"Falling and no one catching me."

My thumbs wipe at her tears, and I guide her eyes back to me. "I will catch you. You just have to trust me. I'm trying hard to be the man worthy of a woman like you."

There's a knock at the door, and the sound makes Claire jump. I look toward the door and realize that we have been in here long enough for speculation to be made.

"Someone's going to notice," Claire says nervously.

"So be it."

I open the door and come face to face with Penny. I let out a groan over her eager eyes as they flip-flop between looking at Claire and then back to me.

"Hi guys," she says sweetly. "What have you been up to?"

"Hi Penny," I respond, pulling Claire with me. "Quit looking at us like that."

She smiles so big that I want to mess up her hair, just like I used to do when we were kids. I am not in the right state of mind for her good mood over this. She basically has already told me she knows Claire and I are together—and fully supports it.

"I just wanted to tell you that the slideshow is about to start. Everyone is in the theater room."

"You have a theater room?" Claire asks, as we follow Penny down the stairs to the newly renovated basement.

"It was my dad's DIY project over the winter. It wasn't completed yet at Christmas, otherwise, we probably would have been watching family movies in it."

She just nods as we make our way down the steps.

"Mom is a lover of all things holidays. She would have put on a sappy movie where the main characters don't like Christmas, but then get stuck in the mountains in a little village where they learn the true meaning of the holiday."

"And kiss during the first snow of the year," Claire adds.

"See, you know exactly what type of movie we would have all had to endure," I joke.

Claire allows me to hold her hand as we find a seat in the back row of leather recliners with Penny. Dad elevated each row, with the back being the highest row. Lights are built into the floor steps, and Mom purchased a popcorn machine to make it even more authentic. Framed movie posters fill the walls.

I relax into the recliner, kicking up my feet as the music starts and the first picture on the screen is of what I assume is Angie as a baby.

"Aww," Claire coos.

Everyone laughs as Graham's baby pictures are filtered in. Some are professional, while others are the embarrassing ones Mom always took of us kids. She would routinely remind us that she was saving her stash for when we planned to get married. She did not lie.

The show progresses with some family photos with Angie featuring her deceased mom and brother. Her dad must have helped to get the photos to the videographer who put the presentation together. Based on the sniffling coming from Angie, who is sitting right beside him in the front row, she was not expecting to see them.

"She looks just like her mom," Claire whispers.

I am featured in some of Graham's pictures, and while it is good to hear Claire laugh, I am shocked over the half nude ones of me warming up for high school wrestling practice that mom decided to include in the show. Graham and I would often train and compete together. I didn't even know Mom took some of these. I can only imagine the others she has in her arsenal.

"You look like you were ready to hurt someone," Claire mutters, leaning into me.

When I look over at her, I can see her biting her bottom lip even in the darkness of the room. I can smell the shampoo she washes her hair with, and I will never tire of breathing in her scent. She looks up at me and I wiggle my eyebrows, making her giggle.

"I had a lot of pent-up energy in my teenage years, and wrestling helped me channel it. Competing was better than me just going around hitting people just because they pissed me off."

"What were you pissed off about?"

I shrug. "Probably nothing. Just the fact I was an immature teen, learning to deal with my fluctuating emotions. Wrestling gave me an outlet."

Claire nods. "That was cheerleading for me," she says softly. "If I was in a bad mood, I would find structure in the routine. I liked that cheering brought out my spirit, but what I really loved was putting my own spin on the movements. I could still be creative. Too bad..." She pauses and I now know why she had to quit.

"Tara was a fucking bitch?" I conclude.

"Yeah."

I still can't get over the irony that with over seven billion people on the planet, we would have the same person screw us over at completely different times in our lives.

"I'm sorry you went through that as a teenager, baby, and that there was no one in your life to lean on for support."

Claire sucks her bottom lip back between her teeth again.

"For years I blamed her for ruining my life."

Claire looks at me, while the slideshow plays in the background. "And now you don't?"

I shake my head *no*. "If anything, Tara gave me the

prime example of what I didn't want in life, so that when I found the person I did want, it would be obvious. Claire, it's obvious now. I struggled to find my way before, but I'm without doubt telling you that—"

"Nic..."

I need her to understand. I need her to give me—*us*—a chance to find our way again. "What if all of our pain was meant to be endured so we could get to this very moment in time?" I ask, completely ignoring the slideshow.

"What if all of these circumstances are just a bunch of coincidences?" she counters.

"What if I—"

"Psst!" Penny hisses, causing me to look over Claire's shoulder to glare at her.

"What?" I mouth.

"Show's over. Move it along or get another room," she teases. "Before Mom notices and starts to plan another—"

I give Penny a look and then pull Claire out of her seat, ushering her back up to the main floor. Penny is right behind us and looking for drama, probably to fill the void left from being at the therapy facility. Staying here with Mom and Dad has to get boring after a while. So, I cut her some slack and don't make a big deal out of it.

When we get into the living room, everyone is saying their goodbyes and giving Angie hugs and Graham some slaps on the back. Mom and Dad escort the guests outside to their vehicles, and when Claire starts to leave as well, I pull her to me and give her a questioning look.

"I just need to grab my bag."

"I don't want you to go."

"It doesn't feel right to stay," she says sadly. "Plus,

aren't Graham and Angie going to need to sleep apart before the wedding?"

"They already are in separate rooms," I point out with a grin. I'm sure my brother is doing none of the separate rooms shit and sneaking into Angie's room as soon as the house quiets, but who am I to judge? I would be doing the same damn thing.

Claire puts her hands on her hips and narrows her eyes up at me. "You don't honestly believe that, do you?"

I shrug. "Not any of my business. Want to watch one of those sappy movies that I described earlier?"

"A Christmas movie? Now?"

"Maybe one where someone always ends up with a rare disease toward the middle and we wait until the end to see if they die?"

"That sounds like a horrible idea," she giggles. "I want comedy." Then reality hits and she frowns. "I really should go."

"You really should stay."

"But what would your parents think?"

I shrug nonchalantly. "Probably that I'm making the single best decision of my life."

"You cannot possibly know that."

I glance at my watch. "It's late. You are staying."

"You are bossy."

"Just bask in the freedom of not having to make a decision. It's been decided."

"Fine."

27

CLAIRE

I should have found a ride back to my one-room box, because lying on Nic's bed while he fumbles with the TV, wearing only low-hanging sweatpants and a fitted T-shirt, is not my idea of relaxing.

I feel the complete opposite of relaxed. I am wound tight like a coil, ready to come undone at the first sight of his exposed skin. That is what Nic does to me, and while I used to think he knew his effect on me, now I am not quite sure he knows the extent to which I find him attractive. Otherwise, he would probably use it against me any chance he got —or just become a nudist.

"I thought you were an expert in electronics and all," I tease, making him turn back to me with a sexy grin.

"Perhaps you are making me nervous."

"Me?" I ask innocently. "You're the one walking around wearing lingerie."

"Lingerie?" he asks, pausing his task to look down at his outfit. "I'm wearing gray sweatpants."

"Exactly." I exaggeratedly lick my lips. "If only you understood the appeal of what they do to a woman."

He huffs out a laugh in disbelief. "I feel like a piece of meat being analyzed to see if it is ready to be eaten."

"I recently have taken a liking to meat," I comment nonchalantly, earning a chuckle in reply.

"Maybe if you stop looking at me as if I'm your next meal, I can get the show started."

"I'm enjoying the show right here."

Nic smirks and his eyes twinkle with mischief. I love our playful times and will miss the bantering if we go back to just being coworkers-who-sometimes-get-naked-and-have-intercourse. "Well, when your little pussy is begging for release, don't get mad at me when I withhold the fun as a punishment."

"You think you hold all the power, don't you?" I goad.

"You can't resist me," he challenges.

Then I have a little fun by stretching my whole body out on top of his bed like a lazy starfish. I yawn and allow my legs to spread casually, while the red satin pajama set I am wearing coats my skin like molten lava. My little science experiment is working, and I must have caught Nic's attention because once he notices my movement, he stalks over to me and climbs on top—balancing his weight on his arms.

"Don't tease me if you don't plan to take me." His words come out as a growl.

"Maybe that was my plan all along."

"You are such a bad girl," he chides.

"I remember once upon a time, you told me you like bad girls. Ones who know the score," I add, staring straight into his eyes. I could get lost here. I can feel his breath on my skin and it warms me. It is like our hearts beat as one. I've never felt this connected to anyone. He makes me go crazy. One second I want to run and the next I want to rip his clothes off. "This round, I need *you* to understand the score. I have my hormones all out of whack, and I can either take care of myself or use you. Which shall it be? Because the bathroom incident just warmed me up."

I've always been sure of my sexuality but just hearing my wanton words makes me wonder if I have an alter ego just waiting to burst out of me. Nic gives me the unspoken confidence to be myself—even if I sound a bit deprived.

Nic's eyes smolder and darken to a navy blue shade. "I've never stopped wanting you, baby. You are so freaking be—"

"Ah, ah, ah," I interrupt, holding up my manicured finger and waving it back and forth. "Less talk. More action."

Nic doesn't need any convincing while he tears off my clothes, lines himself up at my entrance, and sinks inside me from tip to root. I have been primed and ready to go ever since leaving the bathroom where we reacquainted ourselves with each other after a dry spell. My insides are still freshly lubricated from his last entry, so I don't need time to adjust.

"Is this what you want?" he asks, biting my earlobe.

I nod and suck my bottom lip into my mouth. "Harder."

Nic stops midstroke to get my attention. "You sure, baby? I don't want to bruise you."

"I'm sure."

And just like that, we get our groove back, and I meet every thrust by lifting my hips off the mattress in the same rhythmic dance we seem to do with each other. Nic is my home away from home, and no matter how things change, there is one thing that will always remain the same—my inability to resist his charm. Or his body in those damn gray sweatpants.

My orgasm is sudden and unexpected. My body is changing and everything feels different—but in the best kind of way—at least sexually. Nic rolls and tucks me to his side, slipping out and making me instantly miss the fullness. I know that I will be sore in the morning like he warned. He didn't go easy on me, and part of me is glad about it. Yes, the baby is changing everything, but it is comforting to know that Nic claims he will still find me attractive. It shouldn't matter. I am torturing us both by riding the fence between being together and being apart, but I blame him for tonight's encounter because he asked me to stay. He knows I can't resist that look he gives me.

After several minutes, Nic gets up, and I groan over my heat source vacating the bed. I watch through slanted eyes as he goes back over to the TV and fumbles with his phone. "You must really have your heart set on a chick flick. Who would have ever guessed?"

Nic laughs and then grabs the remote while invading the cocoon I created for myself since his departure. "Just watch." He hits play and one of my favorite love songs that I always sing to in the car starts.

"I love this song," I say softly. My eyes are fixated on the TV when a picture of me appears on the screen. I am walking into Hoffman Headquarters and my hair is blowing in the wind. I look up at Nic with confusion, but he just places a finger to my lips to shush me.

"Just watch," he reiterates.

I turn my attention back to the screen and wait as my image fades and then another one fills up the frame—but this time it is of me and Nic under the Welcome to Vegas sign.

There are pictures at Red Rock Canyon, the pancake shop, and from the night I went on a bashing spree at the break-everything warehouse—which also was the night we first had sex.

"When did you do this? And why?"

"I have been working on it for weeks and wanted to show you just how I see you."

"And how is that?" I ask.

"I see you as if you are the most beautiful sunflower in an empty field. You are wild and free. No one can compare to your beauty, and when I am around you, it is like nothing else exists."

I don't know what to say, so I just turn my attention to the screen and watch as picture after picture fills up the frame to the rhythm of the music. I didn't even realize some of these pictures existed. I imagine some were taken from security footage, and the idea of being watched should freak me out more than it does. Have I just gotten used to it?

That's the fear I have with being with Nic. Is he going to do things "in my best interest" but not give me a choice? He seems to run by his own set of rules. I refuse to lose myself entirely in a relationship, then one day wake up and not even recognize who I am.

The song changes over and some pictures of us together flood the screen. Nic pulls me closer and draws lazy circles on my back, sending tingles up my spine. He went through a lot of work to make this slideshow, and when it ends, I am left speechless and confused.

Can I truly be happy denying myself the love that Nic is learning to freely offer? He is doing everything I thought I wanted him to do for months. Now that he is opening up and being vulnerable, what am I doing? I'm keeping him at arm's length. Is the timing all wrong? Am I missing my chance at a lifetime of happiness because I am afraid to take a leap of faith and trust the man who has let me down in the past?

"You're being awfully quiet," Nic says absently, while shutting off the TV when the show ends.

"There's just a lot on my mind."

"I know, baby. And I want to reassure you that I will wait."

"Wait? For what exactly?" I ask, turning my attention to his face so I can see his eyes. That's where I can find the truth.

"For you to realize that we are meant for each other."

"Maybe we were."

"*Are.*"

I shake my head. "I'm struggling with this pregnancy. I'm an adult who is dealing with trauma that started in my childhood."

"I'm sorry, baby girl," Nic says, kissing my forehead. "Your family doesn't deserve you. How well you turned out despite having a shitty past is a testament to just how amazingly resilient you are as a human. You never cease to amaze me. No child ever needs to grow up feeling unwanted or as a burden."

"That's what I'm desperately trying to avoid for this baby."

"This baby is going to be loved, Claire. It has you as a mommy," he says with such reverence that I can't help but cry. "Oh baby, don't cry. If only you would be open to trusting me to take care of you." He places soft kisses on my forehead and breathes into my hair. His strength is my comfort.

"Your family is going to hate me if you are with me and Ethan ends up being the father."

He sighs. "Even if that happens—which it won't—I am a grown man and don't let the opinions of others dictate my own. I will stand up and fight for what I want."

"And if he is the father, he'll stop at nothing to rip this baby from me."

"And I'll stop at nothing to protect what I already feel is mine," he growls. "Wash your mind of that fucking prick, because if he threatens you one more time, he might not breathe another day."

"Nic…"

"Forget him, Claire. I'm still trying to do right by you for all the past pain I caused you. I went about everything the wrong way. And saying sorry right now seems pathetic compared to the weight of my transgressions, yet I am out of options that will be substantial enough for you to see that I am here. I am here, baby girl. And I'm not going anywhere. I'm done being emotionally inept. I'm done pretending that life would be better without the chance of heartbreak, when having the chance in and of itself is what causes me to actually live."

I take a deep breath, hold it, and then let it out. "Everything is just so complicated."

"True love is gritty and raw. It's that feeling deep inside the soul. Claire, you are interwoven into my thoughts when I wake up and when I go to sleep. We are like grains of sand mixed together, no longer able to be separated. That's what you do to me. You make me want to try to be better. Give us a chance, baby. I want you. I will always want you."

"I want you too, Nic. I've only been trying to convince myself that I don't and it's a lie." I lift my head to gain access to his lips. "I am tired of holding back," I say as I keep kissing him. "I'm done lying to myself."

Nic's eyes light up, and his body releases tension that I never noticed he was carrying until his muscles relax. He lets out an exhale and then devours my lips, kissing me with such passion that I feel like I am being worshipped.

I'm not naive enough to think that this journey is not going to have struggles or obstacles to get over. However, I am tired of trying to do this by myself. Maybe everything leading up to this very moment was meant to teach me that sometimes it is okay to not be okay. Right now, I am hurting and terrified about what will happen with my future, but with certainty, I want Nic to be in it.

He rolls me to my back and kisses down my exposed neck and bare chest. He lays his head on my stomach and whispers, "Did you hear that, little one? Your mommy is finally coming to her senses. Took her long enough, eh?"

I shake with laughter as Nic continues lower and settles between my thighs. He pulls my glistening lips apart and slips in two fingers. I feel like a blob of nerves and incapable of doing much other than lying back and enjoying the ride.

"I love you, Nic," I cry out, as I am overcome by all the pleasure he wants to give to me.

"I love you more."

I wake up rested and without regrets the next morning, ready to get my best friend married off to the love of her life. I feel different now that I have finally found mine at the same time. It took me long enough to accept the inevitable, but Nic is that for me. He's my once in a lifetime love.

I turn my head to look at his sleepy face. He is wrapped around me, holding me to him so tightly that if I move a certain way it hurts to breathe. He has a leg draped over my hips and my back is to his front. I can tell he is asleep based on the way he is breathing. We exhausted each other last night, and just when I think he cannot possibly raise the bar, he does.

While there are a lot of things still left to figure out, I know without doubt that I want to go through the fire with Nic by my side.

I trust that he will protect me from Ethan.

I trust that he will be a good daddy to this baby.

Nic starts to stir and nuzzles his face into my hair, breathing in my scent. He murmurs in his sleep how good I smell, and I smile over his inability to let me go—even as I try to wiggle free of his hold.

"Not letting you go ever again," he murmurs.

"I have to pee."

"Oh well," he says slowly, making me laugh.

"Stop making me laugh or I really will pee."

Nic finally relents and sits up. Before I can even roll out of bed, he scoops me up and carries me off into his attached bathroom. Setting me on the toilet, he leans against the vanity and crosses his arms.

"I can't pee with you watching," I say seriously. He places a hand over his eyes, and I can't help but laugh. "I still can't."

"Better get used to it. I am going to see a whole lot more in the delivery room."

I groan. "Yeah, I am seeing way too many too-much-information posts on some of the first-time mom blogs I am on." I finish up and flush, joining Nic at the sink.

"There's no part of you that I won't love, Claire. I can handle it."

I look at him in the reflection of the mirror. "I'm slowly starting to believe you."

"Good. Because the only thing that scares me is losing you again."

I don't have words of comfort to offer him. I can only try to include him as much as I can with what is going on in my head. I wash my hands and turn to face Nic. "I am spending the morning with the girls. We are getting glammed up and going to have brunch."

He nods and kisses my forehead. "I'm doing the same with the guys, minus the glam part. Might even hit up a gun range to shoot some things."

I make a face. "I hate guns. They scare me."

"As they should, if you don't know how to handle one," he explains, his tone serious. "But being with me means that

I do have them. I keep them unloaded and locked up." He tugs me closer at the hips. "Does that bother you?"

I think about my answer for a few seconds and then shake my head no. "I know that you and Graham have a thing for privacy and security, so I understand that you would want some protection."

"It's more than a *thing*, Claire. It's an obsession." His eyes darken. "We protect what is ours. And baby? You're mine now. You always were mine. Even when we were apart, I was always trying to protect you."

"I'm not like Angie, though, Nic. She accepts the guards and all the protocols to be with Graham. I'm not so sure I can do all of that."

His eyes soften, but his jaw doesn't relax. "I can't let go of my need to keep you safe."

"I'm not in any danger. Ethan won't want to physically hurt me now that he knows I'm pregnant."

Nic glances away, and I can tell he is battling inside between giving me my freedom and locking me away in some proverbial tower.

"Men like me always have enemies, Claire. Even if they take their time revealing themselves. Going public with our relationship will only make it obvious to anyone against me that I have a weakness, yet I want the whole world to know that you are mine. Only mine. I am done taking things for granted, but I refuse to keep this a secret for much longer."

"I can take care of myself, Nic. I'm not some clueless bimbo."

"I know that, baby."

"Why do I get the feeling you aren't telling me everything? Has something happened? I know Angie told me that there were some security breaches at HH."

"I don't want you to worry about it, baby. I'm handling it and have people I trust working for me to handle it."

"But you and Graham are in danger? Again?" I probe.

Nic sighs and runs a hand down the back of his neck. I can see the slight tic to his jaw and the way his breathing gets more labored. "I can't go about my day if I don't know that I have taken some safety measures to keep you safe. It is imperative that I do."

"Like tracking me?" I inquire, propping my hands on my hips.

"That's part of it, yes."

"I can't do a shadow," I protest. "Please. Having someone following me will make me paranoid. I already feel extra eyes on me at HH. It makes me twitchy."

"How about if you don't know they are around?"

"I'll know."

"You don't now."

I let out a long exhale and I am about to ask him to repeat himself, but I heard him loud and clear. "I thought we just fought about this. Did you not learn anything from that conversation?"

"I never agreed to not keep tabs, baby. I just promised myself to be extra discreet."

"No," I say flatly.

"No?"

"If you are going to insist on doing this to me, then you need to tell me everything so I at least feel like you are not invading my privacy. Who is watching me? Where are the trackers? How long have you been keeping tabs on me and will you stop if you find that I am actually safe?"

"You really want to hash this out now?" Nic asks with a sigh. "Before you eat?"

I narrow my eyes at him. Does he think I'm cranky and less flexible if I don't eat? Well, he does have a point, because I am. "Yes."

"Then get in the shower and we can do it while I wash your hair."

I start the water and give it a minute to warm. Nic goes in first and pulls me to him. "Don't get distracted," I warn, as he runs soapy hands up and down my arms and back.

"I do not have someone regularly following you at HH, but ever since you got a new phone, I have lost access to the tracking device I installed on your old one. I still have one in your car."

"Why?"

"It started out as a way to make sure you were not used as a bargaining chip to harm Graham or Angie. Being best friends with my brother's wife makes you an important person of interest. Graham and I made some enemies when we took down the ring last year, and while we are trying to keep a low profile and never had to testify, we are still overly cautious about any retaliation."

I allow the water to cascade down my face as I listen to Nic share the details that I should have demanded long ago. "You said it started out that way, but what changed and what are you doing now?"

"I became obsessed. It was comforting to know you got back to your apartment or you arrived to work or you got to the gym on schedule. I used the added knowledge as a way to cope with my own insecurities, masking everything under the umbrella category of it-was-for-your-own-good. Then after Vegas, I couldn't resist any longer. I knew Ethan was a horrible match for you. While I was very commitment-averse, I still wanted to pursue you for selfish reasons and make sure that you had everything you needed. The tracker was just a bonus to me being able to find you at all times. What started out as a favor to Graham to make sure you were not used as a weapon to harm his fiancée later became my way of being able to sleep at night—knowing you were safe. But with this level of insight, also came a jealous rage when I found out you were still accessing the Entice Escorts database and pursuing dates for money."

"My parents were supposed to be paying for my college tuition," I explain. "For years I believed that, but then my mom dropped the bombshell on me right before Vegas that I was really the one stuck with the bill. With interest being elevated due to the length of time it would take me to repay back the loan, I knew I was going to have to get another job. Being an escort is a quick way to make money and not have to commit to a nine-to-five job."

"You never have to worry about money again, baby. I've been waiting for the day that you accepted our relationship, and I planned to wipe your debt away."

"You knew about it?" I ask in shock.

"Yes. I made it my priority to learn everything I could about you. Between Collins, my friend Asher who lives in California, and a couple of hired associates, I was able to make sure your new apartment had added security features and learned that you were getting bogged down with debt."

"Damn," I exhale, allowing a shiver to run through me,

despite the water being very hot. "I should be scared over your level of obsession."

Nic pulls me to him. "But you're not?"

"I'm flattered. But you are a bit over the top."

"Only when it comes to you, baby. No one else has ever had my heart so tied up in knots. You are my present and my future. From this day forward, I want it all."

I don't have the right words to say, so I just stand up on tiptoes to kiss his lips, while my hands slither down between us to massage his cock.

"Hmm," I hum.

"You enjoying yourself?" he asks with a humorous edge to his tone.

I shake my head. "No. I'm rather bored."

He huffs out a laugh, tangling his fingers in my damp hair. "Are you now?"

Keeping my gaze laser focused on his eyes, I slowly lower myself onto the smooth tiled floor. Nic tries to stop me, but I'm too determined to show him how much I appreciate him helping me to see what was in front of me all along.

"Claire, you're pregnant…"

I flatten my tongue and scrape it across the side of his hardening cock from root to tip, flicking it at the end. I sit my butt farther back on my feet. "Do you have a point?" I do the same thing along the other side, feeling Nic's fingers wrapping around my hair.

He lets out a labored breath and shifts his weight, as he leans against the wall. "You shouldn't be kneeling on a hard floor."

I give him a half smile, while placing a finger in front of

my lips. "Shhh…you're talking way too much. Do I need to get my ball gag out?"

"What?" he asks, then bursts out into laughter when he realizes I'm joking. "Wait, you can't be serious."

"Try me."

He holds his hands up, as he lets me continue my road trip with my mouth, savoring this quiet moment where I can have some control. Without warning, I push my mouth forward, swallowing him whole. I squeeze my thumbs into the palms of my hands, taking advantage of the little trick that helps to avoid setting off my gag reflex.

Pulling back, I glance up at Nic, who has his head tilted back against the shower wall. His eyes are hooded, and I smile at the ability to give him a fraction of the pleasure he gives to me.

I continue back to my rhythm of sucking and licking, using my hands to help twist and pull his hard cock. The water pelts down around us, while our moans merge into the steam.

"I'm close," he bites out, thrusting his hips forward.

In.

Out.

In.

Out.

It just takes a few more rounds, and I feel the first splash of his cum hit the back of my throat.

"Fuck!" Nic barks, as I swallow him a little deeper. Just a little farther.

His cock twitches inside my mouth several times, as the sweet and salty liquid stimulates my tastebuds. He tastes so good.

Sliding him out, I lick my lips and then yelp as Nic's strong arms pull me up. I wrap my legs around his waist, molding my body to his.

"Well, that was fun," I say softly, kissing his neck.

"You are full of surprises."

I shrug, while still keeping my head tucked into the contours of his chest. "I got thirsty."

"Ha," he says with a huff, "well, then I'm glad I could quench it for you."

"You sure taste delicious."

Nic shuts off the water and wraps me in a towel the size of a blanket. "All of my clothes are in my room. Can I borrow something of yours so I can get down the hall without embarrassing myself?"

Nic's eyes wiggle. "I love it when you wear my clothes. I love it even better when I can take them off of you. Go pick something out," he says, staying back in the bathroom as he pulls out his supplies to shave.

I move into the bedroom and over to his suitcase. I rummage through to dig for something comfy to wear. As I move a sweatshirt, I notice a catalog hidden beneath a few folded pairs of pants. Looking across the top, I see a couple holding a baby. I leaf through the pages and find Sharpie circles over some of the items, as well as scribbled notes in the margins.

"Wow, I wasn't expecting to find this," I call over to him.

"Oh boy, hopefully it's not my teenage collection of nudie magazines."

"Pretty sure those types of magazines were obsolete when you were a teen," I comment with a laugh. Nic is older than I am by several years, but the age difference never bothered me. Similarly, Angie and Graham have a gap —except theirs is even bigger.

"I was a more visual person though," he says, moving his body into the frame of the door. He has a towel wrapped around his waist. It is situated low on his hips so I can still enjoy the V of his muscles. Like liquid heat, his eyes scan over my naked body. I lost my towel when I entered the room. I just never expected to take this long to find an outfit to throw on. Despite just spending time in the shower together, it is like Nic can't get enough of me. "Still am."

I saunter over to him and hold up the baby magazine. I point to the front cover. "This."

"That."

"Why do you have it packed in your bag?" I ask, flipping through the pages, reading his little barely legible notes.

"I was educating myself and making a list of all the items I want to buy for the baby."

"Oh. But this was before I agreed to be with you."

"Baby, I would have made sure you had everything you needed, even if it would have taken you longer to see what I already saw with us."

"Did you learn anything from all your research?" I ask, curious at his findings.

"Tons. But the most important finding I found was how expectant mothers get super horny and need to be"—he pauses while thinking of the best way to phrase his words— "cared for."

"Is that so?" I ask, trying to hold back the smile that wants to break loose.

"So, I expect you to want sex regularly, and I think I may be able to handle that challenge."

"Maybe I'm the exception to the rule."

Nic's eyes light up with mirth. "No doubt. Knowing your current appetite for my dick, you'll probably just want to stay molded together every waking moment."

I smack his arm, as he fake winces. "Stop. I'm horny, yes. But I'm not some nymphomaniac."

"Maybe you'll be that by the time you hit your second trimester. Challenge accepted."

"You are crazy."

"I'm utterly crazy for you, Claire. Does that bother you?"

I smile over his words and stretch up to kiss his lips. "I'm done being scared of how deep you can love me. I'm all in."

"All in," he repeats.

28

NIC

I stand beside Claire, waiting for our turn to walk down the rose-covered aisle. Harp music is playing, and I can feel my heart beating out of my chest. Today Graham is tying the knot, and I can't be any happier for him to have found his person. He and Angie belong together, and watching their relationship develop from the start helped me see how love can change someone.

Graham has always been rigid and unyielding. When he sets his mind on something, there is no stopping him. So once he put his eyes on Angie, it was no surprise that she couldn't resist his charm. She gets all the credit for helping Graham to soften. There is something about her that allows him to be his true self—flaws and all. I should know; Claire has done the equivalent thing for me. I know it is cliché to say that she has made me a better man, but it is one hundred percent true. She has breathed life back into me when I thought I would never love anyone again.

Claire fidgets and then slowly brings her bouquet of

flowers up to her nose to smell. I can tell she is nervous based on how her left foot is tapping on the green grass. I want to pull her to me and kiss the hell out of her. I don't give a damn who sees, and the only thing that stops me is that I am not selfish enough to take any focus away from my brother and his bride.

Today isn't about us. It is about them.

Guests are lined up on elegant white chairs, waiting anxiously for the start of the ceremony. Trees are decorated with hanging flowers and glass crystals. It is late afternoon, and the golden light from the slowly setting sun casts a warm glow on everything in its path.

Every time I look at my girl, I feel like the air is being pulled from my lungs. She is that beautiful. How did I get so lucky for her to accept me into her heart? I vow to cherish the love she has to give to me. We fought hard to get to this place, and the journey leading us to this moment was not easy. I refuse to let Claire slip away by taking her for granted. Life is always full of curveballs, but every turn was worth the risk if it brought us to where we are now.

Penny and Collins are ahead of us, setting the tone and the pace for the start of the ceremony. The wedding planner is at our side, hidden behind a wall of greenery, giving us the nod to go.

"You ready, baby?" I ask, looking down at my angel of a girl. She is glowing in an elegant, long rose-gold dress with a satin bow that is embellished with little rhinestones. Her hair is twisted up and held together with a barrette that is covered in sparkling diamonds. Just when I think she could not be any more stunning, she smiles up at me. It's that look in her eyes reflecting the love I have for her back at me that is enough to stop my heart.

"I'm ready," she whispers. "Please don't let me fall."

"I'll always be there to catch you, baby." We link arms and I lead her down the aisle, where our family and friends are situated on both sides staring at us as we make our way to the altar at the end. We separate, Claire moving to stand beside Penny, and I move to stand between Collins and Graham, who is waiting for the first sighting of his bride.

Zander is playing the piano, while the harpist strums along. We listen to the melodic rendition of Andrea Bocelli's "The Prayer," sung by the vocalist, as we all anticipate Angie and her dad coming down the aisle. It is a dedication to her mom and twin brother who cannot be here in the physical sense today.

I look over at Claire across the way and give her a small smile. I don't care who notices the exchange, because after today, I will be telling everyone I know that my heart is taken by the strongest woman I know. Claire is different from everyone else I ever dated or had a tryst with. She doesn't put up with my shit and has no fear in telling me what's on her mind. She is bold and snarky when necessary, but sweet and sophisticated as well. I've met my match.

Once the prelude song finishes, the instrumental version of Canon in D starts to play and the guests stand at attention, looking back up the aisle to see Angie and her dad make their appearance. If Disney needed another princess, I am sure Angie would meet the standard in her layered wedding dress. As she walks closer, with her eyes fixed only on Graham, I can tell that she is crying through her smile. Her pure white dress is made mostly of lace. Little flowers are sewn into the top sheer layer, adding dimension to an otherwise simple dress.

The officiant moves to stand between Graham and Angie, as her dad uncovers the veil from her face and places her hands into his son-in-law's. Words are exchanged between the men and their mutual respect is evident on their faces. There was a time when neither Graham nor I believed her dad would be able to make it here today. Angie and her dad have battled their vices and are living proof that patience and dedication can triumph.

"Family and friends, we are gathered together to bear witness to this wonderful couple who are about to embark on the ultimate journey of a lifetime—marriage." The officiant motions for us all to sit down. I take my seat in the front row, beside my dad. Claire fluffs Angie's dress with the grace of a dancer and takes the bouquet from her hands before taking a seat herself.

Angie beams up at Graham as he smiles an encouraging smile to give her the confidence she needs to make this public declaration. "Today and every day after, I say 'I do' to you. I choose you today. I choose you tomorrow. And I choose you for forever. You are the piece of my heart that I did not know was missing. Thank you, Graham Xavier Hoffman, for loving me."

I take my eyes off of Angie to look at my brother who is crying. Holy fuck. My heart sinks as he pulls out a tissue from his pocket and wipes at his eyes. There is so much emotion reflected back to his bride that I wonder if he will be able to recite his vows. I look over at my girl and see that she is fighting back the tears that I know she would easily shed if she had some privacy. I hate seeing her cry.

"My sweet Angie. You make it easy to love you. You are selfless and kind. Feisty and gentle. Your love is a gift, and I will spend the rest of my life treasuring it. You are all mine."

"As you are mine," she mouths.

"It is now time for the rings," the officiant announces, taking the rings from a little box that he has on a podium. "Graham, repeat after me. With this ring, I thee wed."

Graham echoes the words, and then slides the ring onto Angie's finger. He kisses the ring and then places her hand over his heart. The custom-made diamond ring sparkles in the light from the setting sun.

Taking my hand out of my pocket, I turn my ring that I wear as a reminder of my once toxic desire to never get married. I have worn this ring since my heart was broken, vowing to myself that I would never make the kind of commitment I am witnessing today.

It seems silly wearing it now. So much has changed.

Sliding off the ring, I rotate it and then slip it back into my pocket. I glance over at my girl, who I catch watching me. I can only hope she realizes just how strong my love is for her. I'm never letting her go.

"And now it is your turn, Angie," the officiant says softly.

"With this ring, I thee wed," she says, sliding Graham's band onto his finger. She kisses it and places his hand over her heart.

"By the state of Oregon, it is my pleasure to announce Mr. and Mrs. Graham Hoffman, our newly married husband and wife. Graham, you may…" The officiant pauses as Graham swoops in and kisses Angie with such ferocity that the entire bridal party rises and cheers them on. He spins her around as she lifts her feet off the ground.

"Yeah!" I yell, rooting for them with my fist in the air.

Zander starts playing the piano recessional music, and I meet Claire halfway to walk her back up the aisle. We pass by the rows of guests, and everyone is bursting with excitement to go back into the mansion to kick off the reception.

"Are you okay?" I ask Claire, who seems quiet. She looks a little pale, and I wonder if it is just from trying not to cry.

"I'm just a little lightheaded. Watching them say their vows really made my heart smile."

"When was the last time you ate?" I ask, waving to a few friends of the family I haven't seen in a while. I turn my attention back to Claire when she doesn't answer right away. I frown as she looks deep in thought. "Baby, when?"

"This morning for brunch. I just had something small, and now I am feeling the drop in my blood sugar, I think. I'm fine, really. No need to fuss over me. We have bridal party obligations to perform."

"I'm going to get you something to snack on before the main dinner. My duty to care for you far outweighs anything else."

Claire places a hand on my arm. "No, we have to greet the guests and such. I have to make sure Angie's dress stays smoothed out and help her remove her veil for the reception."

I ignore her protests and flag down one of the staff members who is dressed in a black suit and bowtie. "I am going to need a glass of juice and some crackers. And maybe some cheese."

"Of course, sir."

"You didn't have to do that. I'm an adult and can wait for the meal."

"You are pregnant and need to take care of yourself. Good thing you have me."

"Are you going to be like this the entire pregnancy?"

I shrug. "Probably worse. You know how I love to take everything to the extreme."

"Lovely," she groans, making me smile.

"Keep it up, and I'll buy you one of those motorized scooters so you can stay off your feet. Oh, and those comfy slip-on silicone shoes with the holes all over them. Because the days of you wearing those death traps"—I point down to her heels—"are going to be over."

"I am pregnant, not crippled."

The staff member returns and hands over a plate and a glass of a burgundy liquid. I lift the glass to Claire's lips for her to take a sip. "Good?"

She smiles. "It's cranberry juice with ginger ale. Tastes delicious, thank you."

I feed her a cracker with cheese and we sit in the garden on a bench, watching as the crowd disperses and enters the mansion for the reception.

"I think we have to go take pictures," she says between bites.

"Don't rush. I am sure we'll have plenty of time to do everything. Here, give me your feet and I can rub them while you snack."

"I could get used to this special treatment, you know."

"That's the plan, baby. I got to earn my place in your

heart," I tease. "But at least there's two entry points—through your stomach and through your feet."

"This is true," she giggles.

"Stop or everyone is going to notice," Claire scolds, as she pushes away the hand that I have resting on her ass.

The photographer is posing us around the newlyweds, and I am having way too much fun teasing Claire. Getting her to blush is now my new favorite hobby. Despite her tone of voice, I know she is enjoying the attention because she can't help but shiver every time I move closer to her. It is a game we like to play with each other to see who gives in first.

"Going public with my feelings for you is a reality, Claire. I want the entire world to know you are off the market."

"Pretty sure no one is paying me any attention. No need to get the ruler out to size up dicks."

I laugh over her bold remark just as the photographer reminds us to be serious. I clear my throat and hold my hands up in apology as Graham gives me some side-eye. When there is a transition to another outdoor setting, I lean in closer to Claire to whisper, "Pretty sure you are oblivious to how appealing you are to men."

She shrugs. "Whatever. I'll be hugely pregnant soon and no one will even give me a second glance. Lucky you, you have me all to yourself."

"Damn straight I do," I say with a smack to her ass. She jumps into the air and looks around to see if anyone noticed.

Claire pouts out her bottom lip and looks up at me through her dark eyelashes. "Does that mean I can't catch the bouquet during the reception?"

"Correct."

"Why not? Afraid some other man is going to slide his hands up my legs to place the garter?" She taps a finger along her jaw. "Come to think of it, that kinda sounds fun. I think I will veto your demand."

A deep growl builds low in my throat. "If you want to be responsible for his hands being broken, then go for it," I say flatly.

Claire swallows hard and then follows the photographer's directive to take a few pictures with just her and Angie. She adds a sway to her hips as she walks away from me. That girl better watch it or she is going to find herself pulled away from the party so I can stuff her full of my dick. She brings out every predatory, animalistic impulse in me. And dammit, I think she actually likes it. Sneaky little minx.

I watch from the sidelines as the two girls stand back-to-back and then turn toward the camera with a giggle. The photographer then asks them to lean against the railing of a little footbridge that goes over a koi pond.

We wrap up the photo session and then hop in golf carts to ride around the grounds before we have to go into the mansion for the formal introductions.

"Remind me why I can't drive this thing?" Claire asks, crossing her arms over her chest.

"Because I value all three of our lives."

"Oh, c'mon. I'm not that bad," she huffs.

"You pretty much are."

She smacks me on the arm, making the cart swivel.

"I've never gotten in an accident before and only have a few minor incidents on my record."

"I'm sure none of them were your fault," I respond sarcastically.

"Oh, you have some nerve!"

"Your driver starts on Monday and will be driving you to work."

Claire turns so fast that I jerk from the suddenness of her movements. "My driver?"

"Yup," I confirm.

Someone is trying their best to get me to distrust those I once trusted. Whoever thinks it's in their best interest to double-cross me hasn't experienced just how dark my revenge can get. Until everything settles, I'm not taking Claire's safety for granted. Whatever concessions I've made to allow her some level of independence may no longer apply. With Graham gone soon on his honeymoon, it'll be up to me to keep everything afloat.

"I don't need a driver."

"Yes, you do."

"Who is he?" she inquires, facing the front again.

"Me."

"You."

"I want you to move in with me—officially. We can then spend a few months planning out our dream home before the baby arrives."

"You want to build?" she asks, emotion evident in her tone.

"I want to build a life with you, baby. The house is just part of the process."

Claire turns toward me again, and when I look into her

eyes, I see hope and happiness. Everything I never thought I would want is now entwined with Claire's acceptance of her and me becoming an *us*.

"Thank you for accepting me," she says softly.

"Thank you for giving me space to realize it is you that I want. I'm never letting you go."

"Good. Because I play for keeps. And we both know how good I am at gambling."

I laugh over the memory of her in Vegas. She definitely knows how to work a table. "You are worth the risk, baby."

"I'll be reminding you of that when I'm driving you nuts with all the stupid shit I'll most likely do."

Placing a chaste kiss on her forehead, I tickle her sides. "No doubt."

29

NIC

I finish spinning my girl for the bridal party dance and take my seat at the linen-covered table that faces the guest tables.

"Drink some more water," I remind Claire. "I don't want you lightheaded again."

"So bossy."

"You like it."

She leans into me. "No, I like your cock inside me, and in order for that to happen, I need to accept the less thrilling parts of you. Which means I have to learn to deal with your jealousy, possessiveness, and poor understanding of how I like to drive."

I want to kiss the smirk right off her lips and pull her away just to show her how much my cock worships her, but the DJ's voice cuts through the crowd, silencing everyone.

"Ladies and gentlemen, please give a round of applause to the father of the bride, who is going to say a few words to his daughter and son-in-law."

Everyone claps as he makes his way to the center of the

dance floor and turns his attention toward Angie. The DJ hands him the microphone and smacks hands with him in an encouraging gesture.

"For those of you who don't know me, I am Angie's dad. I have made a lot of mistakes in my lifetime, Angie, but marrying your mother was not one of them. She embodied everything good in this world, and I am so glad that you were able to get to know her for as long as you did before she passed. You and your brother, James, enthralled her and were her pride and joy. Your mother wrote this letter the day before she took her last breath. She wrote a letter for you and one for James. James has his letter buried with him. I have been holding onto yours until the day you married the man of your dreams. I made a promise to your mother that I would ensure that you would not settle for anything less than what you deserved. And I am honored to say that I held up my vow to her."

Angie's dad clears his throat and takes a sip of his water, obviously trying to cover the fact that he wants to cry. I look over at my girl and she has tears cascading down her cheeks. I touch her thigh and hand her a napkin. We just finished up dinner, and while the cake is getting cut, we are doing the speeches that we prepared.

"I'm going to read the letter as my speech, because your mom always had a way with words and because it was one of her last requests that I am honored to fulfill. 'Dearest Angela, from the first moment I realized I was pregnant with you, I would dream about all of your future milestones. Your first word, your first step, your first boo-boo. I would think about how happy I would be to watch you graduate. I knew without any doubt that you would make me proud—

just for being you. I would dream about the day you would say vows to the man you love. I watched you grow. You were always so feisty as a toddler. My little sweet and sour girl. I know life is not going to be easy for you after I go. I know you are going to struggle. And while I have bargained with God to give me more time here, I know that it is inevitable that I am going to miss some of your milestones. Just know that I am with you—even if not in the physical sense. Know that I love you, am proud of you, and rejoice in the day that you fall head over heels and marry the guy of your dreams.'"

Boxes of tissues are passed around, and the sound of noses blowing fills up the space.

"I think I'm next," Claire chokes out, emotion flooding through her body.

"You'll do great. Just breathe."

When Claire's name is announced to speak next, I help pull out her chair and squeeze her hand in encouragement.

"Hi. I'm Claire," she says with a wave. "I met Angie when I moved from the East Coast to attend River Valley University. We were two different people who were both looking for fresh starts. Angie, I knew early on that we were going to be best friends. You always try to see the good in people, and it is through your perseverance that you taught me so many things. You taught me that life is too short. When we put off things for tomorrow, we are really gambling with time. You taught me to hug those I love, to be bold with how I use my words, and that challenges in life are just learning opportunities. I miss cohabitating with you, but I get why things have changed. Enter Graham. From the moment we first met, I knew you had your eyes set on my best friend. I get why we didn't get along at our first encounter. Or the second. Or the third." The guests laugh over her exaggerated way of saying the words slowly. "Maybe we are too much alike. Once I saw how protective and kind you were toward Angie, I knew that I was going to eventually have to say goodbye to the notion of seeing her as just mine. While I typically don't like to share, I will make this exception for you. You bring a joy to her life and a stability that she needs to flourish and grow. Thank you for being there for her when she needed someone who wasn't afraid of the hard work it took to get her to today. I get that she can be difficult and challenging and stubborn—"

"Hey!" Angie speaks up, making a face at Claire.

"We both know it's true, Angie. It's part of your charm." Angie breaks out into a smile and Claire continues with her speech. "Anyhoo, if anyone is up for this task, it is you, Graham. You have breathed life into my friend, and I will forever be thankful to you. However, if you do her wrong—in any way—I will cut you, watch you bleed out, and then bury your body." Claire waits for the eruption of laughter to stop and then she raises up her glass of sparkling water that she is white knuckling, probably from performance anxiety. "Cheers to the married couple. May your lives be full of belly laughs, crazy stories, and endless milestones. I love you both and wish you nothing but happiness."

"Hear, hear!" the guests filling the ballroom chant.

"Next up is the brother of the groom, Nic Hoffman," the DJ announces.

I wait until Claire is back at the table. I pull out her chair for her to sit and run a hand over her bare shoulder. "You did amazing, baby."

"Thank you," she exhales. "Just glad it's over."

I make my way to the dance floor, bumping fists with the DJ. I clutch the microphone and smile at the audience. "I'm Nic. The easier going of the brothers." I wink and earn some laughs and a snicker from Graham who knows my mellow nature is just a facade masking how I really feel. I know how intense I can be. All the Hoffmans have it in our blood. "And a tad bit more handsome."

"Boo!" Graham yells, making me laugh.

"Just teasing," I chuckle. "Needless to say, I know Graham pretty damn well. We grew up inseparable, played sports together, and now even manage to work together. Graham, you are the best brother. You have paved the road of what a leader should be. I look up to you, I respect you, and I am honored to call you brother. You deserve happiness, and I'm thrilled that you found it with the one woman who is your match." I pause and turn my attention toward my sister-in-law. "Angie, you really are perfect for Graham. He needs someone like you in his life. Someone to talk back, fight with him, and drive him utterly insane. You do all of that, and I thank you for it. He needs that challenge. For a man set in his ways, you have proven that even old dogs can be trained."

"Hey," Graham grunts out.

"It's true. Before you, Graham went through life doing whatever the hell he wanted. Now he has to get through you, and I'd be lying if I said it isn't entertaining to sit back and watch him deal with the strong woman that you are. You are the perfect addition to our family, and we all

welcome you with open arms. I love you and wish you all
the luck in the world in dealing with my brother—because
you may need it. Let's raise up our glasses and toast to the
happy couple. To health and happiness!"

"Cheers!"

When I make it back to my seat, Claire rubs my thigh
and whispers, "That was really sweet."

"Sweet?" I ask, trying to think back over all my words.

"Just thought it was nice how you welcomed Angie into
your family."

"I welcome you too, baby. You are the most important
thing to me. You are not just an option; you are my everything. I will forever put you and the baby first."

"Thank you," she mouths, the words stuck in her throat.

I tug her toward me and kiss her forehead. My mom and
dad catch the movement from their table and smile back at
me. I know they know. Penny probably couldn't keep her
mouth shut over it. I'm just glad that they seem to approve.
It is one less hurdle to cross.

The evening wraps up with us going outside to bid
farewell to the newlyweds, watch a fireworks show, and
listen to a live concert that is set up around the pool.

I have Claire in front of me and my arms wrapped over
her midsection when I feel the presence of someone coming
up from behind me. I turn my attention away from the
artists to see Collins. His expression is impenetrable, and I
know from the tic of his jaw that something is wrong.

"Baby, I need to take care of something," I say softly in
her ear. "Go stand with Penny."

"What?" she asks, looking behind me to see Collins
standing rigid in the moonlight. "Something's wrong? Is it

Ethan? He's going to sue me and take the baby, isn't he? I can tell by your eyes something just happened…"

"Please just go be with Penny while I handle whatever it is."

I hate seeing the uncertainty in her eyes, but I know that Collins would never interrupt an intimate moment unless it was serious.

I walk with him through the gardens, away from all listening ears while he finds the words to tell me what is going on.

"There's been another break-in," he says bluntly.

"At HH?"

"No."

"Where then?" I snap. I am angry with the entire situation—not with him.

"Miss Nettles's apartment."

"Fuck," I growl. "Who? Did they take anything? Was it caught on the cameras? Clues to a motive?"

"Whoever gained access appears to have tripped the security cameras prior to entering. It wasn't a forced entry, so I would assume they had access to a key."

"Fuck," I hiss.

"There's a note."

I look back to where I left Claire with Penny. "Dammit, what did it say?"

"It said, 'Revenge is sweet but Claire is sweeter.'"

I feel like I am going to pass out. "This doesn't make sense. It's also damn well ballsy to go to her residence."

"Agree."

The sound of my phone buzzing alerts me of an incoming text. It's from Tyler.

Tyler: A female broke into Claire's place but the motive is unclear

Nic: How do you know the gender? All the security cameras had a recording glitch apparently.

Tyler: Because I never stopped keeping tabs on Claire's place despite you kicking me off the assignment...and I set up my own devices in unobtrusive areas outside the building, in the hallway near her room, and in the lobby. Female average height but in a ski mask.

Nic: Send me stills if you have them.

Within seconds, Tyler sends over what I need. Collins and I make eye contact, as curse words fly out of my mouth. I relay the message exchange.

"Do you believe him?" Collins asks.

"Yes. I've only ever doubted Tyler when evidence pointed to his betrayal. But men like us don't get caught. And the evidence was so strikingly concrete that it had to be fabricated. So, I trust him."

Collins nods. "Double crossing you would not be wise."

Glancing back up the hill toward the mansion, I find Claire rocking on her heels beside Penny. I hate seeing her this agitated. "Yeah, but *someone* sure has a death wish. But who? That's basically what it boils down to. Have you kept intel on my ex, Tara?"

"Yes," Collins says softly. "She's back in Virginia. I've been keeping tabs on her and all of her credit card records, and the security camera footage proves she hasn't left the state in weeks. That said, she went from being in a decent amount of debt to suddenly being financially stable."

"I didn't give in to her demands for more money, that's for sure. Definitely keep watch on her. I don't trust her at all. She's volatile at best. Figure out who cleared her debt just to be thorough."

"Understood. What about Ethan's fiancée, Deena?" Collins asks, appearing to be thinking out loud. "Could she be involved?"

I glance again at the photos that Tyler sent over. "Assuming these are authentic, it could be her."

"Would Maxwell use her as bait?"

"He's stupid enough to think he can't be touched. So nothing would surprise me. And it would be just like Ethan to use his woman to try to gather evidence against Claire. He wants to take her to court. Says she showed up at his residence and beat the shit out of him." I leave out the part that both women are pregnant. Now is not the time to open up about it. But could Deena be searching Claire's place for proof? Does she think Claire is lying about her pregnancy? I mean, why would she do that?

"Taking her to court wouldn't serve him well—especially with as much dirt as we have on him."

"No argument there." Then a thought hits me from a database search I did a few days ago. "I know I mentioned this already the other day via text, but I've discovered photos of Eugene and my personal assistant, Brenna, together. Granted, her hair was stark black prior to her going blonde. I may not have noticed her in the photos if I wasn't already looking for discrepancies. I just can't shake this feeling that something seems off with her."

"Tell me more about Eugene. There wasn't a huge digital footprint to be found online."

We take a few steps, moving farther away from the noise. "Dan and Eugene were vying for the exact position I have currently. So, maybe there was tension there? I told Brenna not to report to work basically until I'm back in the office. I wanted to be sure she wasn't using her position as a way of infiltrating the business."

"I think it's best to act like nothing is wrong until we put all of the puzzle pieces together. If you pull back too much, it draws red flags to your behavior and will make it harder to learn the truth."

"Exactly."

"How did Eugene get let go?"

"A lot of the security breaches happened on his watch. The logical reaction was to skim the fat on any of the weak links."

Collins clears his throat. "I thought Brenna was actually starting to get interested in Dan."

"Dan, really?"

"The past few times I was there, it seemed that she was going out of her way to be where he could be on her breaks."

That's the thing about Collins. He's always been more than a bodyguard. He has an incredible set of instincts, and what he brings to the table is always valuable.

I run a hand through my hair. "I'm over this. I want to fire every person on the payroll and start from scratch. That's how angry I am. Shit…"

"What?"

"Brenna never went through the full interview process, and I may have gotten sloppy hiring her. I figured she was on a trial basis so I didn't have to worry about committing to someone permanent. But what if I cut too many corners and hired someone who was nefarious?"

Pacing along the pathway, Collins sighs. "You'd have your motive if she was with your disgruntled employee. Eugene is pissed he lost the job, so he uses Brenna to get closer to you and Claire as a way to provide him with information."

"Maybe all this time, Brenna has been inching closer to Claire. Plus, getting me fired up could put me at risk of making rash decisions based on my fears." The fastest way to get to me is through those I love. And I'm madly in love with Claire.

"It's all theory though," Collins reminds me, as if it's an afterthought. "There's still Kevin and Leo, the two former guards who accosted Claire, to consider."

"Yeah, but they are followers. I don't see them orchestrating any of this nonsense."

I rub a hand at my forehead. I have a migraine forming as I frantically try to figure out how to keep my girl from being caught in the collateral war being waged as revenge against me. Targeting her just made things go from bad to catastrophic, because I will bury any person who tries to do her harm.

But what if Brenna is caught in the middle of a love triangle between Eugene and Dan? And how does that all play out?

Sure, firing them all would make it harder to access the

building without a badge. However, I need to understand why someone is hell-bent on destroying everything I care about.

"Nothing touches Claire," I say flatly. "Without going into details, she is the most important priority in my life right now. She and my family. Hell, she *is* my family."

"Whatever you need, consider it done."

"I'm tired of shutting Tyler out. Get ahold of him and tell him to get to HH to provide on-site surveillance around the clock until I can get there. Hopefully for a weekend, everything is calm on that front."

I turn on my phone and find Asher's name in my list of contacts.

Nic: There's a crisis here and it is affecting my entire life. I need help.

Asher: Must be important if you are asking

Nic: It is

Asher: I'll book the first flight I can get

Nic: Appreciate this, man. I owe you

Relief rushes over me as I know I will soon have fresh eyes, in person, looking over this whole mess with me. Asher and I have a history, and he is someone I trust like a brother. With Graham and Angie soon taking their honeymoon, I need to have extra men on deck if I'm going to figure out what is happening seemingly right under my nose.

I'm about to text Asher a quick summary of the new events when I hear the sound of panting coming from up ahead. I turn and find Penny running toward me, panic evident on her face.

"What's wrong?" I ask, holding her elbows as I seek information. "Is it Claire? Where is she?"

"She is freaking out. She just got a horrible text from an unknown caller."

"Fuck. Where is she?"

"She's with her friend Blake."

I jog up to where guests are still gathered outside, Collins and Penny not far behind. I scan the crowd until I spot Claire. Weaving around clusters of people, I reach her and hug her to me.

"Let me see your phone, baby."

She hands it over with trembling fingers, and when I pull open the text chain, I want to smash something. It is a photo of her, rather than a text. I look at Claire who appears to be leaving Portland General.

"When was this taken?" I ask, trying to put the pieces together.

"Just a few days ago. I was at the hospital because I fell and started to bleed." Her words come out as a whisper so those around us do not hear her announcement that she is pregnant. "I'm okay though."

Nothing about this fucking situation is okay. But I keep my cool. The last thing Claire and the baby need right now is more stress. "I'm trying to figure this all out, baby. I know you are disturbed that you are being watched or followed by someone, but I'm going to do everything in my power to protect you."

"I trust you."

I kiss the top of her head and hold her tightly to me. It is an honor to have Claire's trust, and while she is freaking out, on the inside I am too. I want those who are behind all of this to suffer a slow torture. While the list of potential suspects grows, I am getting further and further away from figuring out who is ultimately responsible.

30

CLAIRE

Agreeing to let Nic into my heart comes with a lot of stipulations. For starters, he is refusing to let me stay alone in my apartment, reciting some big monologue about making up for lost time and taking advantage of every opportunity to explore living together under the same roof.

I know he is spooked from the mysterious text message, and I also know he is keeping things from me. He may see it as protecting me, but he also doesn't realize how much I overthink just about everything in my life. These secrets are messing with my mental state, but no matter how many times I ask, he just reassures me that I will be safe.

I am enjoying a bowl of cereal on his sofa when he walks out from his office down the hallway and joins me. I offer up a spoonful of carbs, which he accepts, and then place my sore feet onto his lap for rubbing.

Even in this building, I know that security has been tightened. I can't even go to get the mail without seeing extra "residents"—dressed in nondescript clothes—

watching what I'm doing. When I bring this to Nic's attention, he vaguely reminds me that my safety matters most to
him and that he's handling it.

"I may need you to conduct your Plus None business
remotely," he says hesitantly. He presents his statement like
it is still being decided, but from the look in his eyes, I can
already tell his mind is made up.

"No. I can't do that," I say simply. "I can tolerate a lot of
things, but I can't accept what you are proposing."

"Claire…"

"Don't *Claire* me, Nic. This is my career and it brings
me happiness. I am a cofounder and need to step up to the
plate while Angie is on her honeymoon. She leaves today.
Who knows, maybe she and Graham are at their destination
by now."

He sighs and then runs one hand down the back of his
neck. "What if I told you it is no longer safe to be at HH?"

"I would find you utterly paranoid. I have to be safer
being close to you and in the same building than I would be
if you were to leave me and keep me locked up somewhere.
I have a business to run, Nic. I already have anxiety over
what my job is going to look like when I am eight months
pregnant or what it will look like with a newborn. I have a
lot to juggle, and I fear losing this opportunity because I
can't juggle motherhood and a career." Women put an unbe-
lievable amount of pressure on themselves to do everything,
and quite frankly it is exhausting trying to keep up with
societal norms.

"You don't need to w—"

"Shhh!" I wave my hands in front of his lips, trying to
get him to stop with the bullshit. He should know better.

While we haven't exactly chatted about gender roles or expectations or financial contributions, he should know me enough by now, and my determination to have a life outside of him shouldn't surprise him in the slightest.

"But you don't—"

"Stop. This is not about you. This is about me and my quest to figure this whole career and mommyhood thing out on my own. I don't need you throwing shade my way and making everything even more complicated."

"I am putting more guards on you. My friend Asher is arriving today, and we need to hash out a plan. But first, get ready to go. Today's the day for the big paternity test."

"I'm more interested in the results that will be ready in a few days," I say grimly.

"May the best man win," Ethan jeers at us, with his lawyer and a three-bodyguard escort in tow. Apparently he thought I might *make a scene* or refuse to show up. Or perhaps he's projecting his insecurities of guilt onto me, when he's the one who should worry about the law.

Tucking me to his side, Nic kisses my forehead. "Don't worry about him, baby girl. Not even his entourage can protect him from me if he missteps or breathes out of turn. I said it once and I'll say it again—he'll never take this baby from you, no matter how delusional his mind can get."

Glancing at Ethan, I find him smugly looking over at me. He has his arm around Deena, and his face is still wearing the marks from where Nic hit him in my apartment. Why she decided to show up with him, dressed like she is going to high tea, beats me. I think he just brought her to add to the drama and be present in a public place with lots of witnesses.

I turn my shoulder away from the nauseatingly happy couple so I can block them out of my vision—and hopefully my mind. Nic leads me down the hall away from the clinic's entrance so we can catch a completely different elevator and not be forced to ride with them.

"At least we got to see the baby," Nic comments, wrapping an arm around me.

Ethan insisted on seeing for himself that I was even pregnant. Like I would pretend or falsify records to be in this nightmare with him just for funsies. What did I ever see in that narcissistic asshat? In my defense, I didn't have very good logic or self-esteem when we first met. That might have been some of my appeal. Ethan could tell me some sweet words, and I would easily take them at face value. It makes flipping the switch and still maintaining a fuck-buddy—what I ended up turning out to be—easier when trust is first established. In a way, I feel like I was groomed for his abuse.

Sicko.

I'm done using men as a way of validating my own self-worth. That is what years of emotional abuse can do to the heart and mind. I'm just glad that who I am in my core was not completely tarnished. Sure, I think about what life would have been like for me if I had two parents—hell, even one—that showed me what unconditional love is. But you can't pick your family, you can only choose to grow up and surround yourself with people who bring you joy. I found my joy. I am just glad I healed enough to recognize what really matters.

Nic checks his phone and types out a message.

"Everything okay?" I ask, linking arms with him. I am going to need to keep my mind busy while we wait a couple of days for the test results. I would love to drown myself in work to stay occupied, but just from the fear penetrating through Nic's body, I know that I have to give him what he needs. Right now, he needs reassurance that I can follow his safety rules.

"Asher just landed. He wants to meet at HH just to take a look around the building and see if I am missing something."

I nod and frown. "I know you don't think it's safe, but can I go just to touch base with my employees and draft a plan to maybe only work a half day or two in the physical office, but then do the rest at home? I can try to work remotely this week while you figure things out."

Nic turns toward me, and the love reflected back through his eyes is enough to make me shiver. "Thank you," he whispers, visibly relieved at my concession. "I can see you trying to accommodate my wishes, and for that"—he bends to kiss my forehead—"I am very grateful."

I reach for his hands and give them a squeeze. "We are in this together, right?"

He nods and this time captures my lips. "In this together, baby," he says, helping me into the passenger side of his car. He moves my hair over my left shoulder and kisses my exposed neck before shutting the door. The chill from the air-conditioned clinic evaporates off my skin as the heat from his touch lingers and spreads. I watch as he finds his place in the driver's seat, starts the engine, and switches into reverse. He places his hand behind my seat as he expertly backs the car up with ease and then heads out of the parking lot.

I fix my hair behind my ear and catch the sparkle of my new earrings in the mirror.

"Those new?" Nic asks, glancing over to look at my new diamond studs. They are way bigger than anything I have ever owned.

"Angie gave me and Penny a set from the Jealousy line from Graham's company. It was a gift for being a bridesmaid."

"Diamonds suit you, baby."

I touch my fingers against the stones. I love them.

Nic drives in silence to HH, but I know his broody mood has nothing to do with his feelings toward me and everything to do with his fears. With Graham on his honeymoon, Nic is losing one more person he trusts to help him solve some mystery, which seems to be getting exponentially more dangerous, based on how many calls he's—

His phone buzzes in the cup holder, and before I can look at it, Nic snatches it up and breathes out a string of curse words.

"Unknown caller?" I ask, looking at his face for any clues.

He grunts out a confirmation.

"Can I see it?"

"No," he barks. He runs a hand angrily through his hair, as I can hear his breathing pick up. "I'm sorry, Claire. I'm losing my mind with worry, and if anything happens to you, I'll go crazy."

I shift in my seat. "I wish you'd tell me what's going on. I deserve to know."

"Whoever is behind this is going to pay," he says, taking a few deep breaths. "I'll feel better when Asher is finally here to give another perspective on the situation."

"You guys went to college together on the East Coast?" I ask, trying to change the subject.

"Yeah. He and his now wife moved to Silicon Valley and are expecting their first child."

"Oh, how nice," I say softly. "Do you even want children, Nic? Maybe you will decide one day it is not what you want."

"I didn't think I wanted any, baby. But that was because I was so set on never settling down and on going through life alone. I was afraid to get hurt again, and it was easier for me to give up on hope than it was to gamble with trust. You showed me that the chance of getting a broken heart is worth taking the risk if what is waiting at the end of the tunnel is you. Thank you for our baby. What is a part of you, is also a part of me. I told you this before, I don't need a test to confirm what I already feel inside."

"I love you with every ounce of my heart."

"Feeling's mutual, my love. But how about you—did you always want kids?"

"No. I worry that I won't be a good mommy. I don't have much experience with babies, and I had the worst role model growing up. So, don't be surprised if I suck at this whole parenthood thing."

Nic places his hand on my leg, and I cover his with mine. Maybe there will come a day when I don't let any of my insecurities through, but for now I just have to hope I can learn through my own experiences and break the cycle that keeps running on a loop inside my head.

"I hate that your family," Nic starts to say but then shakes his head. "No. Let's not even give them that title. I hate that the people who were supposed to care for you sacrificed you on the altar of their own selfish desires. But you are bigger than that, Claire. You radiate acceptance and love and strength. You aren't going to be just a good mother. You are going to be the best mother, because you know exactly what it feels like to be ignored, neglected, and treated like trash. Use the pain of your past to change the future. Channel your energy in making this child never doubt that it is loved."

Nic's words are like poetry to my soul. He may claim he is not romantic. But what is more intimate than a man who can be honest and real? That to me is the definition of sexy.

I pull his hand up to my lips and kiss his palm. We are just a block away from HH, and the nerves of going in to talk with my employees who have been keeping the company afloat while I handled some of the wedding responsibilities is getting to me. We are a start-up that requires devotion and long hours. Now I have some drama surfacing over someone potentially using me to get to Nic. If the cofounders are taking huge chunks of time off from work, what message does that send to our employees?

"Can I walk you to your office?" Nic asks quietly as he parks his car on the street outside of the building.

"Sure." I open the car door to get out and see several workers making their way in through the main lobby, most likely from their lunch break.

"Hey man," a voice calls from down the sidewalk.

We turn to find a sandy-brown-haired man walking toward us, his strides long and steady.

"This must be Claire," the man says, holding out his hand to shake mine. "I'm Nic's best friend, role model, person he looks up to, and—"

"This is Asher," Nic says, cutting him off with a smirk. "My modest best friend."

Asher chuckles and gives Nic a once-over.

"Nice to finally meet you," I say with a smile.

Nic and Asher smack hands and do a half-hug-pat-on-the-back thing. I rock on my feet as I watch the men give each other looks that convey some message that I can't interpret. I'm assuming they want to catch up but also don't want to have my head filled with all of the drama that seems to be erupting like a volcano around us.

Asher looks toward the entrance to the building. "I wasn't expecting so much hustle and bustle. Seems pretty hyper today."

He's right. There are a lot of extra people entering HH today.

"That's because I have maintenance workers checking over the electrical work in the building."

Nic glances at the entrance as employees enter. I know he loves working here and is much happier than he's ever been being with his brother. Surely things will go back to normal soon.

Turning to me, he gives me a side squeeze. "Baby, I will walk you to your office like I promised."

"I'll be fine, really. You guys catch up."

Nic looks around and then raises his phone to his ear. "Do you mind escorting Claire?"

As if on cue, a tall man exits a parked car I didn't even notice was occupied. Pulling the sunglasses from his eyes, he makes eye contact with me. Sheesh, he's intense. Then he shakes hands with Asher, as if their acquaintance goes beyond the surface.

"Baby, this is my associate, Tyler." Turning to the man I've never seen before, he gives him a direct look. "Do you mind walking Claire to her office? She can show you where it's located."

"So, you're my shadow?"

Tyler tips his head down. "But only because I'm scared of not following his orders." He nudges Nic with his elbow lightly. "He can be pretty hostile when it comes to you."

"Don't I know it," I say with a weak laugh, as Asher makes some snide comment. I am trying not to get freaked out, but with this many men surrounding me, I'm worried that this whole crisis is bigger than all of us. Nic might have trust issues, but so do I.

"I'll see you in a bit," Nic says, pulling me to him gently as I try to walk away. He moves his hands up to my face, and my eyes widen with uncertainty with what his next move is going to be. When I'm about to ask him, he swoops down and places a gentle kiss on my lips in front of his best friend and employee. It's too hot for the streets of Portland, but the tingling sensation coursing through my body doesn't seem to care. There is no doubt in my mind about whether or not this development will spread like wildfire amongst the entire staff. I am sure it has already started in the break rooms. People sure love their gossip. "You are mine. And the world deserves to know it." He kisses away my hesitation, making me lean into him and open up more.

"All yours," I say softly, blushing over his attention. He makes me melt inside, and if we weren't in the middle of a dumpster fire, I would try to coerce him into having office sex again—this time with me doing all the initiation.

"I'll walk in with you both as to not cause confusion at the security checkpoints," Nic offers. "Ready to go in?"

I nod, feeling the pangs of nervous energy taking hold. I follow with my entourage as Nic gets us through security and onto an empty elevator. Tyler doesn't make small talk with me, and I am thankful for the silence. There's an aura of authority surrounding him. No wonder Nic hired him. They probably both geek out over passcodes and fingerprint scanners and such.

Stepping into Plus None causes my body to relax. I am in my element, and just being here helps my mind focus on what needs to be done.

"I will be outside waiting for you. If you need anything, come get me."

I wave a hand behind me. There's too much fussing over me happening this morning, and it'll be good to separate myself from it—if just for an hour.

Sitting down at my desk, I put a flash drive into the machine and start copying over my work to the storage device and then log out. I call an emergency meeting in the conference room and start delegating workers to handle a revised timeline, the manufacturing components, and basically choose a temporary second-in-command based on the few weeks of work I have seen from the crew. It is a lot of thinking on my feet, and after I put closure on the meeting, I feel mentally exhausted and ready for a nap.

Maybe it's the baby causing me this level of tiredness or

perhaps it is the stress of the unknown surrounding nearly every aspect of my life. Someone is threatening me. While I haven't received any more texts, I know there's a monster lurking in the corner, waiting to pounce. I feel it…

It's in the way Nic has been holding me tighter.

It's in the way my dreams are drifting into nightmares.

There's an eerie quiet in the office space, and when I glance around it appears everyone has left for their lunch break. My stomach growls with anticipation of my next meal. This baby needs to eat.

Standing up, I meander into the break room and pull a yogurt and a can of ginger ale from the fridge. I busy myself with peeling back the label and licking off the excess that settles on it. Food tastes so good to me right now—even things I wouldn't normally eat.

Then I hear it…

The sound of the door opening and the calm footsteps of someone behind me. I slowly turn around and lock eyes with the man who seems to have a little crush on me.

Do grown-ass men even have crushes? Or is that something that is only meant for teenage boys? Who knows. Regardless, now that I am fully committed to Nic, I bet he'll back off and probably feel silly for even trying with me.

That's what this is about, right? He probably heard that Nic and I are together and this is his last-ditch effort to make his case.

Dan is not sporting his normally impeccable attire. Instead, he has on a maintenance worker's jumpsuit and a matching ball cap with a company's logo across the front.

"I missed you."

I let out a laugh that I try not to make awkward. The

feeling's definitely not mutual. "Oh, I'm sure it was extra quiet while I was gone."

Taking a step closer, Dan's eyes trail down my body. I feel a shiver run down my spine, and it isn't the good kind. Something is wrong. He looks crazed...on edge.

I just need to get out of this room and get to Tyler. He'll know what to do.

Act normal, Claire.

I try my best to steady my breathing and to not sway on my feet.

"The wedding go okay?" he inquires. It's small talk, yet nothing about it actually feels small.

"Yeah, it was absolutely beautiful."

"That's great."

"Yup."

"And Graham is gone..."

Fuck.

"Nic has his hands full..."

Double fuck.

"And the overbearing asshole guarding you outside the office is bleeding from his head..."

My heart skips, and I feel the energy wash right out of me. I'm going to faint. Gripping the counter behind me, I try to reach for a knife. But Dan is too—

"Ahhh..." I wail, as my hair gets yanked toward him.

He spins me around, locking his forearm into my throat and pulling my back to his front.

I try to scream, but the words get stuck in the pressure he keeps applying to my windpipe. Dammit.

Leaning down into my ear, he whispers, "I never

expected to like you. But finding you attractive is going to make my entire plot at revenge even sweeter."

"Mfph…"

"Sometimes a surprise is better than the expected."

My mind numbs over the phrase. It is the same one that was left for me on a notecard in my office without a name. I thought it was from Nic. I thought it was in reference to the baby that has been the best unexpected event in my life.

I get a sick feeling in the pit of my stomach. Even my best effort at trying to wiggle free is futile.

"Shhh…don't worry." His hand splays over my belly, giving it an unwanted caress. "I'm going to take such good care of you."

I try to form the word "help," but it just comes out as "haaaaapp" and there's no one in the office to hear it anyway.

"I love how beautiful things grow from dirt."

Oh no. Does he know I'm pregnant? Please, no. My little bump is starting to become a little more protruded, but I haven't told many people. Only a handful actually know.

"Remember the day you fell after leaving the smoothie shop? I followed you to Portland General. And while you didn't see me there, we both shared in learning that the baby you are carrying is doing just fine."

I struggle against his hold, managing only to exhaust myself further. So he's the unknown caller who sent me the hospital photo when I was at Angie and Graham's wedding reception… And he's the one who sent me a nameless note soon after learning I was pregnant.

All this time, Dan wasn't developing a little one-sided

crush. Instead he was developing an obsession. All of the mixed messages I could have been sending him run through my head. I was friendly toward him, and if that's all it took for him to develop an attraction, then I'm gravely sorry I even did that.

I'm surprised he lets go of me. I pant for air, relishing in my esophagus being unobstructed. When I look up, I find a sinister smirk plastered on Dan's face.

He looks like the devil.

"I'm sorry if I implied I was interested on a nonplatonic level."

"It wouldn't have stopped me from making a move."

I'm sure it wouldn't. "I'm willing to go on a date with you." It's a lie, but I need to buy some time until Nic gets worried and comes to check on me. I press my side against the counter and try to discreetly use my phone in my pocket without him noticing.

"We are going to do so much more than just date, Claire."

My pulse quickens, and every nerve in my body stands on end. I'm in danger. And if I'm going to get out of here alive, I need to act fast.

"What do you mean?"

"For starters, we are going to go on a little field trip."

Before the words register to my ears, I bolt toward the door and run out of the break room. I dash through my office and into the hallway, where I see an incapacitated Tyler bleeding on the floor.

Tears burst out of my eyes as I think of just how hurt he is but thankful I see the rise and fall of his chest.

I continue running, trying to get to the stairwell. My hand reaches for the door and—

"Oh, no you don't," Dan says, grabbing me forcefully and pulling my body up against his. His hands splay over my belly, and it's like he knows that the baby growing inside is his way to get me to cooperate. It's like he knows the safety of my child trumps the desire to fight back with all my might.

He found the perfect hostage for getting out of here alive—my baby.

I start to scream, and he covers my mouth so quickly that I choke to take in my next fresh breath of air. "Make a noise and the baby you're carrying will be a dead one. Just when I thought you couldn't possibly be any better of a hostage, you go and get yourself knocked up and make yourself even more valuable. For that, I thank you."

Dan lets go of my mouth so I don't hyperventilate. "Why are you doing this?" I cry out, my words sticking to the roof of my mouth like paste.

"You are the perfect revenge to the man who stole my life."

"What?"

"I was in line to be head here. Been working for years trying to develop a stellar reputation. I eliminated the competition with Eugene who also had similar aspirations. But then that asshole Nic comes along and takes everything away from me. Just like that. Nic's the roadblock that is going to be roadkill if you don't play nice."

I struggle to get free, wiggling and stomping on his foot to try to get him to loosen his hold.

The demented clown chuckles with a demonic howl. "You can't get away, sweets. You are the main attraction."

31

NIC

"I feel very uneasy," I admit, showing Asher the control room where I have all of the cameras set up. I sent away all of the staff and just gave some excuse that I'm doing some software updates—which is a lie. I can't afford to tip anyone off with my fears.

"You installed all of these?" Asher asks, looking over all of the equipment and taking some pictures with his phone to reference later, I assume.

"Yeah. As soon as I took on the job, I made it a mission to basically start from scratch. I even cleaned house here and"—I pause as I pinch the bridge of my nose—"got tipped off that one of my former workers is working with your man, Tyler. I now no longer believe it. I think the whole plan was for me to become disloyal to those that deserve my trust."

"Who shared all of this information with you?"

"The second lead security officer here, Dan King."

"What happened with your first?"

"Eugene didn't make the cut. He and Dan were vying for the top position prior to me joining the team. However, Eugene kept having breaches on his watch. So, I fired him."

"And Dan?"

"Trying to make a name for himself. He's a hard worker."

"Then start with him," Asher says flatly. "Let's put a tracker on him and see what he's been up to."

I nod. "I've been thinking the same thing." I've been avoiding using my skill set, but these vague threats have gone on for way too long. "I just wish I knew a motive that would help me to understand why anyone would want to break into HH. I had this place running like a fortress."

"Then it's probably an in-house job."

"Again, I agree with you," I admit. "But that still leaves the question of who is sending my girlfriend photos as threats and breaking into her apartment. The image that Tyler sent over appears to be of a female."

"Perhaps everything is connected? Someone joining forces for a common goal?"

"Yeah...maybe."

"Have you been checking motion during the evening and following through by looking through the recorded footage?"

"Yeah, but I never got any notifications...well, at least not over the past three weeks."

"So, the cleaning crew or night guard doing security sweeps doesn't set off your notifications?" Asher inquires.

I think about it and inwardly scold myself for not cross-referencing the crew schedule with my notification dashboard. "Something is off. I should definitely be getting some sort of warning."

"Maybe you are being tested to see how well you are paying attention. Let's take a look at your sensors. Do you have remote access or just physical?"

"Both."

"Well," Asher says, leaning against one of the tables, "let's turn them all on and see if your dashboard will light up like a Christmas tree. How many people are present in the building right now?"

"Probably around six hundred, give or take. Teams often stagger lunch breaks."

"Surely with that many people, you will get some action," he says coolly.

"I have everything set up in my office behind a hidden locked panel."

"Then let's head there."

I walk Asher out, but before I allow my workers back in, I triple-check that I have everything in its place. We take the stairs, me walking a bit faster than usual. I am anxious and worn out from the stress. I just want to get to my girl and take her home where I know she will be safe. If I could whisk her away to some island out in the middle of nowhere, I would.

When we get to the floor my office is on, everything is calm. Brenna is still off since my coming to the office today was a last-minute decision.

"Does your assistant have access to this office?" Asher asks, watching me unlock my door.

"Not a key if that is what you are referring to," I answer. Does he think Brenna is capable of double-crossing me?

Being thorough is what makes people in this field the best of the best, and it isn't like I haven't thought it myself. "She is being watched though and is most likely involved. She has connections to Eugene and seems to be flirting with Dan while at work."

Asher gives me a look. "That seems mighty suspicious."

"It does. I am working on it. And it seems like the list of people trying to ruin my life is growing as we speak."

I lock the door and move to the wall where I hit a switch under my desk to reveal a hidden compartment where I have the security features that only Graham and Collins know about. Not even Tyler was made privy to just how anal I am when it comes to my security techniques here at HH. Yet there are still breaches, and I'm over it.

I manually change the settings and allow for the sensors to provide feedback during work hours—instead of my previous schedule which only ran after hours.

"Any action?" he asks.

I look down at my phone. "None. Maybe they need more time to turn on."

"Or maybe they were all discovered and shut off at the source," he adds.

I allow his words to penetrate. "I think you are right. We have a mole, and it has to be someone who works security for me to be able to watch me close enough to know my next move."

"I'm going to just meander around the building if you don't mind and see what I can get access to during the workday and test out your checkpoints."

I nod, grabbing my Glock 48 that I keep locked up in a metal box in my closet. I tuck it into the waistband of my pants. It's been a while since I actively carried, and just feeling it against my skin puts me into a dark mental state.

"I'm going to lock up and go get Claire. I'm going to convince her to go back to Hillsboro until I figure out this gigantic mess. I need her one hundred percent safe until Graham is back from his honeymoon to help. Then I'll come back here to brainstorm more with you. If I have to shut down the entire building, so be it."

"Speaking of Claire," Asher says, turning toward me at the door to my office. "Well done, man. She is lovely."

I nod. "Thank you. Took us a while to get to this place, but I am thrilled that we both came to our senses."

"Good, I know how pigheaded you can be."

"Gee, thanks."

"You're welcome," he replies, exiting to go explore.

I pull up Claire's number on my phone and give her a ring to see if she is still waiting for me in her office. Surely, she's finished her list of tasks and is just hanging out with Tyler, driving him nuts with a bunch of questions.

When she doesn't answer, I resort to text.

Nic: Baby? You still waiting for me?

Nic: I need to talk to you

Then I try Tyler's number.

Nic: On my way to Plus None. Everything okay?

Within seconds, I get a kickback message saying that what I sent was undelivered with an error. That's weird.

I can't wait for the day where I'm not second-guessing everything. Today is not that day.

I jog out of my office and see Brenna's panicked face as she gets off the elevator. She looks like she is sick.

"I wasn't expecting you yet." My words come out a bit harsh. I don't know whether or not to trust her. I know she's holding something back.

"I'm so sorry," she blurts out. "Really sorry…"

"Sorry? For what?" I growl. "What did you do?"

"He made me do it. He told me he would kill my boyfriend, and I believed he would. Then he told me if I didn't do as I'm told, he would find me and make me suffer."

"Slow down, Brenna. You're rambling. What the fuck is going on?"

"I broke into Claire's apartment. And I left her that threatening note."

"Dammit, why?"

"I was told to pack her a bag. He is—"

"Who is *he*?" I snap, rage bursting out of my chest. I feel like my entire heart is about to stop beating.

"Dan King."

"*Fuck.*"

"He is going to kill us all to get revenge on you for destroying his life. And I think he wanted Claire to have clothes because he is going to take her with him. He is going to kidnap her!" She lets out a roar of regret, making me tremble with an animalistic need to go find my girl and protect her.

"Well, he'll have to get through me first."

I start to run toward the elevator, as Brenna continues to

fill me in on developing information. I smack the button to retrieve the car and wait.

"She's mine," I growl, entering the elevator alone. I hit the button for the Plus None floor, as the door closes.

That fucker is going to die, and my hands are going to be the ones that squeeze out his last breath.

I say a prayer that I'm not too late to get to Claire. Tyler should be watching her, and I trust him to do his job at protecting her.

My phone buzzes with an incoming call, and it's from Asher.

"Dude, there's candles, pictures, and personal items collected over time of—"

"Claire." I know it before he has to say anything. "My assistant, Brenna, told me it is Dan King pulling all this shit. He wants revenge. I need to get to my girl and get her out of here. I'm not even sure if Dan's in the building, but I'm taking zero chances with her life. He's going to try to hurt her to get to me. Dan wants her. He wants to take her away from me."

"Okay, slow down, man. I can secure all exits. No one is going to take her out of here."

"She won't answer her phone. Tyler's phone isn't working either."

I end the call and crack my knuckles as I try to keep my breathing under control. It is like my brain is running on a motor, and I won't stop until I can get to Claire and make sure that she is safe. Nothing else matters except getting to her.

Suddenly the elevator jerks and then abruptly stops, propelling my body back against the wall. I hit the service call button and wait for one of my men to answer. Static noise fills the small space, letting me know there is someone on the other line listening.

"It's Nic. I'm stuck in the elevator."

"That's the plan."

"Dan, is this you? What's going on?" I ask, trying to keep the anger out of my tone. He doesn't know that I'm on to him.

"Just a little game of revenge."

My mind races at how to get out of here and get to Claire, who I know in my gut is in danger. I quickly hit the fire alarm button, hoping that someone arrives in time to get me out of here. More importantly, I hope the building clears out for everyone's safety or someone sees Claire in need of help and intervenes. From the menacing sound of Dan's voice, I know that every second counts. I look up at the ceiling and see the escape door. However, it's locked and can only be opened from the top—most likely from a rescue team.

"Do you honestly think you will get away with this?" I ask, trying to buy some time. The piercing sound of the alarm comes through the phone, and I wince, thinking my girl is somewhere in the building—scared. I quickly text Collins.

Nic: Dan wants Claire

Nic: stuck in elevator

Nic: I am being set up

Collins: getting help

Nic: let Asher know

"I already have," Dan states matter-of-factly. "I am getting everything I have always wanted—minus my dream job, of course. But I have a wonderful consolation prize in the form of a barely five-foot, beautiful brunette. She's feisty and is going to get marked if she keeps fighting me. But you know how passionate this firecracker can be."

"I'm going to kill you if you harm one hair on her head."

"Tsk-tsk. You don't have the upper hand here, so quit acting like you do."

I use my phone to try to pull up the security camera footage for the Plus None floor, assuming that's where they are located.

The lights inside the elevator flicker and then the emergency ones switch on.

It is no secret to the employees here that there are cameras on every floor and in every department. My security staff knows of their locations and has access to them for monitoring purposes. The motion sensors were my little secret. But with them malfunctioning, it is obvious that Dan was watching me when I didn't realize it. Dan would easily know where my cameras are all located. Thus, he would also know how to restrict my viewing. Dammit. He has cut the power in the building, including the backup supply I have for all of the security cameras. No matter what footage I check, I have lost all access to the building.

"You're hurting me, please stop," a whimpering voice begs.

Claire. Her pleading voice slices through my heart. Fuck. I slam my hand against the metal doors and then dig my fingers into where the two panels meet, prying with all my might for them to open—if only just an inch.

"What do you want?" I yell into the wall's speaker. "Money? Fame? Tell me what you fucking want!"

"I just want to be *you*," he responds simply. "I'm sure with time Claire will grow fond of me. She has such delicate skin. Have you noticed?" He chuckles like a demented demon. "Of course you have. So smooth and flawless. I would hate to mar it with my blade."

"You fucker," I growl.

"Now, now, let's just hope for her sake that she cooperates and can follow the rules. Would be a shame for me to have to get angry."

I just want to be you. What does he even mean? While it may appear that Dan is obsessed with Claire, it is actually me he wants to mimic.

It's all starting to make sense now. Dan was moving up in ranks before I came along. He probably set up some breaches on Eugene's watch to make him look bad. He might have even been privy to why Brenna wanted to work here at HH. That's why he used her to get into Claire's apartment. Getting a key made could have happened while she was on lunch break and left her purse in the office.

Graham hiring me derailed his entire plan to be the top dog. So instead of dealing with his letdown like a man, he's now looking to seek revenge.

I get the doors to separate a bit more, but the safety

feature restricts the opening, locking it at just a measly four inches. I open up the app for the tracking device I have for Claire, completely forgetting about her getting a new phone. Fuck. I see the dot with her location, but it is where her car is—not her body.

I text Asher who should still be in the building.

Nic: service stairwell; only few know about it

Asher: on my way; police called

Unfortunately this is Asher's first time in the building. He has seen pictures of my layout and offered valuable advice, but he doesn't know the floor plan like I do. No one really knows this place like Graham and I do.

Shit.

Dan planned this around Graham not being here in the building. He waited until I was at a disadvantage before he made a move. And taking Claire equates to a death sentence if I find him before the police can intervene.

The call with Dan disconnects, and I try to get him back on the line with no luck. Tipping my head up to the ceiling, I scream at the top of my lungs for someone to get me out of here. I send out an urgent group text to my team and include Graham. I feel helpless stuck here, and my mind is racing for a solution.

Nic: Dan King has a hostage. Claire Nettles. Check the service stairwell. Traitor

Graham immediately calls me. "What the hell?" he answers panting.

"Dan has her."

"Do you still have power? I am trying to access the cameras. Everything is offline."

"He cut it. Emergency lights are on but backup power supply on all cameras is gone. I am stuck in the elevator. He had to be planning this for weeks."

"I'm turning the plane around."

I want to say I am sorry for ruining their honeymoon before it even really started, but I know that Claire's life trumps any trip. I would easily do the same if the roles were reversed.

"I love her, Graham."

"I know, Nic. Police are on their way. Keep your head on straight. Come out of this alive so you have a story to tell your grandkids."

I swallow hard. Claire is carrying my child. While the test results won't be back for days, in my heart that baby is mine.

"She's pregnant, Graham."

"What? Whoa. Angie know?"

"Yeah, but Ethan could be the father. We just took the test this morning to find out and are waiting for the results." And to think, we thought that Ethan and Deena were the biggest threat in our lives, when all this time an even greater danger was waiting for us to let our guards down.

The warning message of low battery pops up on my screen. It is like I am in the middle of my worst nightmare, living minute by minute. My phone buzzes, and I glance at the screen to see Dan is calling.

"Got to go. Dan is calling. Please get ahold of everyone you can and tell them Tyler is also missing," I say to Graham, as I click accept for the other line.

I can hear Claire's sobs in the background as Dan shouts out demands for her to move or to stop dragging her feet.

I hate myself for not seeing this sooner. For not putting the clues together that would make me realize he was out for revenge—and now out to steal the love of my life. As plain as day, my focus changes to not caring as much about my own life and worrying with all my energy about Claire's life.

"What do you want?" I scream, feeling helpless.

"All my life," he explains, "I've had to work to get to the top. Here you come along with the last name of Hoffman and just get everything handed to you. Didn't even have to work for it. I mean, it helps that your brother is the CEO here and gave you the job I've been working toward. You ruined everything. I had everything I ever wanted within a fingertip's reach and you snatched it all away with your heavy-handedness to exert your power wherever the wind blew you. Well, this is the perfect revenge."

"Why take Claire down with you? How does she fit into this?"

"If I can't get the job, at least I can get the girl. Nothing like fighting for the one you love, right? Makes this whole mess more fulfilling when I take the one thing you love more than your job title away from you. She would have fallen in love with me if you weren't around."

"Bullshit."

"She's the perfect hostage and leverage against you."

"Lust is not the same as love. We are just fuck buddies."

I try to keep my voice from having any emotion. Maybe if I can convince Dan that Claire doesn't mean to me what he thinks she means, he will let her go and find someone of more value.

"Says the man who has a video stash of recordings of this sweet brunette girl that is going to be mine soon. Nice try. It didn't take me long to see what she means to you. When I discovered your lovely ex-fiancée still had a thing for you, I hatched a plan to fly her here, secretly get her through security, and show up in your office. Granted, she did it for the money I shelled out. She didn't know the extent of my plan or that I was the person orchestrating it all. Not sure it would have changed anything, though. That girl is hungry for cash."

"You are sick."

"And it still didn't work to push Claire away from you. I really thought you would have resorted back to your old bad habits and freed up Claire to be with me. I think I would have found happiness with just that too. This is your fault. You did this."

"So you are butt sore over Claire not wanting you?"

"Yet. She still has a lifetime to fall in love with me. And she will. But let's not get off topic. It's story time after all. Where was I? Oh yes...getting those two bitches on the same plane back to Virginia was the work of the universe. But forcing them to sit beside each other was my version of sweet torment. So, don't give me this garbage that Claire doesn't mean anything to you. Because I know she means *everything* to you. She is your one and only weakness. And I'm getting hard just thinking about what the future holds for us. She is a very passionate woman."

"You fucker!"

Dan lets out an unhinged laugh. "Oh, and congrats on the baby. If it's a boy, we are naming him Danny." I can hear a rustle and then the sound of smacking flesh. "I said to shut up!"

I cringe over the thought of him hitting my girl. Her sniffling sounds filter through the receiver and it propels me—

SCREECH!

The sound of hinges opening comes from the ceiling panel, and I can see Collins's hand reach down with a rope for me to grab. Relief floods through my system, letting me know that there is hope. I hold on to that feeling, allowing it to keep me focused on getting to Claire. I mute the call to not give away my rescue effort, and hit the speaker button to go hands-free. I step onto the handrail to hoist myself higher, grabbing the rope and wrapping it around my hand a few times to get leverage. The call disconnects, and I lose verbal proof of Claire's safety. Scaling the wall with my feet, I climb and get pulled up on top of the roof of the elevator car.

Memories of Claire from the morning flash through my mind. We spent the morning in bed before going to the clinic to do the paternity test. She was so beautiful today wearing a pink-and-red-striped dress. Her new earrings suit her perfectly, and I can't wait to add to her diamond collection.

"Shit," I exhale.

"What?" Collins asks, turning toward me.

"Graham designed earrings for both Penny and Claire as

a bridal party gift from Angie. My phone is about to die. Can I borrow yours?"

Collins quickly hands over his while we figure out how to get out of this hellhole.

"It's Hoffman," Graham answers on the first ring.

"The earrings," I say with hope.

"What about them?"

"Did you put trackers in them? Claire is wearing hers today."

"Yes. Shit, yeah. I'll get the code so you can follow her."

My hands ball into fists thinking of how I want to squeeze the life out of Dan. He'll deserve every miserable second of his death too.

"Check the app," Graham says.

I hang up and get Collins to sign in to the app. I enter in the code to signify to the GPS device to follow that specific tracker.

"I found her," I exhale. "I think Dan is taking her out the back exit. Probably has a car waiting." We use the ladder to climb up to the floor above where the faint light is coming through the opened doors.

"Asher is trying to hunt him down. I have my own men on it. He won't be able to leave with her."

"He may try to hurt her just to punish me."

Collins doesn't comment. He knows that my fear is a real possibility. There's no telling how deranged Dan is or what he is capable of. All of my employees have been background checked and have no criminal record. However, most lunatics who take a hostage don't have a colorful history of offenses. Something just makes them snap, and negotiating is pointless.

I lift myself through the opened doors. "You have a gun on you? I have my Glock."

"Yes, sir. I grabbed the other one out of my lockbox. Here. Take a backup."

He hands me his pistol without waiting for me to even ask. I tuck it into the waistband of my pants, opposite of my Glock. Even though Collins doesn't technically work for me, he is basically family. I trust him with Claire's life and my own. But like most men whose life's mission is to guard and protect, there is an unspoken code that is understood. Collins knows that I'm determined to get Claire to safety no matter what it takes. I don't need to tell him I love her. I think he already knows.

I race to the stairwell and burst through the doors. I jump down multiple steps to hit the landing and then do it again and again until I get to the bottom door that leads out into the lobby. Where is everyone? The police and fire department should be here by now.

My phone vibrates, and I answer it immediately. Claire's quivering voice fills the silence. "Nic."

"Baby? Hold on, I'm coming to get you."

"Bitch," Dan snaps. "I told you just to say hi, not to cry."

I hear sniffling in the background and the sound of some doors opening. "You are going to get sloppy and make some mistakes," I warn. "Wouldn't you rather take me down before you get arrested and endure the rest of your life behind bars?"

"Oh, isn't that cute? You actually are hopeful. By the

way, I tried calling your phone and it died. But lucky you, it looks like Batman found Robin." He's referring to Collins and must have some sort of eyes on us. "Too bad both men suck at getting the girl," Dan snickers.

"Listen here," I snarl, "if you harm one hair on her body…"

"Aww, but what if she likes it rough?"

Without time to give a verbal reaction, I run toward the back entrance through a series of hallways that are typically blocked off from the majority of the employees. Collins takes up the rear as we speed through the maze of corridors and badge-access-only doors. He has to know I'm gunning for him. He has to know that the only way out of this mess is by death or prison time.

"Oh silly, forgetful me," he laughs. "I almost forgot to tell you the little secret that our sweet Claire has been keeping." He pauses, and the scream out of Claire's throat causes me to break. "Should you tell him or should I?"

I hear rustling and then another smack of his hand most likely connecting with her face. I am going to murder him. I quickly change the access code on the back door using the app that is also on Collins's phone. Maybe if I can trap them inside, he won't be able to relocate without trying to use another door or breaking a window. Luckily most of the security features I have installed—some known only to Graham and myself—are backed up on emergency power sources.

"Fine, fine," Dan huffs out a breath. "I'll tell him."

"Tell me what, dammit?"

"Our little Claire is toting some precious cargo."

I stop in my tracks and use my hand to balance me against the wall. "What? You already know she's pregnant."

"Oh yeah, you're right. But she's carrying around more than just a baby. But I'll give you a little hint. It goes BOOM."

My throat dries. "You fucker!"

"She has enough explosives strapped to her to take down this whole building."

"You bastard," I snarl.

"Now, now, now," Dan scolds. "I won't light her up like a firework unless you make me. Otherwise, it ain't goin' to be pretty."

"I'm going to get you."

"I hope you do. Fireworks shows are best enjoyed by a crowd. Come and get me."

32

CLAIRE

"You're hurting me," I cry out, as my hair gets pulled viciously from my scalp.

I am afraid to move; I don't want to set off whatever is strapped to me. Dan forced me into a heavy vest and called it his insurance. The palm of his hand slithers down the side of my face. His eyes now lack the life I used to see when we interacted. It is like the light has dimmed, and he is someone else. I brace myself for his gentleness to be tarnished with an aggressive streak.

BANG!

I flinch and turn my head away from the sound, thinking it is my flesh getting struck—again. But this time it is a gunshot.

Dan's chuckle causes tears to pour from my eyes, as he wrenches my arm to tug me along. "Get ready," he says maniacally. "It's goin' to be showtime. But know for sure we are in this together. We will either leave together or there's going to be an epic murder-suicide. You choose."

If I wasn't carrying a baby I am desperately trying to protect, I would fight. I would claw and hit and spit and run, because dying sounds better than being Dan's whore.

"Your boy toy is pretty slick and made a last-minute change in the code for this door. Maybe he's not so stupid after all." Dan takes the barrel of his pistol that he just used to try to blow through the lock and rubs it down my face, making me jerk from the heat.

I scream out in agony. Dan cups my cheek and leans in closer, trailing his nasty tongue along the burn line. I take a few deep breaths. I can't panic. I need to survive this.

"Why are you doing this to me?" I ask. I'm living in a nightmare that I am unable to wake up from. I have a demonic madman using me as leverage to execute his revenge plan.

"Nic Hoffman stole my life when he decided to come work here. I was in line for a promotion and would have been top dog if it wasn't for him. So what better way to get revenge on the man who took my life than in return taking his?"

"We aren't even together. This baby isn't his. It's my ex's."

"Ha, you're a horrible liar. I've been watching the two of you together since you started working here. You can't keep flipping the switch like you would a light, Claire. Nic showed too many of his cards when he made it clear to the security guards assigned to work the lobby entrance that if they touched you or disrespected you in any way, they would no longer have a job in security anywhere on the West Coast. Most people here just assumed it was because you're the big boss's fiancée's best friend. But I knew better. No man gets that jazzed up unless there are feelings involved. So, as Nic kept tabs on you, I kept tabs on him. Studied his movements. Predicted his next steps. I got him to distrust his right-hand man, Tyler, who I set up to make it look like he was accepting bribes. It was so easy to get your man to doubt those who would have otherwise caught on to my plan before I could execute it. Good thing I used Nic's paranoia and obsession for you against him. Oh, and the help of some photo editing software to make Tyler look like the mole—instead of me."

"*You* are obsessed," I grind out. "A real sicko."

"It didn't have to be this way. I almost got what I wanted to achieve through Tara."

"What? How does freaking Tara fit in?"

"Oh, I tried to pay her off to break you both up. It didn't work, so I had to hatch another plan. This one. But hey doll, look on the bright side. Nic broke you in for me. Enjoy your last moments of freedom, because I'm going to have so much fun tying you to my bed and never letting you stop spreading your legs. There's something extremely sexy about a pregnant woman. I can already tell your tits are coming to life, which is good for me because"—he leans in closer, placing his tongue against the shell of my ear—"I'm a boob man."

Dan pulls me by my arm and pushes me into the hallway. I cover my ears as he breaks open the fire supply box and releases the axe. He pulls open an interior door and hacks through any locks or glass barriers he finds standing in his way.

"Where are we going?" I ask, out of breath from trying to keep up with the pace. "Through the main entrance?

Someone is going to see. Plus, if you have any chance of getting me out of here without being followed, you better get the tracking devices off of me. You know Nic probably plants them in my shoes and in all my jewelry and probably has one on my phone. The man is crazy possessive of me. He wants to know where I'm at all the time. I just recently discovered his whole obsession, and I lost it on him. Didn't change anything. Nic does whatever Nic wants."

Dan tugs me into a dark alcove and runs his nasty eyes over my body. He makes me feel dirty without even touching me. "Why are you even telling me this? Don't you want him to find you?"

"No, not anymore," I say flatly. "I don't want him hurt. I don't want *anyone* hurt. I'll go willingly with you if you promise not to cause physical harm to anyone else. We can call it a sacrifice of one person to save hundreds."

Dan's eyes narrow at mine. I hold his gaze so I can try to portray that I am being honest—even though I would rather die than be his sex slave. That's what I'd be, too, if he gets me out of this building alive. He'll fulfill the horror he just described and keep me as his prisoner.

But this isn't just about me. It is about my unborn child as well. I have to be smart about this if I'm going to be able to escape.

"Aww," Dan coos, "you are so noble."

"It's obvious that someone is going to get hurt during all of this. Promise me you'll protect this baby, and I'll do whatever you want. But you'd be neglectful if you didn't at least try to get all of the items off me that a GPS could be hiding inside. It's not like Nic would ever tell me where he stashes his trackers. I just know he has them on me.

There've been too many coincidences where he showed up where I was and acted like it was a random occurrence. I mean, his brother runs this jewelry company, so I can only assume they are in my belly piercing or"—I try my best to blush, while looking away—"my nipple rings. Mainly because I never take those ones out since he had the pair made special for me."

Dan's eyes light up. "I always knew you'd be a fun one."

I shrug, trying to act the role he has me pegged to play. "Some extra bling doesn't make me a slut."

"But it sure separates you from the prudes."

I swallow hard. "Maybe." The only thing pierced on me are my ears. But those won't allow for the removal of this damn vest. This is my only plan. My only hope.

"I know I can make you love me someday."

I give a weak smile. "Only time will tell."

I wait for Dan's expression to change from indifference to hope. He pushes my back against the wall and tucks his gun in his waistband, while tossing the axe to the floor. He first starts pulling out my diamond studs that were a beautiful gift from Angie, making the backings scatter from his roughness. I barely had a chance to enjoy them before Dan trashes them with his evil touch. His hands reach around my back and carefully rip the Velcro straps that are securing the explosives vest to my body. As soon as the garment meets the floor, I double over in pain.

"Ahhh," I groan, holding my belly. I let out a scream of agony.

"What?" he demands. "What's wrong?"

"It's the baby."

"What? How?" Dan asks, hovering over me to see if he can see anything as to why I am writhing in pain.

And then I act. I thrash my head up, connecting right with his nose. Blood spatters from his face, hitting the wall like angry crimson raindrops. I knee him in the groin and grab the axe with both hands. Whirling it around like a windmill, I crack it against his legs. He deflects just in time, and I only seem to graze him from the force, tearing through the fabric of his jumpsuit pants and slicing what I assume is the top layer of his skin.

But I move.

I bolt through the barely lit hallways, hopefully making my way toward the lobby. I can hear Dan barreling toward me, his panting and painful groans echoing through my ears.

He is going to catch me. And then he is going to make my death a thousand times worse than if I would have just stayed.

I need to get away. I can stay and die, or run and try.

So I run.

And run.

And run.

And I never look back.

The air gets caught in my throat making it impossible to scream or to give warning to my whereabouts. I can hear the sound of the police guiding people out of the building in hushed tones, but I can't get myself to find their location. I run toward a metal door and it is chained off, keeping me locked in a maze with a deranged madman.

I shove myself into a small office space and shut the door, clicking the lock into place. I push the potted plant, the desk, the chair, and everything I can move up against the only access to the room. I feel like I just trapped myself inside a box, hoping it does not become my coffin. At least there is a window, and I am low to the ground. I move to the back of the room and slip down onto the floor in a ball in the corner.

Please find me. Before it is too late.

Images of the entire building going up in a dusty mushroom cloud of smoke pass through my brain. I rock back and forth with my knees bent to my chest, closing my eyes and trying desperately to wait this out. I can't cry because I don't want to feel. I just want to forget I am here.

My eyes fly open as bullets ricochet from the outside hallway, and I put my hands over my ears to try to drown out the sound. Muffled voices echo, and I shiver at the thought of someone I love getting hurt during the exchange.

All this time it's been Dan lurking on the sidelines, waiting for the right time to make his move. How did I not see it sooner?

The handle of the door shakes, and I whimper at the realization that I am going to die alone in this room. My baby and I are going to die at the hands of an evil man. Thoughts of Nic flash through my brain as I think about him finding my body. What about Angie? She can't cope with another loss. She won't be able to mentally survive this. And to think her life is just getting started. It's not fair to do that to her.

I think about the baby I won't ever get to know. I don't even know the gender yet—or the father. I think about the missed opportunities and how Plus None was my chance to support the way women see themselves as strong, independent warriors of their own domain. I have so much to accomplish, and if my life gets snuffed out before I can make my stamp on the world, what a waste it would be. Change doesn't happen overnight, and I need more time to get what I want done.

Stay strong, Claire. It's not over yet. *You need to think and stay calm. Quit thinking like a victim, but rather a survivor.*

At the opposite side of the room, there's what appears to be a closet. Hoisting myself off the floor, I make my way to the doors and open them. I stumble backwards at the glowing light that casts an eerie darkness on the entire room, as my eyes take in the sight.

Holy hell.

Pictures, memorabilia, and pencil drawings line the walls of what appears to be a shrine dedicated to me. Battery-operated candles rest on a little table, along with trinkets and items that belong to me. My fingers touch the hairband I remember misplacing on my lunch break. I see a smoothie cup that has my name scribbled along the side that I must have thrown in the trash at one time. There are news-paper cutouts from the Plus None publicity shoot. There's even a pair of my fucking underwear.

Bile rises in my throat, as I clutch my hands over my mouth to keep it down. I'm going to be sick.

Dan King is a madman.

I look around at the rest of my surroundings, allowing the disgusting feeling in the pit of my stomach to fuel my motivation to get out of here. Going back out into the hallway that is blocked off with chains is not a viable option. There has to be another way to escape and get to safety.

The shaded windows that line the one wall are most likely double-paned and made of thicker glass. There will be no way I can get them to break without hurting myself in the futile attempt. I tip my head back and notice the big air return vent in the corner of the room. I have always been a petite but strong girl. I bet I can fit.

I move the desk over to the wall and stack the chair on top to use it as a step stool. I crawl up onto the desk and then climb onto the chair. Stretching, I use my fingers to try to pull at the metal grate without success. Looking at the screws, I realize I need to get them out first. Hopping down from the chair, I dig through the desk and discover a pair of scissors along with an entire drawer of typical office supplies. I open the scissors and get back up onto the chair. Placing the dulled point into the screw groove, I turn and turn.

It takes me several minutes, but I am able to pull the grate from the wall and expose the dusty hollowed-out metal ducts where the air flows. Hoisting myself up, I slither inside. It smells like I am stuck with my head under dirt. The odor of musk penetrates my nostrils, and I sniffle from the mucus starting to drip from my nose.

I pull up the collar of my dress to protect my airway from breathing in the thick dust. Then, I crawl and crawl and crawl, slowly moving my way through the metal tube. I feel the scratching sensation on my arms and legs, as I get nicked by the metal seams. Sharp joints and metal screws dig into my skin as I slide myself through on my belly. I follow the dark maze until I see the strips of horizontal light. Looking through, I see another office space. I push with my hands and try with all my might to break through. Shove and push and bang.

POP!

Finally, I feel like I might have a chance to get out of here alive. I crawl onto a filing cabinet and then slide down to the carpeted floor. I don't have time to think. I just need to get out as fast as I can. I dart toward the door and turn the handle. I race down the hall and crash right into a wall.

"Claire? Claire! Oh my gosh, Claire!"

I look up and through the fog of tears in my eyes, I see him, surrounded by armed officers with shields.

"Nic."

"Yes, baby girl, it's me. I got you. I got you…"

I feel the rush of warmth fill my body, and for a second, I think I must have died. Maybe from a gunshot or an explosion or from fear. He looks so perfect and whole and beautiful. My words stick in my throat, and I can no longer make a sound. My eyes fill with little black-and-white spots, and then I feel myself drifting—like a helium balloon let go in the wind. I coast and coast and coast…

Until the only thing left is the memory of us.

33

CLAIRE

My head feels like it is a fluffy cloud. My eyes open and several sets are staring back at me expectantly. The sight is so intense that I just shut them again. I must be dead or in a permanent dream-like state. My head feels foggy, and I don't feel like I am inside my own body.

"Baby? We know you are awake." It is Nic. Everything else is fuzzy, but I am certain that is him.

"Heaven is too intense," I groan.

I hear some muffled laughter, and I open one eye to take another look—but only because the suspense is killing me. Then the other one opens. Nic, Graham, Angie, Donna, Germain, Penny, Collins, Asher, and Blake are all waiting around my bed—holding some vigil or ceremony of some sort. Flowers are arranged on every smooth surface, and I can't even see the rest of the room because they are so over-the-top in size. I think there is a window along the opposite side, but it is too claustrophobic in here to really notice.

"This is my funeral," I mumble, my words coming out airy.

"Is she normally this comical?" Asher asks from the sidelines. "Maybe we should get the doctor."

"The medicine they gave her to relax her is just making things a bit wonky, I bet," Donna says softly.

Angie breaks through the group first, joining Nic who seems glued to my side. "You scared the piss out of me, you know that?" she asks, her voice going up an octave with every few words. "Every hour you slept shed time off my own life. Never do that to me again." Graham wraps an arm around her and pulls her away before she bursts into tears— or hits me. He offers me a weak smile, and I can tell that he is relieved.

My brows scrunch together, as I try to figure out how they got back to Portland so fast from their honeymoon. Donna moves toward the bed and pats me on my leg. Germain looks like he just let go of all the pressure in his shoulders. Penny stays back, rocking on her heels, looking like she doesn't know whether to cry or smile.

"How long have I been asleep?" I ask, confusion growing as more time passes.

"Into the next day, so about twelve hours," Nic explains. "You've been admitted for tests and monitoring."

Blake steps out from behind Asher, tears dripping from his eyes. "Claire Bear, don't ever do that again," he says bitterly, pulling me toward him to hug me. "You don't realize how much my life depends on you to be in it." His words make me cry, and I shudder over the memories that will forever be burned into my brain.

"I'm sorry," I mouth, scanning the room so everyone knows. "I'm sorry."

"This was never your fault, Claire," Graham says. "Angie and I turned our plane around as soon as we realized what Dan was doing. We landed and got here as fast as we could."

"So, I'm not dead?" I ask for clarification.

Nic's smile is warm. "No, baby. Everyone important made it out alive."

"It's all over," Graham adds. "And now you can start the next chapter and never have to revisit the one you just endured."

Tears cascade down my cheeks, and Nic tries to wipe each stream with a tissue. "Okay, you all came, you saw, now leave," he says bluntly to those in the room. "My girl needs to eat and get her rest."

I pout out my bottom lip. "But I just slept away half a day."

"I need time with you to myself. Everyone else can go."

"My son," Donna snickers, "a man of great words."

"Let's shuffle out of here," he prompts again, "and give me a chance to really see for myself that Claire is alright."

"We got the point, man," Asher teases, as Nic gently pushes everyone from the room.

"Wh—" I reach for my water pitcher but Nic beats me to it, pouring me a cupful over ice. I take a sip and then try to find my voice again. "Which hospital am I at?"

"Portland General." He walks to the door leading to the hallway and wheels in a food cart meant to feed probably the entire wing I'm on. "I needed to make sure you didn't get any internal injuries at the hands of that"—Nic runs a hand over the back of his neck—"madman."

I know his words are being censored. I am sure he has better descriptors but is refraining for my sake. Truth is, though, I have a few of my own. "Is he dead?" I ask, my voice quivering.

He lines up containers of my favorite things onto a tray and helps me move into an upright position by propping pillows behind my back and adjusting the bed settings. "Yes," he says almost passively. "And my only regret is not getting to him fast enough to do it myself."

"Who did? Police?"

"Tyler."

"Oh, hell, Tyler. Is he okay then? I saw his bloody body on the floor outside of Plus None. Where is he?"

Nic hugs me to him. Pulling back, he puts a plastic spoon into my hands, encouraging me to take the first bite of the oatmeal he had delivered. "I'm so sorry you had to go through everything you went through." He pushes hair off my forehead. "Tyler is fine. He just had a scan done and nothing is broken. He is in the room beside you. I can wheel you over once he wakes up."

"Oh, thank God he's okay."

"He saved us all, Claire. Tyler is a hero."

I reach for a tissue to blow my nose, as tears form in my eyes. "I am just glad we all made it out alive."

"I will never forgive myself for not seeing it sooner. It was right in front of my face. If only I trusted Tyler the whole time…"

I take a few more bites of my food—mainly to appease

Nic but also because it is so delicious. "We all make mistakes, Nic."

"It was that asshole Dan who"—Nic looks away and takes a deep breath—"was feeding me lies hinting that Tyler was double-crossing me. He put the doubt in my mind about one of my most trusted employees. I had Collins working to see if the speculation was warranted or not, and while nothing was found to incriminate Tyler, the damage to the trust we established was already done. And when I realized he was telling me the truth, Dan had already solidified his plan to run off with you."

"I thought Dan was just a guy who may have had a crush on me. We would run into each other on breaks throughout the building or outside during lunch. Now, looking back, he was probably stalking me and learning my patterns. I found the"—my body shudders—"shrine."

"Damn, baby," Nic says with a sigh. "I was hoping you'd never see that. I just found out about it yesterday. I will forever regret missing all the signs."

"I was so scared," I cry. "I thought Dan was going to blow everything up or lose his patience with me or hurt you. And the baby. He wanted to take me and—" I tremble, not being able to complete my sentence. There's no point reliving the fear and the memories.

"It's over, baby. You are safe. And I vow to protect you always. I should have never let you go into the building. That guilt and regret will be carried by me for the rest of my life."

"Nic?"

Taking my hands in his, he kisses each one. "Hmm?"

"Remember the guard who accosted you when you first started working at HH?"

"Yeah, Kevin?"

"I think he was helping Dan."

"I'm aware, baby. He's in custody now. Dan never thought he would get caught and got sloppy. Kevin was completely expendable to him, but that's on him for going into the darkness. Dan tried to throw Kevin to me as a traitor just to get the focus off of himself. The scum wanted to destroy me."

"Wow..."

"But don't worry. Everyone involved will pay. With the amount of evidence at HH alone, there's no way for Kevin to ever step foot outside of a prison."

I nod in relief. "He had me meet with him recently at a cafe. Was very ominous and vague about having information I would like to know. He basically told me you were tracking me."

"Never doubt my love for you, Claire. If tracking you helps me protect you, please accept it."

"I see things so clearly now. I'm sorry I never told you what I knew. I just didn't think anything was connected."

"I know." Nic sighs. "I just don't know what I would have done if you'd been hurt yesterday. You are my happiness. You are my whole world."

"Tara was..." My voice cracks as I sniffle.

"Shh...I know. Dan told me before he died. And I'm having my men look into it to make sure she really is innocent in all of this and just wanted money. Brenna was involved too, but it was to protect her boyfriend, Eugene."

"The employee you fired?"

"Yes. Basically, Brenna came to work for me to try to prove Eugene's innocence. She suspected Dan had something to do with him being fired and apparently would flirt with Dan to try to manipulate him. He just got caught in the collateral damage like so many others and desperately wanted to clear his name. I owe him a job."

My hands move over my stomach, resting on top of the stark white freshly laundered sheet. "Is the baby okay?"

Nic nods and smiles. "Yes, the little gummy bear looks perfect."

I giggle. "So you named our baby gummy bear?" I use the word *our* without even thinking about it. This is our baby. If Ethan ends up sharing DNA with it, then we can worry about custody issues later. As far as what a daddy represents, Nic will be amazing—I finally have zero doubts.

"Yeah, at least until we find out the gender," he says proudly.

It warms my insides to know he is excited about the baby. Even though it took me some time to accept the reality, I am thrilled to be embarking on parenthood with the man I love. Sure, we did things unconventionally, but that's just how we are. There's no script. There's no rule book. We can author our own story.

I snuggle into the bed that cannot be the normal one they offer patients here. It is too soft and comfy. "I'm so tired," I whisper, allowing my eyes to close.

"You rest, baby. I'll watch over you while you sleep."

My eyes open, and I can't tell what time it is based on the darkness of the room with the blinds shut. Maybe I slept a week and didn't realize it. I was that tired, so I would not be surprised if I did. I hear rustling from the side of the room and turn on the table lamp to see what is happening.

Nic is pacing the room and periodically doing weird stretches.

"What are you doing? Pilates? Some yoga?"

He turns his attention to me, and his smile lights up the room. My eyes scan down his body, and it is then that I notice the baby carrier strapped to him with a doll inside. "I am checking this contraption for quality and safety."

"Don't government agencies do things like that?"

"Yeah, I don't trust those though." He bends and then the doll slips right out and falls to the floor—headfirst. "Ahhh!" he gasps, grabs it, and holds it up to his face for comfort. "It's okay, you are fine."

"You've gone and lost your mind." I can't help but laugh. "You know that, right?"

"You can thank me later when I write a nasty letter to this company explaining that their product is faulty and unsafe. Should be recalled."

I just shake my head and watch him take his notepad out and write a few things down. I notice the pile of baby products on the pullout sofa and giggle to myself as he goes through each one and "tests" it for his seal of approval.

"You know that even if a product is safe now, it can be recalled later. Defects happen, even to the best companies."

Nic's attention snaps to me, and he looks at me with adoration. "Exactly. This is why I will need to do my own testing periodically to ensure that everything is working properly."

"I would expect nothing less," I mumble under my breath.

"Did you know that only five percent of parents use car seats correctly?"

I shake my head. "No."

"Five percent, Claire. Think about it. That blows my mind. There's all these rules too. No fluffy coat is to be worn. Rear facing up until a certain weight or height. Chest clip needs to be at armpit level. Oh, and you can't add any extra fancy features post manufacturer production. Even certain laundry detergents can't be used to wash the straps, as it could deteriorate the fabric. And—"

"Nic?"

He stops midstride, mindlessly burping a baby that is incapable of even sucking in air, and stares at me expectantly. "Yes?"

"You need to calm down. You are giving me anxiety."

"Well, you know what gives me anxiety?" he asks, putting his hands on his hips.

"No, but I'm sure you are going to tell me."

"Mommy blogs."

"What? What are you doing on those?" I ask, sitting myself up a little more in my bed.

"Apparently being judgmental according to more than seventy percent of the people commenting on my post. Sheesh. You women are so hard to read on these online platforms. I can't tell if someone is being serious or trolling me."

"What did you post?" I ask, not really sure I even want to know.

"So, I went off on some safe sleep statistics I've been researching and then was factual in my post. Nope. I must have crossed some arbitrary line and then got shamed for it. I don't think you women want facts. You just want to trust your"—he makes a face—"feelings. Like men don't have instincts and are born brainless or something."

"Oh boy."

"Oh yes. But it was my vaccine post that really made a name for myself."

"You need to reel this in."

"This gummy bear means everything to me, and I want to protect it forever."

"You will," I say with confidence. "I have zero doubt. But let's dial it back. Tone it down a bit."

"Just so you know, that *is* me toning it down."

"How did they allow a dad on their mom blog? Asking for a friend..."

Nic looks to be super proud of himself, as he taps a finger against the side of his temple. "I used a creative screen name."

I cringe. "And what is it?"

"Notyomomma."

"Oh my goodness. You are too much."

Nic looks down at the doll he is holding, cradling it to his chest. He fixes the swaddling blanket around it, as if the foot-long plastic toy could possibly feel any shifts in temperature. "If it is a boy," he says thoughtfully, "then I can teach him how to be a good man. If it is a girl, then I will teach every boy who crosses her path how to be a good man."

I burst out laughing over the image. "Help us all if she is a girl. Poor thing will never have a chance to find love with you micromanaging her whole life."

"Damn right. And I won't even feel an ounce of guilt. I know how men are."

"Do you now?" I ask, intrigued at the direction this conversation is going. "Tell me more."

Nic places the baby onto the recliner. "We are sexual beings," he says like it is a fact. "Takers but also givers. Protective and territorial and pumped up on testosterone."

"Meat heads."

Nic scrunches up his face. "Show some respect."

I burst into laughter over our exchange. It feels good to be this comfortable with someone that we can talk freely and openly and without hesitation. Nic is my safe haven. I do not fear being anyone but myself when I'm around him, and that alone is refreshing and different from any other relationship I've had in the past.

My eyes scan over Nic's body. He has changed into fresh clothes that Donna and Germain brought in a bag from his place. Now he has well-worn dark denim jeans on and a short-sleeved gray shirt. He looks smoking hot and all mine. "Go back."

"To which part?" he asks, genuinely confused.

"To the sexual beings part. Let's focus on that and forget about the rest."

Nic's lips lift to a smirk. He then moves over to the recliner and rotates the doll baby the other way to face the chair. "You coming on to me, baby?" he asks over his shoulder.

"I'm trying but you are slow to take the bait."

"Am I?" he asks, walking closer to my hospital bed. He loses the baby carrier, allowing it to fall to the floor. He looks toward the door and verifies that it is closed. "Maybe I am slow playing this hand. Waiting for you to go all in."

"Too slow, if you ask me," I goad. "Either up the ante or I'm going to get bored and fold."

"I don't want to hurt you."

"I feel like all of this," I say, motioning with my hand toward the monitors, "is a bit over the top. I am fine."

"I could have lost you," he points out.

"I could have lost you too. But here we are, and this occasion deserves a celebration. So come and get me."

Nic whips his shirt over his head and is out of his shoes, jeans, and boxers in seconds. He climbs on top of the mattress, bracing his weight on his side, while pulling me toward him. Luckily for me, I am already half undressed and the access is easy. Lifting my sheet, he joins me underneath. His body is like a furnace, and the heat radiates off of him.

"You never cease to amaze me with your appetite."

"I think the thrill of getting caught is making me extra horny," I whisper. "Or maybe it is how your ass wears denim. I should have made you do a twirl."

"I would have complied." He kisses my lips and then lifts one of my legs to rest over his like two pairs of scissors. "I don't want to hurt you."

"I am stronger than you think."

"You are the strongest and most beautiful woman I know."

He trails a hand down my body, stopping at my apex. The pad of his finger teases my clit, circling it with just the right amount of pressure. He moves it lower and then slips it inside my warmth. After a few pumps, he adds a second and then hooks both to try to reach my G-spot.

"Ahh," I call out, feeling my body come to life from just his touch. "Damn, that feels good."

I reach for his cock and pump it with my fist, twisting and pulling with a soft pressure. I know I must be doing something right because the fingers inside me pause as Nic lets out a moan. Feeling powerfully feminine, I suck on his neck and hump his hand that is cupped over my core, all while keeping his cock entertained.

"You trying to end this in record time, my little vixen?"

"I want you to lose control like you make me do so often."

He bites at my lips and increases his pace with his fingers. My breaths come out as pants, while my legs straighten and lock into place from the force of my impending orgasm. My head flies back against the pillow, as I try to keep my head in the game and pump my hand at the same time.

Nic exhales. "I'm close."

The rush hits me like a hurricane, thrashing through me like a tidal wave looking for the comfort of the shore. Nic groans and releases his seed against my belly at the same time. Sweat coats my skin as I come down from my high, and it is then that I notice the sheets beneath me are soaked.

"Did I pee?" I ask, my eyes growing wide.

"No, baby," he says softly. "Not that it would bother me if you did. You don't need to be embarrassed around me. Ever."

"What happened then?"

"I think you just had a super intense orgasm and you squirted."

"Wow. That has never happened to me before." I look down between us and see the damp spot that continues to grow in circumference. "I mean, I've read that some women can do that."

Nic looks so satisfied that he brought me that level of pleasure, as he wipes my stomach clean with the top sheet.

The quick series of knocks on the door startles me, and I turn to see the nurse standing near the wall looking at me with a disappointed glare.

"This isn't a hotel."

"Based on the amount of money I paid for this private room," Nic says sternly, "I would expect the staff to be a little more respectful."

"You are cleared to be discharged, Miss Nettles. Unless you want to stay and enjoy dinner in bed? I was simply coming to inform you that the doctor signed off on the paperwork," she says tersely.

I hope she knows that irking Nic with her snootiness is never good. Maybe she is new to the scene and doesn't realize how much money the Hoffman family dumps into this hospital through charitable donations.

"Good," Nic says with an edge to his tone. "See to it that there is a rush on it. We are through here." Turning to me, he kisses my forehead. "We can eat dinner together in our own bed."

"Yes, sir," the nurse replies, borderline rude.

"What did you do to her?" I ask suspiciously.

"Threatened her job and the entire floor's staff if they didn't give you the best care and to allow us to break pretty much every rule they have."

"Rules?"

"Visiting hour guidelines, number of people allowed to occupy the room regulations, and I also insisted on the private room despite them not having one ready. I had to advocate for Tyler to get the best care as well."

"Making a name for yourself here, Nic Hoffman? Causing a bunch of ruckuses?"

"You know it," he answers sheepishly. "Now let's get you out of here so we can pack up your bags."

"Are we going somewhere?"

"Yes."

"And I should expect you to be mysterious about this?"

Nic gives me a boyish smile. "You should expect to be pampered and relaxed at all times while we are there."

"Good. It's about time you start taking care of my needs," I joke.

Nic tickles my sides, and I laugh until I cry. Life is going to be so much better with him in it. And I can't wait to start this next chapter with him.

34

NIC

I watch from the wooden boardwalk as Claire's hair blows in the wind. She is looking out at the ocean as the setting sun paints the sky with orange, purple, and pink hues. It is like I am living inside of a watercolor painting. We are at my family's beach house in northwest Florida, bordering the shore of the Gulf of Mexico.

After the trauma she endured at the hands of Dan King, it was an easy decision to whisk Claire away for some much needed relaxation. I used Graham's chartered jet and took some time off work. Claire doesn't know that I also invited our friends and family to join us in the morning for brunch. But right now, we need this time to just be us.

My bare feet step onto the warm sand, and the smell of salt fills my nostrils. The pant legs of my beige linen pants are cuffed at the bottom, and my white button-down shirt is tucked into the waistband, secured with a brown leather belt. Claire feels my presence and turns around, her hand waving at me and her smile making her eyes crinkle. Her skin looks even more golden against the contrast of her white cotton dress. I have never seen a more perfect image of her, and I can't help but stop in my tracks to stand in awe of her beauty.

Damn, woman, you take my breath away.

She gets up from her place in the sand and places her book down on her towel. She turns toward me and starts to jog. I join her in a run and catch her as she throws herself into my arms. Spinning her around, I feel the mist in the air from the waves kissing the shore.

"You enjoy some solitude?" I ask, putting my girl back on her feet.

She nods and then stretches up to kiss my lips. "But I much prefer the time we have together."

"Well, lucky you, I'm never letting you go."

"Promise?" She got some sun today, and I can see little brown freckles popping up on her nose. She is adorable.

"With everything that I am. What I feel for you is greater than a moment. You are my dream but also my reality. I want to wake up each day and go to bed each night with you beside me. Claire, I'm not even sure the word love is grand enough to describe what I feel for you. The way I feel right now is the way I feel when I believe there is a future for me. A really damn good future."

"You are my once in a lifetime."

"I know that what we started out as was a trip down an unforeseen path of self-discovery. But during the journey, I found you, Claire. And as much as I wanted to deny what your presence has done in my life, I know now that the only way to keep you is to be honest—with you and with myself. My feelings for you have evolved, baby. I'm not falling in love with you, Claire. I am immersed in it. Head over fucking heels," I say, smoothing her hair that is blowing into her face. I cup her cheeks and relish in the softness of her skin. "I love all your layers. And baby, you have many. You keep me intrigued, and I want to get to know every part of you—not just your body but also your mind and soul."

"I used to wish for the man of my dreams to come rescue me from a life I once thought was empty. But you are not the man I used to draw in my mind. You are better than anything I could have ever dreamed up or imagined. You, Nic Hoffman, have changed my life. You helped me to see myself through a different lens. Your love has changed me for the better. Thank you."

"Sometimes the best moments are the unplanned ones. I never expected to fall in love. I never could have predicted that I would love you more than I did a moment ago."

I kiss Claire on the forehead and then bend down to one knee to kiss the swell of her belly. I look up at her, the sun casting a beautiful glow to her features, and then pull out the ring from my pants pocket that I have been holding on to for several days—just waiting for the perfect moment to show her.

"Claire, I can't promise to not make mistakes. I can only promise to spend the rest of my life trying to be the man you deserve. I vow to love you as my best friend. I vow to love you as my partner. I vow to love you as the mother of my child. And I would be honored to spend the rest of my days loving you as my wife. Please do me this honor and say you'll marry me." I hold up the two-and-a-half-carat plat-inum ring for the sun to catch the angles and make it sparkle. The center princess cut diamond is the main focal point, while the six round diamonds on the band make the ring elegant, but still one of a kind.

Claire's hands cup my cheeks, and she falls to her knees onto the sand. Her lips crash into mine, and the sheer force knocks me back. I laugh against her lips and slide the ring back into my pocket, so I don't lose it in the sand. She crawls on top of me and kisses me with such passion that my skin tingles. My arms wrap around her, and I hold her close to me like she is the most precious gemstone in the entire world.

I love us like this...unfiltered and deliriously happy.

"Claire?"

"Hmm?"

"I'm waiting."

"Oh!" she screams, lifting her head up. "Yes!" Her hands fly up into the air, waving them around like flags of victory. "A million times yes!"

I pick us both up and pull the ring back out, sliding it onto her finger. "You were meant to wear diamonds, baby. You look spectacular in them."

"I love it, Nic. Thank you."

I smile down at my girl and pull out my unicorn selfie stick from my side pocket, showing it to her. "Let's capture this memory," I say, locking my phone into the device.

"You're having way too much fun with this gift I got you."

"It's pretty life changing."

"You goof," she laughs, as I keep snapping pictures of us, even though she's not looking in ninety percent of them.

That's the thing with Claire. Every angle is a good one.

When the excitement settles, I reach into my back pocket and pull out an envelope. "Now that I have your promise to never leave me, let's find out whether the start of our journey will be bumpy or smooth."

Claire's eyes widen when she reads the return address in the upper lefthand corner of the envelope, knowing exactly what is inside. I turn her so we are both looking out at the sun barely visible over the horizon. It shines onto the water, almost blinding us. With arms wrapped around her midsection, I tear through the secured flap and pull out the trifold document. Opening it up, I start to cry.

"It is with 99.9998% certainty that..." My voice gets stuck in my throat, and I stop reading.

"*You* are the father," Claire finishes, twisting in my arms to squeeze hers around me so hard that I worry she will hurt herself in the process.

"Oh baby, this"—I wipe at the tears flowing down my cheeks—"is the greatest gift you could have given me. I'm not only going to be a daddy but this baby's father. I get to be both." I am awestruck with the news as every single nerve in my body ignites with excitement. *I am going to be a father*.

Claire looks up to the sky and whispers, "Thank you." And I couldn't agree more.

Thank you.

I wake to the smell of something baking. I reach over to feel for Claire, and when I am left with just cold sheets in my hands, my eyes pop open. With a glance at my phone, I see that it is barely seven in the morning.

So much has happened since first arriving in Florida, but waking up this early has not been the norm.

Where is my girl?

Surely I tuckered her out enough last night to want to sleep in while we still can. Once the baby arrives, I imagine our entire routine will then be dictated by the tiny gummy bear.

I roll out of bed, slip on a pair of gray jogging pants, and go off in search of my fiancée.

Thinking of Claire as my future bride feels a bit weird for my head to comprehend. Our relationship has had so many ups and downs that getting to this happy state we are both living in makes every day feel like a celebration. She gives me a new purpose, and her love restores the pain of the past and all of the mistakes I have made with her.

I follow the smell into the kitchen and see the back of my sexy girl dressed in the navy and white cheerleading outfit I have been begging her to wear ever since I learned she used to cheer. It is probably the only good thing that has come from her trip back to Virginia, and my eyes are having a feast just watching her do her thing.

Claire is looking out through the wall of glass at the ocean, while stirring a huge metal bowl with a spatula. The oven light is on, and I can see the rise of what looks to be cupcakes. Damn. Can she look any sexier?

I sneak up behind her and place my hand over hers with the spatula, taking over the stirring. I kiss her neck. She has her hair piled high up on top of her head with a huge white bow.

She is a freaking wet dream turned reality.

"Hmm, I was trying to surprise you," she says softly. "I am making you vanilla cupcakes. Just working on the vanilla frosting. You do have a thing for vanilla, right?"

"I have a thing for you," I say with a grunt, feeling my cock come to life over how short her outfit is.

Claire's legs are toned and tanned. If she bends over just a tad, I bet I can see the curve of her lush ass cheeks. I wonder if she is wearing any panties. I better check.

I squat down just enough to run my hand from her knee to the top of her thigh. My fingers search for the fabric where her panties should be located, coming up empty-handed.

"Searching for something?" she asks innocently, turning her body so her butt presses against the counter. She holds up the spatula that is covered in pink frosting. Sticking out her tongue, she licks from the bottom of the silicon spoon to the top, showing me with her open mouth just how much is stuffed inside. She swallows her mouthful and then smacks her lips. "Hmm...I'm full."

"You are my bad girl."

My hands grip her bare ass cheeks under the canopy of her skimpy pleated cheer outfit. I squeeze until she yelps and then lift her so she is sitting up on the countertop. My hands cup her breasts, weighing them. I can already tell her body is developing in ways I never imagined could get better. But that is how it is with Claire. Every new curve or swell adds to the excitement of getting to know her body as it develops. It is thrilling and invigorating to know that the life she is carrying inside is my doing. She is mine in every possible way, and I'm one lucky man to be able to spend forever with her by my side.

I shimmy out of my pants and allow them to fall to my ankles. The sun is up and the kitchen is filled with warmth, but it is really Claire that lights me up inside.

I push up her fitted shirt, exposing her naked breasts for me to kiss and suckle. I lick at her nipples and revel in how responsive they are to my touch. Their color has changed slightly, and they are even more enticing. Flicking up her mini skirt, I can see her glistening pussy in all its delight. Reaching my hand into the metal mixing bowl, I scoop out some pink frosting onto my finger. I smear it onto her folds, standing back to admire my artwork.

"That's a waste of perfectly good icing," she points out with a smirk.

"It's not a waste if I have full intention of eating it and *you*."

"Oh," she says, making her lips form into an O.

"I wonder which is sweeter—the frosting or you."

She leans her weight back on her elbows, tossing her head back toward the window, while bringing her feet up to rest on the counter.

"You are exquisite," I purr.

"And you are teasing me with this slow torture."

I smile, while moving my mouth over her pussy. I lick and suck and feast on her sweetness. I'm in full sugar-rush mode. I glide my tongue from her opening up to her clit and then back down again. When I get her warmed up, I step back and admire my girl in all her glory.

"You are pretty and pink and *perfect*."

I help Claire sit up and slide onto my dick that is painfully hard. I moan at the feel of her coating me with her wet heat. With hands on her hips, I bounce her on me until we are both close to release.

"Ahhh," Claire calls out, arching her back while I keep her from falling.

"Claire!" I yell, releasing as deep as I can into her, marking her.

"I am never going to grow tired of you worshipping my body."

"Good," I say with a satisfied smirk.

The timer goes off on the oven, and we both look toward the sound. I allow Claire to slide down my body one inch at a time, smacking her bare ass cheeks as she walks away to get the pan out before the cupcakes burn.

She jumps into the air and gives me a fake glare. "Ouch."

"You better get dressed before all the guests arrive."

"Guests?" she asks with curiosity. "We're expecting company?"

"Yup," I chirp, not giving anything away. "Oh, and Claire?"

"Hmm?" She follows my eyes down to her now concealed pussy.

"You are definitely sweeter."

I place a blindfold over Claire's freshly made up eyes and kiss each eyelid through the silky fabric. "Ready for your surprise?" I ask, ushering her out the back door onto the deck. The Gulf Coast's springs are very pleasant and invit-ing. I could get used to this type of weather. The sound of the ocean is calming, even though my heart is racing with excitement. I never cared about someone enough to pull off a surprise like this. I just hope that it is welcomed and doesn't backfire on me.

I wave to everyone and help Claire sit down on the cushioned wicker couch, finding my place right beside her. I glance around at the space and am shocked at what can be done in thirty minutes by a crew determined to make this day extra special for my girl.

Claire sure deserves it. She is my everything.

With shaky fingers, I pull off the sash and wait until Claire's eyes focus and come to life.

"Congrats!" everyone cheers, popping streamers and bottles of champagne.

A few people whistle with excitement.

"What is going on?" Claire asks with tears dripping down her cheeks as she takes in the entire scene around her.

Blake, Penny, my parents, Graham, Angie, Collins, Tyler, Asher, and his pregnant wife are clapping their hands and sitting around a huge table that is set up with balloons, presents, and a brunch fit for a royal family. When I proposed the last-minute idea to the group, they were thrilled to be a part of welcoming Claire and our baby in a joint celebration.

"We're here to celebrate you being pregnant and engaged," Angie says, getting out of her seat and moving toward us to give us both a hug.

"You told them?" Claire asks, looking at me with a bit of confusion.

"We've known since you were in the hospital but resisted saying anything until we could have this moment to have a real party," Mom says softly. "We cannot wait to make this all official and have you join our family. You are the perfect addition, and we love you."

"I"—Claire clears her throat and smiles through the tears—"don't know what to say. I never really had anyone do something like this for me before. Thank you."

"Claire Bear," Blake says with pride, "you deserve to be celebrated. You are always there for those you care about, and it is easy to return the love back to you."

I pour myself a glass of champagne and hand Claire the nonalcoholic alternative kind. "To starting the journey of forever with my girl by my side!"

"To making us grandparents," Dad chimes in, holding up his glass, while wrapping an arm around Mom.

"To being best friends and sisters," Angie interjects.

"We love you both," Penny adds, making her way closer to embrace both Claire and me in a hug.

Everyone fills their plates with pastries, quiches, and breakfast meats. Mimosas are served and presents are put in line to be opened.

"Okay, this is from me and Germain," Mom says proudly, handing us a huge box.

We tear through the wrapping paper and pull off the lid to reveal a huge giraffe that when standing is taller than Claire.

"Really, Mom?"

"Yes, son," she hisses. "If they had a bigger one, I would have bought it. It is so much fun shopping for a baby. I cannot wait to see if this child is as stubborn as you are. It would be karma, that's for sure."

We all laugh over my mom's ability to lighten any mood.

"Oh, and there's another part to the gift. It's at the bottom."

I reach inside and pull out a smaller box. Removing the lid and unwrapping the tissue paper, I hold up a golden-brown fleece thing. "Umm, thanks?"

"Turn it around," Mom says, bursting with anticipation.

I flip the item around and then notice it is a giraffe costume for a baby.

"Awww," Claire chants. "That's the cutest thing I've ever seen."

"Wow," I mutter, "I thought I was."

I laugh as Claire hits me on my arm. I will do anything in this lifetime to make her as happy as she is today.

"Your baby is going to make the cutest giraffe," Mom states. "Can't wait to see him or her in that costume."

"Thank you," Claire says, examining the fabric closer.

"Mine next," Penny says, bouncing on her feet with excitement. She was granted an extended release, so having her here with all of us is a blessing. She hands us a small gift bag. "It's a milestone gift. Oh, and it's more for Claire than for you."

I laugh as my girl pulls out the tissue paper and then retrieves the tiny gift box. She lifts the lid and reveals a beautiful white-gold charm bracelet that already has a ring charm and a baby rattle charm attached.

"I figure you can buy more charms as you reach more

events in your life that you want to remember," Penny explains.

"I love it. I want to wear it now," Claire says joyfully. She undoes the clasp and looks at me expectantly to help her snap it into place.

Once the bracelet is secured, I kiss her engagement band and join fingers with hers.

Angie grabs the next box that simply has a bow on top. "This is not necessarily a gift, but a proposal."

Claire takes the box and puts it on her lap. "I'm confused," she says softly.

"Open it and see."

I watch as Claire pulls off the bow on the box and sees the Plus None logo underneath. Lifting the lid, she discovers a maternity lifestyle line in the form of a subscription box.

"Once I found out you were pregnant, I thought about how many other mommies or mommies-to-be out there are struggling to find cute outfits, comfortable shoes, and inspiration. I thought we could extend our box line and embrace moms too. You don't have to answer now, we can—"

"Yes!" Claire says with confidence. "I love this idea, Angie. It is wonderful."

"I also thought you could be the lead for this certain branch. After all, you are going to rock this lifestyle, and what better way to create a brand than to be experiencing it too?"

I smile and hug Claire to me. She has come a long way with her career goals and her confidence. It makes me so happy to stand by someone who is so strong and resilient. I have no doubt she is going to change the world. She is that special. The best leaders are the ones who have some life experience and some bruises that guide their choices.

We eat more food and finish up by cutting a cake that is designed to look like a sunflower—Claire's favorite flower. After all of the presents are opened, we reminisce and share embarrassing stories. I'm pretty sure that is Asher and Graham's favorite part, because they sure think they are hilarious—at my expense.

Regardless, it feels great to laugh and be surrounded by those I love.

"This is the best engagement and baby announcement party. I never expected this. It was a wonderful surprise. Thank you all for throwing this for me," Claire says, her tone full of gratitude and warmth. "You guys sure know how to make a person feel special."

I pull her toward me and kiss her temple. "If you all don't mind, I need to sneak Claire away for a moment."

"Where are we going?" she asks.

"You'll see."

I walk her down the boardwalk that leads onto the beach. We kick off our shoes and make a pile at the end of the wooden platform.

It is around noon and the sun is high in the sky. I have a blanket laid out waiting for us, something I was able to set up while Claire was in the shower earlier.

"What do we have here?" she asks, looking at the quilt and the folded board I have weighed down by a cooler.

"Sit." I help Claire down onto the fabric and join her. I pick up the cooler and pull out the board, unfolding the trifold flaps. I watch as she scans over the magazine cutouts, laughing over my gesture.

"You made me a vision board," she says fondly. She taps her fingers over the picture of the baby and smiles.

"It's not complete. I want you to be a part of adding to it with me. I want your dreams to become our reality."

Claire runs her fingers over the individual letters I cut out to spell the word "forever." She then trails them over the small picture of the Eiffel Tower.

"You want to go back to Vegas?" she asks, looking over at me. "To where our story began?"

"Sure, we can do that. But I thought you would like to see the real tower with me in Paris."

Claire sits up straighter, glancing between the board and me. "Paris?"

"You know, the city in France?" I laugh.

She launches herself at me, making me fall back. "Is that a yes?"

"It's a hell yes."

"Good," I say, sitting us back up again. "I was thinking of going when you hit your second trimester."

"I'm so excited."

I smile. "So am I."

Claire goes back to examining the board, moving her fingers over the tube of vanilla cupcake lip gloss. "I thought you hated my lip gloss."

"I only hated it when you would taunt me with it and test my self-restraint limits."

"I never did that."

"Lies," I say with a chuckle. "So, we now own joint stock in the company that produces your favorite flavor."

"Of course we do," she laughs, shaking her head at me. "You are one of a kind, Nic Hoffman."

She touches the patch of green straw I glued down. It is the same kind of filler you put in baskets for Easter. On top of the fake grass is a yellow excavator sticker. "You have a liking for construction vehicles?"

I chuckle over her sense of humor. "I want to design and build a house with you." I watch as her expression changes and then moisture fills her eyes. "Don't cry, baby. This is a happy moment in time."

"I know. I just..." She pauses to collect herself. "I'm just overcome with emotion."

I squeeze her hands. "I have a building company picked out and some potential plots of land we could buy. But my vision is for us to have a house we can raise children in."

"Children?"

"Assuming you want more. I want a place that is ours, where we can grow old together. I want a house that will be made into a place we can call home."

Claire wraps her arms around me. "I want for our children what I never really had."

"I know, baby."

She pulls back to look into my eyes. I can get lost in hers. "I love the idea of having our own place. But *you* are my home, Nic."

I kiss her lips and we roll onto the quilt. I never imagined I could be this happy with a life I never thought I wanted. I'm just glad I met a girl who could make me see all that I was missing out on and get me to take a chance on her.

Seeing the sunlight coat Claire's skin and the way her eyes crinkle when she is truly happy just lets me know that I found my person. Without any doubt or reservation, I know with confidence that Claire is the one. *My one.*

My girl leans up on an elbow to look at me. "You are the first person in my life who has ever tried to catch me when I fall."

"I'll always catch you. I love you, Claire."

"I'm going to love spending forever with you."

I soak in her beauty, pressing my lips against hers. "Forever won't be long enough."

EPILOGUE
NIC

"So this is happening," I say, more as a statement than as a question.

Graham sighs as he pulls into the parking lot at Soulful Mind in Seattle. I can tell by the way he is tapping his fingers manically along the steering wheel that we are sharing similar thoughts about this whole thing. "I just hope it isn't too soon, and there's no major relapse."

He just got back from his three-week honeymoon in Fiji and is already starting to regress back to looking stressed. I had the luxury of spending a much-needed break with Claire in Paris, showing her all of the sights. She went completely into tourist mode with her vision board as guidance, and needed to be reined in a few times. I assured her we can go back anytime she wants.

"All of her therapists claim she is ready." I'm mainly talking out loud, trying to convince myself that this is what is best for our baby sister, Penny, who insists on getting out of the facility as soon as possible. "She'll be enrolled in a maintenance program, and we can always hire someone to watch out for her."

"That will be nonnegotiable," Graham responds flatly. "And it can't be just anybody. She's already proven to me that she can sneak away from guards."

I rub a hand down the back of my neck. "Oh, I'm aware of how stubborn and determined Penny can be. I'm just glad we're both on the same page when it comes to keeping her safe."

"I've already seen the attention she's gotten from some visitors and part-time work staff. The last thing Penny needs is some loser guy to come along and give her some setbacks. She's come so far."

I nod. "I agree. Penny needs stability and some hobbies to occupy her time. We both know she'll grow bored with Hillsboro before the end of the week. But whatever we decide for security, it has to be nonintrusive and subtle. I'm thinking something light, so she doesn't feel the need to constantly bypass it."

Graham groans, cutting the engine and exiting his side of the car. I slide out of my side and shut the door.

"Let's do this," he says, as we walk toward the main entrance of the therapy center.

Once inside, we see our baby sister resting on a couch in the lobby. My eyes narrow as I take in her new appearance.

Holy hell.

Where did the baggy pants go?

Her brown locks? Gone.

And her makeup? Is she on her way to a pageant?

I turn to look Graham in the eyes, as he conveys the same message I'm sending back to him.

We are in trouble.

ACKNOWLEDGMENTS

Dear Readers,

Thank you for never having enough books. Thank you for taking a big chance on a newer author and trusting me to provide an entertaining experience. Thank you for giving me this opportunity to follow a passion. I appreciate your enthusiasm, your support, and your kindness. You have made this entire journey worth it to me.

I told myself before publishing that if just one person fell in love with my books, then I would feel like I accomplished what I set out to do. Well, through this experience, not only did some of you express how much my books have touched your lives, but you have done the same for me. I am changed because of you.

I can only hope to continue to deliver compelling books that you will find worthy to read.

Thank you for being a part of my journey,

Victoria

ABOUT THE AUTHOR

Victoria Dawson is the creator of books with fiery heroines and possessive heroes. She thrives on writing stories that transcend the minds of readers, allowing them to get lost in the journey to love—and all the drama that entails. Prior to delving heart first into the romance writing world, she taught middle and high school students mathematics for ten years.

Victoria is a unique combination of hopeful realist and hopeless romantic. She is an iced coffee connoisseur, a reality TV enthusiast, and a habitual wearer of stretchy pants. If she is not chasing after her three active children, she is often found scouring social media for her next book boyfriend.

Having grown up in an itty-bitty town in Pennsylvania, Victoria is a little bit country. She currently resides in Maryland with her family.

Never miss a release or an important update by signing up for my newsletter.

www.ingramcontent.com/pod-product-compliance
Lightning Source LLC
Chambersburg PA
CBHW022236020726
47496CB00004B/935

* 9 7 8 1 9 5 9 3 6 4 0 9 2 *